DEVICES
AND
DESIRES

DEVICES AND DESIRES

P. D. James

Alfred A. Knopf 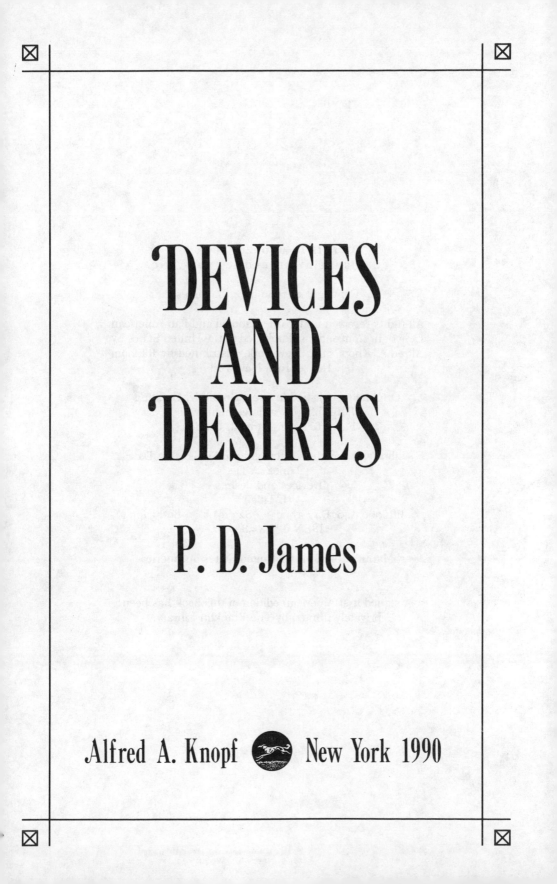 New York 1990

THIS IS A BORZOI BOOK
PUBLISHED BY ALFRED A. KNOPF, INC.

Originally published in Great Britain by Guilding
Publishing by arrangement with
Faber & Faber Limited, London.

Library of Congress Cataloging-in-Publication Data
James, P. D.
Devices and desires.
I. Title.
PR6060.A467D4   1990   823'.914   89-45305
ISBN 0-394-58070-2

Manufactured in the United States of America

A signed first American edition of this book has been
privately printed by The Franklin Library.

Author's Note

This story is set on an imaginary headland on the north-east coast of Norfolk. Lovers of this remote and fascinating part of East Anglia will place it between Cromer and Great Yarmouth, but they must not expect to recognize its topography, nor to find Larksoken Nuclear Power Station, Lydsett Village or Larksoken Mill. Other place names are genuine, but this is merely the novelist's cunning device to add authenticity to fictitious characters and events. In this novel only the past and the future are real; the present, like the people and the setting, exists only in the imagination of the writer and her readers.

BOOK ONE

Friday 16 September
to
Tuesday 20 September

1

The Whistler's fourth victim was his youngest, Valerie Mitchell, aged
fifteen years, eight months and four days, and she died because she
missed the 9.40 bus from Easthaven to Cobb's Marsh. As always, she
had left it until the last minute to leave the disco, and the floor was
still a packed, gyrating mass of bodies under the makeshift strobe
lights when she broke free of Wayne's clutching hands, shouted instructions to Shirl about their plans for next week above the raucous
beat of the music and left the dance floor. Her last glimpse of Wayne
was of his serious, bobbing face bizarrely striped with red, yellow and
blue under the turning lights. Without waiting to change her shoes,
she snatched up her jacket from the cloakroom peg and raced up the
road past the darkened shops towards the bus station, her cumbersome shoulder-bag flapping against her ribs. But when she turned
the corner into the station she saw with horror that the lights on their
high poles shone down on a bleached and silent emptiness and, dashing to the corner, was in time to see the bus already half-way up the
hill. There was still a chance if the lights were against it, and she
began desperately chasing after it, hampered by her fragile, high-
heeled shoes. But the lights were green and she watched helplessly,
gasping and bent double with a sudden cramp, as it lumbered over
the brow of a hill and like a brightly lit ship sank out of sight. "Oh
no!" she screamed after it, "Oh God! Oh no!" and felt the tears of
anger and dismay smarting her eyes.

This was the end. It was her father who laid down the rules in her family, and there was never any appeal, any second chance. After protracted discussion and her repeated pleas, she had been allowed this weekly visit on Friday evenings to the disco run by the church Youth Club, provided she caught the 9.40 bus without fail. It put her down at the Crown and Anchor at Cobb's Marsh, only fifty yards from her cottage. From 10.15 her father would begin watching for the bus to pass the front room where he and her mother would sit half-watching the television, the curtains drawn back. Whatever the programme or weather, he would then put on his coat and come out to walk the fifty yards to meet her, keeping her always in sight. Since the Norfolk Whistler had begun his killings, her father had had an added justification for the mild domestic tyranny which, she half-realized, he both thought right in dealing with his only child and rather enjoyed. The concordat had been early established: "You do right by me, my girl, and I'll do right by you." She both loved him and slightly feared him, and she dreaded his anger. Now there would be one of those awful rows in which she knew she couldn't hope to look to her mother for support. It would be the end of her Friday evenings with Wayne and Shirl and the gang. Already they teased and pitied her because she was treated as a child. Now it would be total humiliation.

Her first desperate thought was to hire a taxi and to chase the bus, but she didn't know where the cab rank was and she hadn't enough money; she was sure of that. She could go back to the disco and see if Wayne and Shirl and the gang between them could lend her enough. But Wayne was always skint and Shirl too mean, and by the time she had argued and cajoled it would be too late.

And then came salvation. The lights had changed again to red, and a car at the end of a tail of four others was just drawing slowly to a stop. She found herself opposite the open, left-hand window and looking directly at two elderly women. She clutched at the lowered glass and said breathlessly: "Can you give me a lift? Anywhere Cobb's Marsh direction. I've missed the bus. Please."

The final desperate plea left the driver unmoved. She stared ahead, frowned, then shook her head and let in the clutch. Her companion hesitated, looked at her, then leaned back and released the rear door.

"Get in. Quickly. We're going as far as Holt. We could drop you at the crossroads."

Valerie scrambled in and the car moved forward. At least they were going in the right direction, and it took her only a couple of seconds to think of her plan. From the crossroads outside Holt it would be less than half a mile to the junction with the bus route. She could walk it and pick it up at the stop before the Crown and Anchor. There would be plenty of time; the bus took at least twenty minutes meandering round the villages.

The woman who was driving spoke for the first time. She said: "You shouldn't be cadging lifts like this. Does your mother know that you're out, what you're doing? Parents seem to have no control over children these days."

Silly old cow, she thought, what business is it of hers what I do? She wouldn't have stood the cheek from any of the teachers at school. But she bit back the impulse to rudeness, which was her adolescent response to adult criticism. She had to ride with the two old wrinklies. Better keep them sweet. She said: "I'm supposed to catch the nine-forty bus. My dad'ud kill me if he thought I'd cadged a lift. I wouldn't if you was a man."

"I hope not. And your father's perfectly right to be strict about it. These are dangerous times for young women, quite apart from the Whistler. Where exactly do you live?"

"At Cobb's Marsh. But I've got an aunt and uncle at Holt. If you put me down at the crossroads, he'll be able to give me a lift. They live right close. I'll be safe enough if you drop me there, honest."

The lie came easily to her and was as easily accepted. Nothing more was said by any of them. She sat looking at the backs of the two grey, cropped heads, watching the driver's age-speckled hands on the wheel. Sisters, she thought, by the look of them. Her first glimpse had shown her the same square heads, the same strong chins, the same curved eyebrows above anxious, angry eyes. They've had a row, she thought. She could sense the tension quivering between them. She was glad when, still without a word, the driver drew up at the crossroads and she was able to scramble out with muttered thanks and watch while they drove out of sight. They were the last human beings, but one, to see her alive.

She crouched to change into the sensible shoes which her parents insisted she wear to school, grateful that the shoulder-bag was now lighter, then began trudging away from the town towards the junction where she would wait for the bus. The road was narrow and unlit, bordered on the right by a row of trees, black cut-outs pasted against the star-studded sky, and on the left, where she walked, by a narrow fringe of scrub and bushes at times dense and close enough to over-shadow the path. Up till now she had felt only an overwhelming relief that all would be well. She would be on that bus. But now, as she walked in an eerie silence, her soft footfalls sounding unnaturally loud, a different, more insidious anxiety took over and she felt the first prickings of fear. Once recognized, its treacherous power ac-knowledged, the fear took over and grew inexorably into terror.

A car was approaching, at once a symbol of safety and normality and an added threat. Everyone knew that the Whistler must have a car. How else could he kill in such widely spaced parts of the county, how else make his getaway when his dreadful work was done? She stood back into the shelter of the bushes, exchanging one fear for another. There was a surge of sound and the cat's-eyes momentarily gleamed before, in a rush of wind, the car passed. And now she was alone again in the darkness and the silence. But was she? The thought of the Whistler took hold of her mind, rumours, half-truths fusing into a terrible reality. He strangled women, three so far. And then he cut off their hair and stuffed it in their mouths, like straw spilling out of a Guy on November 5th. The boys at school laughed about him, whistling in the bicycle sheds as he was said to whistle over the bodies of his victims. "The Whistler will get you," they called after her. He could be anywhere. He always stalked by night. He could be here. She had an impulse to throw herself down and press her body into the soft rich-smelling earth, to cover her ears and lie there rigid until the dawn. But she managed to control her panic. She had to get to the crossroads and catch the bus. She forced herself to step out of the shadows and begin again her almost silent walk.

She wanted to break into a run but managed to resist. The crea-ture, man or beast, crouching in the undergrowth was already sniffing her fear, waiting until her panic broke. Then she would hear the crash of the breaking bushes, his pounding feet, feel his panting breath hot on her neck. She must keep walking, swiftly but silently, holding her bag tightly against her side, hardly breathing, eyes fixed ahead.

And as she walked she prayed: "Please, God, let me get safely home and I'll never lie again. I'll always leave in time. Help me to get to the crossroads safely. Make the bus come quickly. Oh God, please help me."

And then, miraculously, her prayer was answered. Suddenly, about thirty yards ahead of her, there was a woman. She didn't question how, so mysteriously, this slim, slow-walking figure had materialized. It was sufficient that she was there. As she drew nearer with quickening step, she could see the swathe of long blond hair under a tight-fitting beret, and what looked like a belted trench coat. And at the girl's side, trotting obediently, most reassuring of all, was a small black-and-white dog, bandy-legged. They could walk together to the crossroads. Perhaps the girl might herself be catching the same bus. She almost cried aloud, "I'm coming, I'm coming," and, breaking into a run, rushed towards safety and protection as a child might to her mother's arms.

And now the woman bent down and released the dog. As if in obedience to some command, he slipped into the bushes. The woman took one swift backward glance and then stood quietly waiting, her back half-turned to Valerie, the dog's lead held drooping in her right hand. Valerie almost flung herself at the waiting back. And then, slowly, the woman turned. It was a second of total, paralysing terror. She saw the pale, taut face which had never been a woman's face, the simple, inviting, almost apologetic smile, the blazing and merciless eyes. She opened her mouth to scream, but there was no chance, and horror had made her dumb. With one movement the noose of the lead was swung over her head and jerked tight and she was pulled from the road into the shadow of the bushes. She felt herself falling through time, through space, through an eternity of horror. And now the face was hot over hers and she could smell drink and sweat and a terror matching her own. Her arms jerked upwards, impotently flailing. And now her brain was bursting and the pain in her chest, growing like a great red flower, exploded in a silent, wordless scream of "Mummy, Mummy." And then there was no more terror, no more pain, only the merciful, obliterating dark.

2
☒

Four days later Commander Adam Dalgliesh of New Scotland Yard
dictated a final note to his secretary, cleared his in-tray, locked his
desk drawer, set the combination of his security cupboard and prepared to leave for a two-week holiday on the Norfolk coast. The break
was overdue and he was ready for it. But the holiday wasn't entirely
therapeutic; there were affairs in Norfolk that needed his attention.
His aunt, his last surviving relative, had died two months earlier,
leaving him both her fortune and a converted windmill at Larksoken
on the north-east coast of Norfolk. The fortune was unexpectedly large
and had brought its own, as yet unresolved, dilemmas. The mill was
a less onerous bequest but was not without its minor problems. He
needed, he felt, to live in it alone for a week or two before finally
making up his mind whether to keep it for occasional holidays, sell,
or pass it over at a nominal price to the Norfolk Windmill Trust, who
were, he knew, always anxious to restore old windmills to working
order. And then there were family papers and his aunt's books, particularly her comprehensive library of ornithology, to be looked at and
sorted and their disposal decided upon. These were pleasurable tasks.
Even in boyhood he had disliked taking a holiday totally without purpose. He didn't know from what roots of childhood guilt or imagined
responsibility had grown this curious masochism, which in his middle
years had returned with added authority. But he was glad that there
was a job to be done in Norfolk, not least because he knew that the

journey had an element of flight. After four years of silence his new book of poetry, *A Case to Answer and Other Poems*, had been published to considerable critical acclaim, which was surprisingly gratifying, and to even wider public interest which, less surprisingly, he was finding more difficult to take. After his more notorious murder cases, the efforts of the Metropolitan Police press office had been directed to shielding him from egregious publicity. His publisher's rather different priorities took some getting used to and he was frankly glad of an excuse to escape from them, at least for a couple of weeks.

He had earlier said his goodbye to Inspector Kate Miskin, and she was now out on a case. Chief Inspector Massingham had been seconded to the Intermediate Command Course at Bramshill Police College, one more step on his planned progress to a Chief Constable's braid, and Kate had temporarily taken over his place as Dalgliesh's second-in-command of the Special Squad. He went into her office to leave a note of his holiday address. It was, as always, impressively tidy, sparsely efficient and yet feminine, its walls enlivened by a single picture, one of her own abstract oils, a study in swirling browns heightened with a single streak of acid green, which Dalgliesh was growing to like more each time he studied it. On the uncluttered desktop was a small glass vase of freesias. Their scent, at first fugitive, suddenly wafted up to him, reinforcing the odd impression he always got that the office was more full of her physical presence empty than it was when she was seated there working. He laid his note, exactly in the middle of the clean blotter, and smiled as he closed the door after him with what seemed unnecessary gentleness. It remained only to put his head round the AC's door for a final word and he was on his way to the lift.

The door was already closing when he heard running footsteps and a cheerful shout and Manny Cummings leapt in, just avoiding the bite of the closing steel. As always he seemed to whirl in a vortex of almost oppressive energy, too powerful to be contained by the lift's four walls. He was brandishing a large brown envelope. "Glad I caught you, Adam. It is Norfolk you're escaping to, isn't it? If the Norfolk CID do lay their hands on the Whistler, take a look at him for me, will you, check he isn't our chap in Battersea."

"The Battersea Strangler? Is that likely, given the timing and the MO? Surely it isn't a serious possibility?"

"Highly unlikely but, as you know, Uncle is never happy unless every stone is explored and every avenue thoroughly upturned. I've put together some details and the Identikit just in case. As you know, we've had a couple of sightings. And I've let Rickards know that you'll be on his patch. Remember Terry Rickards?"

"I remember."

"Chief Inspector now, apparently. Done all right for himself in Norfolk. Better than he would have done if he'd stayed with us. And they tell me he's married, which might have softened him a bit. Awkward cuss."

Dalgliesh said: "I shall be on his patch but not, thank God, on his team. And if they do lay hands on the Whistler, why should I do you out of a day in the country?"

"I hate the country and I particularly loathe flat country. Think of the public money you'll be saving. I'll come down—or is it up?—if he's worth looking at. Decent of you, Adam. Have a good leave."

Only Cummings would have had the cheek. But the request was not unreasonable, made, as it was, to a colleague his senior only by a matter of months, and one who had always preached co-operation and the common-sense use of resources. And it was unlikely that his holiday would be interrupted by the need to take even a cursory glance at the Whistler, Norfolk's notorious serial killer, dead or alive. He had been at his work for fifteen months now and the latest victim—Valerie Mitchell, wasn't it?—was his fourth. These cases were invariably difficult, time-consuming and frustrating, depending as they often did more on good luck than good detection. As he made his way down the ramp to the underground car-park he glanced at his watch. In three-quarters of an hour he would be on his way. But first there was unfulfilled business at his publisher's.

3
☒

The lift at Messrs. Herne & Illingworth in Bedford Square was almost
as ancient as the house itself, a monument both to the firm's obstinate
adherence to a bygone elegance and to a slightly eccentric inefficiency
behind which a more thrustful policy was taking shape. As he was
borne upwards in a series of disconcerting jerks, Dalgliesh reflected
that success, although admittedly more agreeable than failure, has its
concomitant disadvantages. One of them, in the person of Bill Costello,
Publicity Director, was waiting for him in the claustrophobic fourth-
floor office above.

The change in his own poetic fortunes had coincided with
changes in the firm. Herne & Illingworth still existed insofar as their
names were printed or embossed on book covers under the firm's
ancient and elegant colophon, but the house was now part of a multinational corporation which had recently added books to canned
goods, sugar and textiles. Old Sebastian Herne had sold one of London's few remaining individual publishing houses for eight and a half
million and had promptly married an extremely pretty publicity assistant, who was only waiting for the deal to be concluded before,
with some misgivings but a prudent regard for her future, relinquish-
ing the status of newly acquired mistress for that of wife. Herne had
died within three months, provoking much ribald comment but few
regrets. Throughout his life Sebastian Herne had been a cautious,
conventional man who reserved eccentricity, imagination and occa-

sional risk-taking for his publishing. For thirty years he had lived as a faithful, if unimaginative, husband, and Dalgliesh reflected that, if a man lives for nearly seventy years in comparatively blameless conventionality, that is probably what his nature requires. Herne had died less of sexual exhaustion—assuming that to be as medically credible as puritans would like to believe—than from a fatal exposure to the contagion of fashionable sexual morality.

The new management promoted their poets vigorously, perhaps seeing the poetry list as a valuable balance to the vulgarity and soft pornography of their best-selling novelists, whom they packaged with immense care and some distinction, as if the elegance of the jacket and the quality of the print could elevate highly commercial banality into literature. Bill Costello, appointed the previous year as Publicity Director, didn't see why Faber & Faber should have a monopoly when it came to the imaginative publicizing of poetry, and was successful in promoting the poetry list despite the rumour that he never himself read a line of modern verse. His only known interest in verse was his presidency of the McGonagall Club, whose members met on the first Tuesday of every month at a City pub to eat the landlady's famous steak-and-kidney pudding, put down an impressive amount of drink and recite to each other the more risible efforts of arguably Britain's worst poet ever. A fellow poet had once given Dalgliesh his own explanation: "The poor devil has to read so much incomprehensible modern verse that you can't wonder that he needs an occasional dose of comprehensible nonsense. It's like a faithful husband occasionally taking therapeutic relief at the local cat-house." Dalgliesh thought the theory ingenious but unlikely. There was no evidence that Costello read any of the verse he so assiduously promoted. He greeted his newest candidate for media fame with a mixture of dogged optimism and slight apprehension, as if knowing that he was faced with a hard nut to crack.

His small, rather wistful and childish face was curiously at odds with his Billy Bunter figure. His main problem was apparently whether to wear his belt above or below his paunch. Above was said to indicate optimism, below a sign of depression. Today it was slung only just above the scrotum, proclaiming a pessimism which the subsequent conversation served only to justify. Eventually Dalgliesh said firmly:

"No, Bill, I shall not parachute into Wembley Stadium holding the book in one hand and a microphone in the other. Nor shall I compete with the station announcer by bawling my verses at the Waterloo commuters. The poor devils are only trying to catch their trains."

"That's been done. It's old hat. And it's nonsense about Wembley. Can't think how you got hold of that. No, listen, this is really exciting. I've spoken to Colin McKay and he's very enthusiastic. We're hiring a red double-decker bus, touring the country. Well, as much of the country as we can in ten days. I'll get Clare to show you the rough-out and the schedule."

Dalgliesh said gravely: "Like a political-campaign bus: posters, slogans, loudspeakers, balloons."

"No point in having it if we don't let people know it's coming."

"They'll know that all right with Colin on board. How are you going to keep him sober?"

"A fine poet, Adam. He's a great admirer of yours."

"Which doesn't mean he'd welcome me as a travelling companion. What are you thinking of calling it? Poets' Progress? The Chaucer Touch? Verse on Wheels—or is that too like the WI? The Poetry Bus? That has the merit of simplicity."

"We'll think of something. I rather like Poets' Progress."

"Stopping where?"

"Precincts, village halls, schools, pubs, motorway cafés, anywhere where there's an audience. It's an exciting prospect. We were thinking of hiring a train, but the bus has more flexibility."

"And it's cheaper."

Costello ignored the innuendo. He said: "Poets upstairs; drinks, refreshments downstairs. Readings from the platform. National publicity, radio and TV. We start from the Embankment. There's a chance of Channel Four and, of course, Kaleidoscope. We're counting on you, Adam."

"No," said Dalgliesh firmly. "Not even for the balloons."

"For God's sake, Adam, you write the stuff. Presumably you want people to read it—well, buy it anyway. There's tremendous public interest in you, particularly after that last case, the Berowne murder."

"They're interested in a poet who catches murderers, or a policeman who writes poetry, not in the verse."

"What does it matter as long as they're interested? And don't tell me that the Commissioner wouldn't like it. That's an old cop-out."

"All right, I won't, but he wouldn't."

And there was after all nothing new to be said. He had heard the questions innumerable times and he had done his best to answer them, with honesty if not with enthusiasm. "Why does a sensitive poet like you spend his time catching murderers?" "Which is the more important to you, the poetry or the policing?" "Does it hinder or help, being a detective?" "Why does a successful detective write poetry?" "What was your most interesting case, Commander? Do you ever feel like writing a poem about it?" "The love poems, is the woman you've written them to alive or dead?" Dalgliesh wondered whether Philip Larkin had been badgered about what it felt like to be both poet and librarian, or Roy Fuller on how he managed to combine poetry with law.

He said: "All the questions are predictable. It would save everyone a great deal of trouble if I answered them on tape; then you could broadcast them from the bus."

"It wouldn't be at all the same thing. It's you personally they want to hear. Anyone would think you didn't want to be read."

And did he want to be read? Certainly he wanted some people to read him, one person in particular, and having read the poems he wanted her to approve. Humiliating but true. As for the others: well, he supposed that the truth was that he wanted people to read the poems but not be coerced into buying them, an overfastidiousness which he could hardly expect Herne & Illingworth to share. He was aware of Bill's anxious, supplicating eyes, like those of a small boy who sees the bowl of sweets rapidly disappearing from his reach. His reluctance to co-operate seemed to him typical of much in himself that he disliked. There was a certain illogicality, surely, in wanting to be published but not caring particularly whether he was bought. The fact that he found the more public manifestations of fame distasteful didn't mean that he was free of vanity, only that he was better at controlling it and that in him it took a more reticent form. After all, he had a job, an assured pension and now his aunt's considerable fortune. He didn't have to care. He saw himself as unreasonably privileged compared with Colin McKay, who probably saw him—and who could blame Colin?—as a snobbish, oversensitive dilettante.

He was grateful when the door opened and Nora Gurney, the firm's cookery editor, came briskly in, reminding him as she always did of an intelligent insect, an impression reinforced by the bright exophthalmic eyes behind huge round spectacles, familiar fawn jumper in circular ribbing and flat pointed shoes. She had looked exactly the same since Dalgliesh had first known her.

Nora Gurney had become a power in British publishing by the expedient of longevity (no one could remember when she had first come to Herne & Illingworth) and a firm conviction that power was her due. It was likely that she would continue to exercise it under the new dispensation. Dalgliesh had last met her three months previously at one of the firm's periodic parties, given for no particular reason as far as he could tell, unless to reassure the authors, by the familiarity of the wine and canapés, that they were still in business and basically the same lovable old firm. The guest list had chiefly comprised their most prestigious writers in the main categories, a ploy which had added to the general atmosphere of inadvertence and fractionized unease: the poets had drunk too much and had become lachrymose or amorous as their natures dictated; the novelists had herded together in a corner like recalcitrant dogs commanded not to bite; the academics, ignoring their hosts and fellow guests, had argued volubly among themselves and the cooks had ostentatiously rejected their half-bitten canapés on the nearest available hard surface with expressions of disgust, pained surprise or mild, speculative interest. Dalgliesh had been pinned in a corner by Nora Gurney, who had wanted to discuss the practicality of the theory she had developed: Since every set of fingerprints was unique, could not the whole country be printed, the data stored on a computer and research carried out to discover whether certain combinations of lines and whorls were indicative of criminal tendencies? That way crime could be prevented rather than cured. Dalgliesh had pointed out that, since criminal tendencies were universal, to judge from the places where his fellow guests had parked their cars, the data would be unmanageable, apart from the logistical and ethical problems of mass fingerprinting and the discouraging fact that crime, even supposing the comparison with disease to be valid, was, like disease, easier to diagnose than to cure. It had almost been a relief when a formidable female novelist, vigorously corseted in a florid cretonne two-piece which made her look like a walking sofa, had borne him off to pull out a crumple of parking tickets from her voluminous handbag and angrily demand what he was proposing to do about them.

The Herne & Illingworth cookery list was small but was strong, its best writers having a solid reputation for reliability, originality and good writing. Miss Gurney was passionately committed to her job and her writers, seeing the novels and verse as irritating if necessary adjuncts to the main business of the house, which was to nourish and publish her darlings. It was rumoured that she herself was an indifferent cook, one more indication of the firm British conviction, not uncommon in more elevated if less useful spheres of human activity, that there is nothing so fatal to success as knowing your subject. It didn't surprise Dalgliesh that she had seen his arrival as fortuitous and the chore of delivering Alice Mair's proofs as a near-sacred privilege. She said: "I suppose they've called you in to help catch the Whistler."

"No, that, I'm thankful to say, is a job for the Norfolk CID. Calling in the Yard happens more often in fiction than real life."

"It's convenient that you're driving to Norfolk, whatever the reason. I wouldn't really wish to trust these proofs to the post. But I thought your aunt lived in Suffolk? And surely someone said that Miss Dalgliesh had died."

"She did live in Suffolk until five years ago, when she moved to Norfolk. And, yes, my aunt has died."

"Oh well, Suffolk or Norfolk, there's not a lot of difference. But I'm sorry she's dead." She seemed for a moment to contemplate human mortality and to compare the two counties to the disadvantage of both, then said: "If Miss Mair isn't at home you won't leave this at the door, will you? I know that people are extraordinarily trusting in country districts but it would be quite disastrous if these proofs were lost. If Alice isn't at home her brother, Dr. Alex Mair, may be. He's the Director of the nuclear-power station at Larksoken. But perhaps, on second thoughts, you'd better not hand it to him either. Men can be extremely unreliable."

Dalgliesh was tempted to point out that one of the country's foremost physicists, who was responsible for an atomic-power station and, if the papers were to be believed, was strongly tipped for the new post of nuclear-power supremo, could presumably be trusted with a parcel of proofs. He said: "If she's at home, I'll hand it to Miss Mair personally. If she isn't, I'll keep it until she is."

"I've telephoned to say that it's on its way, so she'll be expecting you. I've printed the address very clearly. Martyr's Cottage. I expect you know how to get there."

Costello said sourly: "He can map-read. He's a policeman, remember."

Dalgliesh said that he knew Martyr's Cottage and had briefly met Alexander Mair but not his sister. His aunt had lived very quietly, but neighbours sharing the same remote district inevitably do get to know each other and, although Alice Mair had been away from home at the time, her brother had made a formal visit of condolence to the mill after Miss Dalgliesh's death.

He took possession of the parcel, which was surprisingly large and heavy and crisscrossed with an intimidating pattern of Sellotape, and was slowly borne downwards to the basement, which gave access to the firm's small car-park and his waiting Jaguar.

4

⊠

Once free of the knotted tentacles of the eastern suburbs, Dalgliesh made good time, and by 3.00 he was driving through Lydsett Village. Here a right turn took him off the coastal road onto what was little more than a smoothly macadamed track bordered by water-filled ditches and fringed by a golden haze of reeds, their lumbered heads straining in the wind. And now, for the first time, he thought that he could smell the North Sea, that potent but half-illusory tang evoking nostalgic memories of childhood holidays, of solitary adolescent walks as he struggled with his first poems, of his aunt's tall figure at his side, binoculars round her neck, striding towards the haunts of her beloved birds. And here, barring the road, was the familiar old farm gate still in place. Its continued presence always surprised him, since it served no purpose that he could see except symbolically to cut off the headland and to give travellers pause to consider whether they really wanted to continue. It swung open at his touch, but closing it, as always, was more difficult, and he lugged and half-lifted it into place and slipped the circle of wire over the gatepost with a familiar sensation of having turned his back on the workaday world and entered country which, no matter how frequent his visits, would always be alien territory.

He was driving now across the open headland towards the fringe of pine trees which bordered the North Sea. The only house to his left was the old Victorian rectory, a square, red-bricked building, incongruous behind its struggling hedge of rhododendron and laurel. To his right the ground rose gently towards the southern cliffs. He could see the dark mouth of a concrete pillbox, undemolished since the war, and as seemingly indestructible as the great hulks of wave-battered concrete, remnants of the old fortifications which lay half-submerged in the sand along part of the beach. To the north the broken arches and stumps of the ruined Benedictine abbey gleamed golden in the afternoon sun against the crinkled blue of the sea. Breasting a small ridge, he glimpsed for the first time the topsail of Larksoken Mill and beyond it, against the skyline, the great grey bulk of Larksoken Nuclear Power Station. The road he was on, veering left, would lead eventually to the station but was, he knew, seldom used, since normal traffic and all heavy vehicles used the new access road to the north. The headland was empty and almost bare; the few straggling trees, distorted by the wind, struggled to keep their precarious hold in the uncompromising soil. And now he was passing a second and more dilapidated pillbox, and it struck him that the whole headland had the desolate look of an old battlefield, the corpses long since carted away but the air vibrating still with the gunfire of long-lost battles, while the power station loomed over it like a grandiose modern monument to the unknown dead.

On his previous visits to Larksoken he had seen Martyr's Cottage spread out beneath him when he and his aunt had stood surveying the headland from the small top room under the cone of the Mill. But he had never been closer to it than the road, and now, driving up to it, it struck him again that the description "cottage" was hardly appropriate. It was a substantial two-storey, L-shaped house standing to the east of the track, with walls partly flint and partly rendered, enclosing at the rear a courtyard of York stone which gave an uninterrupted view over fifty yards of scrub to the grassy dunes and the sea. No one appeared as he drew up and, before lifting his hand to the bell, he paused to read the words of a stone plaque embedded in the flints to the right of the door.

In a cottage on this site lived Agnes Poley, Protestant martyr, burned at Ipswich, 15th August, 1557, aged 32 years. Ecclesiastes Chapter 3, Verse 15.

The plaque was unadorned, the letters deeply carved in an elegant script reminiscent of Eric Gill, and Dalgliesh remembered his aunt telling him that it had been placed there by previous owners in the late 1920s when the cottage was originally extended. One of the advantages of a religious education is the ability to identify at least the better-known texts of scripture, and this was one which it needed no effort of memory to recall. As a delinquent nine-year-old at his prep school, he had once been required by the headmaster to write out in his best handwriting the whole of the third chapter of Ecclesiastes, old Gumboil, economical in this as in all matters, believing that writing lines should combine punishment with literary and religious education. The words, in that round childish script, had remained with him. It was, he thought, an interesting choice of text.

That which hath been is now; and that which is to be hath already been; and God requireth that which is past.

He rang and there was only a short delay before Alice Mair opened the door. He saw a tall, handsome woman dressed with careful and expensive informality in a black cashmere sweater with a silk scarf at the throat and fawn trousers. He would have recognized her from her strong resemblance to her brother, although she looked the elder by some years. She took it for granted that each knew who the other was and, standing aside to motion him in, she said: "It's good of you to be so accommodating, Mr. Dalgliesh. I'm afraid Nora Gurney is implacable. Once she knew you were on your way to Norfolk you were a predestined victim. Perhaps you would bring the proofs through to the kitchen."

It was a distinguished face with the deep-set, widely spaced eyes beneath straight brows, a well-shaped, rather secretive mouth and strong greying hair swept upwards and curled into a chignon. In her publicity photographs she could, he recalled, look beautiful in a somewhat intimidating, intellectual and very English mould. But seen face-to-face, even in the informality of her own house, the absence of a spark of sexuality and, he sensed, a deep-seated reserve, made her seem less feminine and more formidable than he had expected, and she held herself stiffly, as if repelling invaders of her personal space. The handshake with which she had greeted him had been cool and firm and her brief smile was surprisingly attractive. He knew that he was oversensitive to the timbre of the human voice, and hers, although not jarring or unpleasant, sounded a little forced, as if she were deliberately speaking at an unnatural pitch.

He followed her down the hall to the kitchen at the back of the house. It was, he judged, almost twenty feet long and obviously served the triple purpose of sitting room, working place and office. The right-hand half of the room was a well-equipped kitchen with a large gas stove and an Aga, a butcher's chopping block, a dresser to the right of the door holding an assortment of gleaming pots, and a long working surface with a wooden triangle sheathing her assortment of knives. In the centre of the room was a large wooden table holding a stoneware jar of dried flowers. On the left-hand wall was a working fireplace, the two recesses fitted with floor-to-ceiling bookshelves. To each side of the hearth was a high-backed wicker armchair in an intricate closely woven design, fitted with patchwork cushions. There was an open roll-top desk facing one of the wide windows and, to its right, a stable door, the top half open, gave a view of the paved courtyard. Dalgliesh could glimpse what was obviously her herb garden planted in elegant terra-cotta pots carefully disposed to catch the sun. The room, which contained nothing superfluous, nothing pretentious, was both pleasing and extraordinarily comforting and, for a moment, he wondered why. Was it the faint smell of herbs and newly baked dough; the soft ticking of the wall-mounted clock, which seemed both to mark the passing seconds and yet to hold time in thrall; the rhythmic moaning of the sea through the half-open door; the sense of well-fed ease conveyed by the two cushioned armchairs, the open hearth? Or was it that the kitchen reminded Dalgliesh of that rectory kitchen where the lonely only child had found warmth and undemanding, uncensorious companionship, been given hot dripping toast and small forbidden treats?

He placed the proofs on the desk, refused Alice Mair's offer of coffee and followed her back to the front door. She walked out with him to the car and said: "I was sorry about your aunt—sorry for you, I mean. I expect that for an ornithologist death ceases to be terrible once sight and hearing begin to go. And to die in one's sleep without distress to oneself or inconvenience to others is an enviable end. But you had known her for so long that she must have seemed immortal."

Formal condolences, he thought, were never easy to speak or accept and usually sounded either banal or insincere. Hers had been perceptive. Jane Dalgliesh had indeed seemed to him immortal. The very old, he thought, make our past. Once they go it seems for a moment that neither it nor we have any real existence. He said: "I don't think death was ever terrible to her. I'm not sure that I really knew her, and I'm left wishing I'd tried harder. But I shall miss her."

Alice Mair said: "I didn't know her either. Perhaps I should have tried harder too. She was a very private woman, I suspect one of those fortunate people who find no other company more agreeable than their own. It always seems presumptuous to encroach on that self-sufficiency. Perhaps you share it. But if you can tolerate company, I'm having a few people, mostly colleagues of Alex from the power station, to dinner on Thursday night. Would you care to join us? Seven-thirty for eight."

It sounded, he thought, more like a challenge than an invitation. Somewhat to his surprise, Dalgliesh found himself accepting. But then the whole encounter had been a little surprising. She stood regarding him with a serious intensity as he let in the clutch and turned the car, and he had the impression that she was watching critically to see how he handled it. But at least, he thought as he gave a final wave, she hadn't asked him whether he had come to Norfolk to help catch the Whistler.

5
⊠

Three minutes later he raised his foot from the accelerator. Ahead of him, trudging along on the left of the path, was a little group of children, the eldest girl wheeling a push-chair with two smaller children, one each side of her, clutching the bars. Hearing the noise of the car she turned, and he saw a peaked, delicate face framed with red-gold hair. He recognized the Blaney children, met once before, with their mother, walking along the beach. Obviously the eldest girl had been shopping: the folding push-chair had a shelf under the seat lumped high with plastic bags. Instinctively he slowed down. They were unlikely to be in real danger; the Whistler stalked at night, not in broad daylight, and no vehicle had passed him since he left the coastal road. But the child looked grossly overburdened and ought not to be so far from home. Though he had never seen their cottage, he seemed to remember that his aunt had told him that it lay about two miles to the south. He recalled what he knew about them, that their father earned a precarious living as a painter whose innocuous, prettified water-colours were sold in cafés and tourist shops along the coast, and that their mother had been desperately ill with cancer. He wondered whether Mrs. Blaney was still alive. His instinct was to pile the children into the car and drive them home, but that, he knew, was hardly sensible. Almost certainly the eldest child—Theresa, wasn't it?—had been taught not to accept lifts from strangers, particularly men, and he was virtually a stranger. On an impulse he reversed the Jaguar and drove quickly back to Martyr's Cottage. This time the front door was open and a swathe of sunlight lay across the red-tiled floor. Alice Mair had heard the car and came out to him from the kitchen, wiping her hands. He said: "The Blaney children are walking home. Theresa is wheeling a push-chair and trying to cope with the twins. I thought I could offer a lift if I had a woman with me, someone they know."

She said briefly: "They know me."

Without another word she went back into the kitchen, then came out to him, closed the front door after her without locking it and got into the car. Putting it into gear, his arm brushed her knee. He was aware of an almost imperceptible withdrawing, more emotional than physical, a small delicate gesture of self-containment. Dalgliesh doubted whether that half-imagined recoil had anything to do with him personally, nor did he find her silence disconcerting. Their conversation, when they did speak, was brief. He asked: "Is Mrs. Blaney still alive?"

"No. She died six weeks ago."

"How are they managing?"

"Not particularly well, I imagine. But Ryan Blaney doesn't welcome interference. I sympathize. Once he lets down his defences, half the social workers in Norfolk, amateur and professional, will move in on him."

When they drew up beside the little band it was Alice Mair who opened the car door and spoke.

"Theresa, here is Mr. Dalgliesh to give you all a lift. He's Miss Dalgliesh's nephew from Larksoken Mill. One of the twins had better sit on my lap. The rest of you and the push-chair can fit into the back."

Theresa looked at Dalgliesh without smiling and said a grave thank you. She reminded him of pictures of the young Elizabeth Tudor, the same red-gold hair framing a curiously adult face both secretive and self-composed, the same sharp nose and wary eyes. The faces of the twins, softer editions of her own, turned towards her questioningly, then broke into shy smiles. They looked as if they had been dressed in a hurry and not very suitably for a long walk on the headland, even in a warm autumn. One wore a tattered summer dress in pink-spotted cotton with double flounces, the other a pinafore over a checked blouse. Their pathetically thin legs were unprotected. Theresa was wearing jeans and a grubby sweatshirt with a map of London's Underground across the front. Dalgliesh found himself wondering if it had been brought back from a school trip to the capital. It was too large for her and the wide sleeves of limp cotton hung from her freckled arms like rags thrown over a stick. In contrast to his sisters, Anthony was overclad, a bundle of leggings, jumper and a padded jacket topped with a woollen helmet with a bobble pulled well down over his forehead, beneath which he surveyed their busyness, unsmiling, like a stout, imperious Caesar.

Dalgliesh got out of the Jaguar and tried to extricate him from the push-chair, but the anatomy of the chair momentarily defeated him. There was a bar beneath which the child's rigid legs were obstinately stuck. The solid uncooperative bundle was surprisingly heavy; it was like trying to manoeuvre a firm and rather smelly poultice. Theresa gave him a brief, pitying smile, dragged the plastic bags from beneath the seat, then expertly freed her brother and settled him on her left hip while, with the other hand, she collapsed the push-chair, with a single vigorous shake. Dalgliesh took the baby from her while Theresa helped the children into the Jaguar and commanded with sudden fierceness "Sit still." Anthony, recognizing incompetence, grasped Dalgliesh's hair firmly with a sticky hand and he felt the momentary touch of a cheek, so soft that it was like the fall of a petal. Throughout these manoeuvrings Alice Mair sat quietly watching from the car but made no move to help. It was impossible to know what she was thinking.

But once the Jaguar had moved away she turned to Theresa and said in a voice of surprising gentleness: "Does your father know that you're out alone?"

"Daddy has taken the van to Mr. Sparks. It's due for its MOT test. Mr. Sparks doesn't think it's going to pass. And I found we'd run out of milk for Anthony. We have to have milk. And we wanted some more disposable nappies."

Alice Mair said: "I'm giving a dinner party on Thursday evening. If your father agrees, would you like to come and help with the table like you did last month?"

"What are you going to cook, Miss Mair?"

"Put your head close so that I can whisper. Mr. Dalgliesh is going to be one of the guests. I want it to be a surprise."

The pale-golden head leaned forward towards the grey and Miss

Mair whispered. Theresa smiled and then nodded with serious satisfaction in a moment of grave feminine conspiracy.

It was Alice Mair who directed him to the cottage. After about a mile they turned seaward and the Jaguar lurched and bounced down a narrow track between high, untended hedges of bramble and elderberry. The track led only to Scudder's Cottage, the name crudely painted on a board nailed to the gate. Beyond the cottage it widened to provide a rough, gravelled turning, backed by a forty-foot bank of shingle behind which Dalgliesh could hear the crash and suck of the tide. Scudder's Cottage, small-windowed, picturesque under its tiled, dipping roof, was fronted by a flowering wilderness which had once been a garden. Theresa led the way, between grass almost knee-high bordered by a riot of unpruned roses, to the porch, then reached for a key hung high on a nail, less, Dalgliesh supposed, for security reasons than to ensure that it wasn't lost. With Dalgliesh carrying Anthony they passed into the cottage.

It was much lighter than he had expected, largely because of a rear door, now open, which led to a glass extension giving a view of the headland. He was aware of the room's clutter: the central wooden table still covered with the remains of their midday meal, an assortment of plates smeared with tomato sauce, a half-eaten sausage, a large bottle of orangeade uncapped; the children's clothes thrown over the back of a low nursing chair before the fireplace; of the smell of milk and bodies and wood smoke. But what held his attention was a large oil painting propped on a chair and fronting the door. It was a three-quarter portrait in oils of a woman, painted with remarkable power. It dominated the room, so that he and Alice Mair stood for a moment, silently regarding it. The painter had avoided caricature, if only just, but the portrait was, he felt, intended less as a physical likeness than an allegory. Behind the wide, full mouth, the arrogant stare of the eyes, the dark, crimped, Pre-Raphaelite hair streaming in the wind, was a careful delineation of the headland, its objects disposed and painted with the meticulous attention to detail of a sixteenth-century primitive; the Victorian rectory, the ruined abbey, the half-demolished pillbox, the crippled trees, the small white mill like a child's toy and, gaunt against a flaming evening sky, the stark outline of the power station. But it was the woman, painted more freely, who dominated the landscape, arms stretched, the palms facing outwards in a parody of blessing. Dalgliesh's private verdict was that it was technically brilliant, but overwrought and painted, he felt, in hatred. Blaney's intention to produce a study of evil was as clear as if the portrait had been labelled. It was so different from the artist's usual work that without the bold signature, the single surname, Dalgliesh might have wondered if it was, in fact, his work. He recalled Blaney's pallid and innocuous water-colours of the better-known beauty spots of Norfolk—Blakeney, St. Peter Mancroft and the Cathedral at Norwich—which he produced for the local shops. They could have been painted from picture-postcards and probably were. And he could recall seeing one or two small oils hung in local restaurants and pubs, slap-dash in technique and economical of paint, but so different from the prettified water-colours that it was hard to believe that they too were by the same hand. But this portrait was different from either; the wonder was that the artist who could produce this disciplined splurge of colour, this technical artistry and imagination, had been content to churn out meretricious souvenirs for the tourist trade.

"You didn't know I could do it, did you?"

Absorbed in the painting, they hadn't caught his almost silent approach through the open door. He moved round and joined them and stared intently at the portrait, as if seeing it for the first time. His daughters, as though obedient to some unspoken command, grouped themselves around him in what in older children could have been a conscious gesture of family solidarity. Dalgliesh had last seen Blaney six months earlier, splashing alone along the edge of the beach, painting gear slung over his shoulder, and was shocked by the change in the man. He stood a lean six-foot-three in his torn jeans, the checked woollen shirt open almost to the waist, his long grubby feet in the open sandals looking like dry, brown bones. His face was a picture of red ferocity, the straggling red hair and beard, the bloodshot eyes, the gaunt-featured face burnt red by wind and sun, which yet showed on the cheekbones and under the eyes the bruising stain of tiredness. Dalgliesh saw Theresa slip her hand into his while one of the twins moved closer to him and clasped both arms firmly round one of his legs. Dalgliesh thought that however ferocious he might appear to the outside world, his children had no fear of him.

Alice Mair said calmly, "Good afternoon, Ryan," but did not appear to expect an answer. She nodded towards the portrait and went on:

"It's remarkable, certainly. What are you proposing to do with it? I can hardly suppose that she sat for you or that it was commissioned."

"She didn't need to sit. I know that face. I'm showing it at the Norwich Contemporary Arts Exhibition on October third if I can get it there. The van is out of use."

Alice Mair said: "I'll be driving to London within the next week. I could collect it and deliver it if you let me have the address."

He said: "If you like." The response was ungracious but Dalgliesh thought he detected relief. Then Blaney added: "I'll leave it packed and labelled to the left of the door in the painting shed. The light is just above it. You can collect it whenever it suits you. No need to knock." The last words had the force of a command, almost of a warning.

Miss Mair said: "I'll telephone you when I know when I'm going. By the way, I don't think you've met Mr. Dalgliesh. He saw the children on the road and thought of giving them a lift."

Blaney didn't say thank you, but after a moment's hesitation held out his hand, which Dalgliesh grasped. Then he said gruffly, "I liked your aunt. She telephoned offering to help when my wife was ill, and when I said there was nothing she or anyone could do, she didn't keep fussing. Some people can't keep away from a deathbed. Like the Whistler, they get their kicks from watching people die."

"No," said Dalgliesh, "she never fussed. I shall miss her. I'm sorry about your wife."

Blaney didn't reply, but stared hard at Dalgliesh, as if assessing the sincerity of that simple statement, and then said curtly, "Thank you for helping the children," and lifted his son from Dalgliesh's shoulder. It was a clear gesture of dismissal.

Neither of them spoke as Dalgliesh negotiated the track and finally turned onto the higher road. It was as if the cottage had exerted some spell which it was important to throw off before they talked. Then he asked: "Who is that woman in the portrait?"

"I hadn't realized that you didn't know. Hilary Robarts. She's Acting Administrative Officer at the power station. Actually you'll meet her at dinner on Thursday night. She bought Scudder's Cottage when she first arrived here three years ago. She's been trying to get the Blaneys out for some time. There's been a certain amount of feeling about it locally."

Dalgliesh asked: "Why does she want to gain possession? Does she propose to live there?"

"I don't imagine so. I think she bought it as an investment and wants to sell. Even a remote cottage—particularly a remote cottage—has value on this coast. And she has some justice on her side. Blaney did say that his tenancy would be short-term. I think she feels a certain resentment that he used his wife's illness, her death, and now uses the children as an excuse for reneging on his undertaking to leave when she wanted the cottage back."

Dalgliesh was interested that Alice Mair apparently knew so much about local affairs. He had thought of her as essentially a private woman who would be very little concerned with her neighbours or their problems. And what about himself? In his deliberations whether to sell or keep on the Mill as a holiday home he had seen it as a refuge from London, eccentric and remote, providing a temporary escape from the demands of his job and the pressures of success. But how far, even as an occasional visitor, could he isolate himself from the community, from their private tragedies no less than their dinner parties? It would be simple enough to avoid their hospitality, given sufficient ruthlessness, and he had never lacked that when it came to safeguarding his privacy. But the less tangible demands of neighbourliness might be less easily shrugged away. It was in London that you could live anonymously, could create your own ambience, could deliberately fabricate the persona which you chose to present to the world. In the country you lived as a social being and at the valuation of others. So he had lived in childhood and adolescence in the same country rectory, taking part each Sunday in a familiar liturgy which reflected, interpreted and sanctified the changing seasons of the farming year. It was a world he had relinquished with small regret, and he had not expected to find it again on Larksoken headland. But some of its obligations were here, deep-rooted in this arid and unfertile earth. His aunt had lived as privately as any woman he knew, but even she had visited and tried to help the Blaneys. He thought of the man, bereft and incarcerated in that cluttered cottage behind the great dyke of shingle, listening night after night to the never-ceasing moaning of the tide, and brooding on the wrongs, real or imaginary, which could inspire that hate-filled portrait. It could hardly be healthy for him or for his children. Come to that, Dalgliesh thought grimly, it could hardly be healthy for Hilary Robarts. He asked: "Does he get much official help with the children? It can't be easy."

"As much as he's prepared to tolerate. The local authority has arranged for the twins to attend some kind of day-care centre. They get collected most days. And Theresa, of course, is at school. She catches the bus at the end of the lane. She and Ryan between them cope with the baby. Meg Dennison—she housekeeps for the Reverend and Mrs. Copley at the Old Rectory—thinks we ought to do more for them, but it's difficult to see precisely what. I should have thought she'd had her fill of children as an ex-schoolmistress, and I make no pretence at understanding them." Dalgliesh remembered her whispered confidence to Theresa in the car, the child's intent face and brief transforming smile, and thought that she understood one child at least far better than she would probably claim.

But his thoughts returned to the portrait. He said: "It must be uncomfortable, particularly in a small community, to be the object of so much malevolence."

She understood at once what he meant. "Hatred rather than malevolence, wouldn't you say? Uncomfortable and rather frightening. Not that Hilary Robarts is easily frightened. But she's becoming something of an obsession with Ryan, particularly since his wife's death. He chooses to believe that Hilary practically badgered her into her grave. It's understandable, I suppose. Human beings need to find someone to blame both for their misery and for their guilt. Hilary Robarts makes a convenient scapegoat."

It was a disagreeable story and, coming as it did after the impact of the portrait, it provoked in Dalgliesh a mixture of depression and foreboding which he tried to shake off as irrational. He was glad to let the subject drop and they drove in silence until he left her at the gate of Martyr's Cottage. To his surprise she held out her hand and gave him, once again, that extraordinary attractive smile.

"I'm glad you stopped for the children. I'll see you, then, on Thursday night. You will be able to make your own assessment of Hilary Robarts and compare the woman with the portrait."

6

⊠

As the Jaguar crested the headland, Neil Pascoe was dumping rubbish into one of the two dustbins outside the caravan, two plastic bags of empty tins of soup and baby food, soiled disposable napkins, vegetable peelings and squashed cartons, already malodorous despite his careful sealing of the bags. Firmly replacing the lid, he marvelled, as he always did, at the difference one girl and an eighteen-month-old baby could make to the volume of household waste. Climbing back into the caravan, he said: "A Jag has just passed. It looks as if Miss Dalgliesh's nephew is back."

Amy, fitting a recalcitrant new ribbon to the ancient typewriter, didn't bother to look up.

"The detective. Perhaps he's come to help catch the Whistler."

"That isn't his job. The Whistler is nothing to do with the Met Police. It's probably just a holiday. Or perhaps he's here to decide what to do with the Mill. He can hardly live here and work in London."

"So why don't you ask him if we can have it? Rent-free, of course. We could caretake, see that no one squats. You're always saying it's antisocial for people to have second homes or leave property empty. Go on, have a word with him. I dare you. Or I will if you're too scared."

It was, he knew, less a suggestion than a half-serious threat. But for a moment, gladdened by her easy assumption that they were a couple, that she wasn't thinking of leaving him, he actually entertained the idea as a feasible solution to all their problems. Well, almost all. But a glance round the caravan restored him to reality. It was becoming difficult to remember how it had looked fifteen months ago, before Amy and Timmy had entered his life; the home-made shelves of orange boxes ranged against the wall which had held his books, the two mugs, two plates and one soup bowl, which had been sufficient for his needs, neatly stacked in the cupboard, the excessive cleanliness of the small kitchen and lavatory, his bed smooth under the coverlet of knitted woollen squares, the single hanging cupboard which had been adequate for his meagre wardrobe, his other possessions boxed and tidily stowed in the chest under the seat. It wasn't that Amy was dirty; she was continually washing herself, her hair, her few clothes. He spent hours carrying water from the tap outside Cliff Cottage to which they had access. He was continually having to fetch new Calor-gas cylinders from the general store in Lydsett Village, and steam from the almost constantly boiling kettle made the caravan a damp mist. But she was chronically untidy: her clothes lying where she had dropped them, shoes kicked under the table, knickers and bras stuffed beneath cushions and Timmy's toys littering the floor and tabletop. The make-up, which seemed to be her sole extravagance, cluttered the single shelf in the cramped shower, and he would find half-empty, opened jars and bottles in the food cupboard. He smiled as he pictured Commander Adam Dalgliesh, that no doubt fastidious widower, making his way through the accumulated mess to discuss their suitability as caretakers at Larksoken Mill.

And then there were the animals. She was incurably sentimental about wildlife, and they were seldom without some maimed, deserted or starving creatures. Seagulls, their wings covered with oil, were cleansed, caged and then let free. There had been a stray mongrel whom they had named Herbert, with a large uncoordinated body and look of lugubrious disapproval, who had attached himself to them for a few weeks and whose voracious appetite for dog meat and biscuits had had a ruinous effect on the housekeeping. Fortunately Herbert had eventually trotted off and to Amy's distress had been seen no more, although his lead still hung on the caravan door, a limp reminder of her bereavement. And now there were the two black-and-white kittens found abandoned on the grass verge of the coast road as they came back in the van from Ipswich. Amy had screamed for him to stop and, scooping up the kittens, had thrown back her head and

howled obscenities at the cruelty of human beings. They slept on
Amy's bed, drank indiscriminately from any saucer of milk or tea put
down for them, were remarkably docile under Timmy's boisterous
caresses and, happily, seemed content with the cheapest kind of
tinned cat food. But he was glad to have them because they too seemed
to offer some assurance that Amy would stay.

He had found her—and he used the word much as he might of
finding a particularly beautiful sea-washed stone—one late-June afternoon the previous year. She had been sitting on the shingle staring
out to sea, her arms clasped round her knees, Timmy lying asleep on
the small rug beside her. He was wearing a blue fleecy sleeping suit
embroidered with ducks from which his round face seemed to have
spilled over, still and pink as a porcelain painted doll, the delicate
lashes brush-tipped on the plump cheeks. And she, too, had something
of the precision and contrived charm of a doll, with an almost round
head poised on a long delicate neck, a snub nose with a splatter of
freckles, a small mouth with a full upper lip beautifully curved and
a bristle of cropped hair, originally fair but with bright orange tips
which caught the sun and trembled in the breeze so that the whole
head seemed for a moment to have a vivid life separated from the rest
of her body and, the image changing, he had seen her as a bright
exotic flower. He could remember every detail of that first meeting.
She had been wearing blue faded jeans, and a white sweatshirt flattened against the pointed nipples and the upturned breasts, the cotton
seeming too thin a protection against the freshening onshore breeze.
As he approached tentatively, wanting to seem friendly but not to
alarm her, she had turned on him a long and curious glance from
remarkable slanted violet-blue eyes.

Standing over her, he had said: "My name's Neil Pascoe. I live
in that caravan on the edge of the cliff. I'm just going to make some
tea. I wondered if you'd like a mug."

"I don't mind, if you're making it." She had turned away at once
and gazed again out to sea.

Five minutes later he had slithered down the sandy cliffs, a mug
of tea slopping in each hand. He heard himself say: "May I sit down?"

"Please yourself. The beach is free."

So he had lowered himself to sit beside her and together they
had stared wordlessly towards the horizon. Looking back on it, he was

amazed both at his boldness and at the seeming inevitability and naturalness of that first encounter. It was several minutes before he had found the courage to ask her how she had got to the beach. She had shrugged.

"By bus to the village and then I walked."

"It was a long way carrying the baby."

"I'm used to walking a long way carrying the baby."

And then under his hesitant questioning the story had come out, told by her without self-pity, almost, it had seemed, without particular interest, as if the events had happened to someone else. It was not, he supposed, an unusual tale. She was living in one of the small private hotels in Cromer on Social Security. She had been in a squat in London but had thought it would be pleasant to have some sea air for the baby for the summer. Only it wasn't working out. The woman at the hotel didn't really want kids and with summer holidays approaching could get a better rate for her rooms. She didn't think she could be turned out but she wasn't going to stay, not with that bitch.

He asked: "Couldn't the baby's father help?"

"He hasn't got a father. He did have a father—I mean, he isn't Jesus Christ. But he hasn't got one now."

"Do you mean that he's dead or that he's gone away?"

"Could be either, couldn't it? Look, if I knew who he was I might know where he was, OK?"

Then there had been another silence, during which she took periodical gulps of her tea and the sleeping baby stirred and gave small pig-like grunts. After a few minutes he had spoken again.

"Look, if you can't find anywhere else in Cromer you can share the caravan for a time." He had added hastily: "I mean, there is a second bedroom. It's very small, only just room for the bunk, but it would do for a time. I know it's isolated here, but it's close to the beach, which would be nice for the baby."

She had turned on him again that remarkable glance, in which for the first time he had detected to his discomfiture a brief flash of intelligence and of calculation.

"All right," she said. "If I can't find anywhere else I'll come back tomorrow."

And he had lain awake late that night, half-hoping, half-dreading that she would return. And she had returned the following afternoon, carrying Timmy on her hip and the rest of her possessions in a back-pack. She had taken over the caravan and his life. He didn't know whether what he felt for her was love, affection or pity, or a mixture of all three. He only knew that in his anxious and overconcerned life his second-greatest fear was that she might leave.

He had lived in the caravan now for just over two years, supported by a research grant from his northern university, to study the effect of the Industrial Revolution on the rural industries of East Anglia. His dissertation was nearly finished but for the last six months he had almost stopped work on it and had devoted himself entirely to his passion, a crusade against nuclear power. From the caravan on the very edge of the sea he could see Larksoken Power Station stark against the skyline, as uncompromising as his own will to oppose it, a symbol and a threat. It was from the caravan that he ran People Against Nuclear Power, with its acronym PANUP, the small organi-zation of which he was both founder and president. The caravan had been a stroke of luck. The owner of Cliff Cottage was a Canadian who, returning to his roots and seduced by nostalgia, had bought it on impulse as a possible holiday home. About fifty years earlier there had been a murder at Cliff Cottage. It had been a fairly commonplace murder, a henpecked husband at the end of his tether who had taken a hatchet to his virago of a wife. But if it had been neither particularly interesting nor mysterious, it had certainly been bloody. After the cottage had been bought, the Canadian's wife had heard graphic ac-counts of spilt brains and blood-spattered walls and had declared that she had no intention of living there in summer or at any other time. Its very isolation, once attractive, now appeared both sinister and repellent. And to compound the problem, the local planning authority had shown themselves unsympathetic to the owner's overambitious plans for rebuilding. Disillusioned with the cottage and its problems, he had boarded up the windows and returned to Toronto, meaning eventually to come back and make a final decision about his ill-advised purchase. The previous owner had parked a large old-fashioned car-avan at the back, and the Canadian had made no difficulty about renting this to Neil for two pounds a week, seeing it as a useful way of having someone to keep an eye on the property. And it was the caravan, at once his home and his office, from which Neil conducted his campaign. He tried not to think about the time, six months ahead, when his grant would finish and he would need to find work. He knew that he had somehow to stay here on the headland, to keep always in view that monstrous building which dominated his imagination as it did his view.

But now to the uncertainty about his future funding was added a new and more terrifying threat. About five months earlier he had attended an open day at the power station during which the Acting Administrative Officer, Hilary Robarts, had given a short preliminary talk. He had challenged almost everything she had said, and what was meant as an informative introduction to a public-relations exercise had developed into something close to a public brawl. In the next edition of his news-sheet he had reported on the incident in terms which he now realized had been unwise. She had sued him for libel. The action was due to be heard in four weeks' time and he knew that, successful or not, he was faced with ruin. Unless she died in the next few weeks—and why should she die?—it could be the end of his life on the headland, the end of his organization, the end of all he had planned and hoped to do.

Amy was typing envelopes, sending out the final copies of the newsletter. A pile was already to hand, and he began folding the pamphlets and inserting them into the envelopes. The job wasn't easy. He had tried to economize with the size and quality, and the envelopes were in danger of splitting. He now had a mailing list of 250, only a small minority of whom were active supporters of PANUP. Most never paid any dues towards the organization, and the majority of the pamphlets went unsolicited to public authorities, local firms and industry in the vicinity of Larksoken and Sizewell. He wondered how many of the 250 were read and thought with a sudden spasm of anxiety and depression of the total cost of even this small enterprise. And this month's newsletter wasn't his best. Rereading one before he put it in the envelope, it seemed to him to be ill organized, to have no coherent theme. The principal aim now was to refute the growing argument that nuclear power could avoid the damage to the environment through the greenhouse effect, but the mixture of suggestions ranging from solar power to replacing light bulbs with those which consumed seventy-five percent less energy seemed naïve and hardly convincing. His article argued that nuclear-generated electricity couldn't realistically replace oil and fossil fuels unless all nations built sixteen new reactors a week in the five years from 1995, a programme impossible to achieve and one which, if practicable, would add intolerably to the nuclear threat. But the statistics, like all his figures, were culled from a variety of sources and lacked authority. Nothing he produced seemed to him genuinely his own work. And the rest of the newsletter was a jumble of the usual scare stories, most of which he had used before: allegations of safety breaches which had been covered up, doubts about the safety of the ageing Magnox stations, the unsolved problem of storing and transporting nuclear waste. And this issue he had been hard put to it to find a couple of intelligent letters for the correspondence page; sometimes it seemed that every crackbrain in north-east Norfolk read the PANUP newsletter but that no one else did.

Amy was picking at the letters of the typewriter, which had a persistent tendency to stick. She said: "Neil, this is a bloody awful machine. It would be quicker to write the addresses by hand."

"It's better since you cleaned it, and the new ribbon looks fine."

"It's still diabolical. Why don't you buy a new one? It would save time in the end."

"I can't afford it."

"You can't afford a new typewriter and you think you're going to save the world."

"You don't need possessions to save the world, Amy. Jesus Christ had nothing: no home, no money, no property."

"I thought you said when I came here that you weren't religious."

It always surprised him that, apparently taking no account of him, she could yet recall comments he had made months earlier. He said: "I don't believe Christ was God. I don't believe there is a God. But I believe in what He taught."

"If He wasn't a God, I don't see that it matters much what He taught. Anyway, all I can remember is something about turning the other cheek, which I don't believe in. I mean, that's daft. If someone slaps your left cheek, then you slap his right, only harder. Anyway, I do know they hung Him up on the cross, so it didn't do Him a lot of good. That's what turning the other cheek does for you."

He said: "I've got a Bible here somewhere. You could read about Him if you wanted to. Make a start with St. Mark's Gospel."

"No thanks. I had enough of that in the home."

"What home?"

"Just a home, before the baby was born."

"How long were you there?"

"Two weeks. Two weeks too bloody many. Then I ran away and found a squat."

"Where was that, the squat?"

"Islington, Camden, King's Cross, Stoke Newington. Does it matter? I'm here now, OK?"

"It's OK by me, Amy."

Lost in his thoughts, he hardly realized that he had given up folding the pamphlets.

Amy said: "Look, if you're not going to help with these envelopes you might as well go and put a new washer on that tap. It's been dripping for weeks and Timmy's always falling about in the mud."

"All right," he said, "I'll do it now."

He took down his tool kit from the high cupboard where it was kept well out of Timmy's reach. He was glad to be out of the caravan. It had become increasingly claustrophobic in the last few weeks. Outside, he bent to talk to Timmy, caged in his playpen. He and Amy had collected large stones from the beach, looking for those with holes in them—and he had strung them onto strong cord and tied them along one side of the playpen. Timmy would spend hours happily banging them together or against the bars or, as now, slobbering against one of the stones in an attempt to get it into his mouth. Sometimes he would communicate with individual flints, a continuous admonitory prattle broken by sudden triumphant squeals. Kneeling down, Neil clutched the bars, rubbed his nose against Timmy's and was rewarded by his huge, heart-tugging smile. He looked very like his mother, with the same round head on a fragile neck, the same beautifully shaped mouth. Only his eyes, widely spaced, were differently shaped, large blue spheres with, above them, straight bushy eyebrows which reminded Neil of pale and delicate caterpillars. The tenderness he felt for the child was equal to, if different from, the tenderness he felt for his mother. He could not now imagine life on the headland without either of them.

But the tap defeated him. Despite his tuggings with the wrench he couldn't get the screw to shift. Even this minor domestic task was apparently beyond his powers. He could hear Amy's derisive voice. You want to change the world and you can't change a washer. After a couple of minutes he gave up the attempt, left the tool box by the cottage wall and walked to the edge of the cliff, then slithered down to the beach. Crunching over the ridges of stones, he went down to the edge of the sea and almost violently wrenched off his shoes. It was thus, when the weight of anxiety about his failed ambitions, his uncertain future became too heavy, that he would find his peace, standing motionless to watch the veined curve of the poised wave, the tumult of crashing foam breaking over his feet, the wide intersecting arches washing over the smooth sand as the wave retreated to leave its tenuous lip of foam. But today even this wonder, continually repeated, failed to comfort his spirit. He gazed out to the horizon with unseeing eyes and thought about his present life, the hopelessness of the future, about Amy, about his family. Thrusting his hand in his pocket, he felt the crumpled envelope of his mother's last letter.

He knew that his parents were disappointed in him although they never said so openly, since oblique hints were just as effective: "Mrs. Reilly keeps on asking me, What is Neil doing? I don't like to say that you're living in a caravan with no proper job." She certainly didn't like to say that he was living there with a girl. He had written to tell them about Amy since his parents constantly threatened to visit and, unlikely as this was actually to happen, the prospect had added an intolerable anxiety to his already anxiety-ridden life.

"I'm giving a temporary home to an unmarried mother in return for typing help. Don't worry, I shan't suddenly present you with a bastard grandchild."

After the letter had been posted he had felt ashamed. The cheap attempt at humour had been too like a treacherous repudiation of Timmy, whom he loved. And his mother hadn't found it either funny or reassuring. His letter had produced an almost incoherent farrago of warnings, pained reproaches and veiled references to the possible reaction of Mrs. Reilly if she ever got to know. Only his two brothers surreptitiously welcomed his way of life. They hadn't made university and the difference between their comfortable lifestyle—houses on an executive estate, *en suite* bathrooms, artificial coal fires in what they called the lounge, working wives, a new car every two years and timeshares in Majorca—provided both with agreeable hours of self-satisfied comparisons which he knew would always end with the same conclusion, that he ought to pull himself together, that it wasn't right, not after all the sacrifices Mum and Dad had made to send him to college, and a fine waste of money that had proved.

He had told Amy none of this but would have happily confided had she shown the least interest. But she asked no questions about his past life and told him nothing about hers. Her voice, her body, her smell were as familiar to him as his own, but essentially he knew no more about her now than when she had arrived. She refused to collect any welfare benefits, saying that she wasn't going to have DHSS snoopers visiting the caravan to see if she and Neil were sleeping together. He sympathized. He didn't want them either, but he felt that for Timmy's sake she should take what was on offer. He had given her no money but he did feed both of them, and this was difficult enough on his grant. No one visited her and no one telephoned. Occasionally she would receive a postcard, coloured views usually of London with nondescript, meaningless messages, but as far as he knew she never replied.

They had so little in common. She helped spasmodically with PANUP but he was never sure how far she was actually committed. And he knew that she found his pacifism stupid. He could recall a conversation only this morning.

"Look, if I live next door to an enemy and he has a knife, a gun and a machine gun and I've got the same, I'm not going to chuck mine before he chucks his. I'll say, OK, let the knife go, then the gun maybe, then the machine gun. Him and me at the same time. Why should I throw mine away and leave him with his?"

"But one of you has to make a start, Amy. There has to be a beginning of trust. Whether it's people or nations, we have to find the faith to open our hearts and hands and say, 'Look, I've nothing. I've only my humanity. We inhabit the same planet. The world is full of pain but we needn't add to it. There has to be an end of fear.' "

She had said obstinately: "I don't see why he should chuck his weapons once he knows I've got nothing."

"Why should he keep them? He's got nothing to fear from you any more."

"He'd keep them because he liked the feeling of having them and because he might like to use them some day. He'd like the power and he'd like knowing he had me where he wanted me. Honestly, Neil, you're so naïve sometimes. That's how people are."

"But we can't argue like that any more, Amy. We aren't talking about knives and guns and machine guns. We're talking about weapons neither of us could use without destroying ourselves and probably our whole planet. But it's good of you to help with PANUP when you don't sympathize."

She had said: "PANUP's different. And I sympathize all right. I just think that you're wasting your time writing letters, making speeches, sending out all those pamphlets. It won't do any good. You've got to fight people their way."

"But it's done good already. All over the world ordinary people are marching, demonstrating, making their voices heard, letting the people in power know that what they want is a peaceful world for themselves and their children. Ordinary people like you."

And then she had almost shouted at him: "I'm not ordinary! Don't you call me ordinary! If there are ordinary people, I'm not one of them."

"I'm sorry, Amy. I didn't mean it like that."

"Then don't say it."

The only cause they had in common was a refusal to eat meat. Soon after she arrived at the caravan he had said: "I'm vegetarian but I don't expect you to be, or Timmy." He had wondered as he spoke whether Timmy was old enough to eat meat. He had added: "You can buy a chop occasionally in Norwich if you feel like it."

"What you have is all right by me. Animals don't eat me, and I don't eat them."

"And Timmy?"

"Timmy has what I give him. He's not fussy."

Nor was he. Neil couldn't imagine a more accommodating child nor, for most of the time, a more contented one. He had found the second-hand playpen advertised on a newsagent's board in Norwich and had brought it back on the top of the van. In it Timmy would crawl for hours or pull himself up and stand, precariously balancing, his napkin invariably falling about his knees. When thwarted, he would rage, shutting his eyes tight, opening his mouth and holding his breath before letting out a bellow of such terrifying power that Neil half-expected the whole of Lydsett to come running to see which of them was tormenting the child. Amy never smacked him but would jerk him onto her hip and dump him on her bed saying: "Bloody awful noise."

"Shouldn't you stay with him? Holding his breath like that, he could kill himself."

"You daft? He won't kill himself. They never do."

And he knew now that he wanted her, wanted her when it was obvious that she didn't want him and would never again risk rejection. On the second night at the caravan she had slid back the partition between his bed and hers and had walked quietly up to his bed and had stood gravely looking down at him. She had been completely naked. He had said: "Look, Amy, you don't have to pay me."

"I never pay for anything, at least not like that. But have it your own way." After a pause she had said: "You gay or something?"

"No, it's just that I don't like casual affairs."

"You mean you don't like them, or you don't think you ought to have them?"

"I suppose I mean that I don't think I ought to have them."

"You religious, then?"

"No, I'm not religious, not in the ordinary way. It's just that I think sex is too important to be casual about. You see, if we slept together and I—if I disappointed you—we might quarrel and then you'd walk out. You'd feel that you had to. You'd leave, you and Timmy."

"So what, I walk out."

"I wouldn't want you to do that, not because of anything I'd done."

"Or hadn't done. OK, I expect you're right." Another pause, and then she had added: "You'd mind, then, if I walked out?"

"Yes," he said, "I'd mind."

She had turned away. "I always do walk out in the end. No one has ever minded before."

It was the only sexual advance she had ever made to him, and he knew it would be the last. Now they slept with Timmy's cot wedged between the partition and his bed. Sometimes in the night, wakeful because the child had stirred, he would put out his hands and clasp the bars and long to shake this frail barrier that symbolized the un-bridgeable gulf between them. She lay there, sleek and curved as a fish or a gull, so close that he could hear the rise and fall of her breath faintly echoing the suspiration of the sea. His body ached for her, and he would press his face into the lumpy pillow groaning with the hopelessness of his need. What could she possibly see in him to make her want him, except, as on that one night, out of gratitude, pity, curiosity or boredom? He hated his body, the scrawny legs on which the kneecaps protruded like deformities, the small blinking eyes too closely set, the sparse beard which couldn't disguise the weakness of the mouth and chin. Sometimes, too, he was tormented by jealousy. Without proof he had convinced himself that there was someone else. She would say that she wanted to walk alone on the headland. And he would watch her go with the certainty that she was meeting a lover. And when she returned he would imagine that he could see the glow of the skin, the satisfied smile of remembered happiness, could almost smell that she had been making love.

He had already heard from the university that his research grant wouldn't be extended. The decision wasn't surprising; he had been warned to expect it. He had been saving as much as possible from the grant in the hope of amassing a small sum which would tide him over until he could find a local job. It hardly mattered what. Anything that would pay enough to live and allow him to remain on the headland to carry on the campaign. In theory, he supposed he could organize PANUP from anywhere in the U.K., but he knew that it was irrevocably bound to Larksoken headland, to the caravan, to that concrete mass five miles to the north which had power, apparently, to dominate his will as it did his imagination. He had already put out feelers with local employers, but they hadn't been too keen on employing a well-known agitator; even those who seemed sympathetic to the anti-nuclear cause didn't actually have work on offer. Perhaps they feared that too many of his energies would be diverted to the campaign. And his small capital was draining away with the extra expense of Amy, Timmy and even the cats. And now there was the threat of this libel action, less of a threat than a certainty.

When, ten minutes later, he returned to the caravan, Amy, too, had given up working. She was lying on her bed looking up at the ceiling, Smudge and Whisky curled on her stomach.

Looking down at her, he said abruptly: "If the Robarts legal action goes ahead I'll need money. We're not going to be able to go on as we are. We've got to make plans."

She sat up smartly and stared at him. The kittens, affronted, squealed their protest and fled.

"You mean we might have to leave here?"

The "we" would normally have lifted his heart; now he hardly noticed it.

"It's possible."

"But why? I mean, you aren't going to find anything cheaper than the caravan. Try getting a single room for two pounds a week. We're bloody lucky to have this place."

"But there's no work here, Amy. If I have huge damages to pay I'll have to get a job. That means London."

"What sort of a job?"

"Any sort. I've got my degree."

"Well, I can't see the sense of leaving here even if there isn't any work. You can go to the DHSS. Draw the dole."

"That isn't going to pay damages."

"Well, if you have to go maybe I'll stay on. I can pay the rent here. After all, what's the difference to the owner? He'll get his two quid, whoever pays it."

"You couldn't live here alone."

"Why not? I've lived in worse places."

"On what? What would you do for money?"

"Well, with you gone I could go to the DHSS, couldn't I? They could send their snoopers round and it wouldn't matter. They wouldn't be able to say I was having sex with you then, not if you weren't here. Anyway, I've got a bit in my post-office account."

The casual cruelty of the suggestion struck at his heart. He heard with heavy disgust the note of self-pity which he was unable to suppress. He said: "Is that what you really want, Amy, for me not to be here?"

"Don't be daft, I was only teasing. Honestly, Neil, you should see yourself. Talk about misery. Anyway, it might not happen—the libel action, I mean."

"It's bound to happen unless she withdraws it. They've set a date for the hearing."

"She might withdraw it, or else she might die. She might drown on one of those night swims she takes after the headlines on the nine o'clock news, regular as clockwork, right up to December."

"Who told you that? How do you know that she swims at night?"

"You did."

"I can't remember telling you."

"Then someone else did, one of the regulars in the Local Hero, maybe. I mean, it's no secret, is it?"

He said: "She won't drown. She's a strong swimmer. She wouldn't take foolish risks. And I can't wish her dead. You can't preach love and practise hatred."

"I can—wish her dead, I mean. Maybe the Whistler will get her. Or you might win the action and then she'll have to pay you. That'd be a laugh."

"That's not very likely. I consulted a lawyer at the Citizen's Advice Bureau when I was in Norwich last Friday. I could see he thought it was serious, that she did have a case. He said I ought to get myself a lawyer."

"Well, get one."

"How? Lawyers cost money."

"Get legal aid. Put a note in the newsletter asking for contributions."

"I can't do that. It's difficult enough keeping the newsletter going, what with the cost of paper and postage."

Amy said, suddenly serious: "I'll think of something. There's still four weeks to go. Anything can happen in four weeks. Stop worrying. It's going to be all right. Look, Neil, I promise you that libel action will never come to court." And, illogically, he was, for the moment, reassured and comforted.

7

⊠

It was six o'clock, and at Larksoken Power Station the weekly inter-departmental meeting was drawing to a close. It had lasted thirty minutes longer than usual. Dr. Alex Mair took the view, which he could normally enforce by brisk chairmanship, that little original thought was contributed to a discussion after three hours of talking. But it had been a heavy agenda: the revised safety plan still in draft; the rationalization of the internal structure from the present seven departments to three, under Engineering, Production and Resources; the report of the District Survey Laboratory on their monitoring of the environment; the preliminary agenda for the local Liaison Committee. This annual jamboree was an unwieldy but useful public-relations exercise which needed careful preparation, including as it did rep-resentatives from the interested government departments, local au-thorities, police, fire and water authorities, the National Farmers' Union and the County Landowners' Association. Mair sometimes grudged the work and time it involved but he knew its importance.

The weekly meeting was held in his office at the conference table set in front of the south window. Darkness was falling and the huge pane of glass was a black rectangle in which he could see their faces reflected, like the gaunt, disembodied heads of night travellers in a lighted railway carriage. He suspected that some of his departmental heads, particularly Bill Morgan, the Works Office Engineer, and Ste-phen Mansell, the Maintenance Superintendent, would have preferred a more relaxed setting, in his private sitting room next door, the low, comfortable chairs, a few hours of chat with no set agenda, perhaps a drink together afterwards in a local pub. Well, that was one management style, but it wasn't his.

Now he closed the stiff cover of his folder in which his PA had meticulously tagged all the papers and cross-references, and said dismissively: "Any other business?"

But he was not allowed to get away so easily. On his right, as usual, sat Miles Lessingham, the Operations Superintendent, whose reflection, staring back into the room, looked like a hydrocephalic death's head. Glancing from the image to the face, Mair could see little difference. The stark overhead lights threw deep shadows under the deep-set eyes and the sweat glistened on the wide, rather knobbly forehead with its swathe of fair undisciplined hair. Now he stretched back in his chair and said: "This proposed job—rumoured job, I should say—I suppose we're entitled to ask whether it has been formally offered to you yet? Or aren't we?"

Mair said calmly: "The answer is that it hasn't; the publicity was premature. The press got hold of it somehow, as they usually do, but there's nothing official yet. One unfortunate result of our present habit of leaking any information of interest is that the people most concerned become the last to know. If and when it is official, you seven will be the first to be told."

Lessingham said: "It will have serious implications here, Alex, if you do go. The contract already signed for the new PWR reactor; the internal reorganization, which is bound to create disruption; electricity privatization. It's a bad time for a change at the top."

Mair said: "Is there ever a good time? But until it happens, if it does happen, there's little point in discussing it."

John Standing, the Station Chemist, said: "But the internal reorganization will go ahead, presumably?"

"I hope so, considering the time and energy we've spent planning it. I should be surprised if a change at the top alters a necessary reorganization which is already under way."

Lessingham asked: "Who will they appoint, a Director or a Station Manager?" The question was less innocent than it sounded.

"I imagine a Station Manager."

"You mean that the research will go?"

Mair said: "When I go, now or later, the research will go. You've always known that. I brought it with me and I wouldn't have taken the job if I couldn't have continued it here. I asked for certain research facilities and I got them. But research at Larksoken has always been somewhat of an anomaly. We've done good work, are still doing good work, but logically it should be done elsewhere, at Harwell or Winfrith. Is there any other business?"

But Lessingham was not to be discouraged. He said: "Who will you be responsible to? The Secretary of State for Energy directly or the AEA?"

Mair knew the answer but had no intention of giving it. He said quietly: "That is still under discussion."

"Along, no doubt, with such minor matters as pay, rations, scope of your responsibilities and what you are going to be called. Controller of Nuclear Power has a certain cachet. I like it. But what precisely will you control?"

There was a silence. Mair said: "If the answer to that question were known, no doubt the appointment would have been made by now. I don't want to stifle discussion, but hadn't we better confine it to matters within the competence of this committee? Right, is there any other business?" And this time there was no reply.

Hilary Robarts, the Acting Administrative Officer, had already closed her file. She hadn't taken part in the questioning but the others, Mair knew, would assume that that was because he had already told her the answers.

Even before they had left, his PA, Caroline Amphlett, had come in to take away the teacups and clear the table. Lessingham made it a habit to leave his agenda behind, a small personal protest against the amount of paper which the formal weekly meeting generated. Dr. Martin Goss, head of the Medical Physics Department, had, as always, doodled obsessively. His jotting pad was covered with hot-air balloons, intricately patterned and decorated; part of his mind had obviously been with his private passion. Caroline Amphlett moved, as always, with a quiet, efficient grace. Neither spoke. She had worked for Mair as his PA for the last three years and he knew her now no better than on that morning when she had sat in this same office being interviewed for the job. She was a tall, blonde girl, smooth-skinned, with wide-spaced, rather small eyes of an extraordinary deep blue, who would have been thought beautiful if she had shown more animation. Mair suspected that she used her confidential job as his PA to preserve a deliberately intimidating reserve. She was the most efficient secretary he had ever had and it irked him that she had made it clear that, if and when he moved, she would wish to stay at Larksoken. She had told him that her reasons were personal. That, of course, meant Jonathan Reeves, a junior engineer in the workshop. He had been as surprised and chagrined at her choice as he had at the prospect of taking up a new job with an unknown PA, but there had been an additional and more disturbing reaction. Hers was not a type of female beauty which attracted him, and he had always assumed that she was physically cold. It was disconcerting to think that an acned nonentity had discovered and perhaps explored depths which he, in their daily intimacy, hadn't even suspected. He had sometimes wondered, although with little real curiosity, whether she might not be less compliant, more complicated than he had supposed, had occasionally had a disconcerting sense that the façade she presented to the power station of dedicated, humourless efficiency had been carefully constructed to conceal a less accommodating, more complex personality. But if the real Caroline was accessible to Jonathan Reeves, if she actually liked and wanted that unprepossessing wimp, then she hardly merited the tribute even of his curiosity.

8

He gave his departmental heads time to get back to their offices before
he rang for Hilary Robarts and asked her to come back. It would have
been more usual to have asked her with careful casualness to wait
behind after the meeting, but what he had to say was private and he
had been trying for some weeks now to cut down the number of times
when they were known to be alone together. He wasn't looking forward to the interview. She would see what he had to say as personal
criticism, and that was something which in his experience few women
could take. He thought: "She was my mistress once. I was in love
with her, as much in love as I thought I was capable of being. And
if it wasn't love, whatever that word means, at least I wanted her.
Will that make what I have to say easier or more difficult?" He told
himself that all men were cowards when it came to a showdown with
a woman. That first post-natal subservience, bred of physical depen-
dence, was too ingrained ever to be totally eradicated. He wasn't more
cowardly than the rest of his sex. What was it he had overheard that
woman in the Lydsett stores saying? "George would do anything to
avoid a scene." Of course he would, poor sod. Women, with their
womb-smelling warmth, their talcum powder and milky breasts, had
seen to that in the first four weeks of life.

   He stood up when she came in and waited until she had taken
the chair on the other side of the desk. Then he opened the right-

hand drawer and took out a duplicated news-sheet which he slid across the desk towards her.

"Have you seen this? It's Neil Pascoe's latest news-sheet from PANUP."

She said: "People Against Nuclear Power. That means Pascoe and a few dozen other ill-informed hysterics. Of course I've seen it, I'm on his mailing list. He takes good care that I see it."

She gave it a brief glance, then pushed it back across the desk. He took it up and read: "Many readers will probably have learned by now that I am being sued by Miss Hilary Robarts, the Acting Administrative Officer at Larksoken Power Station, for alleged libel arising from what I wrote in the May issue of the news-sheet. I shall, of course, strenuously defend the action and, as I have no money to pay for a lawyer, will present my own defence. This is just the latest example of the threat to free information and even free speech presented by the nuclear-energy lobby. Apparently now even the mildest criticism is to be followed by the threat of legal action. But there is a positive side. This action by Hilary Robarts shows that we, the ordinary people of this county, are making our impact. Would they bother with our small news-sheet if they weren't running scared? And the libel action, if it comes to trial, will give us valuable national publicity if properly handled. We are stronger than we know. Meanwhile I give below the dates of the next open days at Larksoken so that as many of us as possible can attend and put our case against nuclear power during the question time which normally precedes the actual tour of the station."

She said: "I told you, I've seen it. I don't know why you wasted your time reading it out. He seems determined to aggravate his offence. If he had any sense he'd get himself a good lawyer and keep his mouth shut."

"He can't afford a lawyer. And he won't be able to pay damages." He paused, and then said quietly: "In the interests of the station I think you should drop it."

"Is that an order?"

"I've no power to compel you and you know that. I'm asking you. You'll get nothing out of him, the man's practically penniless, and he isn't worth the trouble."

"He is to me. What he describes as mild criticism was a serious libel and it was widely disseminated. There's no defence. Remember the actual words? 'A woman whose response to Chernobyl is that only thirty-one people were killed, who can dismiss as unimportant one of the world's greatest nuclear disasters, which put thousands in hospital, exposed a hundred thousand or more to dangerous radioactivity, devastated vast areas of land and may result in deaths from cancer amounting to fifty thousand over the next fifty years, is totally unsuitable to be trusted to work in an atomic-power station. While she remains there, in any capacity, we must have the gravest doubts whether safety will ever be taken seriously at Larksoken.' That's a clear allegation of professional incompetence. If he's allowed to get away with that, we'll never get rid of him."

"I wasn't aware that we were in the business of getting rid of inconvenient critics. What method had you in mind?"

He paused, detecting in his voice the first trace of that reedy mixture of sarcasm and pomposity which he knew occasionally affected him and to which he was morbidly sensitive. He went on: "He's a free citizen living where he chooses. He's entitled to his views. Hilary, he's not a worthy opponent. Bring him to court and he'll attract publicity for his cause and do your own no good at all. We're trying to win over the locals, not antagonize them. Let it go before someone starts a fund to pay for his defence. One martyr on Larksoken headland is enough."

While he was speaking she got up and began pacing to and fro across the wide office. Then she paused and turned on him. "This is what it's all about, isn't it? The reputation of the station, your reputation. What about my reputation? If I drop the action now, it will be a clear admission that he was right, that I'm not fit to work here."

"What he wrote hasn't hurt your reputation with anyone who matters. And suing him isn't going to help it. It's unwise to let policy be influenced, let alone jeopardized, by outraged personal pride. The reasonable course is quietly to drop the action. What do feelings matter?" He found that he couldn't remain seated while she was striding to and fro across the office. He got to his feet and walked over to the window, hearing the angry voice but no longer having to face her, watching the reflection of her pacing figure, the swirling hair. He said again: "What do feelings matter? It's the work that is important."

"They matter to me. And that's something you've never understood, have you? Life is about feeling. Loving is about feeling. It was the same with the abortion. You forced me to have it. Did you ever ask yourself what I felt then, what I needed?"

Oh God, he thought, not this, not again, not now. He said, still with his back to her: "It's ridiculous to say that I forced you. How could I? And I thought you felt as I did, that it was impossible for you to have a child."

"Oh no it wasn't. If you're so bloody keen on accuracy, let's be accurate about this. It would have been inconvenient, embarrassing, awkward, expensive. But it wasn't impossible. It still isn't impossible. And for God's sake, turn around. Look at me. I'm talking to you. What I'm saying is important."

He turned and walked back to the desk. He said calmly: "All right, my phrasing was inaccurate. Have a child by all means, if that's what you want. I'll be happy for you as long as you don't expect me to father it. But what we're talking about now is Neil Pascoe and PANUP. We've gone to a lot of trouble here to promote good relations with the local community and I'm not going to have all that good work vitiated by a totally unnecessary legal action, particularly not now when work will soon begin on the new reactor."

"Then try to prevent it. And since we're talking about public relations, I'm surprised you haven't mentioned Ryan Blaney and Scudder's Cottage. My cottage, in case you've forgotten. What am I expected to do about that? Hand over my property to him and his kids rent-free in the interests of good public relations?"

"That's a different matter. It's not my concern as Director. But if you want my opinion, I think you're ill advised to try and force him out simply because you've got a legal case. He's paying the rent regularly, isn't he? And it isn't as if you want the cottage."

"I do want the cottage. It's mine. I bought it and now I want to sell it."

She slumped back into the chair and he, too, sat. He made himself stare into the eyes in which, to his discomfort, he saw more pain than anger. He said: "Presumably he knows that and he'll get out when he can, but it won't be easy. He's recently widowed and he's got four children. There's a certain amount of local feeling about it, I understand."

"I've no doubt there is, particularly in the Local Hero, where Ryan

Blaney spends most of his time and money. I'm not prepared to wait. If we're moving to London in the next three months, there's not much time to get the question of the cottage settled. I don't want to leave that kind of unfinished business. I want to get it on the market as soon as possible."

He knew that this was the moment when he should have said firmly: "I may be moving to London, but not with you." But he found it impossible. He told himself that it was late, the end of a busy day, the worst possible time for rational argument. She was already over-wrought. One thing at a time. He had tackled her about Pascoe and, although she had reacted much as he'd expected, perhaps she would think it over and do what he advised. And she was right about Ryan Blaney: it was none of his business. The interview had left him with two clear intentions more firmly fixed than ever in his mind. She wasn't coming to London with him, nor would he recommend her as Administrative Officer at Larksoken. For all her efficiency, her intelligence, her appropriate education, she wasn't the right person for the job. For a moment it crossed his mind that here was his bargaining card. "I'm not offering you marriage but I am offering you the most senior job you could possibly aspire to." But he knew there was no real temptation. He wouldn't leave the administration of Larksoken in her hands. Sooner or later she was going to have to realize that there would be no marriage and no promotion. But now was the wrong moment, and he found himself wondering wryly when the right moment might be.

Instead he said: "Look, we're here to run a power station efficiently and safely. We're doing a necessary and important job. Of course we're committed to it, we wouldn't be here otherwise. But we're scientists and technicians, not evangelists. We're not running a religious campaign."

"They are, the other side. He is. You see him as an insignificant twit. He isn't. He's dishonest and he's dangerous. Look how he scrubs around in the records to turn up individual cases of leukaemia which he thinks he can ascribe to nuclear energy. And now he's got the latest Comare report to fuel his spurious concern. And what about last month's newsletter, that emotive nonsense about the midnight trains of death trundling silently through the northern suburbs of London? Anyone would think they were carrying open trucks of radioactive waste. Doesn't he care that nuclear energy has so far saved the world from burning five hundred million tons of coal? Hasn't he heard about the greenhouse effect? I mean, is the fool totally ignorant? Hasn't he any conception of the devastation caused to this planet by burning fossil fuels? Has no one told him about acid rain or the carcinogens in coal waste? And when it comes to danger, what about the fifty-seven miners buried alive in the Borken disaster only this year? Don't their lives matter? Think of the outcry if that had been a nuclear accident."

He said: "He's only one voice, and a pathetically uneducated and ignorant one."

"But he's having his effect, and you know it. We've got to match passion with passion."

His mind fastened on the word. We're not, he thought, talking about nuclear energy, we're talking about passion. Would we be having this conversation if we were still lovers? She's demanding from me a commitment to something more personal than atomic power. Turning to face her, he was visited suddenly, not by desire, but by a memory, inconveniently intense, of the desire he had once felt for her. And with memory came a sudden vivid picture of them together in her cottage, the heavy breasts bent over him, her hair falling across his face, her lips, her hands, her thighs.

He said roughly: "If you want a religion, if you need a religion, then find one. There are plenty to choose from. All right, the abbey is in ruins and I doubt whether that impotent old priest up at the Old Rectory has much on offer. But find something or someone: give up fish on Friday, don't eat meat, count beads, put ashes on your head, meditate four times a day, bow down towards your own personal Mecca. But don't, for God's sake, assuming He exists, ever make science into a religion."

The telephone on his desk rang. Caroline Amphlett had left, and it was switched through to an outside line. As he lifted the receiver he saw that Hilary was standing at the door. She gave him a last long look and went out, shutting it with unnecessary firmness behind her.

The caller was his sister. She said: "I hoped I'd catch you. I forgot to remind you to call at Bollard's farm for the ducks for Thursday. He'll have them ready. We'll be six, incidentally. I've invited Adam Dalgliesh. He's back on the headland."

He was able to answer her as calmly as she had spoken.

"Congratulations. He and his aunt have contrived with some skill to avoid their neighbours' cutlets for the last five years. How did you manage it?"

"By the expedient of asking. I imagine he may be thinking of keeping on the mill as a holiday home and feels it's time to acknowledge that he does have neighbours. Or he may be planning to sell, in which case he can risk a dinner party without being trapped into intimacy. But why not give him credit for a simple human weakness—the attraction of eating a good dinner which he hasn't had to cook?"

And it would balance her table, thought Mair, although that was hardly likely to have been a consideration. She despised the Noah's Ark convention which decreed that a superfluous man, however unattractive or stupid, was acceptable; a superfluous woman, however witty and well informed, a social embarrassment.

He said: "Am I expected to talk about his poetry?"

"I imagine he's come to Larksoken to get away from people who want to talk about his poetry. But it wouldn't hurt you to take a look at it. I've got the most recent volume. And it is poetry, not prose rearranged on the page."

"With modern verse, can one tell the difference?"

"Oh yes," she said. "If it can be read as prose, then it is prose. It's an infallible test."

"But not one, I imagine, that the English faculties would support. I'll be leaving in ten minutes. I won't forget the ducks." He smiled as he replaced the receiver. His sister invariably had the power to restore him to good humour.

9

⊠

Before leaving he stood for a moment at the door and let his eyes range round the room as if he were seeing it for the last time. He was ambitious for the new job, had cleverly planned and schemed to get it. And now, when it was almost his, he realized how much he would miss Larksoken, its remoteness, its bleak uncompromising strength. Nothing had been done to prettify the site as at Sizewell, on the Suffolk coast, or to produce the pleasantly laid-out grounds of smooth lawn, flowering trees and shrubs which so agreeably impressed him on his periodic visits to Winfrith in Dorset. A low, curving wall faced with flint had been built on the seaward boundary, behind whose shelter every spring a bright ribbon of daffodils strained and tossed in the March winds. Little else had been done to harmonize or soften the concrete's grey immensity. But this was what he liked, the wide expanse of turbulent sea, browny-grey, white-laced under a limitless sky, windows which he could open so that, at a touch of his hand, the faint continuous boom like distant thunder would instantaneously pour into his office in a roar of crashing billows. He liked best the stormy winter evenings when, working late, he could see the lights of shipping prinking the horizon as they made their way down the coast to the Yarmouth lanes, and see the flashing light ships and the beam from Happisburgh Lighthouse which for generations had warned mariners of the treacherous offshore sands. Even on the darkest night, by the light which the sea seemed mysteriously to absorb and reflect, he could make out the splendid fifteenth-century West Tower of Happisburgh Church, that embattled symbol of man's precarious defences against this most dangerous of seas. And it was a symbol of more than that. The tower must have been the last sight of land for hundreds of drowning mariners in peace and war. His mind, always tenacious of facts, could recall the details at will. The crew of HMS *Peggy*, driven ashore on 19 December 1770, the 119 members of HMS *Invincible* wrecked on the sands on 13 March 1801 when on her way to join Nelson's fleet at Copenhagen, the crew of HMS *Hunter*, the revenue cutter lost in 1804, many of their crews buried under the grassy mounds in Happisburgh Churchyard. Built in an age of faith, the tower had stood as a symbol, too, of that final, unquenchable hope that even the sea would yield up her dead and that their God was God of the waters as He was of the land. But now mariners could see, dwarfing the tower, the huge rectangular bulk of Larksoken Power Station. For those who sought symbols in inanimate objects, its message was both simple and expedient, that man, by his own intelligence and his own efforts, could understand and master his world, could make his transitory life more agreeable, more comfortable, more free of pain. For him this was challenging enough, and if he had needed a faith to live by it would have been starkly sufficient. But sometimes, on the darkest nights, when the waves pounded the shingle like bursts of distant gunfire, both the science and the symbol would seem to him as transitory as those drowned lives, and he would find himself wondering if this great hulk would one day yield to the sea, like the wave-smashed concrete from the last war's defences, and like them become a broken symbol of man's long history on this desolate coast. Or would it resist even time and the North Sea and still be standing when the final darkness fell over the planet? In his more pessimistic moments some rogue part of his mind knew this darkness to be inevitable, although he did not expect it to come in his time, maybe not even in his son's. He would sometimes smile wryly, telling himself that he and Neil Pascoe, on different sides, would understand each other well. The only difference was that one of them had hope.

10
⊠

Jane Dalgliesh had bought Larksoken Mill five years earlier, when she had moved from her previous home on the Suffolk coast. The mill, which was built in 1825, was a picturesque brick tower four storeys high with an octagonal dome cap and a skeleton fantail. It had been converted as a seaside home some years before Miss Dalgliesh had bought it by the addition of a flint-faced two-storey building with a large sitting room, smaller study and kitchen on the ground floor and three bedrooms, two of them with their own bathrooms, on the floor above. Dalgliesh had never asked her why she had moved to Norfolk, but he guessed that the mill's main attraction had been its remoteness, its closeness to notable bird sanctuaries and the impressive view of headland, sky and sea from the top storey. Perhaps she had intended to restore it to working order but with increasing age hadn't been able to summon the energy or enthusiasm to cope with the disturbance. He had inherited it as an agreeable but mildly onerous responsibility, together with her considerable fortune. The origin of that had only become plain after her death. It had been left to her by a noted amateur ornithologist and eccentric with whom she had been friendly for many years. Whether the relationship had gone beyond friendship Dalgliesh would now never know. She had, apparently, spent little of the money on herself, had been a dependable benefactress of the few unusual charities of which she approved, had remembered them in her will but without egregious generosity and had left the residue of her estate to him without explanation, admonition or peculiar protestations of affection, although he had no doubt that the words "my dearly beloved nephew" meant exactly what they said. He had liked her, respected her, had always been at ease in her company, but he had never thought that he really knew her, and now he never would. He was a little surprised how much he minded.

The only change she had made to the property was to build a garage, and after he had unloaded and put away the Jaguar, he decided to climb to the top chamber of the mill while it was still light. The bottom room, with its two huge grinding wheels of burr-granite propped against the wall and its lingering smell of flour, still held an air of mystery, of time held in abeyance, of a place bereft of its purpose and meaning, so that he never entered it without a slight sense of desolation. There were only ladders between the floors and, as he grasped the rungs, he saw again his aunt's long, trousered legs ahead of him disappearing into the chamber above. She had used only the top room of the mill, which she had furnished simply with a small writing table and a chair facing the North Sea, a telephone and her binoculars. Entering it he could imagine her sitting there in the summer days and evenings, working on the papers which she occasionally contributed to ornithological journals and looking up from time to time to gaze out over the headland to the sea and the far horizon, could see again that carved, weather-browned Aztec face with its hooded eyes under the grey-black hair, drawn back into a bun, could hear again a voice which, for him, had been one of the most beautiful female voices he had ever heard.

Now it was late afternoon and the headland lay enriched by the mellow afternoon light, the sea a wide expanse of wrinkled blue with a painter's stroke of purple laid on the horizon. The colours and shapes were intensified by the sun's last strong rays, so that the ruins of the abbey looked unreal, a golden fantasy against the blue of the sea, and the dry grass gleamed as richly as a lush water meadow. There was a window at each of the compass points and, binoculars in hand, he made his slow perambulation. To the west his eyes could travel along the narrow road between the reed beds and the dykes to the flint-walled and Dutch-gabled cottages and the pantiled roofs of Lydsett Village and the round tower of St. Andrew's Church. To the north the view was dominated by the huge bulk of the power station, the low-roofed administration block with, behind it, the reactor building and the great steel, aluminium-clad building of the turbine house. Four hundred metres out to sea were the rigs and platforms of the intake structures through which the cooling sea water passed to the pump house and the circulating water pumps. He moved again to the eastern window and looked out over the cottages of the headland. Far to the south he could just glimpse the roof of Scudder's Cottage. Directly to his left the flint walls of Martyr's Cottage glistened like marbles in the afternoon sun, and less than half a mile to the north, set back among the Californian pines which fringed that part of the coast, was the dull square cottage rented by Hilary Robarts, a neatly proportional suburban villa incongruously set down on this bleak headland and facing inland as if resolutely ignoring the sea. Farther inland, and only just visible from the southern window, was the Old Rectory, set like a Victorian dolls' house in its large, overgrown garden, which, at this distance, looked as neatly green and formal as a municipal park.

The telephone rang. The strident peal was unwelcome. It was to get away from such intrusions that he had come to Larksoken. But the call was not unexpected. It was Terry Rickards saying that he would like to drop in for a chat with Mr. Dalgliesh if it wouldn't be too much bother, and would 9.00 be convenient? Dalgliesh was unable to think of a single excuse why it shouldn't be.

Ten minutes later he left the tower, locking the door after him. This precaution was a small act of piety. His aunt had always kept the door locked, fearing that children might venture into the mill and hurt themselves by tumbling down the ladders. Leaving the tower to its darkness and its solitude, he went into Mill Cottage to unpack and get his supper.

The huge sitting room with its York stone floor, rugs and open fireplace was a comfortable and nostalgic mixture of the old and the new. Most of the furniture was familiar to him from boyhood visits to his grandparents, inherited by his aunt as the last of her generation. Only the music centre and the television set were comparatively new. Music had been important to her, and the shelves held a catholic collection of records with which he could refresh or console himself during the two weeks' holiday. And next door, the kitchen contained nothing superfluous but everything necessary to a woman who enjoyed food but preferred to cook it with a minimum of fuss. He put a couple of lamb chops under the grill, made a green salad and prepared to enjoy the few hours of solitude before the intrusion of Rickards and his preoccupations.

It still surprised him a little that his aunt had finally bought a television set. Had she been seduced into conformity by the excellence of the natural-history programmes and then, like other late converts he had known, sat captive to virtually every offering as if making up for lost time? That at least seemed unlikely. He switched on to see if the set was still working. A jerking pop star was wielding his guitar as the credits rolled, his parodic sexual gyrations so grotesque that it was difficult to see that even the besotted young could find them erotic. Switching off, Dalgliesh looked up at the oil portrait of his maternal great-grandfather, the Victorian bishop, robed but unmitred, his arms in their billowing lawn sleeves confidently resting on the arms of the chair. He had an impulse to say, "This is the music of 1988; these are our heroes; that building on the headland is our architecture and I dare not stop my car to help children home be-cause they've been taught with good reason that a strange man might abduct and rape them." He could have added, "And out there some-where is a mass murderer who enjoys strangling women and stuffing their mouths with their hair." But that aberration, at least, was in-dependent of changing fashions, and his great-grandfather would have had his scrupulous but uncompromising answer to it. And with reason. After all, hadn't he been consecrated bishop in 1880, the year of Jack the Ripper? And probably he would have found the Whistler more understandable than the pop star, whose gyrations would surely have convinced him that man was in the grip of his final, manic St. Vitus's dance.

Rickards came promptly on time. It was precisely 9.00 when Dalgliesh heard his car and, opening the door on the darkness of the night, saw his tall figure striding towards him. Dalgliesh hadn't seen him for more than ten years, when he had been a newly appointed inspector in the Metropolitan CID, and was surprised to see how little he had changed; time, marriage, removal from London, promotion had left no apparent mark on him. His rangy, graceless figure, over six feet high, still looked as incongruous in a formal suit as it always had. The rugged weather-beaten face, with its look of dependable fortitude, would have looked more appropriate above a seaman's guernsey, preferably with RNLI woven across the chest. In profile his face, with the long, slightly hooked nose and jutting eyebrows, was impressive. In full face the nose was revealed as a little too wide and flattened at the base, and the dark eyes, which when he was animated took on a fierce, almost manic gleam, in repose were pools of puzzled endurance. Dalgliesh thought of him as a type of police officer less common than formerly but still not rare: the conscientious and incorruptible detective of limited imagination and somewhat greater intelligence who had never supposed that the evil of the world should be condoned because it was frequently inexplicable and its perpetrators unfortunate.

He gazed round the sitting room at the long wall of books, the crackling wood fire, the oil of the Victorian prelate above the mantelshelf as if deliberately impressing each item on his mind, then sank into his chair and stretched out his long legs with a small grunt of satisfaction. Dalgliesh remembered that he had always drunk beer; now he accepted whisky, but said he could do with coffee first. One habit at least had changed. He said: "I'm sorry that you won't be meeting Susie, my wife, while you're here, Mr. Dalgliesh. She's having our first baby in a couple of weeks, and she's gone to stay with her mother in York. Ma-in-law didn't like the idea of her being in Norfolk with the Whistler on the prowl, not with me working the hours I do."

It was said with a kind of embarrassed formality, as if he, not Dalgliesh, were the host and he was apologizing for the unexpected absence of the hostess. He added: "I suppose it's natural for an only daughter to want to be with her mother at a time like this, particularly with a first baby."

Dalgliesh's wife hadn't wanted to be with her mother, she had wanted to be with him, had wanted it with such intensity that he had wondered afterwards whether she might have felt a premonition. He could remember that, although he could no longer recall her face. His memory of her, which for years, a traitor to grief and to their love, he had resolutely tried to suppress because the pain had seemed unbearable, had gradually been replaced by a boyish, romantic dream of gentleness and beauty now fixed for ever beyond the depredation of time. His newborn son's face he could still recall vividly and sometimes did in his dreams, that white unsullied look of sweet knowledgeable contentment, as if, in a brief moment of life, he had seen and known all there was to know, seen it and rejected it. Dalgliesh told himself that he was the last man who could reasonably be expected to advise or reassure on the problems of pregnancy, and he sensed that Rickards's unhappiness at his wife's absence went deeper than missing her company. He made the usual enquiries about her health and escaped into the kitchen to make the coffee.

Whatever mysterious spirit had unlocked the verse, it had freed him for other human satisfactions, for love; or was it the other way around? Had love unlocked the verse? It seemed even to have affected his job. Grinding the coffee beans, he pondered life's smaller ambiguities. When the poetry hadn't come, the job too had seemed not only irksome but occasionally repellent. Now he was happy enough to let Rickards impose on his solitude to use him as a sounding board. This new benignity and tolerance a little disconcerted him. Success in moderation was no doubt better for the character than failure, but too much of it and he would lose his cutting edge. And five minutes later, carrying in the two mugs and settling back in his chair, he could relish the contrast between Rickards's preoccupation with psychopathic violence and the peace of the mill. The wood fire, now past its crackling stage, had settled into a comfortable glow, and the wind, seldom absent from the headland, moved like a benign, gently hissing spirit through the still and soaring clappers of the mill. He was glad that it wasn't his job to catch the Whistler. Of all murders, serial killings were the most frustrating, the most difficult and the chanciest to solve, the investigation carried on under the strain of vociferous public demand that the terrifying unknown devil be caught and exorcised forever. But this wasn't his case; he could discuss it with the detachment of a man who has a professional interest but no responsibility. And he could understand what Rickards needed: not advice— he knew his job—but someone he could trust, someone who understood the language, someone who would afterwards be gone, who wouldn't remain as a perpetual reminder of his uncertainties, a fellow professional to whom he could comfortably think aloud. He had his team and he was too punctilious not to share his thinking with them. But he was a man who needed to articulate his theories and here he could put them forward, embroider, reject, explore, without the uncomfortable suspicion that his detective sergeant, deferentially listening, his face carefully expressionless, would be thinking, "For God's sake, what's the old man dreaming up now?" Or, "The old man's getting fanciful."

Rickards said: "We're not using Holmes. The Met say the system is fully committed at present, and anyway we've got our own computer. Not that there's much data to feed in. The press and public know about Holmes, of course. I get that at every press conference. 'Are you using the Home Office special computer, the one named after Sherlock Holmes?' 'No,' I say, 'but we're using our own.' Unspoken question: 'Then why the hell haven't you caught him?' They think that you've only got to feed in your data and out pops an Identikit of sonny complete with prints, collar size and taste in pop music."

"Yes," said Dalgliesh, "we're so sated now with scientific wonders that it's a bit disconcerting when we find that technology can do everything except what we want it to."

"Four women so far, and Valerie Mitchell won't be the last if we don't catch him soon. He started fifteen months ago. The first victim was found just after midnight in a shelter at the end of the Easthaven promenade—the local tart, incidentally, although he may not have known or cared. It was eight months before he struck again. Struck lucky, I suppose he'd say. This time a thirty-year-old schoolteacher cycling home to Hunstanton who had a puncture on a lonely stretch of road. Then another gap, just six months, before he got a barmaid from Ipswich who'd been visiting her granny and was daft enough to wait alone for the late bus. When it arrived there was no one at the stop. A couple of local youths got off. They'd had a skinful so weren't in a particularly noticing mood, but they saw and heard nothing, nothing except what they described as a kind of mournful whistling coming from deep in the wood."

He took a gulp of his coffee, then went on: "We've got a personality assessment from the trick cyclist. I don't know why we bother. I could have written it myself. He tells us to look for a loner, probably from a disturbed family background, may have a dominant mother, doesn't relate easily to people, particularly women, could be impotent, un-married, separated or divorced, with a resentment and hatred of the opposite sex. Well, we hardly expect him to be a successful, happily married bank manager with four lovely kids just coming up to GCSE or whatever they call it now. They're the devil, these serial murders. No motive—no motive that a sane man can understand anyway—and he could come from anywhere, Norwich, Ipswich, even London. It's dangerous to assume that he's necessarily working in his own territory. Looks like it, though. He obviously knows the locality well. And he seems to be sticking now to the same MO. He chooses a road intersection, drives the car or van into the side of one road, cuts across and waits at the other. Then he drags his victim into the bushes or the trees, kills and cuts back to the other road and the car and makes his getaway. With the last three murders it seems to have been pure chance that a suitable victim did, in fact, come along."

Dalgliesh felt that it was time he contributed something to the speculation. He said: "If he doesn't select and stalk his victim, and obviously he didn't in the last three cases, he'd normally have to expect a long wait. That suggests he's routinely out after dark, a night worker, mole-catcher, woodman, gamekeeper, that kind of job. And he goes prepared: on the watch for a quick kill, in more ways than one."

Rickards said: "That's how I see it. Four victims so far and three fortuitous, but he's probably been on the prowl for three years or more. That could be part of the thrill. 'Tonight I could make a strike, tonight I could be lucky.' And, by God, he is getting lucky. Two victims in the last six weeks."

"And what about his trademark, the whistle?"

"That was heard by the three people who came quickly on the scene after the Easthaven murder. One just heard a whistle, one said it sounded like a hymn and the third, who was a churchwoman, claimed she could identify it precisely, 'Now the Day Is Over.' We kept quiet about that. It could be useful when we get the usual clutch of nutters claiming they're the Whistler. But there seems no doubt that he does whistle."

Dalgliesh said: " 'Now the day is over / Night is drawing nigh / Shadows of the evening / Fall across the sky.' It's a Sunday-school hymn, hardly the kind that gets requested on *Songs of Praise*, I should have thought."

He remembered it from childhood, a lugubrious, undistinguished tune which as a ten-year-old he could pick out on the drawing-room piano. Did anyone sing that hymn now? he wondered. It had been a favourite choice of Miss Barnett on those long dark afternoons in winter before the Sunday school was released, when the outside light was fading and the small Adam Dalgliesh was already dreading those last twenty yards of his walk home, where the rectory drive curved and the bushes grew thickest. Night was different from bright day, smelled different, sounded different; ordinary things assumed different shapes; an alien and more sinister power ruled the night. Those twenty yards of crunching gravel, where the lights of the house were momentarily screened, were a weekly horror. Once through the gate to the drive, he would walk fast, but not too fast, since the power that ruled the night could smell out fear as dogs smell out terror. His mother, he knew, would never have expected him to walk those yards alone had she known that he suffered such atavistic panic, but she hadn't known and he would have died before telling her. And his father? His father would have expected him to be brave, would have told him that God was God of the darkness as He was of the light. There were after all a dozen appropriate texts he could have quoted. "Darkness and light are both alike to Thee." But they were not alike to a sensitive ten-year-old boy. It was on those lonely walks that he had first had intimations of an essentially adult truth, that it is those who most love us who cause us the most pain. He said: "So you're looking for a local man, a loner, someone who has a night job, the use of a car or van and a knowledge of *Hymns Ancient and Modern*. That should make it easier."

Rickards said: "You'd think so, wouldn't you."

He sat in silence for a minute, then said: "I think I'd like just a small whisky now, Mr. Dalgliesh, if it's all the same to you."

It was after midnight when he finally left. Dalgliesh walked out with him to the car. Looking out across the headland, Rickards said: "He's out there somewhere, watching, waiting. There's hardly a waking moment when I don't think of him, imagine what he looks like, where he is, what he's thinking. Susie's ma is right. I haven't had much to give her recently. And when he's caught, that'll be the end. It's finished. You move on. He doesn't, but you do. And by the end you know everything, or think you do. Where, when, who, how. You might even know why if you're lucky. And yet, essentially, you know nothing. All that wickedness, and you don't have to explain it or understand it or do a bloody thing about it except put a stop to it. Involvement without responsibility. No responsibility for what he did or for what happens to him afterwards. That's for the judge and the jury. You're involved, and yet you're not involved. Is that what appeals to you about the job, Mr. Dalgliesh?"

It was not a question Dalgliesh would have expected even from a friend, and Rickards was not a friend. He said: "Can any of us answer that question?"

"You remember why I left the Met, Mr. Dalgliesh."

"The two corruption cases? Yes, I remember why you left the Met."

"And you stayed. You didn't like it any more than I did. You wouldn't have touched the pitch. But you stayed. You were detached about it all, weren't you? It interested you."

Dalgliesh said: "It's always interesting when men you thought you knew behave out of character."

And Rickards had fled from London. In search of what? Dalgliesh wondered. Some romantic dream of country peace, an England which had vanished, a gentler method of policing, total honesty? He wondered whether Rickards had found it.

BOOK TWO

**Thursday 22 September
to
Friday 23 September**

1

⊠

It was 7.10 and the saloon bar of the Duke of Clarence pub was already smoke-filled, the noise level rising and the crowd at the bar three feet deep. Christine Baldwin, the Whistler's fifth victim, had exactly twenty minutes to live. She sat on the banquette against the wall, sipping her second medium sherry of the evening, deliberately making it last, knowing that Colin was impatient to order the next round. Catching Norman's eye, she raised her left wrist and nodded significantly at her watch. Already it was ten minutes past their deadline, and he knew it. Their agreement was that this was to be a pre-supper drink with Colin and Yvonne, the limit both of time and alcohol consumption clearly understood between her and Norman before they left home. The arrangement was typical of their nine-month-old marriage, sustained less by compatible interests than by a carefully negotiated series of concessions. Tonight it had been her turn to give way, but agreeing to spend an hour in the Clarence with Colin and Yvonne didn't extend to any pretence that she actually enjoyed their company.

She had disliked Colin since their first meeting; the relationship at a glance had been fixed in the stereotyped antagonism between newly acquired fiancée and slightly disreputable old schoolmate and drinking partner. He had been best man at their wedding—a formidable pre-nuptial agreement had been necessary for that capitulation—and had carried out his duties with a mixture of incompetence, vulgarity and irreverence which, as she occasionally enjoyed telling Norman, had spoilt for her the memory of her big day. It was typical of him to choose this pub. God knew, it was vulgar enough. But at least she could be certain of one thing: it wasn't a place where there was a risk of meeting anyone from the power station, at least not anyone who mattered. She disliked everything about the Clarence, the rough scrape of the moquette against her legs, the synthetic velvet which covered the walls, the baskets of ivy spiked with artificial flowers above the bar, the gaudiness of the carpet. Twenty years ago, it had been a cosy Victorian hostelry, seldom visited except by its regulars, with an open fire in winter and horse brasses polished to whiteness hung against the black beams. The lugubrious publican had seen it as his job to repel strangers and had employed to that end an impressive armoury of taciturnity, malevolent glances, warm beer and poor service. But the old pub had burnt down in the 1960s and been replaced by a more profitable and thrusting enterprise. Nothing of the old building remained, and the long extension to the bar, dignified by the name Banqueting Hall, provided for the undiscriminating a venue for weddings and local functions and on other nights served a predictable menu of prawns or soup, steak or chicken, and fruit salad with ice cream. Well, at least she had put her foot down over dinner. They had worked out their monthly budget to the last pound, and if Norman thought she was going to eat this overpriced muck with a perfectly good cold supper waiting in the refrigerator at home and a decent programme on the telly, he could forget it. And they had better uses for their money than to sit here drinking with Colin and his latest tart, who had opened her legs to half Norwich if rumour was to be believed. There were the hire-purchase repayments on the sitting-room furniture and the car, not to mention the mortgage. She tried again to meet Norman's eye, but he was rather desperately keeping his attention on that slut Yvonne. And that wasn't proving difficult. Colin leaned over to her, his bold treacle-brown eyes half-mocking, half-inviting, Colin Lomas, who thought every woman would swoon when he beckoned.

"Relax, darling. Your old man's enjoying himself. It's your round, Norm."

Ignoring Colin, she spoke to Norman: "Look, it's time we were going. We agreed we'd leave at seven."

"Oh, come on, Chrissie, give the lad a break. One more round."

Without meeting her eyes, Norman said: "What'll you have, Yvonne? The same again? Medium sherry?"

Colin said: "Let's get on to spirits. I'll have a Johnnie Walker."

He was doing it on purpose. She knew that he didn't even like whisky. She said:

"Look, I've had enough of this bloody place. The noise has given me a head."

"A headache? Nine months married and she's started the headaches. No point in hurrying home tonight, Norm."

Yvonne giggled.

Christine said, her face burning, "You were always vulgar, Colin Lomas, but now you're not even funny with it. You three can do what you like. I'm going home. Give me the car keys."

Colin leaned back and smiled. "You heard what your lady wife said. She wants the car keys."

Without a word, shame-faced, Norman took them out of his pocket and slid them over the table. She snatched them up, pushed back the table, struggled past Yvonne and rushed to the door. She was almost crying with rage. It took her a minute to unlock the car, and then she sat shaking behind the wheel, waiting until her hands were steady enough to switch on the ignition. She heard her mother's voice on the day when she had announced her engagement: "Well, you're thirty-two, and if he's what you want I suppose you know your own mind. But you'll never make anything of him. Weak as water, if you ask me." But she had thought that she could make something of him, and that small semi-detached house outside Norwich represented nine months of hard work and achievement. Next year he was due for promotion at the insurance office. She would be able to give up her job as secretary in the Medical Physics Department at Larksoken Power Station and start the first of the two children she had planned. She would be thirty-four by then. Everyone knew that you shouldn't wait too long.

She had only passed her driving test after her marriage, and this was the first time that she had driven unaccompanied at night. She drove slowly and carefully, her anxious eyes peering ahead, glad that, at least, the route home was familiar. She wondered what Norman would do when he saw that the car had gone. Almost certainly he would expect to find her sitting there, fuming but ready to be driven home. Now he'd have to rely for a lift on Colin, who wouldn't be so keen on coming out of his way. And if they thought that she was going to invite Colin and Yvonne in for a drink when they arrived, they would get a shock.

The thought of Norman's discomfiture at finding her gone cheered her a little, and she pressed her foot down on the accelerator, anxious to distance herself from the three of them, to reach the safety of home. But suddenly the car gave a stutter and the engine died. She must have been driving more erratically than she thought, for she found herself half-slewed across the road. It was a bad place to be stranded, a lonely stretch of country lane with a thin band of trees on either side, and it was deserted. And then she remembered. Norman had mentioned that they needed to fill up with petrol and must be sure to call at the all-night garage after they left the Clarence. It was ridiculous to have let the tank get so low, but they had had an argument only three days earlier on whose turn it was to call at the garage and pay for the petrol. All her anger and frustration returned. For a moment she sat there, beating her hands impotently on the wheel, desperately turning the key in the ignition, willing the engine to start. But there was no response. And then irritation began to give way to the first tricklings of fear. The road was deserted and, even if a motorist came by and drew up, could she be certain that he wasn't a kidnapper, a rapist, even the Whistler? There had been that horrible murder on the A3 only this year. Nowadays you could trust no one. And she could hardly leave the car where it was, slewed across the road. She tried to recall when she had last passed a house, an AA box, a public telephone, but it seemed to her that she had been driving through deserted countryside for at least ten minutes. Even if she left the dubious sanctuary of the car, she had no clue to the best direction in which to seek help. Suddenly a wave of total panic swept across her like nausea and she had to resist the urge to dash from the car and hide herself among the trees. But what good would that do? He might be lurking even there.

And then, miraculously, she heard footsteps and, looking round, saw a woman approaching. She was dressed in trousers and a trench coat and had a mane of fair hair beneath a tight-fitting beret. At her side, on a leash, trotted a small, smooth-haired dog. Immediately all her anxiety vanished. Here was someone who would help her push the car into the side of the road, who would know in which direction lay the nearest house, who would be a companion on her walk. Without even troubling to slam the door of the car, she called out happily and ran smiling towards the horror of her death.

2

⊠

The dinner had been excellent and the wine, a Château Potensac '78, an interesting choice with the main course. Although Dalgliesh knew of Alice Mair's reputation as a cookery writer, he had never read any of her books and had no idea to what culinary school, if any, she belonged. He had hardly feared being presented with the usual artistic creation swimming in a pool of sauce and accompanied by one or two undercooked carrots and mangetouts elegantly arranged on a side plate. But the wild ducks carved by Alex Mair had been recognizably ducks, the piquant sauce, new to him, enhanced rather than dominated the taste of the birds and the small mounds of creamed turnip and parsnip were an agreeable addition to green peas. Afterwards they had eaten orange sorbet followed by cheese and fruit. It was a conventional menu but one intended, he felt, to please the guests rather than to demonstrate the ingenuity of the cook.

The expected fourth guest, Miles Lessingham, had unaccountably failed to arrive, but Alice Mair hadn't rearranged her table, and the empty chair and unfilled wineglass were uncomfortably evocative of Banquo's ghost. Dalgliesh was seated opposite Hilary Robarts. The portrait, he thought, must have been even more powerful than he realized if it could so dominate his physical reaction to the living woman. It was the first time they had met, although he had known of her existence, as he had of all the handful of people who lived, as the Lydsett villagers said, "t'other side of the gate." And it was a little strange that this was their first meeting; her red Golf was a frequent sight on the headland, her cottage had frequently met his eyes from the top storey of the mill. Now, physically close for the first time, he found it difficult to keep his eyes off her, living flesh and remembered image seeming to fuse into a presence both potent and disturbing. It was a handsome face, a model's face, he thought, with its high cheek-bones, long, slightly concave nose, wide full lips and dark angry eyes deeply set under the strong brows. Her crimped springing hair, held back with two combs, fell over her shoulders. He could imagine her posed, mouth moistly open, hips jutting, and staring at the cameras with that apparently obligatory look of arrogant resentment. As she leaned forward to twitch another grape from the bunch and almost toss it into her mouth, he could see the faint freckles which smudged the dark forehead, the glisten of hairs above a carved upper lip.

On the other side of their host sat Meg Dennison, delicately but unfussily peeling her grapes with pink-tipped fingers. Hilary Robarts's sultry handsomeness emphasized her own very different look, an old-fashioned, carefully tended but unselfconscious prettiness which re-minded him of photographs of the late 1930s. Their clothes pointed up the contrast. Hilary wore a shirt-waister dress in multicoloured Indian cotton, three buttons at the neck undone. Meg Dennison was in a long black skirt and a blue-patterned silk blouse with a bow at the neck. But it was their hostess who was the most elegant. The long shift in fine dark-brown wool worn with a heavy necklace of silver and amber hid her angularity and emphasized the strength and regularity of the strong features. Beside her Meg Dennison's prettiness was diminished almost to insipidity and Hilary Robarts's strong-coloured cotton looked tawdry.

The room in which they were dining must, he thought, have been part of the original cottage. From these smoke-blackened beams Agnes Poley had hung her sides of bacon, her bundles of dried herbs. In a post slung over that huge hearth she had cooked her family's meals and, perhaps, at the end had heard in its roaring flames the crackling fagots of her dreadful martyrdom. Outside the long window had passed the helmets of marching men. But only in the name of the cottage was there a memory of the past. The oval dining table and the chairs were modern, as were the Wedgwood dinner service and the elegant glasses. In the drawing room, where they had drunk

their pre-dinner sherry, Dalgliesh had a sense of a room which deliberately rejected the past, containing nothing which could violate the
owner's essential privacy: no family history in photograph or portrait,
no shabby heirlooms given room out of nostalgia, sentimentality or
family piety, no antiques collected over the years. Even the few pictures, three recognizably by John Piper, were modern. The furniture
was expensive, comfortable, well designed, too elegantly simple to be
offensively out of place. But the heart of the cottage wasn't there. It
was in that large, warm-smelling and welcoming kitchen.

He had only been half-listening to the conversation, but now he
forced himself to be a more accommodating guest. The talk was general, candlelit faces leaned across the table and the hands which
peeled the fruit or fidgeted with the glasses were as individual as the
faces. Alice Mair's strong but elegant hands with their short nails,
Hilary Robarts's long, knobbled fingers, the delicacy of Meg Dennison's pink-tipped fingers, a little reddened with housework. Alex Mair
was saying: "All right, let's take a modern dilemma. We know that
we can use human tissue from aborted foetuses to treat Parkinson's
disease and probably Alzheimer's. Presumably you'd find that ethically
acceptable if the abortion were natural or legal but not if it were
induced for the purpose of providing the tissue. But you can argue
that a woman has a right to the use that she makes of her own body.
If she's particularly fond of someone who has Alzheimer's and wants
to help him by producing a foetus, who has the right to say no? A
foetus isn't a child."

Hilary Robarts said: "I notice that you assume the sufferer to be
helped is a man. I suppose he'd feel entitled to use a woman's body
for this purpose, as he would any other. But why the hell should he?
I can't imagine that a woman who's actually had an abortion wants
to go through that again for any man's convenience."

The words were spoken with extreme bitterness. There was a
pause; then Mair said quietly: "Alzheimer's is rather more than an
inconvenience. But I'm not advocating it. In any case, under present
law, it would be illegal."

"Would that worry you?"

He looked into her angry eyes. "Naturally it would worry me.
Happily it isn't a decision that I shall ever be required to make. But
we're not talking about legality, we're talking about morality."

His sister asked: "Are they different?"

"That's the question, isn't it? Are they, Adam?"

It was the first time he had used Dalgliesh's Christian name. Dalgliesh said: "You're assuming there's an absolute morality independent of time or circumstance."

"Wouldn't you make that assumption?"

"Yes, I think I would, but I'm not a moral philosopher."

Mrs. Dennison looked up from her plate a little flushed and said: "I'm always suspicious of the excuse that a sin is justified if it's done to benefit someone we love. We may think so, but it's usually to benefit ourselves. I might dread the thought of having to look after an Alzheimer's patient. When we advocate euthanasia is it to stop pain or to prevent our own distress at having to watch it? To conceive a child deliberately in order to kill it to make use of its tissue, the idea is absolutely repugnant."

Alex Mair said: "I could argue that what you are killing isn't a child and that repugnance at an act isn't evidence of its immorality."

Dalgliesh said: "But isn't it? Doesn't Mrs. Dennison's natural repugnance tell us something about the morality of the act?"

She gave him a brief, grateful smile and went on: "And isn't this use of a foetus particularly dangerous? It could lead to the poor of the world conceiving children and selling the foetuses to help the rich. Already, I believe, there's a black market in human organs. Do you think a multimillionaire who needs a heart-lung transplant ever goes without?"

Alex Mair smiled. "As long as you aren't arguing that we should deliberately suppress knowledge or reject scientific progress just because the discoveries can be abused. If there are abuses, legislate against them."

Meg protested: "But you make it sound so easy. If all we had to do was to legislate against social evils, Mr. Dalgliesh would be out of work, for one."

"It isn't easy but it has to be attempted. That's what being human means, surely, using our intelligence to make choices."

Alice Mair got up from the table. She said: "Well, it's time to make a choice now on a somewhat different level. Which of you would like coffee and what kind? There's a table and chairs in the courtyard. I thought we could switch on the yard lights and have it outside."

They moved through to the drawing room, and Alice Mair opened the French windows leading to the patio. Immediately the sonorous booming of the sea flowed into and took possession of the room like a vibrating and irresistible force. But once they had stepped out into the cool air, paradoxically, the noise seemed muted, the sea no more than a distant roar. The patio was bounded on the road side by a high flint wall which, to the south and east, curved to little more than four feet to give an unimpeded view across the headland to the sea. The coffee tray was carried out by Alex Mair within minutes and, cups in hand, the little party wandered aimlessly among the terra-cotta pots like strangers reluctant to be introduced or like actors on a stage set, self-absorbed, pondering their lines, waiting for the rehearsal to begin.

They were without coats and the warmth of the night had proved illusory. They had turned as if by common consent to go back into the cottage when the lights of a car, driven fast, came over the southern rise of the road. As it approached its speed slackened.

Mair said: "Lessingham's Porsche."

No one spoke. They watched silently as the car was driven at speed off the road to brake violently on the turf of the headland. As if conforming to some pre-arranged ceremony, they grouped themselves into a semi-circle with Alex Mair a little to the front, like a formal welcoming party but one bracing itself for trouble rather than expecting pleasure from the approaching guest. Dalgliesh was aware of the heightening tension; small individual tremors of anxiety which shivered on the still, sea-scented air, unified and focused on the car door and on the tall figure which unwound from the driver's seat, leapt easily over the low stone wall and walked deliberately across the courtyard towards them. Lessingham ignored Mair and moved straight to Alice. He took her hand and gently kissed it, a theatrical gesture which Dalgliesh felt had taken her by surprise and which the others had watched with an unnaturally critical attention.

Lessingham said gently: "My apologies, Alice. Too late for dinner, I know, but not, I hope, for a drink. And, God, do I need one."

"Where have you been? We waited dinner for forty minutes." It was Hilary Robarts who asked the obvious question, sounding as accusatory as a peevish wife. Lessingham kept his eye on Alice. He said: "I've been considering how best to answer that question for the last twenty minutes. There are a number of interesting and dramatic possibilities. I could say that I've been helping the police with their enquiries. Or that I've been involved in a murder. Or that there was a little unpleasantness on the road. Actually it was all three. The Whistler has killed again. I found the body."

Hilary Robarts said sharply: "How do you mean, found? Where?"

Again Lessingham ignored her. He said to Alice Mair: "Could I have that drink? Then I'll give you all the gory details. After unsettling your seating plan and delaying dinner for forty minutes, that's the least I owe you."

As they moved back into the drawing room, Alex Mair introduced Dalgliesh. Lessingham gave him one sharp glance. They shook hands. The palm which momentarily touched his was moist and very cold. Alex Mair said easily: "Why didn't you ring? We would have kept some food for you."

The question, conventionally domestic, sounded irrelevant, but Lessingham answered it. "Do you know, I actually forgot. Not all the time, of course, but it honestly didn't cross my mind until the police had finished questioning me, and then the moment didn't seem opportune. They were perfectly civil, but I sensed that my private engagements had a pretty low priority. Incidentally, you get absolutely no credit from the police for finding a body for them. Their attitude is, rather, 'Thank you very much, sir, very nasty, I'm sure. Sorry you've been troubled. But we'll take over now. Just go home and try to forget all about it.' I have a feeling that that isn't going to be so easy."

Back in the drawing room Alex Mair threw a couple of thin logs onto the glowing embers and went to get the drinks. Lessingham had refused whisky but had asked for wine. "But don't waste your best claret on me, Alex. This is purely medicinal." Almost imperceptibly they edged their chairs closer. Lessingham began his story deliberately, pausing at times to take gulps of the wine. It seemed to Dalgliesh that he was subtly altered since his arrival, had become charged with a power both mysterious and oddly familiar. He thought: He has acquired the mystique of the story-teller, and, glancing at the ring of fire-lit and intent faces, he was suddenly reminded of his first village school, of the children clustered round Miss Douglas at three o'clock on a Friday afternoon for the half-hour of story-time, and felt a pang of pain and regret for those lost days of innocence and love. He was surprised that the memory should have come back so keenly and at such a moment. But this was to be a very different story, and one unsuited to the ears of children.

Lessingham said: "I had an appointment with my dentist in Norwich at five o'clock and then briefly visited a friend in the Close. So I drove here from Norwich, not from my cottage. I'd just turned right off the B1150 at Fairstead when I nearly crashed into the back of this unlit car skewed across the road. I thought it was a damn silly place to park if someone wanted to take a leak in the bushes. Then it crossed my mind that there could have been an accident. And the right-hand door was open; that seemed a bit odd. So I drew into the side and went to take a look. There was no one about. I'm not sure why I walked into the trees. A kind of instinct, I suppose. It was too dark to see anything and I wondered whether to call out. Then I felt a fool and decided to leave it and mind my own business. And it was then that I almost tripped over her."

He took another gulp of the wine. "I still couldn't see anything, of course, but I knelt down and groped about with my hands. And it was then that I touched flesh. I think I touched her thigh, I can't be sure. But flesh, even dead flesh, is unmistakable. So I went back to the car and got my torch. I shone it on her feet and then slowly up her body to her face. And then, of course, I saw. I knew it was the Whistler."

Meg Dennison asked gently: "Was it very terrible?"

He must have heard in her voice what she obviously felt, not prurience but sympathy, an understanding that he needed to talk. He looked at her for a moment as if seeing her for the first time, then paused, giving the question serious thought.

"More shocking than terrible. Looking back, my emotions were complicated, a mixture of horror, disbelief and, well, shame. I felt like a voyeur. The dead, after all, are at such a disadvantage. She looked grotesque, a little ridiculous, with thin clumps of hair sticking out of her mouth as if she were munching. Horrible, of course, but silly at the same time. I had an almost irresistible impulse to giggle. I know it was only a reaction to shock, but it was hardly admirable. And the whole scene was so, well, banal. If you had asked me to describe one of the Whistler's victims, that's exactly how I should have seen her. You expect reality to be different from imaginings."

Alice Mair said: "Perhaps because the imaginings are usually worse."

Meg Dennison said quietly: "You must have been terrified. I know I should have been. Alone and in darkness with such horror."

He shifted his body towards her and spoke as if it were important that she, of all those present, should understand.

"No, not terrified, that was the surprising part. I was frightened, of course, but only for a second or two. After all, I didn't imagine he'd wait around. He'd had his kicks. He isn't interested in men anyway. I found myself thinking the ordinary, commonplace thoughts: I mustn't touch anything. I mustn't destroy the evidence. I've got to get the police. Then, walking back to the car, I started rehearsing what I'd say to them, almost as if I were concocting my story. I tried to explain why it was that I went into the bushes, tried to make it sound reasonable."

Alex Mair said: "What was there to justify? You did what you did. It sounds reasonable enough to me. The car was a danger slewed across the road. It would have been irresponsible just to drive on."

"It seemed to need a lot of explaining, then and later. Perhaps because all the subsequent police sentences began with 'why.' You get morbidly sensitive to your own motives. It's almost as if you have to convince yourself that you didn't do it."

Hilary Robarts said impatiently: "But the body—when you first went back for the torch and saw her, you were certain she was dead?"

"Oh yes, I knew she was dead."

"How could you have known? It could have been very recent. Why didn't you at least try to resuscitate her, give her the kiss of life? It would have been worth overcoming your natural repugnance."

Dalgliesh heard Meg Dennison make a small sound between a gasp and a groan. Lessingham looked at Hilary and said coolly: "It would have been if there had been the slightest point in it. I knew she was dead, let's leave it at that. But don't worry, if I ever find you *in extremis* I'll endeavour to overcome my natural repugnance."

Hilary relaxed and gave a little self-satisfied smile, as if gratified to have stung him into a cheap retort. Her voice was more natural as she said: "I'm surprised you weren't treated as a suspect. After all, you were the first on the scene, and this is the second time you've been—well, almost—in at the death. It's becoming a habit."

The last words were spoken almost under her breath, but her eyes were fixed on Lessingham's face. He met her glance and said, with equal quietness: "But there's a difference, isn't there? I had to watch Toby die, remember? And this time no one will even try to pretend that it isn't murder."

The fire gave a sudden crackle, and the top log rolled over and fell into the hearth. Mair, his face flushed, kicked it viciously back. Hilary Robarts, perfectly calm, turned to Dalgliesh.

"But I'm right, aren't I? Don't the police usually suspect the person who finds the body?"

He said quietly: "Not necessarily."

Lessingham had placed the bottle of claret on the hearth. Now he leaned down and carefully refilled his glass. He said: "They might have suspected me, I suppose, but for a number of lucky circumstances. I was obviously out on my lawful occasions. I have an alibi for at least two of the previous killings. From their point of view I was depressingly free of blood. I suppose they could see I was in a mild state of shock. And there was no sign of the ligature which strangled her, nor of the knife."

Hilary said sharply: "What knife? The Whistler's a strangler. Everyone knows that's how he kills."

"Oh, I didn't mention that, did I? She was strangled all right, or I suppose she was. I didn't keep the torchlight on her face longer than was necessary. But he marks his victims, apart from stuffing their mouths with hair. Pubic hair, incidentally. I saw that all right. There was the letter *L* cut into her forehead. Quite unmistakable. A detective constable who was talking to me later told me that it's one of the Whistler's trademarks. He thought that the *L* could stand for 'Larksoken' and that the Whistler might be making some kind of statement about nuclear power, a protest perhaps."

Alex Mair said sharply: "That's nonsense." Then added more calmly: "There's been nothing on television or in the papers about any cut on the victim's foreheads."

"The police are keeping it quiet, or trying to. It's the kind of detail they can use to sort out the false confessions. There have been half a dozen of those already, apparently. There's been nothing in the media about the hair either, but that piece of unpleasantness seems to be generally known. After all, I'm not the only one to have found a body. People do talk."

Hilary Robarts said: "Nothing has been written or said, as far as I know, about it being pubic hair."

"No, the police are keeping that quiet too, and it's hardly the sort of detail you print in a family newspaper. Not that it's so very surprising. He isn't a rapist, but there was bound to be some sexual element."

It was one of the details which Rickards had told Dalgliesh the previous evening but one, he felt, which Lessingham could well have kept to himself, particularly at a mixed dinner party. He was a little surprised at his sudden sensitivity. Perhaps it was his glance at Meg Dennison's ravaged face. And then his ears caught a faint sound. He looked across to the open door of the dining room and glimpsed the slim figure of Theresa Blaney standing in the shadows. He wondered how much of Lessingham's account she had heard. However little, it would have been too much. He said, hardly aware of the severity in his voice: "Didn't Chief Inspector Rickards ask you to keep this information confidential?"

There was an embarrassed silence. He thought, They had forgotten for a moment that I'm a policeman. Lessingham turned to him.

"I intend to keep it confidential. Rickards didn't want it to become public knowledge and it won't. No one here will pass it on."

But that single question, reminding them of who he was and what he represented, chilled the room and changed their mood from fascinated and horrified interest to a half-shameful unease. And when, a minute later, he got up to say his goodbyes and thank his hostess, there was an almost visible sense of relief. He knew that the embarrassment had nothing to do with the fear that he would question, criticize, move like a spy among them. It wasn't his case and they weren't suspects, and they must have known that he was no cheerful extrovert, flattered to be the centre of attraction while they bombarded him with questions about Chief Inspector Rickards's likely methods, the chance of catching the Whistler, his theories about psychopathic killers, his own experience of serial murder. But merely by being there he increased their awakening fear and repugnance at this latest horror. On each of their minds was imprinted the mental image of that violated face, the half-open mouth stuffed with hair, those staring, sightless eyes, and his presence intensified the picture, brought it into sharper focus. Horror and death were his trade and, like an undertaker, he carried with him the contagion of his craft.

He was at the front door when, on impulse, he turned back and said to Meg Dennison: "I think you mentioned that you walked from the Old Rectory, Mrs. Dennison. Could I walk home with you—that is, if it's not too early for you?"

Alex Mair was beginning to say that he, of course, would drive her, but Meg extricated herself clumsily from her chair and said a little too eagerly: "I'd be grateful if you would. I would like the walk and it would save Alex getting out the car."

Alice Mair said: "And it's time Theresa was on her way. We should have driven her home an hour ago. I'll give her father a ring. Where is she, by the way?"

Meg said: "I think she was next door clearing the table a minute ago."

"Well, I'll find her and Alex can drive her home."

The party was breaking up. Hilary Robarts had been slumped back in her chair, her eyes fixed on Lessingham. Now she got to her feet and said: "I'll get back to my cottage. There's no need for anyone to come with me. As Miles has said, the Whistler's had his kicks for tonight."

Alex Mair said: "I'd rather you waited. I'll walk with you once I've taken Theresa home."

She shrugged and, without looking at him, said: "All right, if you insist. I'll wait."

She moved over to the window, staring out into the darkness. Only Lessingham stayed in his chair, reaching again to fill his glass. Dalgliesh saw that Alex Mair had silently placed another opened bottle in the hearth. He wondered whether Alice Mair would invite Lessingham to stay the night at Martyr's Cottage or whether he would be driven home later by her or her brother. He would certainly be in no state to drive himself.

Dalgliesh was helping Meg Dennison into her jacket when the telephone rang, sounding unnaturally strident in the quiet room. He felt her sudden shock of fear and for a moment, almost involuntarily, his hands strengthened on her shoulders. They heard Alex Mair's voice.

"Yes, we've heard. Miles Lessingham is here and gave us the details. Yes, I see. Yes. Thank you for letting me know." Then there was a longer silence, then Mair's voice again. "Completely fortuitous, I should say, wouldn't you? After all, we have a staff of five hundred and thirty. But naturally everyone at Larksoken will find the news deeply shocking, the women particularly. Yes, I shall be in my office tomorrow if there's any help I can give. Her family have been told, I suppose? Yes, I see. Good night, Chief Inspector."

He put down the receiver and said: "That was Chief Inspector Rickards. They've identified the victim. Christine Baldwin. She is— she was—a typist at the station. You didn't recognize her, then, Miles?"

Lessingham took his time refilling his glass. He said: "The police didn't tell me who she was. Even if they had, I wouldn't have re-membered the name. And no, Alex, I didn't recognize her. I suppose I must have seen Christine Baldwin at Larksoken, probably in the canteen. But what I saw earlier tonight wasn't Christine Baldwin. And I can assure you that I didn't shine the torch on her longer than I needed to satisfy myself that she was beyond any help that I could give."

Without looking round from the window, Hilary Roberts said: "Christine Baldwin. Aged thirty-three. Actually, she's only been with us for eleven months. Married last year. Just transferred to the Medical Physics Department. I can give you her typing and shorthand speeds if you're interested." Then she turned round and looked Alex Mair in the face. "It looks as if the Whistler's getting closer, doesn't it, in more ways than one."

3

The final goodbyes were said and they stepped out from the smell of wood smoke, food and wine from a room which Dalgliesh was beginning to find uncomfortably warm into the fresh sea-scented air. It took a few minutes before his eyes had adjusted to semi-darkness and the great sweep of the headland became visible, its shapes and forms mysteriously altered under the high stars. To the north the power station was a glittering galaxy of white lights, its stark geometric bulk subsumed in the blue-black of the sky.

They stood for a moment regarding it; then Meg Dennison said: "When I first came here from London it almost frightened me, the sheer size of it, the way it dominates the headland. But I'm getting used to it. It's still disturbing but it does have a certain grandeur. Alex tries to de-mystify it, says its function is just to produce electricity for the National Grid efficiently and cleanly, that the main difference between this and any other power station is that you don't have beside it a huge pyramid of polluting coal-dust. But atomic power to my generation always means that mushroom cloud. And now it means Chernobyl. But if it were an ancient castle standing there against the skyline, if what we looked out at tomorrow morning were a row of turrets, we'd probably be saying how magnificent it is."

Dalgliesh said: "If it had a row of turrets it would be a rather different shape. But I know what you mean. I should prefer the headland without it, but it's beginning to look as if it had a right to be there."

They turned simultaneously from contemplating the glittering lights and looked south to the decaying symbol of a very different power. Before them, at the edge of the cliff, crumbling against the skyline like a child's sand castle rendered amorphous by the advancing tide, was the ruined Benedictine abbey. He could just make out the great empty arch of the east window and beyond it the shimmer of the North Sea, while above, seeming to move through and over it like a censer, swung the smudged yellow disc of the moon. Almost without conscious will they took their first steps from the track onto the rough headland towards it. Dalgliesh said: "Shall we? Can you spare the time? And what about your shoes?"

"Reasonably sensible. Yes, I'd like to, it looks so wonderful at night. And I don't really need to hurry. The Copleys won't have waited up for me. Tomorrow, when I have to tell them how close the Whistler is getting, I may not like to leave them alone after dark. This may be my last free night for some time."

"I don't think they'd be in any real danger as long as you lock up securely. So far all his victims have been young women and he kills out of doors."

"I tell myself that. And I don't think they'd be seriously frightened. Sometimes the very old seem to have moved beyond that kind of fear. The trivial upsets of daily living assume importance but the big tragedies they take in their stride. But their daughter is constantly ringing up to suggest they go to her in Wiltshire until he's caught. They don't want to, but she's a strong-minded woman and very insistent, and if she telephones after dusk and I'm not there it will increase the pressure on them." She paused and then said: "It was a horrible end to an interesting but rather strange dinner party. I wish Mr. Lessingham had kept the details to himself, but I suppose it helped him to talk about it, especially as he lives alone."

Dalgliesh said: "It would have needed superhuman control not to have talked about it. But I wish he'd omitted the more salacious details."

"It will make a difference to Alex, too. Already some of the women staff demand to be escorted home after the evening shifts. Alice has told me that that isn't going to be easy for Alex to organize. They'll only accept a male escort if he has an unbreakable alibi for one of the Whistler murders. People cease to be rational even when they've known and worked with someone for the last ten years."

Dalgliesh said: "Murder does that, particularly this kind of murder. Miles Lessingham mentioned another death: Toby. Was that the young man who killed himself at the station? I seem to remember a paragraph in one of the papers."

"It was an appalling tragedy. Toby Gledhill was one of Alex's most brilliant young scientists. He broke his neck by throwing himself down on top of the reactor."

"So there was no mystery about it?"

"Oh no, absolutely none, except why he did it. Mr. Lessingham saw it happen. I'm surprised you remember it. There was very little about it in the national press. Alex tried to minimize the publicity to protect his parents."

And to protect the power station, thought Dalgliesh. He wondered why Lessingham had described Gledhill's death as murder, but he didn't question his companion further. The allegation had been spoken so quietly that he doubted whether she had in fact heard it. Instead he asked: "Are you happy living on the headland?"

The question did not appear to surprise her but it did surprise him, as did the very fact that they were walking so companionably together. She was curiously restful to be with. He liked her quiet gentleness with its suggestion of underlying strength. Her voice was pleasant, and voices were important to him. But six months ago none of this would have been enough to make him invite her company for longer than was politely necessary. He would have escorted her back to the Old Rectory and then, a minor social obligation performed, turned with relief to walk alone to the abbey, drawing his solitude around him like a cloak. That solitude was still essential to him. He couldn't tolerate twenty-four hours in which the greater part wasn't spent entirely alone. But some change in himself, the inexorable years, success, the return of his poetry, perhaps the tentative beginning of love, seemed to be making him sociable. He wasn't sure whether this was something to be welcomed or resisted.

He was aware that she was giving his question careful thought.

"Yes, I think that I am. Sometimes very happy. I came here to escape from the problems of my life in London and, without really meaning to, I came as far east as I could get."

"And found yourself confronting two different forms of menace, the power station and the Whistler."

"Both frightening because both mysterious, both rooted in a horror of the unknown. But the menace isn't personal, isn't directed specifically against me. But I did run away and, I suppose, all refugees carry with them a small burden of guilt. And I miss the children. Perhaps I should have stayed and fought on. But it was becoming a very public war. I'm not suited to the role of popular heroine of the more reactionary press. All I wanted was to be left alone to get on with the job I'd been trained for and loved. But every book I used, every word I spoke was scrutinized. You can't teach in an atmosphere of rancorous suspicion. In the end I found I couldn't even live in it."

She was taking it for granted that he knew who she was; but, then, anyone who had read the papers must know that.

He said: "It's possible to fight intolerance, stupidity and fanaticism when they come separately. When you get all three together it's probably wiser to get out, if only to preserve your sanity."

They were approaching the abbey now, and the grass of the headland was becoming more hillocky. She stumbled and he put out his hand to steady her. She said: "In the end it came down to just two letters. They insisted that the blackboard should be called the 'chalkboard.' Black or chalk. I didn't believe, I still don't believe that any sensible person, whatever his colour, objects to the word 'blackboard.' It's black and it's a board. The word 'black' in itself can't be offensive. I'd called it that all my life, so why should they try to force me to change the way I speak my own language? And yet, at this moment, on this headland, under this sky, this immensity, it all seems so petty. Perhaps all I did was to elevate trivia into a principle."

Dalgliesh said: "Agnes Poley would have understood. My aunt looked up the records and told me about her. She went to the stake, apparently, for an obstinate adherence to her own uncompromising view of the universe. She couldn't accept that Christ's body could be present in the sacrament and at the same time physically in heaven, at God's right hand. It was, she said, against common sense. Perhaps Alex Mair should take her as patron of his power station, a quasi-saint of rationality."

"But that was different. She believed her immortal soul was in jeopardy."

Dalgliesh said: "Who knows what she believed? I think she was probably activated by a divine obstinacy. I find that rather admirable."

Meg said: "I think Mr. Copley would argue that she was wrong, not the obstinacy, but her earthbound view of the sacrament. I'm not really competent to argue about that. But to die horribly for your own common-sense view of the universe is rather splendid. I never visit Alice without standing and reading that plaque. It's my small act of homage. And yet I don't feel her presence in Martyr's Cottage. Do you?"

"Not in the slightest. I suspect that central heating and modern furniture are inimical to ghosts. Did you know Alice Mair before you came here?"

"I knew no one. I answered an advertisement by the Copleys in *The Lady*. They were offering free accommodation and food to someone who would do what they described as a little gentle housework. It's a euphemism for dusting, but of course it never works out like that. Alice has made a great difference. I hadn't realized how much I was missing female friendship. At school we only had alliances, offensive or defensive. Nothing ever cut across political divisions."

Dalgliesh said: "Agnes Poley would have understood that atmosphere too. It was the one she breathed."

For a minute they walked in silence, hearing the rustle of the long grasses over their shoes. Dalgliesh wondered why it was that, when walking towards the sea, there came a moment when its roar suddenly increased, as if a menace, quiescent and benign, had suddenly gathered up its power. Looking up at the sky, at the myriad pinpricks of light, he seemed to feel the turning earth beneath his feet and sense that time had mysteriously come to a stop, fusing into one moment the past, the present and the future: the ruined abbey, the obstinately enduring artifacts of the last war, the crumbling cliff defences, the windmill and the power station. And he wondered whether it was in such a disorientating limbo of time, listening to the ever-restless sea, that the previous owners of Martyr's Cottage had chosen their text. Suddenly his companion stopped and said: "There's a light in the ruins. Two small flashes, like a torch."

They stood still and watched in silence. Nothing appeared. She said, almost apologetically: "I'm sure I saw it. And there was a shadow, something or somebody moving against the eastern window. You didn't see it?"

"I was looking at the sky."

She said with a note of regret: "Well, it's gone now. I suppose I could have imagined it."

And when, five minutes later, they made their way cautiously over the humpy grass into the heart of the ruins, there was no one and nothing to be seen. Without speaking they walked through the gap of the east window and onto the edge of the cliff and saw only the moon-bleached beach stretching north and south, the thin fringe of white foam. If anyone had been there, thought Dalgliesh, there was plenty of opportunity for concealment behind the hunks of concrete or in the crevices of the sandy cliff. There was little point and no real justification in attempting to give chase, even if they had known the direction in which he had disappeared. People were entitled to walk alone at night. Meg said again: "I suppose I could have imagined it, but I don't think so. Anyway, she's gone now."

"She?"

"Oh yes. Didn't I say? I had the distinct impression it was a woman."

4

⊠

By four o'clock in the morning, when Alice Mair woke with a small despairing cry from her nightmare, the wind was rising. She stretched out her hand to click on the bedside light, checked her watch, then lay back, panic subsiding, her eyes staring at the ceiling, while the terrible immediacy of the dream began to fade, recognized for what it was, an old spectre returning after all these years, conjured up by the events of the night and by the reiteration of the word "murder," which since the Whistler had begun his work seemed to murmur sonorously on the very air. Gradually she re-entered the real world manifested in the small noises of the night, the moan of the wind in the chimneys, the smoothness of the sheet in her clutching hands, the unnaturally loud ticking of her watch and, above all, in that oblong of pale light, the open casement and the drawn curtains which gave her a view of the faintly luminous star-studded sky.

The nightmare needed no interpretation. It was merely a new version of an old horror, less terrible than the dreams of childhood, a more rational, more adult terror. She and Alex were children again, the whole family living with the Copleys at the Old Rectory. That, in a dream, wasn't so surprising. The Old Rectory was only a larger, less pretentious version of Sunnybank—ridiculously named, since it had stood on level ground and no sun ever seemed to penetrate its windows. Both were late Victorian, built in solid red brick, both had a strong curved door under a high peaked porch, both were isolated, each in its own garden. In the dream she and her father were walking together through the shrubbery. He was carrying his billhook and was dressed as he was on that last, dreadful autumn afternoon, a singlet stained with his sweat, the shorts high-cut, showing as he walked the bulge of the scrotum, the white legs, matted with black hair from the knees down. She was worried because she knew that the Copleys were waiting for her to cook lunch. Mr. Copley, robed in cassock and billowing surplice, was impatiently pacing the back lawn, seeming oblivious to their presence. Her father was explaining something to her in that overloud, careful voice which he used to her mother, the voice which said: "I know you are too stupid to understand this, but I will talk slowly and loudly and hope that you won't try my patience too far."

He said: "Alex won't get the job now. I'll see that he doesn't. They won't appoint a man who's murdered his own father."

And as he spoke he swung the billhook and she saw that its tip was red with blood. Then, suddenly, he turned towards her, eyes blazing, lifted it, and she felt its point pierce the skin of her forehead, and the sudden spurt of blood gushing into her eyes. Now wide awake, and breathing as if she had been running, she put her hand up to her brow and knew that the cold wetness she felt was sweat, not blood.

There was little hope of falling asleep again; there never was when she woke in the early hours. She could get up, put on her dressing gown, go downstairs and make tea, correct her proofs, read, listen to the BBC World Service. Or she could take one of her sleeping tablets. God knew they were powerful enough to knock her into oblivion. But she was trying to wean herself from them, and to give in now would be to acknowledge the potency of the nightmare. She would get up and make tea. She had no fear of waking Alex. He slept soundly, even through winter gales. But first there was a small act of exorcism to be performed. If the dream was to lose its power, if she was somehow to prevent it recurring, she must face again the memory of that afternoon nearly thirty years ago.

It had been a warm autumnal day in early October and she, Alex and her father were working in the garden. Her father was clearing a thick hedge of brambles and overgrown shrubs at the bottom of the

shrubbery and out of sight of the house, slashing at them with a
billhook while Alex and she dragged the freed branches clear, ready
to build a bonfire. Her father was underclad for the time of year but
was sweating heavily. She saw the arm lifting and falling, heard the
crack of twigs, felt again the thorns cutting her fingers, heard his
high commands. And then, suddenly, he gave a cry. Either the branch
had been rotten or he had missed his aim. The billhook had sliced
into his naked thigh and, turning, she saw the great curve of red blood
begin to bubble in the air, saw him slowly sink like a wounded animal,
his hands plucking the air. His right hand dropped the billhook and
he held it out to her, shaking, palm upwards, and looked at her be-
seechingly, like a child. He tried to speak but she couldn't make out
the words. She was moving towards him, fascinated, when she felt a
clutch on her arm and Alex was dragging her with him down the
path between the laurels, towards the orchard.

She cried: "Alex, stop! He's bleeding. He's dying. We've got to
get help."

She couldn't remember whether she actually said the words. All
she later remembered was the strength of his hands on her shoulders
as he forced her back against the bark of an apple tree and held her
there, imprisoned. And he spoke a single word.

"No."

Shaking with terror, her heart pounding, she couldn't have broken free even if she had wanted. And she knew now that this pow-
erlessness was important to him. It had been his act and his alone.
Compelled, absolved, she had been given no choice. Now, thirty years
later, lying rigid, her eyes fixed on the sky, she remembered that
single word, his eyes looking into hers, his hands on her shoulders,
the bark of the tree scraping her back through her aertex shirt. Time
seemed to stop. She couldn't remember now how long he had held
her imprisoned, only that it seemed an eternity of immeasurable time.
And then, at last, he gave a sigh and said: "All right. We can go now."

And that, too, amazed her, that he should have been thinking so
clearly, calculating how long it would take. He dragged her after him
until they stood over her father's body. And, looking down at the still-
outstretched arm, the glazed and open eyes, the great scarlet pool
soaking into the earth, she knew that it was a body, that he had gone
forever, that there was nothing she need fear from him ever again.

Alex turned to her and spoke each word loudly and clearly as if she were a subnormal child.

"Whatever he's been doing to you, he won't do it again. Ever. Listen to me and I'll tell you what happened. We left him and went down to climb the apple trees. Then we decided that we'd better get back. Then we found him. That's all there is, it's as simple as that. You don't need to say anything else. Just leave the talking to me. Look at me, look at me, Alice. You understand?"

Her voice, when it came, sounded like an old woman's voice, cracked and tremulous, and the words strained her throat. "Yes, I understand."

And then he was dragging her by the hands, racing across the lawn, nearly pulling her arm from its socket, crashing through the kitchen door, crying aloud so that it sounded like a whoop of triumph. She saw her mother's face draining as if she too were bleeding to death, heard his panting voice.

"It's Father. He's had an accident. Get a doctor quick."

And then she was alone in the kitchen. It was very cold. There were cold tiles under her feet. The surface of the wooden table on which she rested her head was cold to her cheeks. No one came. She was aware of a voice telephoning from the hall, and other voices, other steps. Someone was crying. Now there were more footsteps and the crunch of car wheels on gravel.

And Alex had been right. It had all been very simple. No one had questioned her, no one had been suspicious. Their story had been accepted. She didn't go to the inquest but Alex did, although he never told her what happened there. Afterwards some of the people concerned, their family doctor, the solicitor, a few of her mother's friends, came back, and there was a curious tea party with sandwiches and home-made fruitcake. They were kind to her and Alex. Someone actually patted her head. A voice said, "It was tragic that there was no one there. Common sense and a rudimentary knowledge of first aid would have saved him."

But now the memory deliberately evoked had completed its exorcism. The nightmare had been robbed of its terror. With luck, it might not return for months. She swung her legs out of bed and reached for her dressing gown.

She had just poured the boiling water on the tea and was standing waiting for it to brew when she heard Alex's footsteps on the stairs and, turning, she saw his tall figure blocking the kitchen door. He looked boyish, almost vulnerable, in the familiar corded dressing gown. He pushed both hands through his sleep-tousled hair. Surprised because he was usually a sound sleeper, she said: "Did I disturb you? Sorry."

"No, I woke earlier and couldn't get off again. Holding dinner for Lessingham made it too late for comfortable digestion. Is this fresh?"

"About ready to pour."

He took down a second mug from the dresser and poured tea for them both. She seated herself in a wicker chair and took her mug without speaking.

He said: "The wind's rising."

"Yes, it has been for the last hour."

He went over to the door and unbolted the top wooden panel, pushing it open. There was a sensation of rushing white coldness, scentless, but obliterating the faint tang of the tea, and she heard the deep growling roar of the sea. As she listened it seemed to rise in intensity so that she could imagine, with an agreeable *frisson* of sim-ulated terror, that the low friable cliffs had finally crumbled and that the white foaming turbulence was rolling towards them across the headland, would crash against the door and throw its spume on Alex's face. Looking at him as he stared into the night, she felt a surge of affection as pure and as uncomplicated as the flow of cold air against her face. Its fleeting strength surprised her. He was so much a part of her that she never needed or wanted to examine too closely the nature of her feeling for him. She knew that she was always quietly satisfied to have him in the cottage, to hear his footfalls on the floor above, to share with him the meal she had cooked for herself at the end of the day. And yet neither made demands of the other. Even his marriage had made no difference. She had been unsurprised at the marriage since she had rather liked Elizabeth, but equally unsurprised when it ended. She thought it unlikely that he would marry again, but nothing between them would change, however many wives en-tered, or attempted to enter, his life. Sometimes, as now, she would smile wryly, knowing how outsiders saw their relationship. Those who assumed that the cottage was owned by him, not her, saw her as the unmarried sister, dependent on him for houseroom, companionship, a purpose in life. Others, more perceptive but still nowhere near the truth, were intrigued by their apparent independence of each other, their casual comings and goings, their noninvolvement. She remembered Elizabeth saying in the first weeks of her engagement to Alex, "Do you know, you're a rather intimidating couple?" and she had been tempted to reply, "Oh, we are, we are."

She had bought Martyr's Cottage before his appointment as Director of the power station, and he had moved in by an unspoken agreement that this was a temporary expedient while he decided what to do, keep on the Barbican flat as his main home or sell the flat and buy a house in Norwich and a smaller *pied à terre* in London. He was essentially an urban creature; she didn't see him settling permanently other than in a city. If, with the new job, he moved back to London, she wouldn't follow him, nor, she knew, would he expect her to. Here on this sea-scoured coast she had at last found a place which she was content to call home. That he could walk in and out of it unannounced never made it less than her own.

It must, she thought, sipping her tea, have been after one o'clock when he returned from seeing Hilary Robarts home. She wondered what had kept him. Sleeping lightly as always in the early hours, she had heard his key in the lock, his foot on the stairs, before drifting again into sleep. Now it was getting on for five o'clock. He couldn't have had more than a few hours' sleep. Now, as if suddenly aware of the morning chill, he closed the top half of the door, drove home the bolt, then came and stretched himself out in the armchair opposite her. Leaning back, he cradled his mug in his hands.

He said: "It's a nuisance that Caroline Amphlett doesn't want to leave Larksoken. I don't relish beginning a new job, particularly this job, with an unknown PA. Caroline knows the way I work. I'd rather taken it for granted that she'd come to London with me. It's inconvenient."

And it was, she suspected, rather more than inconvenient. Pride, even personal prestige, was also at stake. Other senior men took their personal assistants with them when changing jobs. The reluctance of a secretary to be parted from her boss was a flattering affirmation of personal dedication. She could sympathize with his chagrin, but it was hardly enough to keep him awake at night. He added:

"Personal reasons, or so she says. That means Jonathan Reeves, presumably. God knows what she sees in him. The man isn't even a good technician."

Alice Mair controlled her smile. She said: "I doubt whether her interest in him is technical."

"Well, if it's sexual she has less discrimination than I gave her credit for."

He wasn't, she told herself, a poor judge of men or women. He rarely made fundamental mistakes and never, she suspected, about a man's scientific ability. But he had no understanding of the extraordinary complexities and irrationalities of human motives, human behaviour. He knew that the universe was complex but that it obeyed certain rules, although, she supposed, he wouldn't have used the word "obey," with its implication of conscious choice. This, he would say, is how the physical world behaves. It is open to human reason and, to a limited extent, to human control. People disconcerted him because they could surprise him. Most disconcerting of all was the fact that he occasionally surprised himself. He would have been at home as a sixteenth-century Elizabethan, categorizing people according to their essential natures: choleric, melancholic, mercurial, saturnine, qualities mirroring the planets that governed their birth. That basic fact established, then you knew where you were. And yet it could still surprise him that a man could be a sensible and reliable scientist in his work and a fool with women, could show judgement in one area of his life and act like an irrational child in another. Now he was peeved because his secretary, whom he had categorized as intelligent, sensible, dedicated, preferred to stay in Norfolk with her lover, a man he despised, rather than follow him to London.

She said: "I thought you said once that you found Caroline sexually cold."

"Did I? Surely not. That would suggest a degree of personal experience. I think I said I couldn't imagine ever finding her physically attractive. A PA who is personable and highly efficient but not sexually tempting is the ideal."

She said dryly: "I imagine that a man's idea of the ideal secretary is a woman who manages to imply that she would like to go to bed with her boss but nobly restrains herself in the interests of office efficiency. What will happen to her?"

"Oh, her job's secure. If she wants to stay at Larksoken there will be plenty of competition to get her. She's intelligent as well as tactful and efficient."

"But presumably not ambitious, else why should she be so eager to remain at Larksoken?" She added: "Caroline may have another reason for wanting to stay in the area. I saw her in Norwich Cathedral about three weeks ago. She met a man in the Lady Chapel. They were very discreet, but it looked to me like an assignation."

He asked, but without real curiosity: "What kind of man?"

"Middle-aged. Nondescript. Difficult to describe. But he was too old to be Jonathan Reeves."

She said no more, knowing that he wasn't particularly interested, that his mind had moved elsewhere. And yet, looking back, it had been an odd encounter. Caroline's blond hair had been bundled under a large beret and she was wearing spectacles. But the disguise, if it was meant as a disguise, had been ineffective. She herself had moved on swiftly, anxious not to be recognized or to seem a spy. A minute later she had seen the girl slowly walking along the aisle, guidebook in hand, the man strolling behind her carefully distanced. They had moved together and had stood in front of a monument, seemingly absorbed. And when, ten minutes later, Alice was leaving the cathedral, she had glimpsed him again. This time it was he who was carrying the guidebook.

Alex made no further comment about Caroline, but after a minute's silence he said: "Not a particularly successful dinner party."

"An understatement. Beta-minus, except, of course, for the food. What's the matter with Hilary? Is she actually trying to be disagreeable or is she merely unhappy?"

"People usually are when they can't get what they want."

"In her case you."

He smiled into the empty fire grate but didn't reply. After a moment she said:

"Is she likely to be a nuisance?"

"Rather more than a nuisance. She's likely to be dangerous."

"Dangerous? How dangerous? You mean dangerous to you personally?"

"To rather more than me."

"But nothing you can't cope with?"

"Nothing I can't cope with. But not by making her Administrative

Officer. She'd be a disaster. I should never have appointed her in an acting capacity."

"When are you making the appointment?"

"In ten days' time. There's a good field."

"So you've got ten days to decide what to do about her."

"Rather less than that. She wants a decision by Sunday."

A decision about what? she wondered. Her job, a possible promotion, her future life with Alex? But surely the woman could see that she had no future with Alex.

She asked, knowing the importance of the question, knowing, too, that only she would dare ask it, "Will you be very disappointed if you don't get the job?"

"I'll be aggrieved, which is rather more destructive of one's peace of mind. I want it, I need it and I'm the right person for it. I suppose that's what every candidate thinks, but in my case it happens to be true. It's an important job, Alice. One of the most important there is. The future lies with nuclear power, if we're going to save this planet, but we've got to manage it better, nationally and internationally."

"I imagine you're the only serious candidate. Surely this is the kind of appointment which they only decide to make when they know they've got the right man available. It's a new job. They've managed perfectly well without a nuclear supremo up to now. I can see that, given the right man, the job has immense possibilities. But in the wrong hands it's just another public-relations job, a waste of public money."

He was too intelligent not to know that she was reassuring him. She was the only person from whom he ever needed reassurance or would ever take it.

He said: "There's a suspicion that we could be getting into a mess. They want someone to get us out of it. Minor matters like his precise powers, who he'll be responsible to and how much he'll be paid have yet to be decided. That's why they're taking so long over the job specification."

She said: "You don't need a written job specification to know what they're looking for. A respected scientist, a proven administrator and a good public-relations expert. They'll probably ask you to take a TV test. Looking good on the box seems to be the prerequisite for anything these days."

"Only for future presidents or prime ministers. I don't think they'll go that far."

He glanced at the clock. "It's already dawn. I think I'll get a couple of hours' sleep." But it was an hour later before they finally parted and went to their rooms.

5

Dalgliesh waited until Meg had unlocked the front door and stepped inside before saying his final good night, and she stood for a moment watching his tall figure striding down the gravel path and into the darkness. Then she passed into the square, tessellated hall with its stone fireplace, the hall which, on winter nights, seemed to echo faintly with the childish voices of Victorian rectors' children and which, for Meg, had always held a faintly ecclesiastical smell. Folding her coat over the ornate wooden newel post at the foot of the stairs, she went through to the kitchen and the last task of the day, setting out the Copleys' early-morning tray. It was a large, square room at the back of the house, archaic when the Copleys had bought the Old Rectory and unaltered since. Against the left-hand wall stood an old-fashioned gas stove so heavy that Meg was unable to move it to clean behind it and preferred not to think of the accumulated grease of decades gumming it to the wall. Under the window was a deep porcelain sink stained with the detritus of seventy years' washing-up and impossible adequately to clean. The floor was of ancient stone slabs, hard on the feet, from which in winter there seemed to rise a damp, foot-numbing miasma. The wall opposite the sink and the window was covered with an oak dresser, very old and probably valuable, if it had been possible to remove it from the wall without its collapse, and the original row of bells still hung over the door, each with its Gothic script: "drawing room," "dining room," "study," "nursery." It was a kitchen to challenge rather than enhance the skills of any cook ambitious beyond the boiling of eggs. But now Meg hardly noticed its deficiencies. Like the rest of the Old Rectory, it had become home.

After the stridency and aggression of the school, the hate mail, she was happy to find her temporary asylum in this gentle household where voices were never raised, where no one obsessively analysed her every sentence in the hope of detecting racist, sexist or fascist undertones, where words meant what they had meant for generations, where obscenities were unknown or at least unspoken, where there was the grace of good order symbolized for her in Mr. Copley's reading of the church's daily offices, Morning Prayer and Evensong. Sometimes she saw the three of them as expatriates, stranded in some remote colony, obstinately adhering to old customs, a lost way of life, as they did to old forms of worship. And she had grown to like both her employers. She would have respected Simon Copley more if he had been less prone to venial selfishness, less preoccupied with his physical comfort, but this, she told herself, was probably the result of fifty years of spoiling by a devoted wife. And he loved his wife. He relied on her. He respected her judgement. How lucky they were, she thought: secure in each other's affection and presumably fortified in increasing age by the certainty that if they weren't granted the grace of death on the same day there would be no lasting separation. But did they really believe this? She would have liked to ask them, but knew that it would have been impossibly presumptuous. Surely they must have some doubts, have made some mental reservations to the creed they so confidently recited morning and night. But perhaps what mattered at eighty was habit, the body no longer interested in sex, the mind no longer interested in speculation, the smaller things in life mattering more than the large and, in the end, the slow realization that nothing really mattered at all.

The job wasn't arduous, but she knew that gradually she was taking on much more than the advertisement had suggested, and she sensed that the main anxiety of their life was whether she would stay. Their daughter had provided all the labour-saving devices: dishwasher, washing machine, spin-dryer, all housed in a disused stillroom near the back door, although until she came the Copleys had been reluctant to use them in case they couldn't turn them off, visualizing the machines whirling away all night, overheating, blowing up, the whole rectory pulsating with an uncontrollable power.

Their only child lived in a manor house in Wiltshire and rarely visited, although she telephoned frequently, usually at inconvenient times. It was she who had interviewed Meg for the Old Rectory, and Meg now found it difficult to connect that confident, tweeded, slightly aggressive woman with the two gentle old people she knew. And she knew, although they would never have dreamed of telling her, perhaps didn't even admit it to themselves, that they were afraid of their daughter. She bullied them, as she would have claimed, for their own good. Their second-greatest fear was that they might be forced to comply with her frequently telephoned suggestion, made purely from a sense of duty, that they should go to stay with her until the Whistler was caught.

Unlike their daughter, Meg could understand why, after retirement, they had used all their savings to buy the rectory and had in old age burdened themselves with a mortgage. Mr. Copley had in youth been a curate at Larksoken when the Victorian church was still standing. It was in that ugly repository of polished pine, acoustic tiles and garish, sentimental stained glass that he and his wife had been married, and in a flat in the rectory, living above the parish priest, that they had made their first home. The church had been partly demolished by a devastating gale in the 1930s, to the secret relief of the Church Commissioners, who had been considering what to do with a building of absolutely no architectural merit serving a congregation at the major festivals of six at the most. So the church had been finally demolished and the Old Rectory, sheltering behind it and proving more durable, had been sold. Rosemary Duncan-Smith had made her views plain when driving Meg back to Norwich station after her interview.

"It's ridiculous for them to be living there at all, of course. They should have looked for a two-bedded, well-equipped flat in Norwich or in a convenient village close to the shops and post office, and to a church, of course. But Father can be remarkably obstinate when he thinks he knows what he wants, and Mother is putty in his hands. I hope you aren't seeing this job as a temporary expedient."

Meg had replied: "Temporary, but not short-term. I can't promise that I'll stay permanently, but I need time and peace to decide on my future. And I may not suit your parents."

"Time and peace. We'd all be glad of that. Well, I suppose it's better than nothing, but I'd be grateful for a month or two's notice when you do decide to go. And I shouldn't worry about suiting. With an inconvenient house and stuck out on that headland with nothing to look at but a ruined abbey and that atomic-power station, they'll have to put up with what they can get."

But that had been sixteen months ago and she was still here.

But it was in that beautifully designed and equipped, but comfortable and homely kitchen at Martyr's Cottage that she had found her healing. Early in their friendship, when Alice had to spend a week in London and Alex was away, she had given Meg one of her spare keys to the cottage so that she could go in to collect and forward her post. On her return, when Meg offered it back, she had said: "Better keep it. You may need it again." Meg had never again used it. The door was usually open in summer, and when it was shut she would always ring. But its possession, the sight and weight of it on her key ring, had come to symbolize for her the certainty and the trust of their friendship. She had been so long without a woman friend. She had forgotten—sometimes she told herself that she had never before known—the comfort of a close, undemanding, asexual companionship with another woman. Before the accidental drowning of her husband four years earlier, she and Martin had needed only the occasional companionship of friendly acquaintances to affirm their self-sufficiency. Theirs had been one of those childless, self-absorbing marriages which unconsciously repel attempts at intimacy. The occasional dinner party was a social duty; they could hardly wait to get back to the seclusion of their own small house. And after his death it seemed to her that she had walked in darkness like an automaton through a deep and narrow canyon of grief in which all her energies, all her physical strength, had been husbanded to get through each day. She thought and worked and grieved only for a day at a time. To allow herself even to think of the days, the weeks, the months or years stretching ahead would have been to precipitate disaster. For two years she had hardly been sane. Even her Christianity was of little help. She didn't reject it, but it had become irrelevant, its comfort only a candle which served fitfully to illumine the dark. But when, after those two years, the valley had almost imperceptibly widened and there was for the first time, not those black enclosing cliffs, but the vista of a normal life, even of happiness, a landscape over which it was possible to believe the sun might shine, she had become unwittingly embroiled in the racial politics of her school. The older members of staff had moved or retired, and the new headmistress, specifically appointed to enforce the fashionable orthodoxies, had moved in with crusading zeal to smell out and eradicate heresy. Meg realized now that she had, from the first, been the obvious, the predestined victim.

She had fled to this new life on the headland and to a different solitude. And here she had found Alice Mair. They had met a fortnight after Meg's arrival, when Alice had called at the Old Rectory with a suitcase of jumble for the annual sale in aid of St. Andrew's Church in Lydsett. There was an unused scullery leading off from a passage between the kitchen and the back door which was used as a collecting point for unwanted items from the headland: clothes, bric-à-brac, books and old magazines. Mr. Copley took an occasional service at St. Andrew's when Mr. Smollett, the vicar, was on holiday, an involvement in church and village life which, Meg suspected, was as important to him as it was to the church. Normally little jumble could be expected from the few cottages on the headland, but Alex Mair, anxious to associate the power station with the community, had put up a notice on the staff board and the two tea chests were usually fairly full by the time the October sale came round. The back door of the Old Rectory, giving access to the scullery, was as a rule left open during daylight hours and an inner door to the house locked, but Alice Mair had knocked at the front door and made herself known. The two women, close in age, both reserved, both independent, neither deliberately seeking a friend, had liked each other. The next week Meg had received an invitation to dinner at Martyr's Cottage. And now there was rarely a day when she didn't walk the half-mile over the headland to sit in Alice's kitchen and talk and watch while she worked.

Her colleagues at school would, she knew, have found their friendship incomprehensible. Friendship there, or what passed for friendship, had never crossed the great divide of political allegiance and in the acrimonious clamour of the staff room could swiftly deteriorate into gossip, rumours, recriminations and betrayal. This peaceable friendship, asking nothing, was as devoid of intensity as it was of anxiety. It was not a demonstrative friendship; they had never kissed, had never indeed touched hands except at that first meeting. Meg wasn't sure what it was that Alice valued in her, but she knew what she valued in Alice. Intelligent, well read, unsentimental, unshockable, she had become the focus of Meg's life on the headland.

She seldom saw Alex Mair. During the day he was at the power station, and at weekends, reversing the normal peregrination, he was at his London flat, frequently staying there for part of the week if he had a meeting in town. She had never felt that Alice had deliberately kept them apart, fearing that her brother would be bored by her friend. In spite of all the traumas of the last three years, Meg's inner self was too confidently rooted to be prone to that kind of sexual or social self-abasement. But she had never felt at home with him, perhaps because, with his confident good looks and the air of arrogance in his bearing, he seemed both to represent and to have absorbed something of the mystery and potency of the power he operated. He was perfectly amiable to her on the few occasions when they did meet; sometimes she even felt that he liked her. But their only common ground was in the kitchen of Martyr's Cottage, and even there she was always more at home when he was away. Alice never spoke of him except casually, but on the few occasions, like last night's dinner party, when she had seen them together, they seemed to have the intuitive mutual awareness, an instinctive response to the other's needs, more typical of a long-standing successful marriage than of an apparently casual fraternal relationship.

And for the first time in nearly three years she had been able to talk about Martin. She remembered that July day, the kitchen door open to the patio, the scent of herbs and sea stronger even than the spicy, buttery smell of newly baked biscuits. She and Alice had sat opposite each other, across the kitchen table, the teapot between them. She could remember every word.

"He didn't get many thanks. Oh, they said how heroic he was and the headmaster said all the right things at the school memorial service. But they thought that the boys shouldn't have been swimming there anyway. The school disclaimed any responsibility for his death. They were more anxious to escape criticism than to honour Martin. And the boy he saved hasn't turned out very well. I suppose I'm silly to worry about that."

"It would be perfectly natural to hope that your husband hadn't died for someone second-rate, but I suppose the boy has a point of view. It could be an awesome responsibility knowing that someone has died for you."

Meg said: "I tried to tell myself that. For a time I was—well, almost obsessed with that boy. I used to hang about the school waiting for him to come out. Sometimes I had the need almost to touch him. It was as if some part of Martin had passed into him. But he was only embarrassed, of course. He didn't want to see me or talk to me, he or his parents. He wasn't, in fact, a very nice boy, a bully and rather stupid. I don't think Martin even liked him, although he never said so. He was spotty, too—oh dear, that wasn't his fault, I don't know why I even mentioned it."

And she had wondered how it was she was speaking of him at all. For the first time in three years. And that business about her obsession with him—she had never mentioned that to a living soul.

Alice had said: "It's a pity your husband didn't leave him to drown and save himself, but I suppose that on the spur of the moment he didn't weigh up the relative value of a useful teaching career and pimpled stupidity."

"Leave him to drown? Deliberately? Oh, Alice, you know you couldn't do that yourself."

"Perhaps not. I'm perfectly capable of irrational folly. I'd probably pull him out if I could do it without too much danger to myself."

"Of course you would. It's human instinct, surely, to save others, particularly a child."

"It's human instinct, and a thoroughly healthy one in my view, to save oneself. That's why, when people don't, we call them heroes and give them medals. We know they're acting against nature. I can't understand how you can have such an extraordinarily benign view of the universe."

"Have I? I suppose I have. Except for the two years after Martin drowned, I've always been able to believe that at the heart of the universe there is love."

"At the heart of the universe there is cruelty. We are predators and are preyed upon, every living thing. Did you know that wasps lay their eggs in ladybirds, piercing the weak spot in their armour? Then the grub grows and feeds on the living ladybird and eats its way out, tying the ladybird's legs together. Whoever thought of that has, you have to admit, a peculiar sense of humour. And don't quote Tennyson at me."

"Perhaps it doesn't feel anything, the ladybird."

"Well, it's a comforting thought but I wouldn't bet on it. You must have had an extraordinarily happy childhood."

"Oh, I did, I did! I was lucky. I would have liked brothers and sisters, but I don't remember that I was ever lonely. There wasn't much money, but there was a great deal of love."

"Love. Is that so very important? You were a teacher, you ought to know. Is it?"

"It's vital. If a child has it for the first ten years, hardly anything else matters. If he hasn't, then nothing does."

There had been a moment's silence and then Alice had said: "My father died, killed in an accident when I was fifteen."

"How terrible. What kind of accident. Were you there? Did you see it?"

"He cut an artery with a billhook. He bled to death. No, we didn't see it, but we were on the scene soon afterwards. Too late, of course."

"Alex too, and he was even younger. How awful for you both."

"It had its effect on our lives undoubtedly, particularly mine. Why don't you try one of those biscuits? It's a new recipe, but I'm not sure that it's entirely successful. A little too sweet, and I may have overdone the spice. Tell me what you think."

Recalled to the present by the cold of the flagstones numbing her feet, and automatically aligning the cup handles, she suddenly realized why she had remembered that summer teatime in Martyr's Cottage. The biscuits she would add to the tray next morning were a later batch of the same recipe provided by Alice. But she wouldn't take them from the tin until tomorrow. There was nothing more to do tonight except to fill her hot-water bottle. There was no central heating in the Old Rectory, and she seldom switched on the two-bar electric fire in her bedroom, knowing how worried the Copleys were by their fuel bills. Finally, hugging the bottle's warmth to her chest, she checked on the bolts of the front and back doors and made her way up the uncarpeted stairs to bed. On the landing she met Mrs. Copley, dressing-gowned, scurrying furtively to the bathroom. Although there was a cloakroom on the ground floor, the Old Rectory had only one bathroom, a defect which necessitated embarrassed, low-voiced enquiries before anyone upset their carefully worked-out rota by taking an unexpected bath. Meg waited until she heard the main-bedroom door shut before going herself to the bathroom.

Fifteen minutes later she was in bed. She knew rather than felt that she was very tired and recognized the symptoms of an overstimulated brain in an exhausted body, the restless limbs and inability to get comfortable. The Old Rectory was too far inland for her to hear the crash of the waves, but the smell and the throb of the sea were always present. In summer the headland would vibrate with a gentle rhythmic humming which, on stormy nights or at the spring tides, would rise to an angry moan. She slept always with her window open and would drift into sleep soothed by that distant murmur. But tonight it had no power to lull her into unconsciousness. Her bedside book, often reread, was Anthony Trollope's *The Small House at Allington*, but tonight it could no longer translate her to the reassuring, comfortable, nostalgic world of Barsetshire, to croquet on Mrs. Dale's lawn and dinner at the squire's table. The memories of the evening were too traumatic, too exciting, too recent to be easily assuaged by sleep. She opened her eyes to the darkness, a darkness too often populated before sleep by those familiar, reproachful, childish faces, brown, black and white, bending over her, asking why she had deserted them when they loved her and thought that she had loved them. Usually it was a relief to be free of those gentle and accusing ghosts, which in the last few months had visited her less often. And sometimes they were replaced by a more traumatic memory. The headmistress had tried to insist that she go on a racial-awareness course, she who had taught children of different races for over twenty years. There was one scene which for months she had tried resolutely to put out of her mind, that last meeting in the staff room, the circle of implacable faces, brown, black and white, the accusing eyes, the insistent questions. And in the end, worn down by bullying, she had found herself helplessly weeping. No nervous breakdown, that useful euphemism, had been more humiliating.

But tonight even that shameful memory was replaced by more recent and more disquieting visions. She glimpsed again that girlish figure momentarily outlined against the walls of the abbey only to slip away like a wraith and be lost among the shadows of the beach. She sat again at the dinner table and saw in the candlelight Hilary Robarts's dark discontented eyes staring intently at Alex Mair, watched the planes of Miles Lessingham's face fitfully lit by the leaping flames of the fire, saw his long-fingered hands reaching down for the bottle of claret, heard again that measured rather high voice speaking the unspeakable. And then, on the verge of sleep, she was crashing with him through the bushes of that dreadful wood, feeling the briars scratching her legs, the low twigs whipping against her cheeks, staring with him as the pool of light from the torch shone down on that grotesque and mutilated face. And in that twilight world between waking and sleeping she saw that it was a face she knew, her own. She jerked back to consciousness with a little cry of terror, switched on the bedside lamp, reached out for her book and began resolutely to read. Half an hour later the book slipped out of her hand and she fell into the first of the night's uneasy periods of slumber.

6

⊠

It took only two minutes of lying stretched and rigid on his bed for Alex Mair to realize that sleep was unlikely to come. To lie in bed wakeful had always been intolerable to him. He could manage with little sleep, but that was invariably sound. Now he swung his legs out of bed, reached for his dressing gown and walked over to the window. He would watch the sun rise over the North Sea. He thought back over the last few hours, the acknowledged relief of talking to Alice, the knowledge that nothing shocked her, nothing surprised her, that everything he did, if not right in her eyes, was judged by a different standard from the one she rigorously applied to the rest of her life.

The secret that lay between them, those minutes when he had held her shaking body against the tree trunk and stared into her eyes, compelling obedience, had bound them with a cord so strong that it couldn't be frayed, either by the enormity of their shared guilty secret, or by the small rubs of living together. And yet they had never spoken of their father's death. He didn't know whether Alice ever thought of it or whether the trauma had erased it from her mind, so that she now believed the version he had formulated, had taken the lie into her unconscious and made it her truth. When, quite soon after the funeral, seeing how calm she was, he had imagined that possibility and had been surprised at his reluctance to believe it. He didn't want her gratitude. It was degrading even to contemplate that she would feel an obligation towards him. "Obligation" and "gratitude" were words they had never needed to use. But he did want her to know and to remember. The deed was to him so monstrous, so surprising that it would have been intolerable not to have shared it with a living soul. In those early months he had wanted her to know the magnitude of what he had done and that he had done it for her.

And then, six weeks after the funeral, he had suddenly found himself able to believe that it hadn't happened, not in that way, and that the whole horror was a childhood fantasy. He would lie awake at night and see his father's crumbling figure, the leap of blood like a scarlet fountain, would hear the harshly whispered words. In this revised and comforting version there had been a second of delay, no more, and then he had raced for the house shouting for help. And there was a second and even more admirable fantasy in which he had knelt at his father's side, had pressed his clenched fist hard into the groin, quenching the spurting blood, had whispered reassurance into those dying eyes. It had been too late, of course; but he had tried. He had done his best. The coroner had praised him, that precise little man with his half-moon spectacles, his face like a querulous parrot. "I congratulate the deceased's son, who acted with commendable promptness and courage and did everything possible to try to save his father's life."

The relief of being able to believe in his innocence was at first so great that temporarily it overwhelmed him. He had lain in bed night after night drifting into sleep on a tide of euphoria. But he had known, even then, that this self-administered absolution was like a drug in the bloodstream. It was comforting and easy, but it wasn't for him. That way lay a danger more destructive even than guilt. He had told himself: "I must never believe that a lie is the truth. I may tell lies all my life if it's expedient, but I must know them for what they are and I must never tell them to myself. Facts are facts. I have to accept them and face them and then I can learn how to deal with them. I can look for reasons for what I did and call those reasons excuses: what he did to Alice, how he bullied Mother, how I hated him. I can attempt to justify his death, at least to myself. But I did what I did, and he died as he died."

And with that acceptance came a kind of peace. After a few years he was able to believe that guilt itself was an indulgence, that he didn't need to suffer it unless he chose. And then there came a time when he felt a pride in the deed, in the courage, the audacity, the resolution which had made it possible. But that, too, he knew was dangerous. And for years afterwards he hardly thought of his father. Neither his mother nor Alice ever spoke of him except in the company of casual acquaintances who felt the need to utter embarrassed condolences from which there was no escape. But in the family only once was his name mentioned.

A year after the death his mother had married Edmund Morgan, a widowed church organist of mind-numbing dullness, and had retired with him to Bognor Regis, where they lived on his father's insurance money in a spacious bungalow in sight of the sea, in an obsessive mutual devotion which mirrored the meticulous order and tidiness of their world. His mother always spoke of her new husband as "Mr. Morgan." "If I don't talk to you about your father, Alex, it isn't that I've forgotten him, but Mr. Morgan wouldn't like it." The phrase had become a catchword between him and Alice. The conjunction of Morgan's job and his instrument offered endless possibilities of adolescent jokes, particularly when he and their mother were on honeymoon. "I expect Mr. Morgan is pulling out all his stops." "Do you suppose Mr. Morgan is changing his combinations?" "Poor Mr. Morgan, labouring away. I hope he doesn't run out of wind." They were wary, reticent children, yet this joke would reduce them to screams of helpless laughter. Mr. Morgan and his organ releasing them into hysterical laughter had anaesthetized the horror of the past.

And then, when he was about eighteen, reality of another kind intruded itself and he said aloud, "I didn't do it for Alice, I did it for myself," and thought how extraordinary it was that it had taken four years to discover that fact. And yet was it a fact, was it the truth, or was it merely a psychological speculation which in certain moods he found it interesting to contemplate?

Now, looking out over the headland to the eastern sky already flushed with the first faint gold of dawn, he said aloud: "I let my father die deliberately. That is a fact. All the rest is pointless speculation." In fiction, he thought, Alice and I should have been tormented by our joint knowledge, distrustful, guilt-ridden, unable to live apart yet miserable together. Yet since his father's death there had been nothing between him and his sister but companionship, affection, peace.

But now, nearly thirty years later, when he thought he had long come to terms with the deed and his own reaction to it, memory had begun to stir again. It had started with the first Whistler murder. The word "murder" itself constantly on someone's lips, like a sonorous curse, seemed to have the power to evoke those half-suppressed images of his father's face which had become as unclear, as devoid of any life, as an old photograph. But in the last six months his father's image had begun to intrude on his consciousness at odd moments, in the middle of a meeting, across a boardroom table, in a gesture, the droop of an eyelid, the tone of a voice, the line of a speaker's mouth, the shape of fingers splayed to an open fire. His father's ghost had returned in the tangle of late summer foliage, the first fall of the leaves, the tentative autumn smells. He wondered if the same thing was happening to Alice. For all their mutual sympathy, for all the sense he had of their being irrevocably bound together, this was the one question he knew he would never ask.

And there were other questions, one question in particular, which he had no need to fear from her. She wasn't in the least curious about his sexual life. He knew enough psychology to have at least some insight into what those early shaming and terrifying experiences had done to her. Sometimes he thought that she regarded his affairs with a casual, slightly amused indulgence, as if, herself immune to a childish weakness, she was nevertheless indisposed to criticize it in others. Once, after his divorce, she had said: "I find it extraordinary that a straightforward if inelegant device for ensuring the survival of the species should involve human beings in such emotional turmoil. Does sex have to be taken so seriously?" And now he found himself wondering whether she knew or guessed about Amy. And then, as the flaming ball rose from the sea, the gears of time slipped, went into reverse, and he was back only four days ago, lying with Amy in the deep hollow of the dunes, smelling again the scent of sand and grasses and the salt tang of the sea as the late-afternoon warmth drained out of the autumn air. He could recall every sentence, every gesture, the timbre of her voice, could feel again the hairs rising on his arms at her touch.

7

She turned towards him, her head propped on her hand, and he saw the strong afternoon light shafting with gold the cropped brightly dyed hair. Already the warmth was draining from the air, and he knew that it was time they were moving. But, lying there beside her, listening to the susurration of the tide and looking up at the sky through a haze of grasses, he was filled, not with post-coital sadness, but with an agreeable languor, as if the long-committed Sunday afternoon still stretched ahead of them.

It was Amy who said: "Look, I'd better be getting back. I told Neil I wouldn't be more than an hour and he gets fussy if I'm late, because of the Whistler."

"The Whistler kills at night, not in daylight. And he'd hardly venture on the headland. Too little cover. But Pascoe's right to be concerned. There isn't much danger, but you shouldn't be out alone at night. No woman should until he's caught."

She said: "I wish they would catch him. It'd be one thing less for Neil to worry about."

Making his voice carefully casual, he asked: "Doesn't he ever ask where you're going when you sneak out on Sunday afternoons, leaving him to look after the child?"

"No, he doesn't. And the child is called Timmy. And I don't sneak. I say I'm going and I go."

"But he must wonder."

"Oh, he wonders all right. But he thinks people are entitled to their privacy. He'd like to ask but he never will. Sometimes I say to him, 'OK, I'm off now to fuck my lover in the sand dunes.' But he never says a word, just looks miserable because he doesn't like me saying 'fuck.' "

"Then why do you? I mean, why torment him? He's probably fond of you."

"No, he isn't, not very fond. It's Timmy he likes. And what other word is there? You can't call it 'going to bed.' I've only been in your bed with you once, and then you were as jumpy as a cat, thinking that sister of yours might come back unexpectedly. And you can't say we sleep together."

He said: "We make love. Or, if you prefer it, we copulate."

"Honestly, Alex, that's disgusting. I think that word is really disgusting."

"And do you do it with him? Sleep, go to bed, make love, copulate?"

"No, I don't. Not that it's any business of yours. He thinks it would be wrong. That means he doesn't really want to. If men want to they usually do."

He said: "That has been my experience, certainly."

They lay side by side like effigies, both staring at the sky. She seemed content not to talk. So the question had at last been put and answered. It had been with shame and some irritation that he had recognized in himself for the first time the nagging of jealousy. More shaming had been his reluctance to put it to the test. And there were those other questions he wanted to ask but daren't. "What do I mean to you?," "Is this important?," "What do you expect of me?" And, most important of all, but unanswerable, "Do you love me?" With his wife he had known precisely where he was. No marriage had begun with a more definite understanding of what each required of the other. Their unwritten, unspoken, only half-acknowledged pre-nuptial agreement had needed no formal ratification. He would earn most of the money, she would work if and when she chose. She had never been particularly enthusiastic about her job as interior designer. In return his home would be run with efficiency and reasonable econ-omy. They would take separate holidays at least once every two years; they would have at most two children and at a time of her choosing;

neither would publicly humiliate the other, the spectrum of marital offences under this heading ranging from spoiling the other's dinner-party stories to a too-public infidelity. It had been a success. They had liked each other, got on with remarkably little rancour, and he had been genuinely upset, if principally in his pride, when she had left him. Fortunately marital failure had been mitigated by the public knowledge of her lover's wealth. He realized that to a materialistic society losing a wife to a millionaire hardly counted as failure. In their friends' eyes it would have been unreasonably proprietorial of him not to have released her with a minimum of fuss. But to do her justice, Liz had loved Gregory, would have followed him to California money or no money. He saw again in memory that transformed laughing face, heard her ruefully apologetic voice.

"It's the real thing this time, darling. I never expected it and I can still hardly believe it. Try not to feel too bad, it isn't your fault. There's nothing to be done."

The real thing. So there was this mysterious real thing before which everything went down, obligations, habit, responsibility, duty. And now, lying in the dunes, seeing the sky through the rigid stalks of marram grasses, he thought about it almost with terror. Surely he hadn't found it at last and with a girl less than half his age, intelligent but uneducated, promiscuous and burdened with an illegitimate child. And he didn't deceive himself about the nature of her hold on him. No lovemaking had ever been as erotic or as liberating as their half-illicit couplings on unyielding sand within yards of the crashing tide.

Sometimes he would find himself indulging in fantasy, would picture them together in London in his new flat. The flat, as yet unsought, no more than a vague possibility among others, would assume dimensions, location, a horribly plausible reality in which he found himself arranging his pictures carefully on a nonexistent wall, thinking over the disposal of his household goods, the exact location of his stereo system. The flat overlooked the Thames. He could see the wide windows giving a view over the river as far as Tower Bridge, the huge bed, Amy's curved body striped with bands of sunlight from the slatted wooden blinds. Then the sweet, deluding pictures would dissolve into bleak reality. There was the child. She would want the child with her. Of course she would. Anyway, who else could look after it? He could see the indulgent amusement on the faces of his friends, the pleasure of his enemies, the child lurching, sticky-fingered, about the flat. He could smell in imagination what Liz had never let him know in actuality—the smell of sour milk and dirty nappies—could picture the dreadful lack of peace and privacy. He needed these realities, deliberately emphasized, to bring him back to sanity. He was horrified that even for a few minutes he could seriously have contemplated such destructive stupidity. He thought: I'm obsessed by her. All right, just for these last few weeks I'll enjoy my obsession. This late summer would be brief enough, the warm unseasonable days of mellow sunshine couldn't last. Already the evenings were darkening. Soon he would smell the first sour tang of winter on the sea breezes. There would be no more lying in the warm sand dunes. She couldn't visit Martyr's Cottage again; that would be recklessly stupid. It was easy to convince himself that with care, when Alice was in London and no visitors expected, they could be together in his bedroom perhaps even for a whole night, but he knew that he would never risk it. Little on the headland was private for long. This was his St. Martin's summer, an autumnal madness, nothing that the first cold of winter couldn't wither.

But now she said, as if there had been no period of silence between them, "Neil's my friend, OK? Why do you want to talk about him anyway?"

"I don't. But I wish he'd civilize his living arrangements. That caravan is in direct line of my bedroom windows. It's an eyesore."

"You'd need binoculars to see it from your windows. And so is your bloody great power station, an eyesore. That's in everyone's direct line; we all have to look at that."

He put out his hand to her shoulder, warm under the gritty film of sand, and said with mock pomposity: "It's generally agreed that, given the constraints imposed by its function and the site, the power station is rather successful architecturally."

"Agreed by whom?"

"I think so, for one."

"Well, you would, wouldn't you? Anyway, you ought to be grateful to Neil. If he didn't look after Timmy I wouldn't be here."

He said: "That whole thing is primitive. He's got a wood stove in there, hasn't he? If that blows up you won't last a minute, all three of you, particularly if the door jams."

"We don't lock it. Don't be daft. And we let the fire go out at night. And suppose your place blows up. It won't be just the three of us, will it? Bloody hell, it won't. Not only humans either. What about Smudge and Whisky? They've got a point of view."

"It won't blow up. You've been listening to his scare-mongering nonsense. If you're worried about nuclear power ask me. I'll tell you what you want to know."

"You mean while you're poking me you'll explain all about nuclear power? Oh boy, I'll certainly be able to take it in."

And then she turned to him again. The pattern of sand on her shoulder glistened and he felt her mouth moving over his upper lip, his nipples, his belly. And then she knelt over him and the round childish face with its bush of bright hair shut out the sky.

Five minutes later she rolled apart from him and began shaking the sand from her shirt and jeans. Tugging the jeans over her thighs, she said: "Why don't you do something about that bitch at Larksoken, the one suing Neil? You could stop her. You're the boss."

The question—or was it a demand—shocked him out of his fantasy as crudely as if, unprovoked, she had suddenly slapped his face. In their four meetings she had never questioned him about his job, had seldom mentioned the power station except, as on this afternoon, to complain half-seriously that it spoilt the view. He hadn't made a deliberate decision to keep her out of his private and professional life. When they were together, that life hardly entered into his own consciousness. The man who lay with Amy in the dunes had nothing to do with that burdened, ambitious, calculating scientist who ran Larksoken, nothing to do with Alice's brother, with Elizabeth's ex-husband, with Hilary's ex-lover. Now he wondered, with a mixture of irritation and dismay, whether she had deliberately chosen to ignore those invisible keep-out signs. And if he had been unconfiding, then so had she. He knew little more about her now than when they had first encountered each other in the abbey ruins on a blustery August evening less than six weeks earlier, had for a minute stood and gazed and had then moved silently towards each other in a wordless, amazed recognition. Later that evening she had told him that she came from Newcastle, that her widowed father had remarried and that she and her stepmother couldn't get on. She had moved down to London and lived in squats. It had sounded commonplace enough but he hadn't quite believed it, nor, he suspected, did she care whether or not he did. Her accent was more Cockney than north-east. He had never asked about the child, partly from a kind of delicacy but mainly because he preferred not to think of her as a mother, and she had volunteered no information about Timmy or his father.

She said: "Well, why don't you? Like I said, you're the boss."

"Not over my staff's private lives. If Hilary Robarts thinks she has been libelled and seeks redress, I can't prevent her from going to law."

"You could if you wanted to. And Neil only wrote what was true."

"That is a dangerous defence to a libel action. Pascoe would be ill advised to rely on it."

"She won't get any money. He hasn't got any. And if he has to pay costs it will ruin him."

"He should have thought of that earlier."

She lay back with a little thud and for a few minutes they were both silent. Then she said, as casually as if the previous conversation had been trivial small-talk which was already half-forgotten: "What about next Sunday? I could get away late afternoon. OK by you?"

So she bore no grudge. It wasn't important to her, or if it was, she had decided to drop it, at least for now. And he could put from him the treacherous suspicion that their first meeting had been contrived, part of a plan devised by her and Pascoe to exploit his influence with Hilary. But that, surely, was ridiculous. He had only to recall the inevitability of their first coming together, her passionate, uncomplicated animal gusto in their lovemaking, to know that the thought was paranoid. He would be here on Sunday afternoon. It might be their last time together. Already he had half-decided that it had to be. He would free himself from this enslavement, sweet as it was, as he had freed himself from Hilary. And he knew, with a regret which was almost as strong as grief, that with this parting there would be no protests, no appeals, no desperate clinging to the past. Amy would accept his leaving as calmly as she had accepted his arrival.

He said: "OK. About four-thirty, then. Sunday the twenty-fifth."

And now time, which in the last ten minutes seemed mysteriously to have halted, flowed again, and he was standing at his bedroom window five days later watching the great ball of the sun rise out of the sea to stain the horizon and spread over the eastern sky the veins and arteries of the new day. Sunday the 25th. He had made that appointment five days ago and it was one that he would keep. But, lying there in the dunes, he hadn't known what he knew now, that he had another and very different appointment to keep on Sunday 25 September.

8

Shortly after lunch Meg walked across the headland to Martyr's Cottage. The Copleys had gone upstairs to take their afternoon rest, and for a moment she wondered whether to tell them to lock their bedroom door. But she told herself that the precaution was surely unnecessary and ridiculous. She would bolt the back door and lock the front door after her as she left, and she wouldn't be gone for long. And they were perfectly happy to be left. Sometimes it seemed to her that old age reduced anxiety. They could look at the power station without the slightest premonition of disaster, and the horror of the Whistler seemed as much beyond their interest as it was their comprehension. The greatest excitement in their lives, which had to be planned with meticulous care and some anxiety, was a drive into Norwich or Ipswich to shop.

It was a beautiful afternoon, warmer than most in the past, disappointing summer. There was a gentle breeze and from time to time Meg paused and lifted her head to feel the warmth of the sun and the sweet-smelling air moving against her cheeks. The turf was springy beneath her feet and to the south the abbey stones, no longer mysterious or sinister, gleamed golden against the blue, untroubled sea.

She did not need to ring. The door at Martyr's Cottage stood open, as it often did in sunny weather, and she called out to Alice before, in response to her answering voice, moving down the corridor to the kitchen. The cottage was redolent with the zesty smell of lemon overlaying the more familiar tang of polish, wine and wood smoke. It was a smell so keen that it momentarily brought back the holiday she and Martin had spent in Amalfi, the trudge hand-in-hand up the winding road to the mountaintop, the pile of lemons and oranges by the roadside, putting their noses to those golden, pitted skins, the laughter and the happiness. The image experienced in a flash of gold, a flush of warmth to her face, was so vivid that for a second she hesitated at the kitchen door as if disorientated. Then her vision cleared and she saw the familiar objects, the Aga and the gas stove with the nearby working surfaces, the table of polished oak in the middle of the room with its four elegantly crafted chairs, and at the far end Alice's office with the walls covered in bookshelves and her desk piled with proofs. Alice was standing working at the table, wearing her long fawn smock.

She said: "As you can see, I'm making lemon curd. Alex and I enjoy it occasionally and I enjoy making it, which I suppose is sufficient justification for the trouble."

"We hardly ever had it—Martin and I, that is. I don't think I've eaten it since childhood. Mother bought it occasionally as a treat for Sunday tea."

"If she bought it, then you don't know what it ought to taste like."

Meg laughed and settled into the wicker chair to the left of the fireplace. It was pale green and closely woven with arms and an elegant, high curved back. She never asked if she could help in the kitchen, since she knew that Alice would be irritated by an offer which she knew to be impractical and insincere. Help was neither needed nor welcomed. But Meg loved to sit quietly and watch. Was it perhaps a memory of childhood, she wondered, that made watching a woman cooking in her own kitchen so extraordinarily reassuring and satisfying? If so, modern children were being deprived of yet one more source of comfort in their increasingly disordered and frightening world.

She said: "Mother didn't make lemon curd, but she did enjoy cooking. It was all very simple, though."

"That's the difficult kind. And I suppose you helped her. I can picture you in your pinafore making gingerbread men."

"She used to give me a piece of the dough when she was making pastry. By the time I'd finished pounding it, rolling it and shaping it, it was dun-coloured. And I used to cut out shaped biscuits. And, yes, I did make gingerbread men, with currants for their eyes; didn't you?"

"No. My mother didn't spend much time in the kitchen. She wasn't a good cook, and my father's criticism destroyed what little confidence she had. He paid for a local woman to come in daily to cook the evening meal, virtually the only one he ate at home except on Sundays. She wouldn't come at weekends, so family meals then tended to be acrimonious. It was an odd arrangement, and Mrs. Watkins was an odd woman. She was a good cook but worked in a perpetual lather of bad temper, and she certainly didn't welcome children in her kitchen. I only became interested in cookery when I was taking my degree in modern languages in London and spent a term in France. That's how it began. I found my necessary passion. I realized that I didn't have to teach or translate or become some man's overqualified secretary."

Meg didn't reply. Alice had only once before spoken of her family or her past life, and she felt that to comment or question might cause her friend to regret the moment of rare confidence. She leaned comfortably back and watched as the deft, familiar, long-fingered hands moved confidently about their business. Before Alice on the table were eight large eggs in a blue shallow bowl and, beside it, a plate with a slab of butter and another with four lemons. She was rubbing the lemons with lumps of sugar until the lumps crumbled into a bowl, when she would pick up another and again begin patiently working away.

She said: "This will make two pounds. I'll give you a jar to take to the Copleys if you think they'd like it."

"I'm sure they would, but I'll be eating it alone. That's what I've come to tell you. I can't stay long. Their daughter is insisting that they go to her until the Whistler is caught. She rang again early this morning, as soon as she heard the news of the latest murder."

Alice said: "The Whistler's getting uncomfortably close, certainly, but they're hardly at risk. He only stalks at night, and all the victims have been young women. And the Copleys don't even go out, do they, unless you drive them?"

"They sometimes walk by the sea, but usually they take their exercise in the garden. I've tried to persuade Rosemary Duncan-Smith that they're not in danger and that none of us is frightened. But I think her friends are criticizing her for not getting them away."

"I see. She doesn't want to have them, they don't want to go, but the friends, so-called, must be propitiated."

"I think she's one of those masterful, efficient women who can't tolerate criticism. To be fair to her, I think she's genuinely worried."

"So when are they going?"

"Sunday night. I'm driving them to Norwich to catch the eight-thirty, getting into Liverpool Street at ten-fifty-eight. Their daughter will meet them."

"That's not very convenient, is it? Sunday travel is always difficult. Why can't they wait till Monday morning?"

"Because Mrs. Duncan-Smith is staying at her club in Audley Square for the weekend and has taken a room for them there. Then they can all drive down to Wiltshire first thing on Monday morning."

"And what about you? Will you mind being left alone?"

"Not in the least. Oh, I expect I'll miss them when they've gone, but at present I keep thinking of all the work I'll be able to catch up on. And I'll be able to spend more time here, helping with the proofs. I don't think I'll be afraid. I can understand the fear and sometimes I find myself almost playing at being frightened, deliberately dwelling on the horror, as if I'm testing my own nerve. It's all right in the daytime. But when night falls and we're sitting there by the fire, I can imagine him out there in the darkness, watching and waiting. It's that sense of the unseen, unknowable menace which is so disquieting. It's rather like the feeling I get from the power station, that there's a dangerous unpredictable power out on the headland which I can't control or even begin to understand."

Alice said: "The Whistler isn't in the least like the power station. Nuclear power can be understood and it can be controlled. But this latest murder is certainly a nuisance for Alex. Some of the secretaries live locally and bus or cycle home. He's arranging for the staff with cars to take them and pick them up in the morning, but with shift work that means more organizing than you'd expect. And some of the girls are beginning to panic and say they'll only be driven by another woman."

"But they can't seriously think it's a colleague, someone from the power station?"

"They don't seriously think, that's the trouble. Instinct takes over, and their instinct is to suspect every man, particularly if he hasn't an alibi for the last two murders. And then there's Hilary Robarts. She swims almost every evening until the end of October, and sometimes through the winter. She still intends to swim. The chances of her getting murdered may be a million to one, but it's an act of bravado which sets a bad example. I'm sorry about yesterday evening, by the way. Not a very successful dinner party. I owed a meal to Miles and Hilary, but I hadn't realized just how much they dislike each other. I don't know why. Alex probably does, but I'm not really interested enough to ask. How did you get on with our resident poet?"

Meg said: "I liked him. I thought he'd be rather intimidating but he isn't, is he? We walked together to the abbey ruins. They look so wonderful by moonlight."

Alice said: "Appropriately romantic for a poet. I'm glad you didn't find his company disappointing. But I can never look at the moon without visualizing that litter of hardware. Man leaves his polluting mess behind him like metal turds. But it will be full moon on Sunday night. Why not come here for a quiet supper when you get back from Norwich and we'll walk to the ruins together. I'll expect you at nine-thirty. It will probably just be the two of us. Alex usually goes into the power station after a weekend in town."

Meg said regretfully: "I'd love to, Alice, but I'd better not. The final packing and getting them off will be a formidable business, and by the time I get back from Norwich I'll be ready for bed. And I shan't be hungry. I need to make a high tea for them before we leave. I could only stay for an hour, anyway. Mrs. Duncan-Smith says that she'll ring from Liverpool Street to say that they've arrived safely."

Uncharacteristically Alice dried her hands and walked with her to the door. Meg wondered why, in chatting about the dinner party and her walk with Adam Dalgliesh, she hadn't mentioned that mysterious female figure glimpsed among the ruins. It wasn't just that she feared to make too much of it; without Adam Dalgliesh's corroboration she could so easily have been mistaken. Something else, a reluctance she could neither explain nor understand, held her back. As they reached the door and Meg gazed out over the curve of the sunlit headland, she experienced a moment of extraordinary perception in which it seemed to her that she was aware of another time, a different reality, existing simultaneously with the moment in which she stood. The external world was still the same. She saw every detail with a keener eye; the motes of dust dancing in the swathe of sunlight which fell across the stone floor, the hardness of each timeworn slab beneath her feet, every nail mark pitting the great oak door, each individual grass of the tussock at the fringe of the heath. But it was the other world which possessed her mind. And here there was no sunlight, only an everlasting darkness loud with the sound of horse's hooves and tramping feet, of rough male voices, of an incoherent babble as if the tide were sucking back the shingle on all the beaches of the world. And then there was a hiss and crackling of fagots, an explosion of fire, and then a second of dreadful silence broken by the high, long-drawn-out scream of a woman.

She heard Alice's voice: "Are you all right, Meg?"

"I felt strange for a moment. It's over now. I'm perfectly all right."

"You've been overworking. There's too much for you to do in that house. And last night was hardly restful. It was probably delayed shock."

Meg said: "I told Mr. Dalgliesh that I never felt Agnes Poley's presence in this house. But I was wrong. She is here. Something of her remains."

There was a pause before her friend replied. "I suppose it depends on your understanding of time. If, as some scientists tell us, it can go backwards, then perhaps she is still here, still alive, burning in an everlasting bonfire. But I'm never aware of her. She doesn't appear to me. Perhaps she finds me unsympathetic. For me, the dead remain dead. If I couldn't believe that, I don't think I could go on living."

Meg said her final goodbye and walked out resolutely over the headland. The Copleys, facing the formidable decisions of what to pack for an indeterminate visit, would be getting anxious. When she reached the crest of the headland, she turned and saw Alice still standing at the open doorway. She raised her hand in a gesture more like a blessing than a wave and disappeared into the cottage.

BOOK
THREE

Sunday 25 September

1
⊠

By 8.15 on Sunday night Theresa had finished the last of her long-deferred homework and thought she could safely put away her arithmetic book and tell her father that she was tired and ready for bed. He had earlier helped her wash up after supper, the last of the Irish stew, to which she had added extra carrots from a tin, and had settled as he always did in front of the television, slumped back in the battered armchair by the empty fire grate with his bottle of whisky on the floor by his side. Here, she knew, he would sit until the last programme had ended, staring fixedly at the screen but not, she felt, really watching those black-and-white flickering images. Sometimes it was almost dawn when, awake, she would hear his heavy feet on the stairs.

Mr. Jago had rung just after 7.30 and she had answered the telephone and taken a message, saying that Daddy was in his painting shed and couldn't be disturbed. It wasn't true. He had been in the privy at the bottom of the garden. But she hadn't liked to tell that to Mr. Jago, and she wouldn't have dreamed of fetching her father, of knocking on the privy door. Sometimes she thought, with a curiously adult perception, that he took his torch and went there when he didn't really need to, that the ramshackle hut with its cracked door and wide comfortable seat was a refuge for him from the cottage, from the mess and muddle, Anthony's crying, her own ineffectual efforts to take her mother's place. But he must have been on his way back. His ears had caught the ring and, coming in, he had asked her who had telephoned.

"It was a wrong number, Daddy," she had lied, and from habit made a quick act of contrition. She was glad that he hadn't spoken to Mr. Jago. Daddy might have been tempted to meet him at the Local Hero, knowing that it would be safe to leave her in charge for an hour or two, and tonight it was vitally important that he didn't leave the cottage. He had only half a bottle of whisky left, she had checked on that. She would be gone for only forty minutes or so, and if there were a fire, the secret fear which she had inherited from her mother, he wouldn't be too drunk to save Anthony and the twins.

She kissed him briefly on a cheek which was prickly to her lips and smelt the familiar smell of whisky, turpentine and sweat. As always, he put up his hand and gently ruffled her hair. It was the only gesture of affection which he now made to her. His eyes were still on the old black-and-white screen, where the familiar Sunday faces could be glimpsed through an intermittent snowstorm. He wouldn't, she knew, disturb her once the door to the back bedroom she shared with Anthony was closed. Since her mother's death he had never entered her bedroom when she was there, either by night or day. And she had noticed the difference in his attitude towards her, almost a formality, as if in a few short weeks she had grown into womanhood. He would consult her as if she were an adult about the shopping, the next meal, the twins' clothes, even the problem with the van. But there was one subject he never mentioned: her mother's death.

Her narrow bed was directly under the window. Kneeling on it, she gently drew back the curtains, letting moonlight stream into the room, seeking out the corners, laying its swathes of cold, mysterious light on the bed and across the wooden floor. The door to the small box room at the front of the cottage, where the twins slept, was open, and she passed through and stood for a moment looking down at the small humps closely curved together under the bedclothes, then, bending low, listened for the regular hiss of their breath. They wouldn't wake now until the morning. She closed the door and went back into her own room. Anthony lay, as he always did, on his back, his legs splayed like a frog's, his head to one side and both arms stretched high as if trying to seize the bars of the cot. He had wriggled free of his blanket, and she drew it up gently over his sleeping suit. The impulse to snatch him into her arms was so strong that it was almost a pain. But instead she carefully let down the side of the cot and, for a moment, laid her head beside his. He lay as if drugged, his mouth pursed, his eyelids delicately veined films under which she could imagine the upturned, unseeing eyes.

Returning to her own bed, she pushed the two pillows down under the blankets and moulded them to the semblance of her body. Her father was very unlikely to look in, but if the unexpected should happen, at least he wouldn't see in the moonlight an obviously empty bed. She felt beneath it for the small canvas shoulder-bag in which she had placed ready what she knew she would need: the box of matches, the single white household candle, the sharp penknife, the pocket torch. Then she climbed on the bed and opened wide the casement window.

The whole headland was bathed in the silver light which she and her mother loved. Everything was transformed into magic; the outcrops of rock floated like islands of crumpled foil above the still grasses, and the broken, ill-kept hedge at the bottom of the garden was a mystic thicket woven from thin shafts of light. And beyond it, like a silken scarf, lay the wide untrammelled sea. She stood for a moment transfixed, breathing quickly, gathering up her strength, then climbed out onto the flat roof over the extension. It was covered with shingles and she crept forward with infinite care, feeling the grittiness of the stones through the soles of her plimsolls. It was a drop of only six feet and, with the help of the drainpipe, she made it easily, then scurried down the garden, stooping low, to the rotting wooden lean-to at the rear of her father's painting shed, where she and her father kept their bicycles. In the moonlight streaming through the open door she disentangled hers, then wheeled it across the grass and lifted it through a gap in the hedge to avoid using the front gate. It was not until she reached the safety of the sunken lane where the old coastal railway had once run that she dared mount, and began bumping over the humpy grass northwards, towards the fringe of pine trees and the ruined abbey.

The old railway track ran behind the wood of pines which fringed the shore, but here it was less sunken, no more than a gentle depression in the headland. Soon that too would flatten and there would be nothing, not even the rotting planks of old sleepers, to show where the coastal railway had once run, taking Victorian families, with their spades and buckets, their nursemaids, their great portmanteaux, for their summer holiday by the sea. Less than ten minutes later she was in the open headland. She switched off the bicycle lamp, dismounted to check that there was no one in sight and began bumping across the tough turf towards the sea.

And now the five broken arches of the abbey ruins came into sight, gleaming in the moonlight. She stood for a moment and stared in silence. It looked unreal, ethereal, an insubstantial edifice of light which would dissolve at a touch. Sometimes when, as now, she came to it by moon- or starlight, the feeling was so strong that she would put out a hand and touch the stones and feel a physical shock at their rough hardness. Propping her bicycle against the low stone wall, she walked into the space where the great west door must once have been and into the body of the abbey. It was on calm moonlit nights like this when she and her mother would make their little expeditions together. Her mother would say, "Let's go and talk to the monks," and they would cycle here together and walk in companionable silence among the ruined arches or stand hand-in-hand where the altar must once have stood, hearing what those long-dead monks had once heard, but more remotely: the melancholy booming of the sea. It was here, she knew, where her mother liked best to pray, feeling more at home on this rough age-hallowed earth than in that ugly red-brick building outside the village where Father McKee visited every Sunday to say Mass.

She missed seeing Father McKee, missed his jokes, his praise, his funny Irish accent. But since her mother's death he visited only rarely and was never made welcome. She remembered the last time, the briefness of the visit, her father seeing him out of the door, Father McKee's parting words.

"Her dear mother, God rest her, would want Theresa to be regular at Mass and confession. Mrs. Stoddard-Clark would be glad to call for her in the car next Sunday, and she could go back to the Grange afterwards for lunch. Now, wouldn't that be nice for the child?"

And her father's voice: "Her mother isn't here. Your God has chosen to deprive her of her mother. Tess is on her own now. When she feels like going to Mass, she'll go, and she'll go to confession when she has something to confess."

The grass had grown high here, spiked with tall weeds and dried flower-heads, the ground so humpy that she had to walk with care.

She moved up under the highest arch of all, where the great eastern window had once shone in an imagined miracle of coloured glass. Now it was an empty eye through which she could see the gleam of the sea and, above it, the sailing moon. And now, by the light of her torch and very quietly, she began her task. She went over to the wall, knife in hand, and began searching for a large, flat-surfaced stone which would form the basis of her altar. Within minutes she had found one and had prised it loose with her penknife. But there was something hidden in the crevice behind it, a thin piece of cardboard pushed deep into the crevice. She took it out and unfolded it. It was half of a coloured postcard of the west front of Westminster Abbey. Even with the right-hand side cut away, she recognized the familiar twin towers. She turned it over and saw that there were a few lines of message which she couldn't read by moonlight and felt no particular curiosity to decipher. It seemed quite new, but with the date stamp unreadable there was no way of knowing how long it had lain there. Perhaps it had been hidden during the summer season as part of a family game. It didn't worry her; indeed, preoccupied as she was, it hardly interested her. This was the kind of secret message her friends left for each other at school, hidden in the bicycle shed, slipped into a blazer pocket. She hesitated for a moment, started to tear it, then smoothed it out and put it carefully back.

Working her way along the wall, she found another suitable stone and the few smaller ones she needed to prop up the single candle. The altar was soon complete. She lit the candle, the hiss of the match sounding unnaturally loud and the sudden flare of the light almost too bright for her eyes. She let the first blobs of wax fall on the stone, then wedged the candle into it, propped it up with pebbles. Then she sat cross-legged before it and gazed into the candle's steady glow. She knew that her mother would come, unseen but known to be present, silent but speaking clearly. She had only to wait in patience and gaze steadily into the candle's unflickering light.

She tried to empty her mind of everything except the questions which she was here to ask. But her mother's death was too recent, the memory too painful to be shut out of her thoughts.

Mummy hadn't wanted to die in hospital and Daddy had promised that she wouldn't. She had heard his whispered assurances. She knew that Dr. Entwhistle and the district nurse had opposed them both.

There were snatches of conversation she wasn't supposed to overhear but which, standing silently in the darkness of the stairs behind the oak door which led to the sitting room, came to her clearly as if she were standing by her mother's bed.

"You really need twenty-four-hour nursing, Mrs. Blaney, more care than I can give. And you'd be more comfortable in hospital."

"I am comfortable. I have Ryan and Theresa. I have you. You're all so good to me. I don't need anyone else."

"I do what I can, but twice a day isn't enough. It's a lot to expect of Mr. Blaney and Theresa. It's all right saying you've got her, but she's only fifteen."

"I want to be with them. We want to be together."

"But if they're frightened . . . it's difficult for children."

Then that gentle, implacable voice, thin and unbreakable as a reed, carrying the obstinate selfishness of the dying.

"They won't be frightened. Do you think we'd let them be frightened? There isn't anything frightening about birth or death if they've been properly taught."

"There are things you can't teach children, Mrs. Blaney, things you can only experience."

And she, Theresa, had done her best to convince everyone that they were all right, that they could manage. There had been small subterfuges. Before Nurse Pollard and the doctor arrived, she would wash the twins, put on clean dresses, change Anthony's nappy. It was important that everything looked under control so that Dr. Entwhistle and the nurse couldn't say that Daddy couldn't cope. One Saturday she cooked buns and handed them gravely round on a plate, the best plate, her mother's favourite, with the delicately painted roses and the holes in the border where you could thread a ribbon. She remembered the doctor's embarrassed gaze as he said, "No thank you, Theresa, not just now."

"Please have one. Daddy made them."

And as he left he had said to her father: "You may be able to bear this, Blaney, I'm not sure that I can."

Only Father McKee seemed to notice her efforts. Father McKee, who spoke so like an Irishman on the telly that Theresa thought he was doing it on purpose as a joke and tried always to reward him with a laugh.

"My, and isn't it grand the way you have this cottage shining. Couldn't the blessed Virgin herself eat off that floor now? Made by your dad, are they? And very nice too. See, I'm putting one in my pocket for later. Now, you be making a nice cup of tea, that's a good girl, while I chat to your ma."

She tried not to think about the night when they had taken her mother away: waking to hear those awful groaning noises, which had made her think that there was an animal in agony snuffling round the cottage; realizing that the noise wasn't outside at all; the sudden terror; her father's figure in the bedroom doorway commanding her to stay there, not to come out, to keep the children quiet; watching at the window of the little front bedroom with the twins' frightened faces staring from the bed and seeing the ambulance arrive; the two men with the stretcher; that blanket-shrouded figure, quiet now, being carried down the garden path. It was then that she had rushed down the stairs and almost hurled herself at her father's restraining arms.

"Better not, better not. Get her inside."

She wasn't sure who had spoken the words. Then she was breaking free and running after the ambulance as it turned at the bottom of the lane, beating her hands against the closed doors. She remembered her father lifting her in his arms, carrying her back into the cottage. She remembered the strength of him, the smell and roughness of his shirt, her impotently flailing arms. She had never seen her mother again. It was how God had answered her prayers, her mother's prayers, to be able to stay at home, her mother who asked for so little. And nothing Father McKee could say would make her forgive God.

The chill of the September night was seeping through her jeans and jumper, and the small of her back was beginning to ache. For the first time she felt a prick of doubt. And then, in a tremble of the candle flame, her mother was with her. Everything was all right.

There were so many things she needed to ask. Anthony's nappies. The disposable ones were so expensive and so bulky to carry, and Daddy didn't seem to realize how much they cost. Her mother said she should use the terries and rinse them out. Then the twins didn't really like Mrs. Hunter, who came and collected them to take them to the playgroup. The twins must be polite to Mrs. Hunter and not mind. She was doing her best. It was important that they kept going to the playgroup for Daddy's sake. Theresa must tell them that. And then there was Daddy. There was so much to say about him. He didn't go to the pub often because he didn't like to leave them, but there was always whisky in the house. Her mother said that she was not to worry about the whisky. He needed it now, but soon he would begin painting again and then he wouldn't need it so much. But if he really became drunk and there was another bottle in the house, she had better pour it away. She needn't be frightened that it would make him angry. He would never be angry with her.

The silent communication went on. She sat as if in a trance, watching while the wax of the candle slowly burned down. And then there was nothing. Her mother had gone away. Before blowing out the candle, she scraped away the traces of wax from the stone with her knife. It was important that no evidence remained. Then she replaced the stones in the wall. The ruins held nothing for her now but a cold emptiness. It was time to go home.

Suddenly she was overcome with tiredness. It seemed impossible that her legs would carry her as far as the bicycle, and she couldn't face the thought of the bumpy ride across the headland. She didn't know what impulse led her through the great east window to stand on the edge of the cliff. Perhaps it was the need to gather her strength, to look out over the moonlit sea and recapture for a moment that lost communion with her mother. But instead her mind was seized with a very different memory, as recent as that afternoon, and one that was still so frightening that she hadn't spoken of it, even to her mother. She saw again the red car, moving at speed down the lane towards Scudder's Cottage, called the children from the garden, bundled them upstairs and shut the sitting-room door. But later she had stood behind it and listened. It seemed to her that no word of that conversation would ever be forgotten.

First Hilary Robarts's voice: "This place was totally unsuitable for a sick woman who had to undergo long journeys for radiotherapy. You must have known she was ill when you took it. She couldn't manage."

And then her father: "And I suppose you thought that after she'd gone I wouldn't be able to manage either. How many months did you give her? You used to pretend that you were concerned, but she knew what you were at. Watching how much weight she was losing each week, more bone showing through, wrists like sticks, the cancer skin. 'Not much longer now,' you thought. You made a bloody good investment in this cottage. You invested in her death, and you made her life a bloody misery for her last weeks."

"That isn't true. Don't load your guilt on me. I had to come here, there were things I had to see. That patch of damp in the kitchen, the problem with rain coming in the roof. You wanted them seen to, presumably. You were the first to point out that I had obligations as a landlady. And if you won't get out, I shall have to apply for a rise in the rent. What you pay is derisory. It doesn't even cover repairs."

"Try. Go to the Rent Tribunal. Let them come and see for themselves. The freehold may be yours, but I'm the man in possession. And I pay the rent regularly. You can't get me out, I'm not that daft."

"You pay the rent, but for how long? You could get by when you had that part-time teaching job, but I can't see you managing now. I suppose you call yourself an artist, but what you are is a cheap hack painter turning out rubbish for undiscriminating tourists who think any fourth-rate original is better than a first-rate print. But they aren't selling as well now, are they? Those four water-colours Ackworth has in his window have been there for weeks. They're beginning to brown. Even tourists are getting a little particular these days. Junk doesn't sell just because it's cheap."

But the twins, tired of incarceration, began quarrelling, and she had to hurry upstairs to tell them it wouldn't be long now, that they mustn't come out until the witch had gone. Then she crept down again. But it wasn't necessary to descend farther than the fourth step. The voices were shouting now.

"I want to know if you sent that woman here, that bloody social worker from the local authority who came to spy on me and question my children about me. Did you send her?"

The witch's voice was cool, but she could hear every word: "I'm not required to answer that. If I did alert them, then it was about time someone did."

"My God, you're evil, aren't you? You'd do anything to get me and my children out of this cottage. They used to burn people like you four hundred years ago. If it wasn't for the children I'd kill you. But I'm not having them taken into so-called care just for the satisfaction of putting my hands round your throat. But, by God, don't tempt me, don't tempt me. So get out. Get out of my cottage and off my ground. Take your rent and be thankful you're alive to take it. And don't ever interfere with my life again. Not ever, not ever."

The witch said: "Don't be hysterical. That's all you're good for, threats and violence. If the local authority took those children into care, it would be the best thing for them. Oh, I dare say you'd like to kill me. Your sort always react to reason with threats and violence. Kill me and expect the state to support your children for the next fifteen years. You're ridiculous and pathetic."

And then her father's voice, not shouting any more but so quiet that she could only just catch the words: "If I do kill you, no one will lay their hands on me or my children. No one."

With the reliving of that last awful encounter came anger, and the anger flowing into her legs seemed to give them strength. She could cope now with the ride home. And it was time she was leaving. And then she saw that the beach was no longer empty. Suddenly she began shaking like a young puppy and then backed into the shelter of the arch. To the north, running down from the pine trees towards the sea, was a woman, her dark hair streaming, her white body almost naked. And she was shouting, shouting in triumph. It was the witch, Hilary Robarts.

2

⊠

Hilary ate an early supper. She wasn't hungry, but she took a French
roll from the freezer and heated it in the oven, then made herself a
herb omelette. She washed up and left the kitchen tidy, then took
papers from her briefcase and settled down at the sitting-room table
to work. There was a paper to be written about the implications of
the reorganization for her department, figures to be collated and presented, an argument for the redeployment of staff logically and elegantly presented. The task was important to her and normally she
would have enjoyed it. She knew that she could be faulted when it
came to personnel management, but no one had been able to criticize
her as organizer and administrator. Shuffling the papers, she wondered how much, if at all, she would miss it when she and Alex were
married and in London. She was surprised how little she cared. This
part of her life was over and she would relinquish it without regret,
this overtidy cottage which had never been her own and never could
be, the power station, even her job. And now there would be a different
life, Alex's job, her status as his wife, entertaining the right people in
the right way, some carefully chosen voluntary work, travel. And there
would be a child, his child.

This overpowering need for a child had strengthened in the last
year, growing in intensity as his physical need for her decreased. She
tried to persuade herself that a love affair, like a marriage, couldn't
always be maintained at the same pitch of sexual or emotional ex-

citement, that essentially nothing had changed between them and nothing really could. How much commitment, physical or emotional, had there been at the start of the relationship? Well, that had suited her all right at the time; she hadn't wanted any more than he was prepared to give, a mutually satisfactory exchange of pleasure, the kudos of being his half-acknowledged mistress, the careful dissimulation when they were in company together, which was hardly necessary or successful and wasn't seriously meant to be but which, for her part at least, had held a powerful erotic charge. It was a game they played: their almost formal greeting before meetings or in the presence of strangers, his twice-weekly visits to her cottage. When she had first come to Larksoken she had looked for a modern flat in Norwich and had, for a time, rented one close to the city centre. But once the affair began it was necessary to be near him, and she had found a holiday cottage less than a quarter of a mile from Martyr's Cottage. He was, she knew, both too proud and too arrogant to visit her surreptitiously, sneaking out at night like a randy schoolboy. But no degrading pretence was required; the headland was invariably deserted. And he never stayed the night. The careful rationing of her company seemed almost a necessary part of the relationship. And in public they behaved as colleagues. He had always discouraged informality, too many first names, except to his immediate colleagues, too much easy camaraderie. The station was as disciplined as a tightly run ship in wartime.

But the affair, begun with such discipline, such emotional and social propriety, had deteriorated into messiness and longing and pain. She thought she knew the moment when the need for a child had begun to grow into an obsession. It was when the theatre sister at that expensive and discreet nursing home, only half-concealing her disapproval and disgust, had taken away the kidney-shaped bowl with that quivering mass of tissue which had been the foetus. It was as if her womb, so clinically robbed, was taking its revenge. She hadn't been able to conceal her longing from Alex, even though she knew that it repelled him. She could hear again her own voice, truculent, whining, an importunate child, and could see his look, half-laughing, of simulated dismay which she knew concealed a genuine repugnance.

"I want a child."

"Don't look at me, darling. That's one experiment I'm not prepared to repeat."

"You have a child, healthy, living, successful. Your name, your genes will go on."

"I've never set store on that. Charles exists in his own right."

She had tried to argue herself out of the obsession, forcing the unwelcome images on her unreceptive mind, the broken nights, the smell, the constant demands, the lessening of freedom, the lack of privacy, the effect on her career. It was no good. She was making an intellectual response to a need where intellect was powerless. Sometimes she wondered if she was going mad. And she couldn't control her dreams, one in particular. The smiling nurse, gowned and masked, placing the newborn baby in her arms, herself looking down at the gentle, self-contained face bruised with the trauma of birth. And then the sister, grim-visaged, rushing in and snatching the bundle away. "That isn't your baby, Miss Robarts. Don't you remember? We flushed yours down the lavatory."

Alex didn't need another child. He had his son, his living hope, however precarious, of vicarious immortality. He might have been an inadequate and scarcely known parent, but he was a parent. He had held in his arms his own child. That wasn't unimportant to him, whatever he might pretend. Charles had visited his father last summer, a golden-bronzed, hefty-legged, sun-bleached giant who had seemed in retrospect to blaze through the station like a meteor, captivating the female staff with his American accent, his hedonistic charm. And Alex, she saw, had been surprised and slightly disconcerted by his pride in the boy, attempting unsuccessfully to conceal it with heavy-handed banter.

"Where is the young barbarian, swimming? He'll find the North Sea an unwelcome change from Laguna Beach."

"He tells me he proposes to read law at Berkeley. There's a place waiting for him in step-papa's firm, apparently, once he qualifies. Next thing, Liz will be writing to say that he's engaged to some socially acceptable sophomore, or do I mean preppy?"

"I'm managing to feed him, by the way. Alice has left me a recipe for hamburgers. Every shelf of the refrigerator is stuffed with ground beef. His vitamin-C requirements seem abnormally high, even for a boy of his height and weight. I press oranges constantly."

She had squirmed in a mixture of embarrassment and resentment; the pride and the juvenile humour had both seemed so out of character, almost demeaning. It was as if he, as much as the typists, had been captivated by his son's physical presence. Alice Mair had left for London two days after Charles had arrived. Hilary wondered whether this had been perhaps a ploy to give father and son some time alone together or whether—and more likely, from what she knew or guessed of Alice Mair—it had been a reluctance both to spend time cooking for the boy and to witness his father's embarrassing excess of paternalism.

She thought again of his last visit, when he had walked home with her after the dinner party. She had deliberately sounded reluctant to be escorted, but he had come and she had meant that he should. After she had finished speaking, he had said quietly: "That sounds like an ultimatum."

"I wouldn't call it that."

"What would you call it, then, blackmail?"

"After what's happened between us, I'd call it justice."

"Let's stick to 'ultimatum.' 'Justice' is too grandiose a concept for the commerce between us two. And like every ultimatum it will have to be considered. It's usual to set a time limit. What's yours?"

She had said: "I love you. In this new job you're going to need a wife. I'm the right wife for you. It could work. I'd make it work. I could make you happy."

"I'm not sure how much happiness I'm capable of. Probably more than I've any right to. But it isn't in anyone's gift, not Alice's, not Charles's, not Elizabeth's, not yours. It never has been."

Then he had come over to her and kissed her on the cheek. She had turned to cling to him, but he had put her gently aside.

"I'll think about it."

"I'd like to announce it soon, the engagement."

"You're not thinking of a church wedding, I suppose. Orange blossom, bridesmaids, Mendelssohn's 'Wedding March,' 'The Voice That Breathed o'er Eden.' "

She had said: "I'm not thinking of making either of us ridiculous, now or after marriage. You know me better than that."

"I see, just a quick, painless turning-off at the local registrar's office. I'll give you my decision next Sunday night, after I get back from London."

She had said: "You make it sound so formal."

And he had replied: "But it has to be formal, doesn't it, the response to an ultimatum?"

He would marry her and, within three months, he would know that she had been right. She would win because, in this, her will was stronger than his. She remembered the words of her father. "There's only this one life, girlie, but you can live it on your own terms. Only the stupid and the weak need to live like slaves. You've got health, looks, brains. You can take what you want. All you need is the courage and the will." The bastards had nearly got him in the end, but he had lived life on his own terms and so would she.

Now she tried to put thoughts of Alex, of their future, on one side and concentrate on the task in hand. But she couldn't settle. Restless, she went through the kitchen into the small back parlour, which held her wine store, and brought out a bottle of claret. She took down a glass from the dresser and poured. Taking her first mouthful, she felt on the corner of her lip the minute scrape of a chip. It was intolerable to her to drink from a chipped glass. Instinctively she took down another and emptied the first glass into it. She was about to throw the defective glass away when she hesitated, her foot on the pedal of the refuse bin. It was one of a set of six that Alex had given her. The defect, unnoticed before, was slight, little more than a roughness on the brim. The glass could be used to hold flowers. She had a picture of them, snowdrops, primroses, small sprigs of rosemary. When she had finished drinking, she washed up both glasses and turned them over to drain. The bottle of claret she left uncorked on the table. It had really been too cold to drink, but in another hour it would be about right.

It was time for her swim, just after nine, and tonight she wouldn't bother with the news. Upstairs, in her bedroom, she stripped naked, put on the bottom half of a black bikini and over it her blue-and-white track suit. On her feet she wore old sandals, the leather stained and toughened by sea water. From the hall peg she took down a small steel locket on a leather thong just large enough to hold her Yale key, which she wore round her neck when swimming. It had been Alex's gift for her last birthday. Touching it, she smiled and felt, strong as the metal against her fingers, the certainty of hope. Then she took a torch from the drawer in the hall table and, closing the door carefully behind her, set off for the beach, her towel slung over her shoulder.

She smelt the resin of the pines before she passed between their slim, spiky trunks. There were only fifty yards of sandy path, thick with their fallen needles, between her and the shore. It was dimmer here, the moon glimpsed fitfully, sailing in majestic splendour above the high spires of the trees now seen and now obscured, so that for a few seconds she had to switch on her torch. And now she passed out of the shadows and saw before her the white moon-bleached sand and the tremble of the North Sea. Dropping her towel in her usual place, a small hollow on the fringe of the wood, she slipped off her track suit and stretched her arms high above her head. Then she kicked off her sandals and began running, over the narrow band of shingle, over the dusty sand above the watermark, over the smooth, sea-washed eddies of the foam, splashing through the small waves which seemed to be falling without a sound, to hurl herself at last into cleansing peace. She gasped at the coldness of it, fierce as a pain. But almost at once that passed, as it always did, and it seemed to her that the water gliding over her shoulders had taken on her own body warmth and that she swam cocooned in self-sufficiency. With her strong rhythmic crawl she struck out from the shore. She knew how long she could safely stay in: just five minutes before the cold struck again and it was time to return. And now she stopped swimming and lay for a moment on her back, floating, looking up at the moon. The magic worked again as it always did. The frustrations, the fears, the anger of the day fell away and she was filled instead with a happiness which she would have called ecstasy, except that "ecstasy" was too ostentatious a word for this gentle peace. And with the happiness came optimism. Everything was going to be all right. She would let Pascoe sweat for another week, then withdraw her action. He was too unimportant even to hate. And her solicitor was right, possession of Scudder's Cottage could wait. It was increasing in value every month. The rent was being paid, she was losing nothing. And the daily irritations of the job, the professional jealousies, the resentments, what did they matter now? That part of her life was coming to an end. She loved Alex, Alex loved her. He would see the sense of everything she had said. They would be married. She would have his child. Everything was possible. And then for a moment there came a deeper peace in which even none of this mattered. It was as if all the petty preoccupations of the flesh were washed away and she was a disembodied spirit floating free, looking down at her body spread-eagled under the moon, and could feel a gentle, undemanding sorrow for this earth-grounded creature who could find only in an alien element this sweet but transitory peace.

But it was time to get back. She gave a vigorous kick, twisted herself over and began her powerful crawl towards the shore, towards that silent watcher waiting for her in the shadow of the trees.

3

⊠

Dalgliesh had spent Sunday morning revisiting Norwich Cathedral and St. Peter Mancroft before lunching at a restaurant on the outskirts of the city where he and his aunt two years previously had eaten an unpretentious but excellently cooked meal. But here too time had wrought its changes. The exterior and the décor were deceivingly the same but it was quickly apparent that both proprietor and chef had changed. The meal, arriving with suspicious promptness, had obviously been cooked elsewhere and heated up, the grilled liver a grainy slab of indistinguishable grey meat blanketed with a synthetic, glutinous sauce and accompanied by potatoes which were underdone and cauliflower which was a mush. It was not a luncheon to deserve a wine, but he fortified himself with cheddar and biscuits before setting out on the afternoon's programme, a visit to the fifteenth-century Church of St. Peter and St. Paul at Salle.

During the last four years it had been rare for him to visit his aunt without driving with her to Salle, and she had left with her will a request that her ashes should be strewn in the churchyard there without ceremony and by him on his own. He knew that the church had exerted a powerful influence on her, but she had not, as far as he knew, been a religious woman, and the request had a little surprised him. It had seemed so much more likely that she would have wanted her physical remains thrown to the winds on the headland, or that she would have left no instructions, regarding this as a simple matter

of expedient disposal requiring neither thought on her part nor ceremony on his. But now he had a task to perform, and one of surprising
importance to him. In recent weeks he had been visited by the nagging
guilt of a duty unfulfilled, almost a spirit unpropitiated. He found
himself wondering, as he had before in his life, at man's insistent
need for ritual, for the formal acknowledgement of each rite of passage.
Perhaps this was something his aunt had understood and in her quiet
way had made provision for.

He turned off the B1149 at Felthorpe to take the country roads
across the flat country. It was unnecessary to consult the map. The
magnificent fifteenth-century tower with its four pinnacles was an
unmistakable landmark, and he drove towards it along the almost
deserted roads with the familiar sense of coming home. It seemed
strange that his aunt's angular figure wasn't beside him, that all that
remained of that secretive but powerful personality was a plastic package, curiously heavy, of white grit. When he reached Salle he parked
the Jaguar a little down the lane and made his way into the churchyard. As always, he was struck that a church as magnificent as a
cathedral could be so isolated yet seem utterly right among these quiet
fields, where its effect was less of grandeur and majesty than of an
unpretentious and reassuring peace. For a few minutes he stood quietly listening and heard nothing, not even a bird song or the rustle
of an insect in the tall grasses. In the frail sunlight the surrounding
trees were flushed with the first gold of autumn. The ploughing was
over, and the brown crust of the crumbled fields stretched in their
Sunday calm towards the far horizon. He walked slowly round the
church, feeling the weight of the package dragging at his jacket
pocket, glad that he had chosen a time between services and wondering whether it might not have been courteous, perhaps even necessary, to obtain the consent of the parish priest before carrying out
his aunt's wishes. But he told himself that it was too late to think of
that now, glad to be spared explanations or complications. Making
his way to the eastern fringe of the churchyard, he opened the package
and tipped out the ground bones like a libation. There was a flash of
silver and all that remained of Jane Dalgliesh sparkled among the
brittle autumn stalks and the tall grasses. He knew the customary
words for such an occasion; he had heard them often enough on his
father's lips. But the ones which came unbidden to his mind were

the verses from Ecclesiastes carved on the stone outside Martyr's Cottage, and in this timeless place beside the dignity of the great church it seemed to him that they were not inappropriate.

The west door was unlocked and before leaving Salle he spent fifteen minutes in the church revisiting old pleasures: the carvings on the oak stalls, peasants, a priest, animals and birds, a dragon, a pelican feeding its young; the mediaeval wineglass pulpit, which after five hundred years still showed traces of its original colouring; the chancel screen; the great east window, which once had glowed in the glory of red, green and blue mediaeval glass but which now let in only the clear Norfolk light. As the west door clanged gently behind him, he wondered when he would return or if he would return at all.

It was early evening before he got home. What he had eaten of lunch had been stodgily filling, so that he was less hungry than he had expected. He heated up the last of yesterday's home-made soup and followed it with biscuits and cheese and fruit and then kindled the fire and sat on the low chair before it, listening to Elgar's Cello Concerto and making a start on the job of sorting out his aunt's photographs. Tipping them out of their faded envelopes he sorted them with his long fingers on the low mahogany table. It was a task which induced a gentle melancholy from which an occasional scribbled identification on the back of a print, a remembered face or incident would stab him into pain. And the Elgar was an appropriate accompaniment, the plaintive notes evoking those long, hot Edwardian summers known to him only from novels and poetry, the peace, the certainty, the optimism of the England into which his aunt had been born. And here was her fiancé, looking ridiculously young in his captain's uniform. The photograph was dated 4 May 1918, only a week before he was killed. He gazed for a moment intently at that handsome, debonair young face which, God knew, must by then have seen enough of horror, but it told him nothing. Turning it over, Dalgliesh saw that it bore a pencilled message written in Greek. The young man was to have read classics at Oxford, and his aunt had studied Greek with her father. But he knew no Greek; their secret was safe enough with him and soon would be safe forever. The hand which had formed these fading characters had been dead now for seventy years, the mind that had first created them for nearly two thousand. And here in the same envelope was one of his aunt herself at about the same age. It must have been one she had sent to her fiancé at the front or given to him before he left for war. One corner was stained browny-red with what must be his blood. Perhaps the photograph had been returned to her with the rest of his effects. She stood in her long skirt with the high-buttoned blouse, laughing, her hair in two wings on either side and bound above the temples. Over the years her face had always had distinction, but he saw almost with a shock of surprise that once she had been beautiful. And now her death had freed him for a voyeurism which in her life would have been repugnant to them both. And yet she hadn't destroyed the photographs. She must have known, realist that she was, that other eyes than hers would eventually see them. Or did extreme old age free one from all such petty considerations of vanity or self-esteem as the mind gradually distanced itself from the devices and desires of the flesh? It was with a sense of irrational reluctance, almost of betrayal, that eventually he threw both photographs into the fire and watched them curl, blacken and finally flare into ash.

And what was he to do with all these undocumented strangers, the women, sloping-bosomed, under immense hats piled with ribbons and flowers, the cycling parties, the men knickerbockered, the women with their long, bell-shaped skirts and their straw boaters; the wedding parties, bride and bridesmaids almost hidden behind their immense bouquets, the chief participants grouped in recognized hierarchy and staring into the lens as if the click of the shutter could for a second halt time, hold it in thrall, proclaiming that this rite of passage at least had importance, binding the ineluctable past to the unseeable future? As an adolescent boy he had been obsessed with time. For weeks before the summer holidays he would feel a sense of triumph that now he had time by the forelock and could say, "Go as quickly as you like and the holiday will be here. Or, if you must, go slowly, and the summer days will last longer." Now, in middle age, he knew of no contrivance and no promised pleasure which could halt the inexorable thudding of those chariot wheels. And here was a photograph of himself in his prep-school uniform, taken in the rectory garden by his father, a stranger ridiculously overclad in cap and striped blazer standing almost to attention, facing the lens as if defying the terror of leaving home. That, too, he was glad to see the end of.

When the concerto was finished, the half-bottle of claret empty, he shuffled the remaining photographs together, placed them in the bureau drawer and decided to shake off melancholy with a brisk walk by the sea before bed. The night was too calm and beautiful to be wasted in nostalgia and futile regrets. The air was extraordinarily still, and even the sound of the sea was muted as it stretched, pale and mysterious, under the full moon and the bright pattern of stars. He stood for a moment under the soaring wings of the mill, then began walking vigorously over the headland towards the north, past the fringe of pines, until, three-quarters of an hour later, he decided to make for the beach. He half-slid down the sandy decline and saw before him the great square hunks of concrete half-buried in the sand, the curls of rotting iron springing from them like bizarre antennae. Moonlight, strong as the last light of the setting sun, had changed the texture of the beach, so that each grain of sand seemed separately illuminated, every pebble mysteriously unique. Suddenly he had a childish impulse to feel the sea washing over his feet and, taking off his shoes and socks, he stuffed the socks in his jacket pocket and, tying the laces, slung the shoes round his neck. The water, after the first sting of cold, was almost blood-warm, and he splashed vigorously along the fringe of the waves, pausing from time to time to look back at his footprints as he had as a child. Now he had reached the narrow strip of pine trees. There was, he knew, a narrow path which cut inland through them past Hilary Robarts's cottage to the road. It was the simplest way of regaining the headland without having to scramble up the friable cliffs to the south. Sitting on a ridge of shingle he tackled the familiar problem of the paddler: how, with an inadequate handkerchief, to rid the spaces between his toes of the gritty dusting of tenacious sand. That achieved, socks and shoes replaced, he trudged through the pebbles to the shoreline.

When he reached the powdery sand on the upper reaches of the beach, he saw that someone had been here before him: to his left was a double line of naked footprints, the mark of running feet. These, of course, would be Hilary Robarts's. She must as usual have taken her nightly swim. Subconsciously he noticed how distinct they were. She must have left the beach nearly an hour and a half ago, yet on this windless night the indentations were as plain in the dry sand as if they had just been made. The path through the trees lay in front of him, leading out of moonlight into the enclosing shadows of the pine wood. And the night was suddenly darker. A low blue-black cloud had momentarily covered the moon, its ragged edges silvered with light.

He switched on his torch and played it over the path. It caught the gleam of something white to his left, a sheet of newspaper, perhaps, a handkerchief, a discarded paper bag. Feeling no more than mild curiosity, he stepped from the path to investigate. And then he saw her. Her distorted face seemed to leap up at him and hang suspended in the bright glare of the torchlight like a vision from a nightmare. Staring down, and for a moment transfixed, he felt a shock in which incredulity, recognition and horror fused into a second which made his heart leap. She was lying in a shallow depression of flattened marram grass, hardly a hollow but deep enough for the grasses on each verge to shield her body until he was almost on top of her. To her right, and partly beneath her, was a crumpled beach towel, striped in red and blue and above it, placed precisely side-by-side, a pair of open sandals and a torch. Beside them, neatly folded, was what looked like a blue-and-white track suit. It must have been the edge of this which had first caught his eye. She lay on her back, the head towards him, the dead eyes upturned as if they had been fixed on him in a last, mute appeal. The small bush of hair had been pushed under the upper lip, exposing the teeth, and giving the impression of a snarling rabbit. A single black hair lay across her cheek and he had an almost irresistible impulse to kneel and pluck it away. She was wearing only the bottom half of a black bikini, and that had been pulled down over her thighs. He could clearly see where the hair had been sliced away. The letter *L* precisely in the centre of the forehead looked as if it had been cut with deliberation, the two thin lines precisely at right angles. Between the splayed and flattened breasts with their dark aureolas and pointed nipples, milk-white against the brown skin of her arms, rested a key-shaped metal locket on a chain. And as he gazed down, slowly moving the torchlight over her body, the cloud moved from the face of the moon and she lay stretched out before him clearly, the naked limbs pale and bloodless as the bleached sands and as clearly visible as if it were day.

He was inured to horror; few manifestations of human cruelty, violence or desperation were unfamiliar to his practised eye. He was too sensitive ever to view a violated body with crude indifference, but only in one recent case, his last, had this sensitivity caused him more than momentary inconvenience. And with Paul Berowne at least he had been warned. This was the first time he had almost stumbled over a murdered woman. Now, as he looked down on her, his mind analysed the difference between the reaction of an expert summoned to the scene of the crime knowing what to expect and this sudden exposure to ultimate violence. He was interested both in the difference and in the detachment which could so coolly analyse it.

Kneeling, he touched her thigh. It felt icy cold and as synthetic as inflated rubber. If he prodded it the mark of his fingers would surely remain. Gently he ran them through her hair. It was still slightly damp at the roots but the ends were dry. The night was warm for September. He looked at his watch: 10.33. He remembered being told, he couldn't recall when or by whom, that it was her practice to take her nightly swim shortly after nine o'clock. The physical signs confirmed what he thought most likely, that she had been dead for less than two hours.

He had seen no footprints on the sand but his and hers. But the tide was ebbing; it must have been high at about 9.00, although the dustiness of the upper levels of the beach suggested that it didn't reach the hollow where she lay. But the most likely path for the murderer to have taken was the one through the wood which she herself must have used. He would have had the protection of the trees and a place in their shadow where he could watch and wait unseen. The ground, with its mat of pine needles on the sand, was unlikely to yield footprints, but it was important that it shouldn't be disturbed. Moving carefully, he backed away from the body, then walked about twenty yards to the south along a ridge of fine shingle. By the light of his torch, half-crouching, he tracked his way through the densely planted pine trees, snapping off the brittle lower twigs as he passed. At least he could be certain that no one had recently passed this way. Within minutes he had gained the road; another ten of brisk walking and he would be at the mill. But the nearest telephone would be at Hilary Robarts's cottage. The probability was that the cottage was locked, and he had no intention of breaking in. It was almost as important to leave the victim's house undisturbed as it was not to violate the scene of the crime. There had been no handbag beside her body, nothing but the shoes and torch neatly placed at the head of the hollow, the track suit and the brightly striped red-and-blue beach towel on which she partly lay. Perhaps she had left the key at home, the cottage unlocked. On the headland, after dark, few people would worry if they left a cottage unlocked for half an hour. It was worth taking five minutes to look.

Thyme Cottage, seen from the windows of the mill, had always struck him as the least interesting house on the headland. It faced inland, a square, uncompromising building with a cobbled yard instead of a front garden and picture windows in modern glass which destroyed any period charm it once might have had and made it look like a modern aberration more appropriate to a rural housing estate than to this sea-scarred and remote headland. On three sides the pines grew so closely that they almost touched the walls. He had wondered from time to time why Hilary Robarts should have chosen to live here, despite its convenient distance from the power station. After Alice Mair's dinner party he thought he knew why. Now all the lights were blazing in the ground-floor rooms, the large rectangle of the picture window to the left reaching almost to the ground and the smaller square to the right, which he thought was probably the kitchen. Ordinarily they would have been a reassuring signal of life, normality and welcome, of a refuge from the atavistic fears of the enclosing wood, the empty moonlit headland. But now those bright, uncurtained windows added to his mounting unease, and as he approached the cottage it seemed to him that there floated between him and those bright windows, like a half-developed print, the mental picture of that dead and violated face.

Someone had been here before him. He vaulted over the low stone wall and saw that the pane of the picture window had been almost completely smashed. Small slivers of glass gleamed like jewels on the cobbled yard. He stood and gazed between the jagged edges of the broken glass into the brightness of the sitting room. The carpet was littered with glass fragments like winking beads of silver light. It was obvious that the force of the blow had come from outside the cottage, and he saw at once what had been used. Below him, face upwards on the carpet, was the portrait of Hilary Robarts. It had been slashed almost to the frame with two right-angled cuts forming the letter *L*.

He didn't try the door to see if it was unlocked. It was more important not to contaminate the scene than to save ten or fifteen minutes in ringing the police. She was dead. Speed was important, but it was not vital. Regaining the road, he set off towards the Mill, half-running, half-walking. And then he heard the noise of a car and, turning, saw the lights coming at him fast from the north. It was Alex Mair's BMW. Dalgliesh stood in the middle of the road and waved his torch. The car slowed and stopped. Looking up to the open right side window, he saw Mair, his face bleached by moonlight, regarding him for a moment with an unsmiling intensity, as if this encounter were an assignation.

Dalgliesh said: "I'm afraid I have shocking news for you. Hilary Robarts has been murdered. I've just found the body. I need to get to a telephone."

The hand lying casually on the wheel tightened, then relaxed. The eyes fixed on his grew wary. But when Mair spoke his voice was controlled. Only in that involuntary spasm of the hand had he betrayed emotion. He said:

"The Whistler?"

"It looks like it."

"There's a telephone in the car."

Without another word he opened the door, got out and stood silently aside while Dalgliesh spent an irritating two minutes getting through to Rickards's headquarters. Rickards wasn't there but, the message given, he rang off. Mair had moved about thirty yards from the car and was staring back at the glitter of the power station, as if dissociating himself from the whole procedure.

Now, walking back, he said: "We all warned her not to swim alone, but she wouldn't listen. But I didn't really believe there was any danger. I suppose all the victims thought that until it was too late. 'It can't happen to me.' But it can and it does. But it's still extraordinary, almost unbelievable. The second victim from Larksoken. Where is she?"

"On the fringe of the pines—where she usually swam, I imagine."

As Mair made a move towards the sea, Dalgliesh said: "There's nothing you can do. I'll go back and wait for the police."

"I know there's nothing I can do. I want to see her."

"Better not. The fewer people who disturb the scene, the better."

Suddenly Mair turned on him. "My God, Dalgliesh, don't you ever stop thinking like a policeman? I said I wanted to see her."

Dalgliesh thought, This isn't my case and I can't stop him by force. But at least he could ensure that the direct path to the body lay undisturbed. Without another word he led the way and Mair followed. Why this insistence, he wondered, on seeing the body? To satisfy himself that she was, in fact, dead, the scientist's need to verify and confirm? Or was he trying to exorcise a horror which he knew could be more terrible in imagination than in reality? Or was there, perhaps, a deeper compulsion, the need to pay her the tribute of standing over her body in the quietness and loneliness of the night before the police arrived with all the official paraphernalia of a murder investigation to violate for ever the intimacies they had shared.

Mair made no comment when Dalgliesh led him to the south of the well-beaten path to the beach and, still without speaking, followed him as he plunged into the darkness and began tracking his way between the shafts of the pines. The pool of light from his torch shone on the brittle spars snapped by his previous breakthrough, on the carpet of pine needles dusted with sand, on dried pine cones and the glint of an old battered tin. In the darkness the strong, resinous smell seemed to intensify and came up to them like a drug, making the air as heavy to breathe as if it were a sultry night in high summer.

Minutes later they stepped out of stultifying darkness into the white coolness of the beach and saw before them, like a curved shield of beaten silver, the moonlit splendour of the sea. They stood for a moment, side-by-side, breathing hard, as if they had come through some ordeal. Dalgliesh's footprints were still visible in the dry sand above the last ridge of pebbles, and they followed them until they stood at the foot of the body.

Dalgliesh thought, I don't want to be here, not with him, not like this, both of us staring down unrebuked at her nakedness. It seemed to him that all his perceptions were preternaturally sharpened in this cold, debilitating light. The blanched limbs, the aureole of dark hair, the gaudy red and blue of the beach towel, the clumps of marram grass, all had the one-dimensional clarity of a colour print. This necessary guard on the body until the police could arrive would have been perfectly tolerable; he was used to the curious undemanding companionship of the recently dead. But with Mair at his side he felt like a voyeur. It was this revulsion, rather than delicacy, which made him move a little apart and stand looking into the darkness of the pines while remaining aware of every slight move and breath of the tall, rigid figure looking down at her with the concentrated attention of a surgeon.

Then Mair said: "That locket round her neck, I gave it to her on twenty-ninth August for her birthday. It's just the right size to hold her Yale key. One of the metalworkers in the workshop at Larksoken made it for me. It's remarkable the delicacy of the work they do there."

Dalgliesh was not inexperienced in the various manifestations of shock. He said nothing. Mair's voice was suddenly harsh.

"For God's sake, Dalgliesh, can't we cover her up?"

With what? thought Dalgliesh. Does he expect me to jerk the towel from under her? He said:

"No, I'm sorry. We mustn't disturb her."

"But it's the Whistler's work. Dear God, man, it's obvious. You said so yourself."

"The Whistler is a murderer like any other. He brings something to the scene and leaves something behind him. That something could be evidence. He's a man, not a force of nature."

"When will the police arrive?"

"They shouldn't be long. I wasn't able to speak to Rickards, but they'll be in touch with him. I'll wait, if you want to leave. There's nothing you can do here."

"I can stay until they take her away."

"That might mean a long wait unless they're able to get the pathologist quickly."

"Then I'll have a long wait."

Without another word he turned and walked down to the edge of the sea, his footprints parallel with Dalgliesh's own. Dalgliesh moved down to the shingle and sat there, his arms round his knees, and watched while the tall figure paced endlessly, backwards and forwards, along the fringes of the tide. Whatever evidence he had on his shoes, it wouldn't be there now. But the thought was ridiculous. No murderer had ever left his imprint more clearly on a victim than had the Whistler. Why, then, did he feel this unease, the sense that it was less straightforward than it seemed?

He wriggled his heels and buttocks more comfortably into the shingle and prepared to wait. The cold moonlight, the constant falling of the waves and the sense of that stiffening body behind him induced a gentle melancholy, a contemplation of mortality including his own.

Timor mortis conturbat me. He thought: In youth we take egregious risks because death has no reality for us. Youth goes caparisoned in immortality. It is only in middle age that we are shadowed by the awareness of the transitoriness of life. And the fear of death, however irrational, was surely natural, whether one thought of it as annihilation or as a rite of passage. Every cell in the body was programmed for life; all healthy creatures clung to life until their last breath. How hard to accept, and yet how comforting, was the gradual realization that the universal enemy might come at last as a friend. Perhaps this was part of the attraction of his job, that the process of detection dignified the individual death, even the death of the least attractive, the most unworthy, mirroring in its excessive interest in clues and motives man's perennial fascination with the mystery of his mortality, providing, too, a comforting illusion of a moral universe in which innocence could be avenged, right vindicated, order restored. But nothing was restored, certainly not life, and the only justice vindicated was the uncertain justice of men. The job certainly had a fascination for him which went beyond its intellectual challenge, or the excuse it gave for his rigorously enforced privacy. But now he had inherited enough money to make it redundant. Was this what his aunt had intended by that uncompromising will? Was she in fact saying, Here is enough money to make any job other than poetry unnecessary. Isn't it time that you made a choice?

It wasn't his case. It would never be his case. But by force of habit he timed the arrival of the police, and it was thirty-five minutes before his ears caught the first rustle of movement in the pine wood. They were coming the way he had directed, and they were making a great deal of noise about it. It was Rickards who appeared first, with a younger but solidly built man at his shoulder and four heavily laden officers in a straggle behind them. It seemed to Dalgliesh, rising to meet them, that they were immense, huge moon-men, their features square and blanched in this alien light, bearing with them their bulky and polluting paraphernalia. Rickards nodded but didn't speak other than briefly to introduce his sergeant, Stuart Oliphant.

Together they approached the body and stood looking down at what had been Hilary Robarts. Rickards was breathing heavily, as if he had been running, and it seemed to Dalgliesh that there emanated from him a powerful surge of energy and excitement. Oliphant and the four other officers dumped their equipment and stood silently, a little apart. Dalgliesh had a sense that they were all actors in a film waiting for the director to give the command to shoot, or that a voice would suddenly shout "Cut" and the little group would break up, the victim stretch herself and sit up and begin rubbing her arms and legs and complaining of stiffness and the cold.

Then, still gazing down at the body, Rickards asked: "Do you know her, Mr. Dalgliesh?"

"Hilary Robarts, Acting Administrative Officer at Larksoken Power Station. I met her first, last Thursday, at a dinner party given by Miss Mair."

Rickards turned and gazed towards the figure of Mair. He was standing motionless with his back to the sea but so close to the surf that it seemed to Dalgliesh that the waves must be washing over his shoes. He made no move towards them, almost as if he were waiting for an invitation or for Rickards to join him.

Dalgliesh said: "Dr. Alex Mair. He's the Director of Larksoken. I used the telephone in his car to call you. He says he'll stay here until the body is removed."

"Then he's in for a long wait. So that's Dr. Alex Mair. I've read about him. Who found her?"

"I did. I thought I made that plain when I telephoned."

Either Rickards was deliberately extracting information he already knew, or his men were singularly inefficient at passing on a simple message.

Rickards turned to Oliphant. "Go and explain to him that we'll be taking our time. There's nothing he can do here except to get in the way. Persuade him to go home to bed. If you can't persuade, try ordering. I'll talk to him tomorrow."

He waited until Oliphant had started scrunching over the ridge of shingle, then called: "Oliphant. If he won't move, tell him to keep his distance. I don't want him any closer. Then get the screens round her. That'll spoil his fun."

It was the kind of casual cruelty which Dalgliesh didn't expect from him. Something was wrong with the man, something that went deeper than professional stress at having to view yet another of the Whistler's victims. It was as if some half-acknowledged and imperfectly suppressed personal anxiety had been violently released by the sight of the body, triumphing over caution and discipline.

But Dalgliesh too felt a sense of outrage. He said: "The man isn't a voyeur. He's probably not altogether rational at present. After all, he knew the woman. Hilary Robarts was one of his senior officers."

"He can't do her any good now, even if she was his mistress." Then, as if acknowledging the implied rebuke, he said: "All right, I'll have a word with him."

He began running clumsily over the shingle. Hearing him Oliphant turned and together they went up to that silent, waiting figure on the fringe of the sea. Dalgliesh watched as they conferred; then they turned and began walking up the beach, Alex Mair between the two police officers as if he were a prisoner under escort. Rickards returned to the body, but it was obvious that Oliphant was going to accompany Alex Mair back to his car. He switched on his torch and plunged into the wood. Mair hesitated. He had ignored the body as if it were no longer there, but now he looked over at Dalgliesh as if there were unfinished business between them. Then he said a quick good night and followed Oliphant.

Rickards didn't comment on Mair's change of mind or on his methods of persuasion. He said: "No handbag."

"Her house key is in that locket round her neck."

"Did you touch the body, Mr. Dalgliesh?"

"Only her thigh and the hair to test its wetness. The locket was a gift from Mair. He told me."

"Lives close, does she?"

"You'll have seen her cottage when you drove up. It's just the other side of the pine wood. I went there after I found the body, thinking it might be open and I could telephone. There's been an act of vandalism, her portrait thrown through the window. The Whistler and criminal damage on the same night—an odd coincidence."

Rickards turned and looked full at him. "Maybe. But this wasn't the Whistler. The Whistler's dead. Killed himself in a hotel at Easthaven, sometime around six o'clock. I've been trying to reach you to let you know."

He squatted by the body and touched the woman's face, then lifted the head and let it drop. "No rigor. Not even the beginning of it. Within the last few hours, by the look of her. The Whistler died with enough sins on his conscience, but this . . . this"—he stabbed his finger violently at the dead body—"this, Mr. Dalgliesh, is something different."

4

Rickards rolled on his search gloves. The latex, sliding over his huge fingers, made them look almost obscene, like the udders of a great animal. Kneeling, he fiddled with the locket. It sprang open and Dalgliesh could see the Yale key nestling inside it, a perfect fit. Rickards extracted it, then said: "Right, Mr. Dalgliesh. Let's go and take a look at that criminal damage."

Two minutes later he followed Rickards up the path to the front door of the cottage. Rickards unlocked it and they passed into a passage running to the stairs and with doors on either side. Rickards opened the door to the left and stepped into the sitting room with Dalgliesh behind him. It was a large room running the whole length of the cottage, with windows at each end and a fireplace facing the door. The portrait lay about three feet from the window, surrounded by slivers of glass. Both men stood just inside the door and surveyed the scene.

Dalgliesh said: "It was painted by Ryan Blaney, who lives at Scudder's Cottage, farther south on the headland. I saw it first on the afternoon I arrived."

Rickards said: "A funny way of delivering it. Sat for him, did she?"

"I don't think so. It was painted to please himself, not her."

He was going to add that Ryan Blaney would, in his view, be the last person to destroy his work. But then he reflected that it hadn't, in fact, been destroyed. Two single cuts in the form of an *L* wouldn't be too difficult to repair. And the damage had been as precise and deliberate as those cuts on Hilary Robarts's forehead. The picture hadn't been slashed in fury.

Rickards seemed for a moment to lose interest in it. He said: "So this is where she lived. She must have been fond of solitude. That is, if she lived alone."

Dalgliesh said: "As far as I know she lived alone."

It was, he thought, a depressing room. It was not that the place was uncomfortable; it held the necessary furniture, but the pieces looked as though they were rejects from someone else's house, not the conscious choice of the occupant. Beside the fireplace with its fitted gas fire were two armchairs in synthetic brown leather. In the centre of the room was an oval dining table with four discordant chairs. On either side of the front window were fitted bookshelves, holding what looked like a collection of textbooks and assorted novels. Two of the lower and taller shelves were packed with box files. Only on the longest wall, facing the door, was there any sign that someone had made this room a home. She had obviously been fond of water-colours, and the wall was as covered with them as if it had been part of a gallery. There were one or two which he thought he could recognize, and he wished he could walk over to examine them more closely. But it was possible that someone other than Hilary Robarts herself had been in this room before them, and it was important to leave the scene undisturbed.

Rickards closed the door and opened the opposite one, on the right of the passage. This led to the kitchen, a purely functional, rather uninteresting room, well enough equipped but in stark contrast to the kitchen at Martyr's Cottage.

Set in the middle of the room was a small wooden table, vinyl-covered, with four matching chairs all pushed well in. On the table was an uncorked bottle of wine with the cork and the metal opener beside it. Two plain wineglasses, clean and upturned, were on the draining board.

Rickards said: "Two glasses, both washed, by her or her killer. We'll get no prints there. And an open bottle. Someone was drinking with her here tonight."

Dalgliesh said: "If so he was abstemious. Or she was."

Rickards with his gloved hand lifted the bottle by its neck and slowly turned it.

"About one glass poured. Maybe they planned to finish it after her swim." He looked at Dalgliesh and said: "You didn't come earlier into the cottage, Mr. Dalgliesh? I have to ask everyone she knew."

"Of course. No, I didn't come earlier into the cottage. I was drinking claret tonight, but not with her."

"Pity you hadn't been. She'd be alive now."

"Not necessarily. I might have left when she went to change for her swim. And if she did have someone with her here tonight, that's probably what he did." He paused, wondered whether to speak, then said: "The left-hand glass is slightly cracked at the rim."

Rickards lifted it to the central light and turned it slowly.

"I wish I had your eyesight. It's hardly significant, surely."

"Some people strongly dislike drinking from a cracked glass. I do myself."

"In which case why didn't she break it and chuck it away? There's no point in keeping a glass you aren't prepared to drink from. When I'm faced with two alternatives, I start by taking the more likely. Two glasses, two drinkers. That's the common-sense explanation."

It was, thought Dalgliesh, the basis of most police work. Only when the obvious proved untenable was it necessary to explore less likely explanations. But it could also be the first fatally easy step into a labyrinth of misconceptions. He wondered why his instinct insisted that she had been drinking alone. Perhaps because the bottle was in the kitchen, not in the sitting room. The wine was a 1979 Château Talbot, hardly an all-purpose tipple. Why not carry it into the sitting room and do it justice in comfort? On the other hand, if she was alone and had needed only a quick swig before her swim, she might hardly have bothered. And if two people had been drinking in the kitchen, she had been meticulous in pushing back the chairs. But it was the level of the wine that seemed to him almost conclusive. Why uncork a fresh bottle to pour only two half-glasses? Which didn't, of course, mean that she wasn't later expecting a visitor to help finish it.

Rickards seemed to be taking an unnatural interest in the bottle and its label. Suddenly he said gruffly:

"What time did you leave the mill, Mr. Dalgliesh?"

"At nine-fifteen. I looked at the carriage clock on the mantelpiece and checked my watch."

"And you saw no one during your walk?"

"No one, and no footprints other than hers and mine."

"What were you actually doing on the headland, Mr. Dalgliesh?"

"Walking, thinking." He was about to add: "And paddling like a boy," but checked himself.

Rickards said consideringly: "Walking and thinking."

To Dalgliesh's oversensitive ears he made the activities sound both eccentric and suspicious. Dalgliesh wondered what his companion would say if he had decided to confide. "I was thinking about my aunt and the men who loved her, the fiancé who was killed in 1918 and the man whose mistress she might or might not have been. I was thinking of the thousands of people who have walked along that shore and who are now dead, my aunt among them, and how, as a boy, I hated the false romanticism of that stupid poem about great men leaving their footprints on the sands of time, since that was essentially all that most of us could hope to leave, transitory marks which the next tide would obliterate. I was thinking how little I had known my aunt and whether it was ever possible to know another human being except on the most superficial level, even the women I have loved. I was thinking about the clash of ignorant armies by night, since no poet walks by the sea at moonlight without silently reciting Matthew Arnold's marvellous poem. I was considering whether I would have been a better poet, or even a poet at all, if I hadn't also decided to be a policeman. More prosaically, I was, from time to time, wondering how my life would be changed for better or worse by the unmerited acquisition of three-quarters of a million."

The fact that he had no intention of revealing even the most mundane of these private musings, the childish secrecy about the paddling, induced an irrational guilt, as if he were deliberately withholding information of importance. After all, he told himself, no man could have been more innocently employed. And it was not as if he were a serious suspect. The idea would probably have struck Rickards as too ridiculous even for consideration, although with logic he would have had to admit that no one who lived on the headland and had known Hilary Robarts could be excluded from the enquiry, least of all because he was a senior police officer. But Dalgliesh was a witness.

He had information to give or withhold, and the knowledge that he would have no intention of withholding it didn't alter the fact that there was a difference now in their relationship. He was involved, whether he liked it or not, and he didn't need Rickards to point out that uncomfortable reality. Professionally it was none of his business, but it was his business as a man and a human being.

He was surprised and a little disconcerted to discover how much he had resented the interrogation, mild as it had been. A man was surely entitled to walk along the beach at night without having to explain his reasons to a police officer. It was salutary for him personally to experience this sense of privacy violated, of virtuous outrage, which the most innocent of suspects must feel when faced with police interrogation. And he realized anew how much, even from childhood, he had disliked being questioned. "What are you doing? Where have you been? What are you reading? Where are you going?" He had been the much-wanted only child of elderly parents, burdened by their almost obsessive parental concern and overconscientiousness, living in a village where little the rector's son did was safe from scrutiny. And suddenly, standing here in this anonymous, overtidy kitchen, he recalled vividly and with heartstopping pain the moment when his most precious privacy had been violated. He remembered that secluded place, deep in the laurels and elderberries, at the bottom of the shrubbery, the green tunnel of leaves leading to his own three square yards of moist, mould-rich sanctuary, remembered that August afternoon, the crackle of bushes, the cook's great face thrust between the leaves. "Your ma thought you'd be in here, Master Adam. Rector wants you. What do you do in there, hiding yourself away in all those mucky bushes? Better be playing out in the sunshine." So the last refuge, the one he had thought totally secret, had been discovered. They had known about it all the time.

He said: "Oh God from You that I could private be."

Rickards looked at him. "What was that, Mr. Dalgliesh?"

"Just a quotation that came into my mind."

Rickards didn't reply. He was probably thinking: "Well, you're supposed to be a poet. You're entitled." He gave a last, searching look around the kitchen, as if by the intensity of his gaze he could somehow compel that unremarkable table and four chairs, the opened bottle of wine, the two washed glasses to yield up their secret.

Then he said: "I'll lock up here and set someone on guard until tomorrow. I'm due to meet the pathologist, Dr. Maitland-Brown, over at Easthaven. He'll take a look at the Whistler and then come straight on here. The forensic biologist should have arrived from the lab by then. You wanted to see the Whistler yourself, didn't you, Mr. Dalgliesh? This seems as good a time as any."

It seemed to Dalgliesh a particularly bad time. One violent death was enough in one night, and he was seized with a sudden longing for the peace and solitude of the mill. But there seemed no prospect of sleep for him until the early hours of the morning, and there was little point in objecting. Rickards said:

"I could drive you over and bring you back."

Dalgliesh felt an immediate revulsion at the thought of a car journey tête-à-tête with Rickards. He said: "If you'll drop me at the mill, I'll take my own car. There won't be any reason for me to linger at Easthaven, and you may have to wait."

It surprised him a little that Rickards was willing to leave the beach. Admittedly he had Oliphant and his minions; procedures at the scene of a murder were well established, they would be competent to do what was necessary, and until the forensic pathologist arrived the body couldn't be moved. But he sensed that it was important to Rickards that he and Dalgliesh together should see the Whistler's body, and he wondered what forgotten incident in their joint pasts had led to that compulsion.

5

⊠

Balmoral Private Hotel was the last house of an undistinguished twentieth-century terrace at the unfashionable end of the long promenade. The summer lights were still strung between the Victorian lampposts, but they had been turned off and now swung in uneven loops like a tawdry necklace which might scatter its blackened beads at the first strong wind. The season was officially over. Dalgliesh drew up behind the police Rover on the left-hand side of the promenade. Between the road and the glittering sea was a children's playground, wire-enclosed, the gate padlocked, the shuttered kiosk pasted with fading and half-torn posters of summer shows, bizarrely shaped ice creams, a clown's head. The swings had been looped high, and one of the metal seats, caught by the strengthening breeze, rapped out a regular tattoo against the iron frame. The hotel stood out from its drabber neighbours, sprucely painted in a bright blue which even the dull street lighting could hardly soften. The porch light shone down on a large card with the words "Under new management. Bill and Joy Carter welcome you to Balmoral." A separate card underneath said simply "Vacancies."

As they waited to cross the road while a couple of cars cruised slowly past, the drivers peering for a parking space, Rickards said: "Their first season. Done quite well up to now, so they say, despite the bloody awful summer. This won't help. They'll get the ghouls, of course, but parents will think twice before booking in with the kiddies for happy family hols. Luckily the place is half-empty at present. Two cancellations this morning, so they've only got three couples, and they were all out when Mr. Carter found the body, and, so far, we've managed to keep them in happy ignorance. They're in bed now, presumably asleep. Let's hope they stay that way."

The earlier arrival of the police must have alerted some of the locals, but the plainclothes officer unobtrusively on duty inside the porch had dispersed any curious bystanders, and now the road was empty except for a little group of four or five people about fifty yards down on the seaward side. They seemed to be muttering together, and as Dalgliesh glanced at them they began moving aimlessly, as if stirred by the breeze.

He asked: "Why here, for God's sake?"

"We know why. There's a hell of a lot we don't know, but at least we know that. They've got a part-time barman here, Albert Upcraft, seventy-five if he's a day. He remembers. He's a bit vague about what happened yesterday, but there's nothing wrong with his long-term memory. The Whistler came here as a kid, apparently. His auntie— his dad's sister—was manager here twenty years ago. Used to take him off his mum's hands for a free holiday when the place was quiet. Mainly when Mum had a new man and the new uncle didn't want the kid around. Sometimes he was here for weeks at a time. No trouble to anyone. Helped with the guests, picked up the odd tip, actually went to Sunday school."

Dalgliesh said: "Now the day is over."

"Well, his day's over, all right. He booked in at two-thirty this afternoon. Asked for the same room, apparently. Single at the back. Cheapest in the house. The Carters should be grateful for small mercies. He might have chosen to go out in style, best double bedroom, private bathroom, view of the sea, the lot."

The constable at the door saluted, and they passed through the lobby into the hall, and into a smell of paint and polish overlaid with the faint tang of lavender disinfectant. The cleanliness was almost oppressive. The lurid flowered carpet was covered with a narrow strip of perspex. The wallpaper was obviously new, a different pattern on each wall, and a glimpse through the open door of the dining room showed tables set for four with shining white cloths and small vases of artificial flowers, daffodils, narcissi and bulbous roses. The couple who came from the back to meet them were as spruce as their hotel. Bill Carter was a dapper little man who looked as if he came fresh from the ironing board, the creases down his white shirtsleeves and the front of his trousers knife-sharp, his tie neatly knotted. His wife was wearing a summer dress in a flowered crimplene under a knitted white sweater. She had obviously been crying. Her plump, rather childish face under the carefully set blond hair was bloated and bruised red, as if she had been struck. Her disappointment at seeing just the two of them was pathetically evident.

She said: "I thought you'd come to take him away. Why can't you take him away?"

Rickards didn't introduce Dalgliesh. He said soothingly: "We will, Mrs. Carter, as soon as the pathologist has seen him. He shouldn't be long now. He's on his way."

"Pathologist? That's a doctor, isn't it? Why do you want a doctor? He's dead, isn't he? Bill found him. His throat's cut. How much deader can you get?"

"He won't be with you much longer, Mrs. Carter."

"The sheet's covered with blood, Bill says. He wouldn't let me in. Not that I want to see. And the carpet, ruined. Blood's terrible to get out, everyone knows that. Who's going to pay for the carpet and the bed? Oh God, I thought things were really coming right for us at last. Why did he come back here to do it? Not very nice, was it, not very considerate?"

"He wasn't a considerate man, Mrs. Carter."

Her husband put his arm round her shoulders and led her away. Less than half a minute later he reappeared and said: "It's the shock, naturally. She's upset. Well, who wouldn't be? You know the way up, Mr. Rickards. Your officer is still there. I won't come up with you, if you don't mind."

"That's all right, Mr. Carter, I know the way."

Suddenly Bill Carter turned and said: "Get him out soon, sir, for God's sake."

For a moment Dalgliesh thought that he, too, was crying.

There was no lift. Dalgliesh followed Rickards up three flights of stairs, down a narrow passage towards the back and a short turn to the right. A young detective constable got up from his chair outside the door and with his left hand opened it, then flattened himself against the wall. The smell seemed to gust out of the room at them, a strong effluvium of blood and death.

The light was on and the main bulb in its cheap pink shade hung low and shone full on the horror on the bed. It was a very small room, little more than a box room, with a single window too high to give a view of more than the sky, and enough space only for the single bed, a chair, a bedside cabinet and a low chest of drawers with a mirror hung above it which served as a dressing table. But this room, too, was obsessively clean, making that unclean thing on the bed even more horrible. Both the gaping throat with its white corrugated vessels and the sagging mouth above it seemed to be stretched in protest or outrage at this violence to decency and order. There were no preliminary cuts visible, and that single act of annihilating violence must, Dalgliesh thought, surely have taken more strength than was possible from the childish hand lying, fingers curved, on the sheet and fixed now in its blackening carapace of dried blood. The knife, six inches of bloodied steel, lay close beside it. For some reason he had undressed himself for death and lay now wearing only a vest and pants and a pair of short blue nylon socks which looked like the onset of putrefaction. On the chair beside the bed a dark-grey striped suit was neatly folded. A blue-striped drip-dry shirt was hung from the back of the chair with the tie folded over it. Under the chair his shoes, well worn but polished to mirror brightness, were precisely placed side-by-side. They looked small enough for a girl.

Rickards said: "Neville Potter, aged thirty-six. Scrawny little sod. You wouldn't believe he'd got the strength in those arms to throttle a chicken. And he came properly dressed in his Sunday best to meet his Maker, but then thought better of it. Probably remembered that his ma wouldn't like him getting blood on his best suit. You should meet Ma, Mr. Dalgliesh. She's a real education, that one. She explains a lot. But he's left the evidence. It's all there, all laid out for us. Neat little devil, wasn't he?"

Dalgliesh edged himself round the end of the bed, being careful not to tread in the blood. On the top of the chest of drawers were the Whistler's weapons and his trophies: a leather dog-lead, neatly curled, a blond wig and blue beret, a clasp-knife, a lamp with a battery ingeniously fixed to the centre of a metal headband. Beside these was a pyramid of tangled bushy hair, blond, dark brown, red. In front of the careful arrangement was a page of paper torn from a notebook with the single written message in biro, printed like a child's. "It was getting worse. This is the only way I know to stop myself. Please look after Pongo." The "Please" was underlined.

Rickards said: "His dog. Pongo, for God's sake."

"What did you expect him to be called, Cerberus?"

Rickards opened the door and stood with his back to the gap, breathing deeply, as if hungry for fresh air.

He said: "He and his ma lived on one of the caravan sites outside Cromer. Been there for twelve years. He was a general handyman, did any easy repairs, kept an eye on the place at night, dealt with complaints. The boss has another site outside Yarmouth, and he would go there some nights to relieve the permanent chap. A bit of a loner. Had a small van and the dog. Married a girl he picked up on the site there years ago but it only lasted four months. She walked out on him. Driven out by Ma or by the smell of the caravan. God knows how she stuck it for four months."

Dalgliesh said: "He was an obvious suspect. You must have checked him."

"His ma gave him an alibi for two of the murders. Either she was drunk and didn't know whether he was there or not, or she was covering up for him. Or, of course, she couldn't give a bloody damn one way or the other." He said with sudden violence, "I thought we'd learned by now not to take that kind of alibi at its face value. I'm having a word with the DC who interviewed them, but you know how it is. Thousands of interviews, checks, the stuff all put on the computer. I'd give a dozen computers for a DC who can sense when a witness is lying. My God, haven't we learned anything from the Yorkshire Ripper fiasco?"

"Didn't your man search the van?"

"Oh, they searched the van, all right. They showed a modicum of initiative. It was clean. He cached his stuff elsewhere. Probably picked it up every evening, watched, waited, chose his moment." He gazed down at the head contraption and said: "Ingenious, isn't it? As his ma says, he was always clever with his hands."

The small rectangle of sky outside the single high window was blue-black pricked with a single star. It seemed to Dalgliesh that he had experienced half a lifetime of sensations since he had woken that morning to the cool sea-scented autumnal dawn, to the beginning of a day which had included that calm, meditative walk under the soaring roof of St. Peter Mancroft; the nostalgic, self-indulgent pain induced by those faded photographs of the long-dead; the rush and pull of the tide over his naked feet; the mingled shock and recognition as his torch shone on Hilary Robarts's body. It was a day which, stretching interminably, seemed to have embraced all seasons. So this was one way of stretching time, time which for the Whistler had stopped with that great gush of blood. And now, at the end of the day, he had come to this neat box of an execution shed, imposing on his mind as if it were a memory the picture of a skinny child lying supine on that same bed and watching through the high window the same single star while arranged on the chest of drawers with careful art were the trophies of his day: the tips in pennies and sixpences, the shells and coloured stones from the beach, the dried swathe of pustulated seaweed.

And he himself was here because Rickards had willed it, had wanted him here in this room and at this time. He could have viewed the Whistler's body tomorrow in the mortuary, or, since he could hardly claim that he hadn't the stomach for it, on the autopsy table, to confirm what hardly needed confirmation, that this scrawny killer wasn't the once-glimpsed, six-foot Battersea Strangler. But Rickards had needed an audience, had needed him, Dalgliesh, against whose dreadfully experienced and unshockable calm he could hurl the bitterness and frustrations of failure. Five women dead, and the murderer a suspect they had interviewed and cleared early in the enquiry. The smell of that failure would linger, at least in his own nostrils, long after the media interest, the official enquiries had run their course. And now there was this sixth death, Hilary Robarts, who might not have died and certainly wouldn't have died as she had if the Whistler had been stopped in his tracks earlier. But Dalgliesh sensed that something more keenly personal even than professional failure was fuelling Rickards's anger, with its uncharacteristic spurts of verbal brutality, and he wondered whether it had something to do with his wife and the coming child.

He asked: "What will happen to the dog?"

Rickards seemed not to notice the irrelevance of the question.

"What do you think? Who's going to take on an animal that has been where he's been, seen what he's seen?" He looked down at the stiffening corpse and, turning to Dalgliesh, said harshly: "You pity him, I suppose."

Dalgliesh didn't reply. He could have said: "Yes, I pity him. And his victims. And you. And myself occasionally, come to that." He thought: Yesterday I was reading *The Anatomy of Melancholy*. Odd. Robert Burton, that seventeenth-century Leicestershire rector, had said all that could be said at such a moment, and the words came to him as clearly as if he had spoken them aloud.

"Of their goods and bodies we can dispose; but what shall become of their souls God alone can tell; His mercy may come *inter pontem et fontem, inter gladium et jugulum*, betwixt the bridge and the brook, the knife and the throat."

Rickards shook himself violently, as if suddenly seized with cold. It was an odd gesture. Then he said: "At least he's saved the country his keep for the next twenty years. One argument for keeping his kind alive instead of putting them down is that we can learn from them, stop it happening again. But can we? We've got Stafford banged up, Brady, Nielson. How much have we learned from them?"

Dalgliesh said: "You wouldn't hang a madman, presumably?"

"I wouldn't hang anyone, I'd find a less barbaric method. But they aren't mad, are they? Not until they're caught. Until then they cope with life like most other people. Then we discover that they're monsters and decide, surprise, surprise, to classify them as mad. Makes it seem more comprehensible. We don't have to think of them as human any more. We don't have to use the word 'evil.' Everyone feels better. Do you want to see the mother, Mr. Dalgliesh?"

"There's no point in it. He obviously isn't our man. I didn't for a moment suppose that he would be."

"You should see the mother. She's a right bitch, that one. And do you know what her name is? Lillian. *L* for 'Lillian.' That's something for the trick cyclist to chew over. She made him what he was. But we can't check on people and decide who's fit to have kids, let alone fit to bring them up. And I suppose that when he was born she must have felt something for him, had some hopes for him. She could hardly know what she'd brought forth. You never had a child, did you, Mr. Dalgliesh."

"I had a son. Briefly."

Rickards kicked the door gently, looking away. He said: "Bloody hell, I'd forgotten. Sorry. Wrong time to ask, for both of us."

There were confident footsteps mounting the stairs, and now they had reached the passage. Dalgliesh said: "It sounds as if the pathologist has arrived."

Rickards made no reply. He had moved over to the chest of drawers and, with his forefinger, gently urged the tangle of hairs across the polished wood.

He said: "There's one sample which we won't find here. Hilary Robarts's. Forensic will look to make doubly sure, but it won't be here. And now I start looking for a very different murderer. And, by God, Mr. Dalgliesh, this time I'm going to get him."

6
⊠

Forty-five minutes later Rickards was back at the scene of the murder. He seemed to have passed beyond conscious tiredness and to be operating in a different dimension of time and space, in which his mind worked with unnatural clarity while his body had become almost weightless, a creature of light and air, as unsubstantial as the bizarre scene in which he moved and spoke and gave his orders. The pale, transparent disc of the moon was eclipsed by the glare of the mounted lights which illumined and solidified the hard outlines of trees and men and equipment, yet paradoxically robbed them of their form and essence so that they were, at one and the same time, revealed and clarified and transformed into something alien and strange. And always, beyond the masculine voices, the scrunch of feet on pebbles, the sudden flap of canvas in a tentative breeze, was the continual fall and suck of the tide.

Dr. Anthony Maitland-Brown had driven from Easthaven to the scene in his Mercedes and had arrived first. He was already gowned and gloved and crouching by the body by the time Rickards caught up with him. Wisely he left him to it. M.B. strongly disliked being watched while he made his preliminary examination at the scene and was apt to protest with a peevish "Do we really need all these people standing around?" if anyone came within ten feet of him, as if police photographer, scene-of-crime officer and forensic biologist were all so many snap-happy sightseers. He was an elegant and extraordinarily handsome man, over six feet tall, who had once, in youth—so it was rumoured—been told that he looked like Leslie Howard and had spent subsequent years sedulously promoting the image. He was amicably divorced, comfortably well off—his mother had bequeathed him a private income—and well able to indulge his twin passions of clothes and the opera. In his free time he escorted a succession of young and extremely pretty actresses to Covent Garden and Glyndebourne, where they were apparently content to endure three hours of boredom for the prestige of his company or, perhaps, the *frisson* of knowing that the elegant hands which poured their wine or helped them out of the Mercedes were commonly engaged with more bizarre activities. Rickards had never found him an easy colleague but recognized that he was a first-class forensic pathologist, and God knew they were rare enough. Reading M.B.'s lucid and comprehensive autopsy reports, he could forgive him even his aftershave.

Now, moving away from the body, he stirred himself to greet the recent arrivals, photographer, cameraman, forensic biologist. The stretch of beach fifty yards each side of the murder scene had been efficiently roped off, and plastic sheeting laid over the path, now lit by a string of overhead lights. He was aware of his sergeant's disciplined excitement at his side.

Stuart Oliphant said: "We've found a print, sir. About forty yards into the copse."

"On grass and pine needles?"

"No, sir, on sand. Someone, a kid perhaps, must have tipped some from a bucket. The print's a good one, sir."

Rickards followed him into the wood. The whole of the path had been protected, but at one place a marker had been driven into the soft ground at the right-hand side. Sergeant Oliphant drew back the plastic, then lifted the box covering the print. In the glow of the overhead lights slung along the path it showed clearly, a dusting of moist sand over the pine needles and flattened grass, covering no more than six inches by four, and printed on it the intricate pattern of the sole of a right shoe.

Oliphant said: "We found it soon after you left, sir. Only the one, but it's pretty clear. The photographs have been taken, and the measurements will be at the lab this morning. Size ten by the look of it. They'll be able to give us confirmation pretty quickly, but it's hardly necessary. It's a trainer shoe, sir. A Bumble. You know the make, the one that has a picture of a bee on the heel. And it has the outline of a bee on the sole. You can see the curve of the wing here, sir. It's quite unmistakable."

A Bumble trainer. If you wanted a print you could hardly hope for anything more distinctive. Oliphant voiced his thoughts: "Common enough, of course, but not all that common. Bumbles are the most expensive on the market, the Porsche of trainers. Most of the kids with money like to have them. It's a bloody silly name. Part of the firm is actually owned by a man called Bumble, and they've only been on the market for a couple of years, but he promotes them fairly vigorously. I suppose he hopes that the name will catch on, that people will start yelling for their Bumbles as they do for their wellie-boots."

Rickards said: "It looks fresh enough. When did we last get rain? Late on Saturday night, wasn't it?"

"About eleven. It was over by midnight, but it was a heavy shower."

"And there's no tree cover on this part of the path. The print's perfectly smooth. If it was made before midnight on Saturday I'd expect some spotting. Interesting that there's only the one and that it's pointing away from the sea. If someone wearing Bumble trainers came along this path any time on Sunday, you'd expect to find at least one similar print on the upper reaches of the beach."

"Not necessarily, sir. The shingle comes up almost as high as the path in places. We'd get no prints if he stayed on the pebbles. But if it was made on Sunday before she died, would it still be here? She must have come along this path."

"No reason why she would have trodden on it. It's well to the right of the path. It's odd, though. Too plain, too distinctive, too opportune. You could almost believe it's been deliberately made to deceive us."

"They sell Bumble trainers at the sports shop in Blakeney, sir. I could send a chap to buy a pair of size ten as soon as they open."

"See that he's in plain clothes and buys them as an ordinary purchaser. I need confirmation of the pattern before we start asking people to turn out their shoe cupboards. We're going to be dealing with intelligent suspects. I don't want a balls-up at the beginning of the case."

"Pity to waste time, sir. My brother owns a pair of Bumbles. The print's unmistakable."

Rickards said obstinately: "I need confirmation, and I want it fast."

Oliphant replaced the box and the plastic cover, then followed him back to the beach. Rickards was uncomfortably aware of the almost physical weight of resentment, antagonism and slight contempt which seemed to flow from the sergeant. But he was lumbered with the man. Oliphant had been part of the team bearing the brunt of the Whistler investigation and, although this admittedly was a different enquiry, it would be difficult to replace him without causing personal or logistical problems which Rickards was anxious to avoid. During the fifteen-month hunt for the Whistler, his mild dislike of the sergeant had grown into an antipathy which he knew to be not wholly reasonable and which he had tried to discipline in the interests both of the investigation and of his own self-regard. A serial murder was difficult enough without personal complications.

He had no real evidence that Oliphant was a bully; he only looked like one. He was six feet of disciplined flesh and muscle, dark and conventionally handsome with rather pudgy features, full-lipped and hard-eyed, with a fleshy chin like a doughnut, dented in the middle with a deep dimple. Rickards found it difficult to keep his eyes off it. His repugnance to the man had elevated it to a deformity. Oliphant drank too much, but that was an occupational hazard for a policeman. The fact that Rickards had never seen him actually drunk only increased the offence. A man shouldn't be able to put away that amount of alcohol and still stand firmly on his feet.

He was meticulous in his attitude to senior officers, respectful without being servile, but subtly managed to give Rickards the impression that he wasn't quite measuring up to the standards Oliphant had privately set for him. He was popular enough with the less sensitive probationers; the others wisely kept clear of him. Rickards told himself that, if he were ever in trouble, Oliphant was the last police officer he would wish to see on his doorstep. Oliphant would probably regard that sentiment as a compliment. And there had never been from the public even the whisper of a complaint against him. That too, unreasonably, made Rickards suspicious. It suggested that where his interests were at stake the man was devious enough to act against his essential nature. He was unmarried but managed, without the crudity of actual boasting, to give the impression that women found him irresistible. Probably a number did, but at least he kept clear of his colleagues' wives. In all, he represented most of the qualities in a young detective which Rickards disliked: aggression only controlled because control was prudent, a frank relish for power, too much sexual assurance and an inflated opinion of his own capabilities. But those capabilities weren't negligible. Oliphant would make Chief Inspector at least and might go higher. Rickards had never managed to bring himself to use his sergeant's nickname of Jumbo. Oliphant, so far from resenting a sobriquet both childish and basically unsuitable, seemed to tolerate, even to like it, at least in those colleagues he had privately authorized to use it. Less favoured mortals only used it once.

Maitland-Brown was ready to make his preliminary report. Drawing himself up to his full six feet three inches, he peeled off his gloves and tossed them to a DC, rather like an actor casually divesting himself of part of his costume. It wasn't his custom to discuss his findings at the scene. He did, however, condescend to announce them.

"I'll do the autopsy tomorrow and let you have a report by Wednesday. I doubt whether there will be any surprises. On a preliminary examination it's clear enough. Death by strangulation. The implement was smooth and two centimetres in width, perhaps a belt, a strap or a dog lead. She was a tall, well-muscled woman. It would have taken strength but not inordinate strength, given the advantage of surprise. He probably stood in the shelter of the pines, then stepped out and slung the strap over her head as soon as she got back from the swim. She had just time to pick up her towel. She made one or two convulsive movements with the feet; you can see where the grass is marked. I estimate on the present evidence that she died between eight-thirty and ten."

Maitland-Brown had pronounced and clearly expected no questions. Nor was there need for any. He put out a hand for his coat, which was obligingly handed to him by a DC, then took his leave. Rickards almost expected him to bow.

Rickards looked down at the corpse. Now, with the head, hands and feet covered with plastic, she looked for a second like a gift-wrapped toy, a plaything for someone with expensive and peculiar tastes, an artifice of latex and synthetic hair, glass eyes, a mere simulation of a living woman. Oliphant's voice seemed to come from a far distance.

"Commander Dalgliesh didn't come back with you, then, sir?"

"Why should he? This isn't his pigeon. He's probably in bed."

He thought, And I wish to God I were too. Already the day was crowding in on him, as if physical weight were being piled on an exhausted body; the press conference about the Whistler's suicide, the Chief Constable, the press officer, this new investigation, suspects to be interviewed, facts established, the whole cumbersome business of a murder investigation set in motion with the knowledge of his previous failure dragging like a stone on his heart. And somehow or other he had to find time to ring Susie.

He said: "Mr. Dalgliesh is a witness, not the investigating officer."

"A witness, but hardly a suspect."

"Why not? He lives on the headland, he knew the girl, he knew how the Whistler killed. He may not be a serious suspect in our eyes, but he makes his statement like everyone else."

Oliphant looked at him stolidly. He said: "That'll be a new experience for him. Let's hope he enjoys it."

BOOK FOUR

Monday 26 September

1
⊠

Anthony woke her, as he usually did, just after 6.30. Theresa wrenched her mind through clogging layers of sleep to the familiar morning sounds, the creak and rock of the cot and the sniffs and grunts as Anthony grasped the rails and pulled himself up. She smelt the familiar nursery smell, compounded of baby talc, stale milk and a sodden nappy. She felt for the switch of the bedside light under the grubby shade with its fringe of dancing Bambis and, opening her eyes, stared into Anthony's and was rewarded by his wide, gummy smile and his ritual small bounces of pleasure, which shook the cot. Gently opening the door of the twins' room she could see that they were still asleep, Elizabeth a curled lump on the far end of the bed, Marie on her back, one arm flung out. If she could change and feed Anthony before he became fretful, they would sleep for another half-hour, thirty more minutes of peace for her father.

She would look after Elizabeth and Marie for her mother's sake as long as they needed her and with all her strength, but it was Anthony whom she loved. For a moment she lay still regarding him, enjoying this moment of their quiet, mutual pleasure in each other. Then he let go of the cot rail with one hand, raised one leg in a parody of a clumsy ballet dancer, collapsed onto his mattress, then rolled over onto his back, stuffed his fist into his mouth and began noisily sucking. Soon he would tire of this substitute comfort. She swung her legs out of bed, waited for a moment until she felt the physical flow of strength into arms and legs, then went over to the cot, let down the side and gathered him into her arms. She would change him downstairs on newspaper spread on the kitchen table, then strap him into his high chair so that he could watch her while she heated his milk. By the time he was fed the twins would be awake and she would be free to help dress them ready for Mrs. Hunter from the Welfare to collect them and drive them to the playgroup. Then there would be breakfast for her father and herself before it was time to set out with her father and Anthony to walk to the crossroads where she would pick up the school bus.

She had just turned off the gas under the saucepan of milk when the telephone rang. Her heart lurched, then settled into a rhythmic pounding. She snatched at the receiver, hoping that she had been quick enough to stop it waking her father. George Jago's voice came over strongly, conspiratorial, husky with excitement.

"Theresa? Is your dad up yet?"

"No, not yet, Mr. Jago. He's still asleep."

There was a pause as if he were thinking; then he said: "OK, don't disturb him. When he wakes, tell him Hilary Robarts is dead. Last night. Murdered. Found on the beach."

"You mean the Whistler got her?"

"Looked like that—meant to look like that, if you ask me. But it couldn't have been. The Whistler was dead, been dead three hours or more. Like I told you last night. Remember?"

"Yes, I remember, Mr. Jago."

"Good thing I rang last night, isn't it? You told him, your dad? You told your dad about the Whistler?"

She heard under the excitement the insistent note of anxiety. "Yes," she said, "I told him."

"That's all right, then. Now, you tell him about Miss Robarts. Ask him to give me a ring. I've got a call to take a party to Ipswich, but I'll be back about twelve. Or I could have a word with him now, if he's quick."

"He wouldn't be quick, Mr. Jago. He's sound asleep. And I'm trying to feed Anthony."

"All right. But you tell him, mind."

"Yes, I'll tell him."

He said: "Good thing I rang last night. He'll know why."

She put down the receiver. Her hands were wet. She wiped them on her nightdress and went over to the stove. But when she picked up the pan of milk, her hands were shaking so violently that she knew she wouldn't be able to pour it into the narrow neck of the bottle. She took it over to the sink and, very carefully, managed to half-fill it. Then she unstrapped Anthony and seated herself in the low nursing chair before the empty fireplace. His mouth opened, and she plugged in the teat of the bottle and watched as he began his vigorous chomping, his eyes, suddenly vacant, fixed on hers, his two chubby hands raised, palms down, like the paws of an animal.

It was then that she heard the creak of the stairs, and her father came in. He never appeared in front of her in the mornings without what he used as a dressing gown: an old raincoat buttoned to the neck. Above it his face under the sleep-tousled hair was grey and swollen, the lips unnaturally red.

He said: "Was that the phone?"

"Yes, Daddy, Mr. Jago."

"What did he want, then, at this hour?"

"He rang to say that Hilary Robarts is dead. She's been murdered."

Surely he would notice how different her voice sounded. It seemed to her that her lips were so dry that they would look bloated and deformed, and she bent her head low over the baby so that he shouldn't see her. But her father didn't look at her and he didn't speak. With his back to her he said: "The Whistler, then, was it? Got her, did he? Well, she was asking for it."

"No, Daddy, it couldn't have been the Whistler. Remember Mr. Jago phoned us last night at half past seven to say that the Whistler was dead. He said this morning he was glad he rang to tell us and that you would know why."

Still he didn't speak. She heard the hiss of water from the tap into the kettle and watched him as he took it slowly back to the table and plugged it in, then took down a mug from the shelf. She was aware of the thudding of her heart, of Anthony's warm body against her arm, of her chin gently resting on his downy head. She said: "What did Mr. Jago mean by that, Daddy?"

"He meant that whoever killed Miss Robarts meant to blame it on the Whistler. That means the police will only suspect people who didn't know that the Whistler was dead."

"But you knew, Daddy, because I told you."

Then he turned and said without looking at her: "Your mother wouldn't like you to tell lies."

But he wasn't cross and he wasn't rebuking her. She heard nothing in his voice but a great weariness. She said quietly: "But it isn't a lie, Daddy. Mr. Jago telephoned when you were out in the privy. When you came back I told you."

And then he turned and their eyes met. She had never seen him look more hopeless, more defeated. He said: "That's right, you told me. And that's what you'll tell the police when they ask you."

"Of course, Daddy. I'll tell them what happened. Mr. Jago told me about the Whistler and I told you."

"And do you remember what I said?"

The teat of the bottle had flattened. She took it from Anthony's mouth and shook the bottle to let in the air. He gave an immediate wail of fury, which she plugged with the teat.

She said: "I think you said that you were glad. We would all be safe now."

"Yes," he said, "we're all safe now."

"Does that mean that we won't have to leave the cottage?"

"It depends. We shan't have to leave at once anyway."

"Who will it belong to now, Daddy?"

"I don't know. Whoever she leaves it to in her will, I suppose. They might want to sell it."

"Could we buy it, Daddy? It would be nice if we could buy it."

"That would depend on how much they want. There's no point in thinking about that yet. We're all right for the moment anyway."

She said: "Will the police be coming here?"

"Sure to. Today, most likely."

"Why will they be coming here, Daddy?"

"To find out whether I knew if the Whistler was dead. To ask you if I left the cottage last night. They'll be here, most likely, when you get back from school."

But she wasn't going to school. Today it was important that she didn't leave her father's side. And she had an excuse ready, a stomach cramp. And that, at least, was true, or partly true. Crouched over the lavatory, she had seen that first pink evidence of her monthly period almost with joy.

She said: "But you didn't leave the cottage, did you, Daddy? I was here until I went to bed at a quarter past eight. I could hear you moving down here. I could hear the television."

He said: "The television isn't an alibi."

"But I came down, Daddy. You remember. I went to bed early, at eight-fifteen, but I couldn't sleep and I was thirsty. I came down just before nine o'clock for a drink of water. Then I sat in Mummy's chair, reading. You must remember, Daddy? It was half past nine before I went back to bed."

He gave a groan. He said: "Yes, I remember."

Suddenly Theresa was aware that the twins had entered the kitchen and were standing silently side-by-side by the doorway, regarding their father expressionlessly. She said sharply: "Go back and get dressed. You shouldn't be down here undressed like that, you'll catch cold."

Obediently they turned and padded up the stairs.

The kettle was spouting steam. Her father turned it off but made no move to make the tea. Instead he sat at the table, his head bowed. She thought she heard him whisper: "I'm no good for you, I'm no good for you." She couldn't see his face, but for one terrible moment she thought that he was crying. Still holding the bottle and feeding Anthony, she got up and moved across to him. She had no free hand but she stood very close. She said: "It's all right, Daddy. There's nothing to worry about. It's going to be all right."

2

⊠

On Monday 26 September Jonathan Reeves was working the 8.15-to-14.45 shift and, as usual, he was early at his bench. But it was 8.55 before the telephone rang and he heard the expected voice. Caroline sounded perfectly calm; only the words were urgent.

"I have to see you. Now. Can you get away?"

"I think so. Mr. Hammond isn't in yet."

"Then I'll meet you in the library. At once. It's important, Jonathan."

She had no need to tell him that. She wouldn't be making an assignation during working hours if it weren't important.

The library was housed in the administration block next to the registry. It was part staff sitting room, part library, with three walls covered with shelves, two free-standing racks, and eight comfortable chairs ranged round low tables. Caroline was already waiting when he arrived, standing at the publications display stand and glancing through the latest copy of *Nature*. No one else was there. He moved up to her, wondering if she expected him to kiss her, but then she turned and looked at him and he saw that it would be a mistake. And yet this was their first meeting since Friday night, the night that had changed everything for him. Surely, when they were alone like this, they needn't meet as strangers.

He said humbly: "There's something you want to say."

"In a minute. It's just on nine o'clock. Pray silence for the voice of God."

His head jerked up at her. He was as surprised at her tone as if she had uttered an obscenity. They had never talked about Dr. Mair except on the most superficial level, but he had always taken it for granted that she admired the Director and was happy to be his PA. He recalled overhearing the whispered words of Hilary Robarts when Caroline had walked into a public meeting at Mair's elbow: "Behold, the handmaid of the Lord." That was how they had all seen her, the intelligent, discreet, beautiful but subservient handmaid to a man she was content to serve because she found him worthy of service.

The intercom crackled. There was a background, indecipherable voice and then Mair's measured, serious tones.

"There cannot be anyone on the station who doesn't now know that Hilary Robarts was found dead on the beach last night. She had been murdered. It appeared at first that she was the second Larksoken victim of the Norfolk Whistler, but it now seems almost certain that the Whistler himself died before Hilary. We shall in time find a way of expressing our corporate grief at her loss, as we shall at Christine Baldwin's. In the meantime her death is a matter for police investigation, and Chief Inspector Rickards of the Norfolk CID, who has been responsible for the investigation into the Whistler murders, has taken charge of the case. He will be on the station later in the morning and may ask to interview those of you who knew Hilary best and may be able to help with details of her life. If any of you has any information, however slight, which may assist the police, please get in touch with Chief Inspector Rickards, either when he is here or at the incident room at Hoveton. The telephone number is 499 623."

The intercom crackled and was silent. She said: "I wonder how many drafts it took before he got that right. Innocuous, noncommittal, nothing crudely stated but everything understood. And he didn't irritate us by saying that he could rely on us all to get on with the job, as if we were a bunch of excitable sixth-formers. He never wastes time and words on inessentials. He'll make a good senior civil servant all right."

Jonathan said: "This Chief Inspector Rickards, do you think he'll want to interview all of us?"

"Anyone who knew Hilary. And that will include us. And that's what I want to talk about. When he sees me, I propose telling him that you and I spent the whole of last evening together, from six o'clock until about half past ten. Obviously I'll need you to back me up. And it depends, of course, on whether anyone can disprove it. That's what we have to discuss."

He stood for a moment appalled. "But we weren't! You're asking me to lie. This is a murder investigation. It's terribly dangerous to lie to the police, they always find out."

He knew what he must sound like, a frightened child, petulant, reluctant to take part in a dangerous game. He looked straight ahead, not wanting to meet her eyes, fearful of what he might see there, entreaty, anger, contempt.

She said: "You told me when you rang on Saturday that your parents were going to spend Sunday night at Ipswich with your married sister. They went, didn't they?"

He said miserably: "Yes, they went."

It was because he knew that they wouldn't be at home that he had hoped, had half-expected, that Caroline would suggest that they should be together again in the bungalow. He remembered her words on the telephone: "Look, there are times when a woman needs to be on her own. Can't you understand that? What happened yesterday doesn't mean that we have to spend every second of our time together. I've told you that I love you. God knows, I've shown it. Isn't that enough?"

She said: "So you were alone in the flat yesterday evening. Or weren't you? If anyone called or telephoned, then obviously I've got to think of something else."

"No one called. I was on my own until after lunch. Then I went for a drive."

"What time did you get back? Did anyone see you garaging the car? It's not a large block of flats, is it? Did you meet anyone when you got home? And what about lights from the windows?"

"I left the lights on. We always do when the flat is empty. Mother thinks it's safer, makes it look occupied. And I didn't get back until after dark. I wanted to be alone, to think. I drove to Blakeney and walked on the marshes. I wasn't home until ten-forty-five."

She gave a small contented sigh. "Then it looks all right. Did you meet anyone on the walk?"

"Only in the distance. A couple with a dog. I don't think they could recognize me even if they knew me."

"Where did you eat?" Her voice was sharp, the interrogation relentless.

"I didn't. Not until I got home. I wasn't hungry."

"Well, that's all right, then. We're safe. And no one spied on me in the bungalow. And no one would ring or call. No one ever does."

"Spy." It was, he thought, a strange word to use. But she was right. The bungalow, as uninspired as its name, Field View, stood totally isolated on a dull country road outside Hoveton. He had never been inside it, never even been allowed to escort her home, before they had arrived together on Friday evening, and it had surprised and a little shocked him. She had told him that it was rented furnished from the owners, who had gone to Australia for a year to stay with a married daughter and had decided to stay on. But why had she stayed on? he wondered. Surely there was a more attractive house or cottage somewhere she could have rented, a small flat in Norwich she could have afforded to buy. And, following her inside the front door, he had been struck by the contrast between its meanness, its vulgarity and her serene loveliness. He could picture it now, the dun-coloured carpet in the hall, the sitting room with two walls papered in pink stripes, the other two with huge clusters of roses, the hard sofa and two chairs with their grubby covers, the small reproduction of Constable's *Haywain*, hung too high to be comfortably seen and placed in incongruous proximity to the ubiquitous print of a yellow-faced Chinese girl, the old-fashioned wall-mounted gas fire. And she had done nothing to change it, nothing to impress on it her own personality. It was as if she hardly noticed its deficiencies, its ugliness. It served its purpose. She asked no more of it. And it had served theirs. But even the hall had struck him chill. He had wanted to cry out: "This is our first time together, my first time ever. Can't we go somewhere else? Does it have to be here?"

He said miserably: "I don't think I can do it, not convincingly. Chief Inspector Rickards will know I'm lying. I'll look guilty, embarrassed."

But she had decided to be gentle with him, reassuring. She said patiently: "He'll expect you to be embarrassed. You'll be telling him we spent the evening alone making love. That's convincing enough.

That's natural enough. He'd find it more suspicious if you didn't look guilty. Don't you see, the guilt and embarrassment will make your story more convincing."

So even his inexperience, his insecurity, yes, even his shame were to be used for her ends.

She said: "Look, all we need to do is to transpose the two nights. Friday night becomes yesterday. Don't fabricate, don't invent. Tell them what we did, what we ate, the food, the wine, what we talked about. It will sound true because it will be true. And they can't catch us out by asking about the TV programmes we didn't watch."

"But what happened was private. It was for us alone."

"Not any more. Murder destroys privacy. We made love. No doubt the police will use a coarser word. If they don't speak it, then they'll think it. But we made love in my bedroom, on my bed. You do remember?"

Remember. Oh yes, he remembered. His face flamed. He felt as if his whole body were burning. The tears that welled up despite his desperate will to hold them back were scalding tears. He squeezed his eyes shut so that he need not have to wipe them away. Of course, he remembered. That dull, square little back room, anonymous as a room in some cheap hotel, the mixture of excitement and terror which half-paralysed him, his incompetent fumblings, the whispered endearments which had become commands. She had been patient, experienced, and in the end she had taken charge. Well, he had never been naïve enough to suppose that for her it was the first time. For him, but not for her. But what had happened was, he knew, irrevocable. It was she who had possessed him, not he her, and that possession was more than physical. For a moment he couldn't speak. It was difficult to believe that those grotesque but controlled writhings had anything to do with the Caroline who stood now so close to him, yet so distanced. He noticed with sharpened perception the pristine cleanness of the grey-and-white-striped shirt, cut like a man's, the sway of the long grey skirt, the black-patent court shoes, the simple gold chain and the matching gold cufflinks, the corn-coloured hair sculpted back into the single thick plait. Was this what he had loved, still loved, a boy's romantic ideal, the cold, remote perfection of her? And he knew with an almost audible groan that their first coupling had destroyed more than it had affirmed, that what he had yearned for, still yearned for, and had lost forever, was an unattainable beauty.

But he knew too that she would only have to stretch out a hand and he would follow her again to that bungalow, to that bed.

He said miserably: "But why? Why? They won't suspect you, they can't. It's ridiculous even to think of it. You got on well with Hilary. You get on well with everyone in the station. You're the last person the police will be interested in. You haven't even a motive."

"But I have. I've always disliked her and I hated her father. He ruined Mummy, forced her to spend her last years in poverty. And I lost the chance of a decent education. I'm a secretary, essentially a shorthand-typist, and that's all I'll ever be."

"I've always thought you could be anything you chose."

"Not without education. All right, I know you can get a grant, but I had to leave school and earn as quickly as possible. And it's not only me, it's what Peter Robarts did to Mummy. She trusted him. She put every penny she'd got, every penny Daddy left, into his plastics company. I've hated him all my life, and I hated her because of him. Once the police discover that, I'll get no peace. But if I can produce an alibi, that will be the end. They'll leave us alone, both of us. We only need to say that we were together and there will be the end of it."

"But they can't see what Hilary's father did to your mother as a motive for murder. It's unreasonable. And it was all so long ago."

"No motive for killing another human being is ever reasonable. People kill for the strangest reasons. And I've got a thing about the police. It's irrational, I know, but I've always had it. That's why I'm so careful when I'm driving. I know I couldn't stand up to a real interrogation. I'm frightened of the police."

And she was, he remembered, seizing on this demonstrable truth as if it made the whole request legitimate, reasonable. She was obsessive about the speed limit even when the road was clear, obsessive about wearing her seat belt, the state of her car. And he remembered that time three weeks ago, when she had had her handbag snatched while shopping in Norwich, and despite his protest, hadn't even reported it. He remembered her words. "It's no use, they'll never get it back. We'll only waste their time at the police station. Let it go, there wasn't much in it." And then he thought, "I'm checking up on what she's telling me, verifying it." And he felt an overpowering shame mixed with pity. He heard her voice.

"All right, I'm asking too much. I know how you feel about truth, honesty, your Boy Scout Christianity. I'm asking you to sacrifice your good opinion of yourself. No one likes doing that. We all need our self-esteem. I suppose yours is knowing that you're morally better than the rest of us. But aren't you a bit of a hypocrite? You say you love me, but you won't lie for me. It's not an important lie. It won't hurt anyone. But you can't do it. It's against your religion. Your precious religion didn't stop you going to bed with me, did it? I thought Christians were supposed to be too pure for casual fornication."

"Casual fornication." Each word was like a blow, not a fierce, stabbing pain but a continuous thud like regular deliberate blows on the same bruised flesh. He had never, even in those first marvellous days together, been able to talk to her about his faith. She had made it plain from the beginning that this was a part of his life with which she had neither sympathy nor understanding. And how could he begin to explain that he had followed her into the bedroom without guilt because his need of her was stronger than his love for God, stronger than guilt, stronger than faith, needing no rationalization, no justification other than itself. How, he had told himself, could anything be wrong which every nerve and sinew told him was natural and right, even holy.

She said: "All right, let it go. I'm asking too much."

Stung by the contempt in her voice, he said miserably: "It's not that. I'm not better, I'm not. And you could never ask too much. If it's important to you, of course I'll do it."

She looked at him sharply, as if judging his sincerity, his will. He heard the relief in her voice as she said: "Look, there's no danger. We're both innocent, we know that. And what we tell the police could so easily have been true."

But that was a mistake, and he saw the realization of it in her eyes. He said: "It could have been true, but it isn't."

"And that's what's important to you, more important than my peace of mind, more important than what I thought we felt for each other."

He wanted to ask why her peace of mind needed to be built on a lie. He wanted to ask what they did, in fact, feel for each other, what she felt for him.

She said, looking at her watch: "And after all it will be an alibi for you too. That's even more important. After all, everyone knows how unkind she's been to you since that local radio programme. God's little nuclear crusader. You haven't forgotten that?"

The crudity of the implication, the note of impatience in her voice, all repelled him. He said: "But suppose they don't believe us."

"Don't let's go over all that again. Why shouldn't they believe us? And it hardly matters if they don't. They can't ever prove we're lying, that's what's important. And after all it's natural that we should have been together. It isn't as if we've just started seeing each other. Look, I've got to get back to the office now. I'll be in touch, but we'd better not see each other tonight."

He hadn't expected to see her that night. The news of this latest murder would have been broadcast on local radio, passed from mouth to mouth. His mother would be waiting anxiously for his return from work, avid for news.

But there was something he had to tell her before she left, and somehow he found the courage. He said: "I rang you last night. While I was driving around thinking. I stopped at a phone box and telephoned. You weren't in."

There was a small silence. He glanced nervously at her face, but it was expressionless. She said: "What time was that?"

"About twenty to ten, perhaps a bit later."

"Why? Why did you telephone?"

"The need to talk to you. Loneliness. I suppose I half-hoped that you might change your mind and ask me to come round."

"All right. You might as well know. I was on the headland last night. I took Remus for a run. I left the car down a cart track just outside the village and walked as far as the ruined abbey. I suppose I was there just after ten."

He said in horrified wonder: "You were there! And all the time she must have been lying dead within a few yards of you."

She said sharply: "Not a few yards, more like a hundred. There was never any chance that I'd find her, and I didn't see her killer, if that's what you're thinking. And I stayed on the cliffs. I didn't go down to the beach. If I had, the police would have found my footprints, mine and Remus's."

"But someone might have seen you. It was bright moonlight."

"The headland was empty. And if the murderer was lurking in the trees and saw me, he's hardly likely to come forward. But it's not the happiest position to be in. That's why I need an alibi. I wasn't going to tell you, but now you know. I didn't kill her. But I was there and I've got a motive. That's why I'm asking you to help."

For the first time Jonathan detected in her voice a note of tenderness, almost of pleading. She moved as if to touch him and then drew back, and the tentative gesture, the withdrawal, was as endearing as if she had laid her hand against his face. The hurt and misery of the last ten minutes were swept away in a rush of tenderness. His lips seemed to have thickened so that speech was difficult, but he found the words. He said: "Of course, I'll help. I love you. I won't let you down. You can depend on me."

3

Rickards had arranged with Alex Mair to be at the power station by 9.00 that morning but had planned to call first at Scudder's Cottage to see Ryan Blaney. The visit was one of some delicacy. He knew that Blaney had children, and it would be necessary to question at least the eldest. But this couldn't be done until he had with him a woman police constable, and there had been some delay in arranging this. It was one of those comparatively minor irritations which he found difficult to accept, but he knew that it would be unwise to pay more than a brief visit to the Blaneys without a WPC. Whether or not the man proved to be a serious suspect, he couldn't risk a later allegation that information had been extracted from a juvenile without the observance of proper procedures. At the same time Blaney had a right to know what had happened to his picture, and if the police didn't tell him someone else speedily would. And it was important that he was there to see the man's face when he heard the news, both of the slashed portrait and of Hilary Robarts's murder.

He thought that he had seldom seen a more depressing place than Scudder's Cottage. A thin drizzle was falling, and he saw the cottage and the neglected garden through a shimmering mist which seemed to absorb shapes and colours so that the whole scene was one damp amorphous grey. Leaving DC Gary Price in the car, Rickards and Oliphant made their way up the weed-infested path to the porch. There was no bell, and when Oliphant thudded on the iron knocker the door almost immediately opened. Ryan Blaney stood before them, six foot tall, lank, bleary-eyed, and gave them a long unwelcoming stare. The colour seemed to have drained even from his ruddy hair, and Rickards thought he had never seen a man look so exhausted and yet still be on his feet. Blaney didn't invite them in, and Rickards didn't suggest it. That intrusion had better wait until he was accompanied by a WPC. And Blaney could wait. He was anxious now to get to Larksoken Power Station. He gave the news that the portrait of Hilary Robarts had been slashed and found at Thyme Cottage, but offered no other details. There was no response. He said: "Did you hear me, Mr. Blaney?"

"Yes, I heard you. I knew that the portrait was missing."

"When?"

"Last night, at about nine-forty-five. Miss Mair called for it. She was going to take it to Norwich with her this morning. She'll tell you. Where is it now?"

"We have it, what remains of it. We shall need it for forensic examination. We'll give you a receipt, naturally."

"What good will that do? You can keep it, the picture and your receipt. Slashed to pieces, did you say?"

"Not to pieces, in two clean slashes. Perhaps it can be repaired. We'll bring it with us when we come, so that you can identify it."

"I don't want to see it again. You can keep it."

"We'll need the identification, Mr. Blaney. But we'll talk about it when we see you later today. When, incidentally, did you last see the portrait?"

"Thursday evening, when I wrapped it and left it in the painting shed. I haven't been in the shed since. And what's the good of talking? It was the best thing I've ever done and that bitch destroyed it. Get Alice Mair or Adam Dalgliesh to identify it. They've both seen it."

"Are you saying you know who's responsible?"

Again there was a silence. Rickards broke it by saying: "We'll be with you late this afternoon, probably between four and five, if that's convenient. And we shall have to talk to the children. We'll have a WPC with us. They're at school, I suppose, the children?"

"The twins are at playgroup, Theresa is here. She isn't well. Look, you're not going to all this trouble about a slashed portrait. Since when have the police cared about pictures?"

"We care about criminal damage. But there is something more. I have to tell you that Hilary Robarts was murdered last night."

He stared intently at Blaney's face as he spoke. This was the moment of revelation, perhaps the moment of truth. It was surely impossible for Blaney to hear the news without betraying some emotion: shock, fear, surprise, real or simulated. Instead he said calmly: "You don't have to tell me that either. I knew. George Jago phoned early this morning from the Local Hero."

Did he indeed, thought Rickards, and mentally added George Jago to his list of people to be questioned as soon as possible. He asked: "Will Theresa be in and well enough to speak to us this afternoon?"

"She'll be here and she'll be well enough."

And then the door was closed firmly in their faces.

Oliphant said: "God knows why Robarts wanted to buy that slum in the first place. And she's been trying to force him and the kids out for months. There's been a great deal of feeling about it in Lydsett, as well as on the headland."

"So you told me on the way here. But if Blaney killed her, he'd hardly draw attention to himself by hurling that portrait through the window of Thyme Cottage. And two unrelated criminal acts, murder and malicious damage on the same night, is too great a coincidence to swallow."

It had been a bad start to the day. The drizzle, seeping coldly under the collar of his coat, added to his mild dejection. He hadn't noticed that it was raining on the rest of the headland and could almost believe that Scudder's Lane and that picturesque but sour little hovel generated their own depressing climate. He had a lot to get through before he returned for a more rigorous confrontation with Ryan Blaney, and he wasn't looking forward to any of it. Forcing the gate shut over a clump of weeds on the path, he took a last look at the cottage. There was no smoke from the chimney, and the windows, hazed with salt, were tightly closed. It was difficult to believe that a family lived here, that the cottage hadn't long been abandoned to damp and decay. And then, at the top right-hand window, he glimpsed a pale face framed with red-gold hair. Theresa Blaney was looking down at them.

4

⊠

Twenty minutes later the three police officers were at Larksoken Power Station. A place had been reserved for them in the car-park outside the perimeter fence close to the guard house. As soon as they approached the gate, it was unlocked and one of the security police came out and removed the cones. The preliminaries took only a little time. They were received with almost impassive civility by the uniformed security guard on duty, signed the book and were issued with their lapel badges. The guard telephoned the news of their arrival, reported that the Director's PA, Miss Amphlett, would be with them very shortly and then appeared to lose interest in them. His companion, who had opened the gates and removed the cones, stood casually chatting to a stocky man dressed as a diver and carrying his helmet under his arm, who had apparently been working on one of the water towers. Neither of them seemed particularly interested in the arrival of the police. If Dr. Mair had instructed that they were to be received with courtesy but the minimum of fuss, his staff couldn't have done it better.

Through the window of the guard house they saw a woman, obviously Miss Amphlett, walking unhurriedly down the concrete path. She was a cool, self-possessed blonde who, on arrival, ignored Oliphant's bold stare as if he weren't present and gravely greeted Rickards. But she didn't respond to his smile, either because she thought a smile inappropriate to the occasion or, more likely, because in her view few visitors to Larksoken merited such a personal welcome and a police officer wasn't among them.

She said: "Dr. Mair is ready for you, Chief Inspector," and turned to lead the way. It made him feel like a patient being shown into the presence of a consultant. You could tell a lot about a man from his PA, and what she told him about Dr. Alex Mair reinforced his private imaginings. He thought of his own secretary, tousle-haired, nineteen-year-old Kim, who dressed in the more bizarre extreme of con-temporary youth fashion, whose shorthand was as unreliable as her timekeeping, but who never greeted even the lowliest visitor without a wide smile and the offer, which they were ill advised to accept, of office coffee and biscuits.

They followed Miss Amphlett between the wide lawns to the administration building. She was a woman who induced unease, and Oliphant, obviously feeling the need to assert himself, began to prattle.

"That's the turbine house to our right, sir, and the reactor building and the cooling plant behind it. The workshop is to the left. It's a Magnox thermal reactor, sir, a type first commissioned in 1956. We had it all explained to us when we went round. The fuel is uranium metal. To conserve the neutrons and to allow natural uranium to be used, the fuel is clad in a magnesium alloy called Magnox with a low neutron absorption. That's where the reactor gets its name. They extract the heat by passing carbon-dioxide gas over the fuel in the reactor core. That transfers its heat to water in a steam generator, and the steam drives a turbine coupled to an electric generator."

Rickards wished that Oliphant didn't feel the need to demonstrate his superficial knowledge of nuclear power in the presence of Miss Amphlett, and only hoped that it was accurate. Oliphant went on: "Of course this type of reactor is out of date now. It's being replaced by a PWR pressurized water reactor like the one being built at Sizewell. I've been shown over Sizewell as well as Larksoken, sir. I thought I might as well learn what's going on in these places."

Rickards thought, And if you've learned that, Elephant Boy, you're even cleverer than you think you are.

The room on the second floor of the administration block into which they were shown struck Rickards as immense. It was almost empty, an arrangement of space and light deliberately deployed to make a statement about the man who now rose to his feet behind the huge black modern desk and stood gravely waiting while they walked across what seemed endless yards of carpet. Even as their hands touched, and Alex Mair's grasp was firm and disconcertingly cold, Rickards's eyes and mind took in the salient features of the office. Two of the walls were painted a smooth light grey, but to the east and south sheets of plate glass reached from ceiling to floor, giving a panorama of sky, sea and headland. It was a sunless morning but the air was suffused with a pale ambiguous light, the horizon blurred so that sea and sky were one shimmering grey. Rickards had for a moment the sensation of being weightlessly suspended in outer space in some bizarre and futuristic capsule. And then another image supervened. He could almost hear the throb of the engines and feel the ship shudder as the great surge of ocean divided under the prow.

There was very little furniture. Alex Mair's uncluttered desk, with a high but comfortable armchair for visitors, faced the southern window, before which stood a conference table set with eight chairs. In front of the east window was a display table holding a model of what Rickards presumed was the new pressurized water reactor shortly to be constructed on the site. Even at a glance he could see that it was beautifully made, a marvel in glass and steel and perspex, as intricately crafted as if it were a decorative object in its own right. On the north wall hung the only picture: a large oil showing a man with a rifle on a skinny horse, posed in a bleak landscape of sand and scrubland with, in the background, a range of distant mountains. But the man had no head. Instead he was wearing a huge square helmet of black metal with a slit for the eyes. Rickards found the picture disturbingly intimidating. He had a faint memory that he had seen a copy of it, or of something very like it, before, and that the artist was Australian. He was irritated to find himself thinking that Adam Dalgliesh would have known what it was and who had painted it.

Mair went over to the conference table and lifting one of the chairs, swung it lightly and placed it by the desk. They were to sit facing him. After a moment's hesitation, Gary Price took a chair for himself, placed it behind Mair and unobtrusively took out his notebook. Looking into the grey sardonic eyes, Rickards wondered how Alex Mair saw him, and a snatch of conversation, overheard some years ago in the mess at New Scotland Yard, came unbidden into his mind.

"Oh, Ricky's nobody's fool. He's a bloody sight more intelligent than he looks."

"He'd better be. He reminds me of one of those characters you get in every war film. The poor, honest son-of-a-bitch who always ends up with his face in the mud and a bullet in his chest."

Well, he wasn't going to end with his face in the mud in this enquiry. The room might look as if it were specifically designed to intimidate him, but it was only a working office. Alex Mair, for all his assurance, his rumoured brilliance, was only a man, and if he had killed Hilary Robarts he would end up, as better men than he had done, looking at the sky through iron bars and watching the changing face of the sea only in his dreams.

As they seated themselves, Mair said: "I expect you'll need somewhere to interview people. I've made arrangements for a small room in the Medical Physics Department to be made available when you're finished here. Miss Amphlett will show you the way. I don't know how long you'll need it, but we've moved in a small refrigerator, and there are facilities for making tea or coffee, or, if you prefer, tea and coffee can be brought to you from the canteen. And the canteen staff can, of course, provide you with simple meals. Miss Amphlett will let you have today's menu."

Rickards said: "Thank you. We'll make our own coffee."

He felt at a disadvantage and wondered if this was intended. They would need an interview room and he could hardly complain if this need had been anticipated. But it would have been a better start if he could have taken the initiative, and he felt, perhaps illogically, that there was something demeaning to his job in this careful reassurance that he would get his food and drink. The look bent on him across the desktop was unworried, speculative, almost, he could imagine, slightly judgemental. He knew that he was in the company of power, and the kind of power with which he was unfamiliar: confident intellectual authority. A clutch of chief constables would have been less formidable.

Alex Mair said: "Your Chief Constable has already liaised with the Atomic Energy Authority Constabulary. Inspector Johnston would like a word with you this morning, probably before you begin your general interview. He realizes that the Norfolk Constabulary have the principal responsibility here, but naturally he has an interest."

Rickards said: "We recognize that, and we shall be glad of his co-operation."

And it would be co-operation, not interference. He had already made himself familiar with the duties of the AEAC, and he was aware that there was a potential risk of dissension and overlapping of powers. But this was essentially a matter for the Norfolk CID and was seen as an extension of the Whistler enquiries. If Inspector Johnston was prepared to be reasonable, then so was he, but it was not a problem which he proposed to discuss with Dr. Mair.

Mair opened the right-hand drawer of his desk and took out a manila folder. He said: "This is Hilary Robarts's personnel file. There's no objection to your seeing it, but it merely gives the background information: age, places of education, degrees, career before she came to us in 1984 as deputy to the Administrative Officer. A curriculum vitae from which the vitae is unusually conspicuously absent. The dry bones of a life."

Mair slid it across the desk. The action had a curious finality. A life closed, finished with. Taking it, Rickards said: "Thank you, sir. It will be helpful to have it. Perhaps you could flesh out some of the dry bones for us. You knew her well?"

"Very well. Indeed, for a time we were lovers. That doesn't, I admit, necessarily imply more than physical intimacy, but I probably did know her as well as anyone here on the station."

He spoke calmly and totally without embarrassment, as if it were as unimportant as stating that he and Robarts had shared the same university. Rickards wondered if Mair expected him to seize on the admission. Instead he asked: "Was she popular?"

"She was highly efficient. The two, I find, do not invariably go together. But she was respected and, I think, generally liked by those staff who had dealings with her. She will be greatly missed, probably more deeply than would be more egregiously popular colleagues."

"And missed by you?"

"By all of us."

"When did your affair end, Dr. Mair?"

"About three or four months ago."

"Without rancour?"

"With neither a bang nor a whimper. We had been seeing less of each other for some time before then. My personal future is at present rather unsettled, but I am unlikely to continue as Director for very much longer. One comes to the end of a love affair as to the end of a job, with a natural feeling that a stage of life has run its course."

"And she felt the same?"

"I imagine so. We both had some regrets at the break, but I don't think either of us ever imagined that we were indulging in a grand passion, or indeed expected our relationship to be lasting."

"There was no other man?"

"None that I know of, but, then, there's no reason why I should know."

Rickards said: "So you would be surprised to learn that she wrote to her solicitor in Norwich on Sunday morning to make an appointment to discuss her will and that she told him she was expecting shortly to be married? We found the unposted letter among her papers."

Mair blinked rapidly but otherwise showed no sign of discomposure. He said evenly: "Yes, it would surprise me, but I'm not sure why. I suppose because she seemed to live rather a solitary life here, and it's difficult to see how she could have found time or opportunity to enter into a new relationship. Of course it's perfectly possible that some man from her past has re-emerged and they have come to an arrangement. I'm afraid I can't help you."

Rickards changed the tack of his questioning. He said: "There seems to be a feeling locally that she wasn't much help to you during the public enquiry into the second reactor here. She didn't give evidence to the official enquiry, did she? I can't quite see how she was involved."

"Officially she wasn't. But at one or two public meetings, unwisely, she got embroiled with hecklers, and on one of our open days the scientist who normally escorts the public was off sick and she took his place. She was, perhaps, less tactful than she should have been with some of the questioners. After that I arranged that she wasn't directly involved with the public."

Rickards said: "So she was a woman who provoked antagonism?"

"Not enough, I should have thought, to provoke murder. She was dedicated to the work here and found it difficult to tolerate what she saw as wilful obscurantism. She hadn't a scientific training but she did acquire considerable knowledge of the science done here, and perhaps undue respect for what she saw as expert scientific opinion. I pointed out that it was unreasonable to expect this to be shared by the general public. After all, they've probably been told by experts in recent years that high-rise flats don't collapse, that the London Underground is safe from fire and that cross-Channel ferries can't keel over."

Oliphant, who had until now remained silent, suddenly said: "I was one of the visitors on that open day. Someone asked her about Chernobyl. She made a remark, didn't she, about 'only thirty dead, so what were people worrying about?' Isn't that what she said? It rather begged the question: how many dead would Miss Robarts agree was an unacceptable figure?"

Alex Mair looked at him as if surprised that he could actually speak and, after a moment's contemplation, said: "In comparing the Chernobyl death toll with fatalities in industry and in mining fossil fuels, she was making a perfectly reasonable point, although she could have done it with more tact. Chernobyl is a sensitive subject. We get rather tired of explaining to the public that the Russian RBMK type of reactor had a number of design weaknesses, notably that it had a fast-acting positive power coefficient when the reactor was at low power. The Magnox, AGR and PWR designs don't have this characteristic at any power level, so that a similar accident here is physically impossible. I'm sorry if that sounds overtechnical. What I'm saying is: it won't happen here, it can't happen here and, in fact, it didn't happen here."

Oliphant said stolidly: "It hardly matters whether it happens here or not, sir, if we get the results of it. Wasn't Hilary Robarts suing someone in the community for alleged libel arising out of the meeting I attended?"

Alex Mair ignored him and spoke to Rickards. "I think that's generally known. It was a mistake, I think. She had a legitimate case but she wasn't likely to get satisfaction by going to law."

Rickards asked: "You tried to persuade her not to in the interests of the station?"

"And in her own. Yes, I tried."

The telephone on the desk rang. Mair pressed the button. He said: "This shouldn't take much longer. Tell him I'll ring back in twenty minutes." Rickards wondered whether he had arranged for the call to be put through. As if in confirmation of the suspicion, Mair said: "In view of my past relationship with Miss Robarts, you'll need to know my movements on Sunday. Perhaps I could give them to you now. Both of us have a busy day ahead, I imagine." It was a less-than-subtle reminder that it was time they got down to business.

Rickards kept his voice steady. "That would be helpful, sir." Gary Price bent his head over his notebook as assiduously as if he had just been reprimanded for inattention.

"They're hardly relevant until Sunday evening, but I may as well cover the whole of the weekend. I left here just after ten-forty-five on Friday and drove to London, lunched with an old university friend at the Reform Club and went on at two-thirty to a meeting with the Permanent Secretary at the Department of Energy. I then went to my flat in the Barbican and in the evening attended a performance of *The Taming of the Shrew* at the Barbican Theatre with a party of three friends. If you later need their corroboration, which seems unlikely, I can, of course, give you their names. I drove back to Larksoken on Sunday morning, lunched at a pub en route and arrived home at about four. I had a cup of tea and then went for a walk on the headland and got back to Martyr's Cottage about an hour later. I had a quick supper with my sister at about seven and left for the station at seven-thirty, or soon afterwards. I was working here in the computer room alone until ten-thirty, when I left for home. I was driving along the coast road when I was stopped by Commander Dalgliesh with the news that Hilary Robarts had been murdered. The rest you know."

Rickards said: "Not altogether, Dr. Mair. There was some delay before we arrived. You didn't touch the body?"

"I stood and looked down at her but I didn't touch her. Dalgliesh was rather conscientiously doing his job, or should I say yours. He very rightly reminded me that nothing should be touched and that the scene should be left undisturbed. I went down and walked by the sea until you arrived."

Rickards asked: "Do you usually come into work on Sunday evenings?"

"Invariably if I have had to spend the Friday in London. There is a very heavy pressure of work at present which it is impossible to fit into a five-day week. Actually I only stayed for less than three hours, but they were valuable hours."

"And you were alone in the computer room. Doing what, sir?"

If Mair found the enquiry irrelevant he didn't say so. "I was engaged on my research, which is concerned with the study of reactor behaviour in hypothesized loss-of-coolant accidents. I'm not, of course, the only person working in what is one of the most important areas of research in nuclear-reactor design. There's a great deal of international co-operation in these studies. Essentially what I'm doing is evaluating the possible effects of loss of coolant by mathematical models which are then evaluated by numerical analysis and advanced computer programmes."

Rickards said: "And you're working here at Larksoken alone?"

"At this station I am. Similar studies are being carried out at Winfrith and in a number of other countries, including the U.S.A. As I have said, there's a considerable amount of international co-operation."

Oliphant asked suddenly: "Is that the worst thing that can happen, a loss of the coolant?"

Alex Mair looked at him for a moment as if deciding whether the question coming from such a source warranted an answer; then he said: "The loss of coolant is potentially extremely dangerous. There are, of course, emergency procedures if the normal cooling arrangements fail. The incident at Three Mile Island in the United States has emphasized the need to know more about the extent and nature of the threat posed by that kind of incident. The phenomenon to be analysed is in three main groups: severe fuel damage and core melting, migration of released fission products and aerosols through the primary coolant circuit and the behaviour of fission products in released fuel and steam in the reactor-container building. If you have a genuine interest in the research and enough knowledge to understand it, I can provide you with some references, but this hardly seems the time and place for scientific education."

Oliphant smiled as if gratified by the rebuke. He asked: "Wasn't the scientist who killed himself, Dr. Toby Gledhill, working on the research side here with you? I thought I read something about that in one of the local papers."

"Yes. He was my assistant here. Tobias Gledhill was a physicist who was also an exceptionally talented computer expert. He is very much missed as a colleague and a man."

And that, thought Rickards, disposes of Toby Gledhill. From another man the tribute could have been moving in its simplicity. From Mair it sounded like a bleak dismissal. But, then, suicide was messy and embarrassing. He would find repugnant its intrusion into his neatly organized world.

Mair turned to Rickards. "I have a great deal to do this morning, Chief Inspector, and no doubt you have too. Is this really relevant?"

Rickards said stolidly: "It helps fill in the picture. I suppose you booked in when you arrived here yesterday night and subsequently booked out?"

"You saw something of the system when you arrived. Every member of the staff has a signed identity badge with a photograph and a personal number which is confidential. The number is electronically registered when the man or woman enters the site, and there is in addition a visual check of the badge by the gate staff. I have a total staff of five hundred and thirty people, working in three shifts covering the twenty-four hours. At the weekend there are two shifts—the day staff, coming on from eight-fifteen until twenty-fifteen, and the night, from twenty-fifteen until eight-fifteen."

"And no one could enter or leave undetected, not even the Director?"

"No one, least of all, I imagine, the Director. My check-in time will be recorded, and I was seen arriving and leaving by the gate officer on duty."

"There is no other way into the station except through the gatehouse?"

"Not unless you emulate the heroes of old war films and tunnel deep under the wire. No one was tunnelling here on Sunday night."

Rickards said: "We shall need to know the movements of every member of the staff on the Sunday from early evening until ten-thirty, when Commander Dalgliesh discovered the body."

"Isn't that an unnecessarily large spread of time? Surely she was killed shortly after nine?"

"That seems the most likely time of death, and we expect to get a more accurate estimate from the post-mortem report. At present I prefer to make no assumptions. We have copies of the forms which were distributed in connection with the Whistler enquiry which we would like to issue to all the staff. I imagine that the great majority can be easily eliminated. Most people who have any family or social life can provide an alibi for Sunday evening. Perhaps you could suggest how the forms can be distributed with as little disturbance to the work here as possible."

Mair said: "The simplest and most effective way would be to leave them in the gatehouse. Each member of staff could be given one when he or she checks in. Those staff who are off sick or on leave today will have to receive them at home. I can supply their names and addresses." He paused and then added: "It seems to me highly unlikely that this murder has anything to do with Larksoken Power Station, but as Hilary Robarts worked here and you will be interviewing members of staff, it might be helpful if you have some idea of the layout and organization. My PA has put up a file for you with a diagram of the site, a booklet describing the operation of the reactor, which will help to give you some idea of the different functions carried out, a list of staff by name and grade and a copy of the existing managerial structure and the operations-staff shift rota. If you want to see any particular department, I can arrange for you to be escorted. Certain areas cannot, of course, be entered without protective clothing and a subsequent radiological check."

The file was ready in his right-hand drawer, and he handed it over. Rickards took it and studied the organization chart. After a moment he said: "You have seven divisions, each with a head of department: Medical Physicist, Station Chemist, Operations Superintendent, Maintenance Superintendent, Reactor Physicist, Work Office Engineer and the station Administrative Officer, the post held by Hilary Robarts."

"Temporarily held. The station Administrative Officer died of cancer three months ago and the post has not yet been filled. We are also about to reorganize the internal administration into three main divisions, as at Sizewell, where they have what I think is a more effective and rational system. But the future here is uncertain, as you've probably heard, and there may be a case for waiting until a new Director or Station Manager is in post."

Rickards said: "And at present the station Administrative Officer is responsible to you through the Deputy Director?"

"Through Dr. James Macintosh, that is right. Dr. Macintosh is at present in the States, studying their nuclear installations, and has been for the past month."

"And the Operations Superintendent—Op. Super., as it says here—is Miles Lessingham, who was one of the guests at Miss Mair's dinner party on Thursday."

Alex Mair didn't reply.

Rickards went on: "You've been unfortunate, Dr. Mair. Three violent deaths of members of your staff within the space of two months. First Dr. Gledhill's suicide, then Christine Baldwin's murder by the Whistler and now Hilary Robarts."

Mair asked: "Have you any doubts that Christine Baldwin was killed by the Whistler?"

"None at all. Her hair was found with that of other victims when he killed himself, and her husband, who would normally be the obvious first suspect, has an alibi. He was driven home by his friends."

"And Toby Gledhill's death was the subject of an inquest, 'death while the balance of his mind was disturbed,' that convenient sop to convention and religious orthodoxy."

Oliphant asked: "And was the balance of his mind disturbed, sir?"

Mair turned on him his ironic and speculative gaze. "I have no way of knowing the state of his mind, Sergeant. What I am sure of is that he killed himself and that he did it unaided. No doubt at the time he felt he had sufficient reason. Dr. Gledhill was a manic depressive. He coped courageously with his disability and it rarely interfered with his work. But with that psychological make-up, suicide is always an above-average risk. And if you agree that the three deaths are unrelated, then we needn't waste time on the first two. Or was your statement, Chief Inspector, intended as a general commiseration?"

Rickards said: "Just a comment, sir." He went on: "One of your staff, Miles Lessingham, found Christine Baldwin's body. He told us then that he was on his way to have dinner with you and Miss Mair. I suppose he gave you all a graphic description of his experience. Natural, I'd say. Difficult thing to keep to yourself."

Mair said calmly: "Virtually impossible, wouldn't you say?" He added: "Among friends."

"Which he was, of course. All friends together, including Miss Robarts. So you got all the gory details fresh from the scene. Including the ones he'd been specifically told to keep to himself."

"Which were they, Chief Inspector?"

Rickards didn't reply. Instead he asked: "Could I have the names of everyone who was present in Martyr's Cottage when Mr. Lessingham arrived?"

"My sister and I; Hilary Robarts; Mrs. Dennison, the housekeeper from the Old Rectory and Commander Adam Dalgliesh of the Metropolitan Police. And the Blaney child—Theresa, I think she's called—was helping my sister with the meal." He paused and then added: "These enquiry forms which you're proposing to issue to all members of staff: I suppose it is necessary to take up their time in this way. Isn't it fairly plain what happened here? Surely this is what your people call a copycat murder."

Rickards said: "It was that all right, sir. All the details correct. Very clever, very convincing. Just the two differences. This murderer knew his victim and this murderer is sane."

Five minutes later, following Miss Amphlett down the corridor to the interviewing room, Rickards thought, "And you're a cool customer, mate." No embarrassing expressions of horror and grief, which always sounded insincere. No protestations of innocence. The assumption that no one in his rational mind could suspect you of murder. He hadn't asked for his solicitor to be present, but, then, he didn't need one. But he was far too intelligent to have missed the significance of those questions about the dinner party. Whoever had killed Hilary Robarts had known that she would be swimming by moonlight sometime after nine o'clock yesterday, had known, too, precisely how the Whistler killed his victims. There were quite a number of people who knew one of these facts, but the number who knew both was limited. And six of them had been present at that dinner party at Martyr's Cottage last Thursday night.

5

The interview room which had been assigned to them was a feature-less little office with a view to the west dominated by the great bulk of the turbine house. It was adequately furnished for their purpose, but only just; entirely appropriate, thought Rickards sourly, to visitors whose presence was tolerated but hardly welcomed. There was a modern pedestal desk, obviously brought in from someone's office, three upright chairs and one rather more comfortable one with arms, a small side table with an electric kettle on a tray, four cups and saucers (did Mair expect them to make coffee for the suspects?), a bowl full of wrapped sugar lumps and three caddies. Rickards said: "What have they given us, Gary?"

Gary Price busied himself with the tins. "Coffee bags and tea bags, sir. And there's a tin of biscuits."

Oliphant asked: "What kind of biscuits?"

"Digestive, Sarge."

"Chocolate?"

"No, Sarge, just plain digestives."

"Well, let's hope they're not radioactive. Better get the kettle on, we may as well start with the coffee. Where do they expect us to get water?"

"Miss Amphlett said there was a tap in the cloakroom at the end of the passage, Sarge. The kettle's filled, anyway."

Oliphant tried one of the upright chairs, stretching in it as if to assess its comfort. The wood creaked. He said: "Cold fish, wasn't he? And clever with it. Not much out of him, sir."

"I wouldn't say that, Sergeant. We've learned more about the victim than he probably realizes. Efficient but not much liked, prone to interfere with matters outside her scope of responsibility, probably because she secretly yearned to be a scientist rather than an administrator. Aggressive, uncompromising, intolerant of criticism. Antagonized the locals and from time to time did the station a bit of no good. And, of course, the Director's mistress, for what that was worth."

Oliphant said: "Until three or four months ago. A natural end with no hard feelings on either side. His version."

"And we're never going to get hers, are we? But one thing was odd. When Mair met Mr. Dalgliesh he was on his way home from here. His sister presumably was expecting him, yet, apparently, he didn't telephone her. It never seems to have occurred to him."

"Shocked, sir, something else on his mind. He's just discovered that his ex-girlfriend is the victim of a particularly vicious psychopathic killer. Tends to eclipse brotherly feelings and thoughts of your bedtime cocoa."

"Maybe. I wonder whether Miss Mair rang here to find out why he was delayed. We'll ask."

Oliphant said: "If she didn't ring, I can think of one reason why. She expected him to be late. She thought he was at Thyme Cottage with Hilary Robarts."

"If she didn't ring because she thought that, then she can't have known that Robarts was dead. Right, Sergeant, let's get started. First of all we'll have a word with Miss Amphlett. The boss's PA usually knows more about the organization than anyone, including her boss."

But any information of interest that Caroline Amphlett might have she was adept at concealing. She seated herself in the armchair with the calm assurance of an applicant for a job which she has every confidence of getting, and answered Rickards's questions calmly and without emotion except when he attempted to probe into Hilary Robarts's relationship with the Director. Then when she permitted herself a moue of distaste that anyone could be so vulgarly inquisitive about matters which were not his concern, she answered repressively that Dr. Mair had never confided in her about his private life. She admitted that she knew Hilary Robarts made a habit of swimming at night and kept this up well into the autumn months and sometimes later. She thought the fact was generally known at Larksoken. Miss Robarts had been a strong and enthusiastic swimmer. She was not particularly interested in the Whistler except to take reasonable precautions and avoid walking alone at night, and she knew nothing about his methods except what she had read in the newspapers, that he strangled his victims. She had known about the dinner party at Martyr's Cottage on Thursday, she thought Miles Lessingham might have mentioned it, but no one had discussed with her the events of the evening and she saw no reason why they should. As for her own movements on Sunday, she had spent the whole of the evening, from six o'clock, at her bungalow with her boyfriend, Jonathan Reeves. They had been together continually until he had left, at about 10.30. Her cool glance at Oliphant challenged him to ask her what they had been doing, and he resisted the temptation except to ask what they had drunk and eaten. Asked about her relationship with Hilary Robarts, she said that she had greatly respected her but hadn't particularly liked or disliked her. Their professional relationship had been perfectly friendly, but she couldn't recall ever meeting her outside the power station. As far as she knew, Miss Robarts had no enemies, and she had no idea who could have wished her dead. When the door had closed after her Rickards said: "We'll check her alibi, of course, but there's no hurry. Let young Reeves sweat for an hour or so. I want to check first on the staff who actually worked for Robarts."

But the next hour was unproductive. The people who had worked directly for Hilary Robarts were more shocked than distressed, and their evidence strengthened the image of a woman more respected than liked. But none had an obvious motive, none admitted to knowing precisely how the Whistler had killed and, more to the point, all could produce an alibi for Sunday night. Rickards had hardly expected otherwise.

At the end of the sixty minutes he sent for Jonathan Reeves. He came into the room, white-faced and as stiffly controlled as if it were an execution shed, and Rickards's first reaction was surprise that a woman as attractive as Caroline Amphlett should have chosen such an unlikely mate. It wasn't that Reeves had a particularly unprepossessing face. You couldn't even describe him as plain if you discounted the acne. And his features, taken individually, were good enough. It was the whole face which was somehow unremarkable, ordinary, the kind of face which defeated any attempt at an Identikit image. Rickards decided that it was best described in terms of movement rather than features: the almost continuous blinking behind the horn-rimmed spectacles, the nervous sucking of the lips, his habit of suddenly stretching his neck like a TV comedian. Rickards knew from the list Alex Mair had provided that the staff at Larksoken was predominantly male. Was this the best Amphlett could do for herself? But sexual attraction was irrational anyway. Look at him and Susie. Seeing them together, her friends probably felt an equal surprise.

He left most of the detailed questioning to Oliphant, which was a mistake. Oliphant was always at his worst with a frightened suspect, and he took his time extracting, not without pleasure, a straightforward story which confirmed Caroline Amphlett's account.

Afterwards, when Reeves had been finally released, Oliphant said: "He was as jumpy as a cat, sir. That's why I took my time over him. I think he's lying."

It was, thought Rickards, typical of Oliphant both to assume and to hope for the worst. He said curtly: "Not lying necessarily, Sergeant; just frightened and embarrassed. Tough luck when your first night of passion ends in a not particularly subtle police interrogation. But the alibi seems firm enough, and neither of them has an obvious motive. And there's no evidence that either knew the details of the Whistler's little habits. Let's get on to someone who did. Miles Lessingham."

Rickards had last seen Lessingham at the scene of Christine Baldwin's murder, since he hadn't himself been at the incident room when Lessingham had called in next morning to sign his statement. He realized that the sardonic attempt at humour and the controlled detachment the man had shown at the scene were mainly due to shock and distaste, but he had sensed, too, that Lessingham had a wariness of the police amounting to dislike. It was not an uncommon phenomenon nowadays even among the middle classes, and no doubt he had his reasons. But it hadn't made him easy to deal with then and it didn't now. After the usual preliminaries Rickards asked: "Were you aware of the relationship between Dr. Mair and Miss Robarts?"

"He's the Director, she was Acting Administrator."

"I meant the sexual relationship."

"No one told me. But, not being entirely insensitive to my fellow mortals, I thought it likely that they were lovers."

"And you knew that it had ended?"

"I assumed so. They didn't confide in me when it began and they didn't confide in me when it ended. You'd better ask Dr. Mair if you want details of his personal life. I have enough trouble managing my own."

"But you weren't aware of any difficulties caused by the relationship: resentment, accusations of favouritism, jealousy perhaps?"

"Not from me, I assure you. My interests lie elsewhere."

"And what about Miss Robarts? Did you get the impression that the affair ended without rancour? Did she seem upset, for example?"

"If she was she didn't weep on my shoulder. But, then, mine is hardly the shoulder she would have chosen."

"And you have no idea who killed her?"

"None."

There was a pause; then Rickards asked: "Did you like her?"

"No."

For a moment Rickards was nonplussed. It was a question which he frequently asked in murder investigations and usually to some effect. Few suspects would admit to disliking the victim without blundering into an attempt at explanation or justification. After a moment's silence, during which it was obvious that Lessingham had no intention of amplifying his statement, he asked: "Why not, Mr. Lessingham?"

"There aren't many people I actually like as opposed to tolerate, and she didn't happen to be one of them. There was no particular reason. Does there have to be? You and your sergeant may not like each other, for all I know. It doesn't mean that either of you is planning murder. And, talking about murder, which is why I assume I'm here, I have an alibi for Sunday night. Perhaps I had better give it to you now. I have a thirty-foot sailing boat berthed at Blakeney. I went out with her on the morning tide and stayed out until nearly ten at night. I have a witness to my departure, Ed Wilkinson, who berths his fishing smack next to my boat, but no witness to my return. There was enough wind in the morning to sail, and then I anchored, caught a couple of cod and some whiting and cooked them for lunch. I had food, wine, books and my radio. There was nothing else I needed. It may not be the most satisfactory of alibis, but it has the merit of simplicity and truth."

Oliphant asked: "You had a dinghy with you?"

"I had my inflatable dinghy on the cabin roof. And, at the risk of exciting you, I have to say that I also carried my collapsible bicycle. But I didn't put ashore either at Larksoken headland or anywhere else, not even for the purpose of murdering Hilary Robarts."

Rickards asked: "Did you see Miss Robarts at any time during your trip? Were you in sight of the beach where she died?"

"I didn't go that far south. And I saw no one, dead or alive."

Oliphant asked: "Do you make a habit of sailing alone at the weekend?"

"I don't make a habit of anything. I used to sail with a friend. Now I sail alone."

Rickards asked him next about Blaney's portrait of Miss Robarts. He admitted that he had seen it. George Jago, the publican of the Local Hero at Lydsett, had put it up for a week in the bar, apparently at Blaney's request. He had no idea where Blaney normally kept it, and he had neither stolen it nor destroyed it. If anyone had, he thought it was probably Robarts herself.

Oliphant said: "And thrown it through her own window?"

Lessingham said: "You think she would have been more likely to slash it and chuck it through Blaney's? I agree. But, whoever slashed it, it wasn't Blaney."

Oliphant asked: "How can you be so sure?"

"Because a creative artist, whether he's a painter or a scientist, doesn't destroy his best work."

Oliphant said: "Miss Mair's dinner party—you gave your fellow guests a description of the Whistler's methods, including information we had specifically asked you not to divulge."

Lessingham said coolly: "One could hardly arrive two hours late for a dinner party without some explanation, and mine was, after all, unusual. I thought they were entitled to a vicarious thrill. Apart from that, to keep silent would have needed more self-control than I was capable of at the time. Murdered and mutilated bodies are your trade, of course. Those of us who have chosen less exciting jobs tend to find them distressing. I knew I could trust my fellow guests not to talk to the press, and as far as I know none of them did. Anyway, why ask me what happened on the Thursday night? Adam Dalgliesh was a guest at the dinner party, so you have a more experienced and no doubt, from your point of view, a more reliable witness. I won't say a police spy: that would be unfair."

Rickards spoke for the first time in minutes. He said: "It would also be inaccurate and offensive."

Lessingham turned on him with a cool "Exactly. That's why I haven't used the word. And now, if you've no more questions, I have a power station to run."

6
⊠

It was after midday before the interviews at the power station were completed and Rickards and Oliphant were ready to leave for Martyr's Cottage. They left Gary Price to cope with the enquiry forms and arranged to pick him up after the interview with Alice Mair, which Rickards felt might be more fruitful with two officers rather than one. Alice Mair received them calmly at the door with no apparent sign either of anxiety or of curiosity, glanced perfunctorily at their identity cards and invited them in. They might, Rickards thought, have been technicians arriving later than expected to repair the television set. And they were, he saw, expected to interview her in the kitchen. At first it struck him as an odd choice but then, looking round, he supposed you could hardly call it a kitchen: more like an office, sitting room and kitchen combined. Its size surprised him and he found himself wondering irrelevantly whether she had knocked down a wall to provide such overgenerous working space. He wondered, too, what Susie would think of it and decided that she would find it unsettling. Susie liked her house to be clearly defined by function; the kitchen was for working, the dining room for eating, the lounge for watching television and the bedroom for sleeping and, once a week, for making love. He and Oliphant sat in two cushioned, high-backed wicker chairs on each side of the fireplace. His was extremely comfortable, gently containing his long limbs. Miss Mair took the chair at her desk and swivelled it round to face him.

"My brother, of course, gave me the news of the murder as soon as he got home last night. I can't help you about Hilary Robarts's death, I'm afraid. I was at home the whole of yesterday evening and saw and heard nothing. But I can tell you a little about her portrait. Would you and Sergeant Oliphant care for coffee?"

Rickards would have cared; he found himself unexpectedly thirsty; but he declined for both of them. The invitation had sounded perfunctory, and he hadn't missed her quick glance towards the desk-top stacked with orderly piles of printed pages and a typewritten man-uscript. It looked as if they had interrupted her in the business of proofreading. Well, if she was busy, so was he. And he found himself irritated—unreasonably, he felt—by her self-possession. He hadn't expected to find her in hysterics or under sedation for grief. The victim wasn't her next-of-kin. But the woman had worked closely with Alex Mair, had been a guest at Martyr's Cottage, had, according to Dal-gliesh, dined there only four days ago. It was disconcerting to find that Alice Mair could sit quietly correcting proofs, a job which surely required concentrated attention. The killing of Robarts had taken considerable nerve. His suspicion of her was hardly serious; he didn't really see this as a woman's crime. But he let suspicion enter his mind like a barb and lodge there. A remarkable woman, he thought. Perhaps this interview was going to be more productive than he had expected.

He asked: "You keep house for your brother, Miss Mair?"

"No, I keep house for myself. My brother happens to live here when he is in Norfolk, which naturally is for most of the week. He could hardly administer Larksoken Power Station from his flat in London. If I'm at home and cook dinner, he usually shares it. I take the view that it would be unreasonable to demand that he make himself an omelette merely to affirm the principle of shared domestic responsibilities. But I don't see what relevance my housekeeping ar-rangements have to Hilary Robarts's murder. Could we, perhaps, get on to what happened last night?"

They were interrupted. There was a knock at the door and, with-out an apology, Alice Mair got up and went through to the hall. They heard a lighter, feminine voice, and a woman followed her into the kitchen. Miss Mair introduced her as Mrs. Dennison from the Old Rectory. She was a pretty, gentle-looking woman, conventionally dressed in a tweed skirt and twin set, and was obviously distressed.

Rickards approved both of her appearance and of the distress. This was how he expected a woman to look and behave after a particularly brutal murder. The two men had got up at her entrance, and she took Oliphant's chair while he moved one for himself from the kitchen table.

She turned to Rickards impulsively: "I'm sorry, I'm interrupting, but I felt I had to get out of the house. This is appalling news, Inspector. Are you absolutely certain that it couldn't have been the Whistler?"

Rickards said: "Not this time, madam."

Alice Mair said: "The timing's wrong. I told you that when I rang early this morning, Meg. The police wouldn't be here now if it wasn't. It couldn't have been the Whistler."

"I know that's what you said. But I couldn't help hoping that there'd been a mistake, that he'd killed her and then himself, that Hilary Robarts was his last victim."

Rickards said: "In a sense she was, Mrs. Dennison."

Alice Mair said calmly: "I think it's called a copycat murder. There's more than one psychopath in the world, and that kind of madness can be infectious, apparently."

"Of course, but how horrible! Having started, will he too go on, like the Whistler did, death after death, no one feeling safe?"

Rickards said: "I shouldn't let that worry you, Mrs. Dennison."

She turned to him almost fiercely. "But of course it worries me! It must worry us all. We've lived so long with the horror of the Whistler. It's appalling to think that it's started all over again."

Alice Mair got up. "You need coffee, Meg. Chief Inspector Rickards and Sergeant Oliphant have declined, but I think we need it."

Rickards wasn't going to let her get away with that. He said firmly: "If you're making it, Miss Mair, I think I'll change my mind. I'd be glad of a coffee. You too no doubt, Sergeant."

And now, he thought, there'll be a further delay while she grinds beans and no one can talk above the noise. Why can't she just pour boiling water on coffee grains like everyone else?

But the coffee, when it did come, was excellent, and he found it unexpectedly comforting. Mrs. Dennison took her mug in her hands and cradled it like a child at bedtime. Then she put it down on the hearth and turned to Rickards.

"Look, perhaps you'd rather I went. I'll just have my coffee and then go back to the rectory. If you want to talk to me I'll be there for the rest of the day."

Miss Mair said: "You may as well stay and hear what happened last night. It has its points of interest." She turned to Rickards. "As I told you, I was here the whole of the evening, from half past five. My brother left for the power station shortly after seven-thirty, and I settled down to work on my proofs. I switched on the answerphone to avoid interruptions."

Rickards asked: "And you didn't leave the cottage for any purpose during the whole of the evening?"

"Not until after half past nine, when I left for the Blaneys'. But perhaps I could tell the story in sequence, Chief Inspector. At about ten past eight I switched off the machine, thinking that there might be an important call for my brother. It was then I heard George Jago's message that the Whistler was dead."

"You didn't ring anyone else to let them know?"

"I knew that wasn't necessary. Jago runs his own information service. He'd make sure that everyone knew. I came back into the kitchen and worked on my proofs until about half past nine. Then I thought that I'd collect Hilary Robarts's portrait from Ryan Blaney. I'd promised to drop it in at the gallery in Norwich on my way to London, and I wanted to make an early start next morning. I tend to be a little obsessive about time and didn't want to go even a short distance out of my way. I rang Scudder's Cottage to let him know that I was collecting the portrait, but the number was engaged. I tried several times and then got out the car and drove over. I must have been there within fifteen minutes. I'd written a note to him to slip through the door telling him that I'd taken the picture as arranged."

"Wasn't that a little unusual, Miss Mair? Why not knock at the cottage and collect it from him personally?"

"Because he had taken the trouble to tell me when I first saw it precisely where it was kept and where I could find the light switch to the left of the door. I took that as a reasonable indication that he didn't expect, or indeed want, to be disturbed by a call at the cottage. Mr. Dalgliesh was with me at the time."

"But that was odd, wasn't it? He must have thought it was a good portrait. He wouldn't wish to exhibit it otherwise. You'd think he'd want to hand it over personally."

"Would you? It didn't strike me that way. He's an extremely

private man, more so since the death of his wife. He doesn't welcome visitors, particularly not women who might cast a critical eye on the tidiness of the cottage and the state of the children. I could understand that. I wouldn't have welcomed it myself."

"So you went straight to his painting shed? Where is that?"

"About thirty yards to the left of the cottage. It's a small wooden shack. I imagine that it was originally a washhouse or a smoking shed. I shone my torch on the path to the door, although that was hardly necessary. The moonlight was exceptionally bright. It was unlocked. And if you're now about to say that that, too, was odd, you don't understand life on the headland. We're very remote here and we get into the habit of leaving doors unlocked. I don't think it would ever occur to him to lock his painting shed. I switched on the light to the left of the door and saw that the picture wasn't where I expected."

"Could you describe exactly what happened. The details, please, as far as you can recall them."

"We're talking about yesterday night, Chief Inspector. It isn't difficult to recall the details. I left the light on in the shed and knocked on the front door of the cottage. There were lights on, downstairs only, but the curtains were drawn. I had to wait for about a minute before he came. He half-opened the door but didn't invite me in. I said, 'Good evening, Ryan.' He just nodded, but didn't reply. There was a strong smell of whisky. Then I said, 'I've come to collect the portrait, but it isn't in the shed, or if it is I haven't found it.' Then he said, his speech rather slurred, 'It's to the left of the door, wrapped in cardboard and brown paper. A brown-paper parcel, Sellotaped.' I said, 'Not now.' He didn't reply but came out to me, leaving the door open. We went to the shed together."

"Was he walking steadily?"

"He was very far from steady, but he could certainly keep on his feet. When I said he smelt of drink and his voice was slurred, I didn't mean that he was totally incapable. But I got the impression that he had spent the evening in fairly continuous drinking. He stood in the doorway of the shed with me at his shoulder. He didn't speak for about half a minute. Then all he said was 'Yes, it's gone.' "

"How did he sound?" As she didn't reply he asked patiently, "Was he shocked? Angry? Surprised? Or too drunk to care?"

"I heard the question, Chief Inspector. Hadn't you better ask him how he felt? I'm only competent to describe what he looked like, what he said and what he did."

"What did he do?"

"He turned and beat his clenched hands against the lintel of the door. Then he rested his head against the wood for a minute. It seemed at the time a histrionic gesture, but I imagine that it was perfectly genuine."

"And then?"

"I said to him, 'Hadn't we better telephone the police? We could do it from here if your telephone is working. I've been trying to get through to you, but it's always engaged.' He didn't reply and I followed him back to the cottage. He didn't invite me in, but I stood in the doorway. He went over to the recess under the stairs and then said: 'The receiver isn't properly on. That's why you couldn't get through.' I said again, 'Why not telephone the police now? The sooner the theft is reported the better.' He turned to me and just said, 'Tomorrow. Tomorrow.' Then he went back to his chair. I persisted. I said, 'Shall I ring, Ryan, or will you? This really is important.' He said, 'I will. Tomorrow. Good night.' That seemed a clear indication to me that he wanted to be alone, so I left."

"And during this visit you saw no one other than Mr. Blaney. The children weren't up, for example?"

"I took it the children were in bed. I neither saw nor heard them."

"And you didn't discuss the Whistler's death?"

"I assumed George Jago had telephoned Mr. Blaney, probably before he rang me. And what was there to discuss? Neither Ryan nor I was in a mood for doorstep chatting."

But it was, thought Rickards, a curious reticence on both their parts. Had she been so anxious to get away and he to see her go? Or, for one of them, had an event more traumatic than a missing portrait driven even the Whistler temporarily out of mind?

There was a vital question Rickards needed to ask. The implications were obvious and she was far too intelligent a woman not to see them.

"Miss Mair, from what you saw of Mr. Blaney that night, do you think he could have driven a car?"

"Impossible. And he hadn't a car to drive. He has a small van, but it has just failed its MOT."

"Or ridden a bicycle?"

"I suppose he could have tried, but he'd have been in a ditch within minutes."

Rickards's mind was already busy with calculations. He wouldn't get the results of the autopsy until Wednesday, but if Hilary Robarts had taken her swim, as was her custom, immediately after the headlines to the main news, which on Sundays was at nine-ten, then she must have died at about half past nine. At 9.45 or a little later, according to Alice Mair, Ryan Blaney was in his cottage and drunk. By no stretch of the imagination could he have committed a singularly ingenious murder, requiring a steady hand, nerves and the capacity to plan, and been back in his cottage by 9.45. If Alice Mair was telling the truth, she had given Blaney an alibi. He, on the other hand, would certainly be unable to give one to her.

Rickards had almost forgotten Meg Dennison, but now he looked across to where she sat like a distressed child, hands in her lap, her untasted coffee still standing in the hearth.

"Mrs. Dennison, did you know last night that the Whistler was dead?"

"Oh yes. Mr. Jago telephoned me too, about a quarter to ten."

Alice Mair said: "He probably tried to get you earlier, but you were on the way to Norwich station with the Copleys?"

Meg Dennison spoke directly to Rickards: "I should have been, but the car broke down. I had to get Sparks and his taxi in a hurry. Luckily he could just do it, but he had to go straight on to a job in Ipswich, so he couldn't bring me back. He saw the Copleys safely on the train for me."

"Did you leave the Old Rectory at any time during the evening?"

Mrs. Dennison looked up and met his eyes. "No," she said, "no, after I'd seen them off I didn't leave the house." Then she paused and said, "I'm sorry, I did go out into the garden very briefly. It would be more accurate to say that I didn't leave the grounds. And now, if you'll all excuse me, please, I'd like to go home."

She got up, then turned again to Rickards: "If you want to question me, Chief Inspector, I'll be at the Old Rectory."

She was gone before the two men could get to their feet, almost stumbling from the room. Miss Mair made no move to follow her and, seconds later, they heard the front door close.

There was a moment's silence, broken by Oliphant. Nodding towards the hearth, he said: "Funny. She hasn't even touched her coffee."

But Rickards had a final question for Alice Mair. He said: "It must have been getting on for midnight when Dr. Mair got home yesterday night. Did you ring the power station to find out if he'd left or why he was delayed?"

She said coolly: "It didn't occur to me, Chief Inspector. Since Alex is neither my child nor my husband, I am spared the compulsion of checking on his movements. I am not my brother's keeper."

Oliphant had been staring at her with his sombre, suspicious eyes. Now he said: "But he lives with you, doesn't he? You do talk, don't you? You must have known about his relationship with Hilary Robarts, for example. Did you approve?"

Alice Mair's colour didn't change, but her voice was like steel.

"Either to approve or disapprove would have been as presumptuously impertinent as was that question. If you wish to discuss my brother's private life, I suggest that you do so with him."

Rickards said quietly: "Miss Mair, a woman has been brutally done to death and her body mutilated. She was a woman you knew. In the light of that outrage, I hope you won't feel the need to be oversensitive to questions which are bound to seem at times both presumptuous and impertinent."

Anger had made him articulate. Their eyes met and held. He knew that his were hard with fury, both with Oliphant's tactlessness and her response. But the grey eyes which met his were less easy to read. He thought he could detect surprise, followed by wariness, reluctant respect, an almost speculative interest.

And when, fifteen minutes later, she escorted her visitors to the door, he was a little surprised when she held out her hand. As he shook it, she said: "Please forgive me, Chief Inspector, if I was ungracious. Yours is a disagreeable but necessary job and you are entitled to co-operation. As far as I'm concerned, you will get it."

7

⊠

Even without the garishly painted sign, no one from Norfolk would have been in any doubt about the identity of the local hero after whom the Lydsett pub was named, nor could a stranger fail to recognize the Admiral's hat with the star, the much-decorated chest, the black patch over one eye, the pinned-up, empty sleeve. Rickards reflected that he had seen worse paintings of Lord Nelson but not many. This made him look like the Princess Royal in drag.

George Jago had obviously decided that the interview should take place in the saloon bar, wrapped now in the dim quietness of the late-afternoon doldrums. He and his wife led Rickards and Oliphant to a small pub table, wooden-topped and with ornate cast-iron legs, set close to the huge and empty fireplace. They settled themselves round it rather, thought Rickards, like four ill-assorted people proposing to conduct a séance in appropriately ill-lit seclusion. Mrs. Jago was an angular, bright-eyed, sharp-featured woman who looked at Oliphant as if she had seen his type before and was prepared to stand no nonsense. She was heavily made up. Two moons of bright rouge adorned each cheek, her long mouth was painted with a matching lipstick and her fingers, blood-tipped talons, were laden with a variety of rings. Her hair was so glossily black that it looked unnatural and was piled high in the front in three rows of tight curls and swept upwards and secured with combs at the back and sides. She was wearing a pleated skirt topped with a blouse in some shiny material striped in red, white and blue, buttoned high at the neck and hung about with gold chains in which she looked like a bit-part actress auditioning for the part of a barmaid in an Ealing comedy. No woman could have been less suitably dressed for a country pub, yet both she and her husband, seated side-by-side with the brightly expectant look of children on their best behaviour, looked perfectly at home in the bar and with each other. Oliphant had made it his business to find out something of their past and had relayed the information to Rickards as they drove to the pub. George Jago had previously been the licensee of a pub in Catford, but the couple had moved to Lydsett four years ago, partly because Mrs. Jago's brother, Charlie Sparks, owned a garage and car-hire business on the edge of the village and was looking for part-time help. George Jago occasionally drove for him, leaving Mrs. Jago in charge of the bar. They had settled happily in the village, took a lively part in community activities and appeared not to miss the raucous life of the city. Rickards reflected that East Anglia had accepted and absorbed more eccentric couples. Come to that, it had absorbed him.

George Jago looked more the part of a country publican, a stocky, cheerful-faced man with bright, blinking eyes and an air of suppressed energy. He had certainly expended it on the interior of the pub. The low, oak-beamed saloon bar was a cluttered and ill-arranged museum devoted to Nelson's memory. Jago must have scoured East Anglia in his search for objects with even a tenuous relationship with the Admiral. Above the open fireplace was a huge lithograph of the scene in the cockpit of *Victory* with Nelson romantically dying in Hardy's arms. The remaining walls were covered with paintings and prints, including the principal sea battles, the Nile, Copenhagen, Trafalgar; one or two of Lady Hamilton, including a lurid reproduction of Romney's famous portrait; while commemorative plates were ranged each side of the doors and the blackened oak beams were festooned with rows of decorated memorial mugs—few of them original, to judge from the brightness of the decoration. Along the top of one wall a row of pennants spelled out what was presumably the famous signal, and a fishing net had been slung across the ceiling to enhance the general nautical atmosphere. And suddenly, looking up into the brown tar-tangled netting, Rickards remembered. He had been here before. He and Susie had stopped here for a drink when they had been exploring the coast one weekend in the first winter of their marriage. They hadn't stayed for long; Susie had complained that the bar was too crowded and smoke-filled. He could recall the bench at which they had sat, the one against the wall to the left of the door. He had drunk half a pint of bitter, Susie a medium sherry. Then, with the fire blazing, the flames leaping from the crackling logs and the bar loud with cheerful Norfolk voices, the pub had seemed interestingly nostalgic and cosy. But now, in the dim light of an autumn afternoon, the clutter of artifacts, so few of them either genuine or of particular merit, seemed to Rickards to trivialize and diminish both the building's own long history and the Admiral's achievements. He felt a sudden onrush of claustrophobia and had to resist an impulse to throw open the door and let in fresh air and the twentieth century.

As Oliphant said afterwards, it was a pleasure to interview George Jago. He didn't greet you as if you were a necessary but unwelcome technician of doubtful competence who was taking up his valuable time. He didn't use words as if they were secret signals to conceal thoughts rather than express them, or subtly intimidate you with his superior intelligence. He didn't see an interview with the police as a battle of wits in which he necessarily had the advantage, or react to perfectly ordinary questions with a disconcerting mixture of fear and endurance, as if you were secret police from a totalitarian dictatorship. All in all, he pointed out, it made a pleasant change.

Jago admitted cheerfully that he had telephoned the Blaneys and Miss Mair shortly after 7.30 on Sunday with news that the Whistler was dead. How did he know? Because one of the police on the enquiry had telephoned home to let his wife know it was all right for their daughter to go alone to a party that night and the wife had telephoned her brother Harry Upjohn, who kept the Crown and Anchor outside Cromer, and Harry, who was a friend of his, had rung him. He remembered exactly what he had said to Theresa Blaney.

"Tell your dad they've found the Whistler's body. He's dead. Suicide. Killed himself at Easthaven. No need to worry now."

He had phoned the Blaneys because he knew that Ryan liked his pint at night but hadn't dared to leave the children while the Whistler was at large. Blaney hadn't come in that evening, but that didn't really signify. With Miss Mair he had left the message on her answering machine in much the same terms. He hadn't telephoned Mrs. Dennison because he thought she would be on her way to Norwich with the Copleys."

Rickards said: "But you did ring her later?"

It was Mrs. Jago who explained. "That was after I reminded him. I was at half-past-six Evensong and, afterwards, I went home with Sadie Sparks to settle arrangements for the autumn jumble sale. She found a note from Charlie to say that he'd been called out on two urgent jobs, taking the Copleys to Norwich and then fetching a couple from Ipswich. So when I got back I told George that Mrs. Dennison hadn't driven the Copleys to the train and that he ought to phone her straight away to tell her about the Whistler. I mean, she'd be more likely to get a good night's rest knowing he was dead than wondering if he was lurking in the rectory bushes. So George rang."

Jago said: "It was close on nine-fifteen by then, I reckon. I would have telephoned later anyway, expecting she'd be back by half past nine."

Rickards said: "And Mrs. Dennison answered the phone?"

"Not then she didn't. But I tried again about thirty minutes later and got her then."

Rickards asked: "So you didn't tell any of them that the body had been found at the Balmoral Hotel?"

"Didn't know, did I? All I was told by Harry Upjohn was that the Whistler had been found and that he was dead. I dare say the police kept it quiet—where exactly he was found, I mean. You wouldn't want a lot of morbid sightseers round the place. Nor would the hotel manager, come to that."

"And early this morning you rang round again to say that Miss Robarts had been murdered. How did you discover that?"

"Saw the police cars passing, didn't I? So I got on my bike and went up to the gate. Your chaps had left it open, so I shut it again and waited. When they came back I opened the gate for them and asked what was up."

Rickards said: "You seem to have an extraordinary talent for extracting information from the police."

"Well, I know some of them, don't I? The local chaps, anyway. They drink in the Hero. The driver of the first car through wouldn't say anything. Nor would the driver of the mortuary van. But when the third car came through and stopped while I opened and shut the gate again, I asked who was dead and they told me. I mean, I know a mortuary van when I see one."

"Who exactly told you?" asked Oliphant belligerently. George Jago turned on him his bright and innocent comedian's gaze.

"Couldn't say, could I? One policeman is much like another. Someone told me."

"So you rang round early this morning? Why then? Why wait?"

"Because it was after midnight by then. Folk like a bit of news but they like their sleep more. But I rang Ryan Blaney first thing today."

"Why him?"

"Why not? When you've got news it's human nature to pass it on to an interested party."

Oliphant said: "And he was certainly an interested party. Must have come as something of a relief."

"Might have done, might not. I didn't speak to him. I told Theresa."

Oliphant said: "So you didn't speak to Mr. Blaney either when you rang last night or this morning. Bit odd, wasn't it?"

"Depends how you look at it. The first time he was in his painting shed. He doesn't like being called to the phone when he's working. No point, anyway. I told Theresa and she told him."

Rickards said: "How do you know she told him?"

"Because she said so when I rang this morning. Why shouldn't she tell him?"

"But you can't know for certain that she did?"

Mrs. Jago said suddenly: "And you can't know for certain that she didn't. What does it matter, anyway? He knows now. We all do. We know about the Whistler and we know about Miss Robarts. And maybe if you'd caught the Whistler a year ago Miss Robarts would still be alive."

Oliphant asked quickly: "What do you mean by that, Mrs. Jago?"

"What they call a copycat murder, isn't it? That's the talk in the village, anyway, apart from those who still think the Whistler did it and you've got your times all wrong. And old Humphrey, of course, who thinks it was the Whistler's ghost still on the job."

Rickards said: "We're interested in a portrait of Miss Robarts which was painted recently by Mr. Blaney. Have either of you seen it? Did he talk about it?"

Mrs. Jago said: "Of course we've seen it. Had it hanging in the bar, didn't we? And I knew that it would bring bad luck. It was an evil picture if ever I saw one."

Jago turned to his wife and explained with patient emphasis: "I don't see how you can say a picture is evil, Doris, not a picture. Things can't be evil. An inanimate object is neither good nor evil. Evil is what is done by people."

"And what is thought by people, George, and that picture came out of evil thoughts, so I say that picture was evil."

She spoke firmly but with no trace of obstinacy or resentment. Obviously this was the kind of marital argument, conducted without acrimony, and with scrupulous fairness, which they both relished. For a few minutes their attention was solely on each other.

Jago went on: "Granted it wasn't the kind of picture you'd want to hang on your sitting-room wall."

"Or in the bar, come to that. Pity you ever did, George."

"Right enough. Still, I reckon it didn't give anyone any ideas they didn't have already. And you can't say that it was evil, not a picture, Doris."

"All right, suppose you get an instrument of torture, something used by the Gestapo." Mrs. Jago looked round the bar as if among its clutter she might reasonably expect to find an example. "I'd say that thing was evil. I wouldn't give it houseroom."

"You could say it was used for an evil purpose, Doris; that's different."

Rickards asked: "Why exactly did you hang the portrait in the bar?"

"Because he asked me, that's why. I usually find room for one or two of his small water-colours, and sometimes he sells them and sometimes not. I always tell him they've got to be seascapes. I mean, it's all the Admiral here, isn't it, it's all nautical. But he was dead keen on having this up, and I said I'd keep it for a week. He brought it down on his bike on Monday the twelfth."

"In the hope of selling it?"

"Oh, it wasn't for sale, not that picture wasn't. He made that very plain."

Oliphant said: "So what was the point of putting it up?"

"That's what I said." Jago turned triumphantly to the sergeant as if recognizing a fellow expert in logic. " 'What's the point in putting it up if you don't want to sell it?' I said. 'Let them look at it,' he said. 'I want them to see it. I want the whole world to see it.' A bit optimistic, I thought. After all, we're not the National Gallery."

"More like the National Maritime Museum really," said Doris surprisingly and beamed at them happily.

"Where did you find room for it?"

"On that wall opposite the door. Took down the two pictures of the Battle of the Nile, didn't I?"

"And how many people did see it in those seven days?"

"You're asking me how many customers I had. I mean, if they came in they saw it. Couldn't hardly miss it, could they? Doris wanted to take it down, but I promised I'd keep it up until the Monday, so I did. Glad when he came and took it away, though. Like I said, it's all commemorative here. It's all the Admiral. It didn't seem to go with the décor. It wasn't here long. He said he'd call for it on the morning of the nineteenth and he did."

"Did anyone from the headland or the power station see it?"

"Those who came in. The Local Hero isn't really their regular local. Most of them want to get away from the place at the end of the day, and who's to blame them? I mean, living over the shop is all right, but not that shop."

"Was there much talk about it? Did anyone ask where he kept it, for example?"

"Not to me. I reckon most of them knew where he kept it. I mean, he talked a bit about his painting shed. And if he had wanted to sell, he wouldn't have got any offers. I'll tell you someone who did see it, though. Hilary Robarts."

"When was this?"

"The evening after he brought it in, about seven o'clock. She does come in here from time to time. Never drinks much, just a couple of dry sherries. Takes them over to the seat by the fire."

"Alone?"

"Usually she is. Once or twice she had Dr. Mair with her. But she was alone that Tuesday."

"What did she do when she saw the picture?"

"Stood and looked at it. The pub was pretty full at the time, and everyone fell silent. You know how it is. They were all watching. I couldn't see her face, because her back was to me. Then she walked over to the bar and said: 'I've changed my mind about drinking here. Obviously you don't welcome customers from Larksoken.' Then she went out. Well, I welcome customers from anywhere if they can hold their drink and don't ask for credit, but I didn't reckon she'd be much loss."

"So she wasn't particularly popular on the headland?"

"I don't know about the headland. She wasn't particularly popular in this pub."

Doris Jago said: "Scheming, she was, to turn the Blaneys out of Scudder's Cottage. And him a widower trying to bring up four kids. Where did she think he was going to go? He gets family allowance and other bits of welfare help, but that isn't going to find him another cottage. But I'm sorry she's dead, of course. I mean, you have to be, don't you? It's not a nice thing to happen to anybody. We'll be sending a wreath from the Local Hero."

"Was that the last time you saw her?"

Mrs. Jago said: "The last time George did. I saw her on the headland yesterday afternoon. Must have been only a few hours before she died. I said to George: Maybe I was the last person to see her alive, well, me and Neil Pascoe and Amy. You don't think at the time, do you? We can't see into the future, nor wouldn't want to. Sometimes I look at that power station and wonder if we'll all end up dead on the beach."

Oliphant asked how it came she was on the headland.

"Delivering the church magazine, wasn't I? I always do on the last Sunday afternoon in the month. Collect them after morning service, then take them round after dinner. Lunch to you, maybe, we call it dinner."

Rickards had called the main meal dinner all his life and still did, despite his mother-in-law's unceasing campaign to raise his social status. Her midday meal was luncheon and her evening meal dinner even if it consisted, as it often did, of sardines on toast. He wondered what they had eaten today. He said: "I didn't realize that people on the headland were church-goers, other than the Copleys, of course."

"And Mrs. Dennison. Very regular, she is. I can't say the others actually come to church—well, not to say actually attend—not to the services, but they do take the parish magazine." Mrs. Jago's tone suggested that there were depths of irreligion to which even the headlanders would hardly sink. She added: "All except the Blaneys, of course. Well, they wouldn't, being RC. At least she was RC, poor dear, and the children are of course. I mean, they have to be, don't they? I don't think Ryan's anything. He's an artist. I never delivered to Scudder's Cottage even when his wife was alive. Anyway RCs don't have parish magazines."

George Jago said: "I wouldn't say that, Doris. I wouldn't go that far. They might."

"We've lived here for four years, George, and Father McKee is in the bar often enough and I've never seen one."

"Well, you wouldn't, would you?"

"I might have, George, if there was one to see. They're different from us. No Harvest Festival and no parish magazines."

Her husband explained patiently: "They're different because they have different dogmas. It's all to do with dogma, Doris, it's nothing to do with Harvest Festival and parish magazines."

"I know it's to do with dogma. The Pope tells them that the blessed Virgin Mary ascended into heaven, and they all have to believe it. I know all about dogma."

Before Jago could open his mouth to dispute this claim to infallibility, Rickards said quickly: "So you delivered the magazines to the headlanders yesterday afternoon. When precisely?"

"Well, I reckon I started off at about three, or maybe a bit after. We have a latish dinner on Sundays, and we didn't get started on the spotted-dick pudding much before two-thirty. And then George loaded the dishwasher and I got ready to go. Say three-fifteen, if you want to be particular."

Jago said: "You were well gone by three-fifteen, Doris. I'd say it was nearer three-ten."

Oliphant said impatiently: "I don't think five minutes matters either way."

George Jago turned on him a glance of nicely judged surprise and mild rebuke. "They might. They could be crucial. I'd say five minutes in a murder investigation could be crucial."

Mrs. Jago added her reproof: "One minute could be crucial if that was the actual minute she died. Crucial for her, anyway. I don't see how you can say they don't matter."

Rickards thought it was time to intervene: "I agree that five minutes could be important, Mr. Jago, but hardly these five minutes. Perhaps your wife would tell us exactly what she did and saw."

"Well, I got on my bicycle. George always offers to drive me, but he has enough driving in the week and I don't like to bother him to get out the car. Not Sundays. Not after roast beef and spotted dick."

"It'd be no trouble, Doris. I've told you that. No trouble."

"I know, George. Haven't I just said you'd be willing enough? I like the exercise and I'm always back before dark." She turned to Rickards and explained: "George never liked me to be out after dark, not with the Whistler around."

Oliphant said: "So you left between three-ten and three-fifteen and cycled off over the headland."

"With the church magazines in the basket, same as usual. First I went to the caravan. I always go to the caravan first. It's a bit tricky now with Neil Pascoe."

"How is it tricky, Mrs. Jago?"

"Well, he's asked us more than once to put out his magazine—*Nuclear Newsletter*, he calls it—in the bar for people to buy or maybe read for free. But George and I have always set our faces against it. I mean, we get some of the staff from Larksoken in the pub and it's not nice, is it, to be faced with a paper saying that what you're doing is wicked and ought to be put a stop to. Not when all you want is a quiet drink. Not everybody in Lydsett agrees with what he's doing. You can't deny that Larksoken Power Station has brought more business into the village, and jobs too. And you've got to trust people, haven't you? I mean, if Dr. Mair says nuclear power is safe, then it probably is. Then again, you can't help wondering, can you?"

Rickards said patiently: "But Mr. Pascoe took the church magazine?"

"Well, it's only ten pence, and I suppose he likes to know what's going on in the parish. When he first arrived on the headland—two years ago, it was now—I called on him and asked if he'd like to take the magazine. He seemed a bit surprised but he said he would and paid his ten pence, and he's had it ever since. If he doesn't want it he's only got to say so."

Rickards asked: "And what happened at the caravan?"

"I saw Hilary Robarts, same as I said. I gave Neil the magazine and collected the money and was having a bit of a chat with him

inside the caravan when she drove up in that red Golf of hers. Amy
was outside with the kid, bringing in some of his clothes from a
washing line they'd rigged up there. When he saw the car Neil got
out of the caravan and went over and stood by Amy. Miss Robarts got
out of the car and they both stood looking at her, not speaking, just
standing side-by-side watching her. It wasn't much of a welcoming
committee, but, then, what would you expect? Then, when Miss Robarts got within six yards or so of them, Timmy trotted over to her
and grabbed at her slacks. He's a friendly little beggar and he didn't
mean any harm. You know how kids are. But he'd been mucking
about in that muddy patch under the tap and started smearing the
stuff all over her trousers. She pushed him away none too gently. The
kid fell flat on his bum and started bawling, and then all hell was let
loose."

Oliphant asked: "What was said?"

"Now, that I can't exactly remember. There were a lot of words
used which you don't expect to hear on a Sunday. Some beginning
with *F* and some beginning with *C*. Use your imagination."

Rickards said: "Were any threats made?"

"Depends what you mean by threats. There was a lot of shouting
and screaming. Not Neil. He was just standing there, looking so white
I thought he was going to faint. It was Amy who was making the
most noise. Anyone would think Miss Robarts had gone for the kid
with a knife. I can't remember the half of it. Ask Neil Pascoe. Miss
Robarts didn't seem to notice that I was there. Ask Amy and Neil.
They'll tell you."

Rickards said: "You tell me too. It's helpful to get different people's
views of an incident. You get a more accurate picture that way."

Jago interposed: "More accurate? Different maybe. It'd only be
more accurate if they were all telling the truth."

For a moment Rickards feared that Mrs. Jago was prepared to
challenge the assertion with another demonstration of semantics. He
said: "Well, I'm sure that you're telling the truth, Mrs. Jago. That's
why we're starting with you. Can you remember what was actually
said?"

"I think Miss Robarts said that she had called to say that she was
thinking of dropping her legal action but that now she would bloody
well go ahead with it and she hoped it would ruin them both. 'You
and your whore.' Charming, wasn't it?"

"She used those precise words?"

"And a good few others which I can't exactly remember."

"What I mean is, Mrs. Jago, Miss Robarts was the one making the threats?"

For the first time Mrs. Jago seemed uneasy; then she said: "Well, she always was the one making the threats, wasn't she? Neil Pascoe wasn't suing her."

"What happened next?"

"Nothing. Miss Robarts got into the car and drove away. Amy lugged the kid into the caravan and slammed the door. Neil looked so miserable I thought he'd burst out crying, so I thought I'd say something to cheer him up."

"What was that, Mrs. Jago?"

"I said she was a vicious evil-minded bitch and one day someone would do her in."

Jago said: "Not very nice, Doris. Not on a Sunday."

Doris Jago said complacently: "Not very nice any day of the week, but I wasn't far wrong, was I?"

Rickards asked: "What happened then, Mrs. Jago?"

"I got on with delivering the magazines, didn't I? First of all I went to the Old Rectory. I don't usually call there, because the Copleys and Mrs. Dennison are usually at morning service and collect their own magazines, but they weren't there yesterday and I was a bit worried. Thought something might be wrong. But it was just that they were too busy packing to attend. The Copleys were off to stay with their daughter in Wiltshire. Nice for them, I thought, and it'll give Mrs. Dennison a bit of a rest. She offered me a cup of tea but I said I wouldn't wait, because I could see she was busy getting on with their high tea. But I did sit in the kitchen with her for five minutes and had a bit of a chat. She said that some of the staff at Larksoken had given some very nice children's clothes for the jumble which might fit the Blaney twins, and she wondered whether Ryan Blaney would be interested. She'd price them up and then he could have his choice before they were taken off for the sale. We've done that once before, but we have to manage it very tactfully. If Ryan thought we were offering charity he wouldn't take the clothes. But it isn't a charity, is it? It's in aid of church funds. I see him when he comes into the pub, and Mrs. Dennison thought that the suggestion might come better from me."

"And after calling at the Old Rectory?"

"Then I went on to Martyr's Cottage. Miss Mair has a bill enclosed with the magazine every six months, so I never bother to collect the ten pence. Sometimes she's busy and sometimes she just isn't there, so I usually just put the magazine through the letter box."

"Did you see whether she was at home on Sunday?"

"I never saw skin nor hide of her. Then I went on to the last cottage, where Hilary Robarts lived. She'd got home by then, of course. I could see the red Golf outside the garage door. But I don't usually knock with her either. She isn't the kind of woman who'd welcome you in for five minutes' chat and a cuppa."

Oliphant said: "So you didn't see her?"

"I'd already seen her, hadn't I? If you're asking whether I saw her again, the answer is no, I didn't. But I heard her."

Mrs. Jago paused for effect. Rickards asked: "How do you mean you heard her, Mrs. Jago?"

"I heard her through the letter box, didn't I, when I was pushing the magazine through? And a fine old argument she was having with somebody. I'd say it was a real row. The second of the day for her. Or, maybe, the third."

Oliphant asked: "What do you mean by that, Mrs. Jago?"

"Just wondered, that's all. It struck me when she arrived at the caravan she was pretty wrought up. High colour. Edgy. You know."

"You could tell that just by looking at her from the caravan door?"

"That's right. Call it a gift."

Rickards asked: "Could you tell whether she was speaking to a man or a woman?"

"Could be either. I only heard the one voice, and that was hers. But she had someone in with her for certain, unless she was shouting at herself."

"What time would this be, Mrs. Jago?"

"About four o'clock, I reckon, or a little after. Say I got to the caravan at twenty-five past three and away by twenty-five to four. Then there was the quarter of an hour at the Old Rectory, which would bring me up to five to four, and then the ride across the headland. It must have been soon after four."

"And after that you went home?"

"That's right. And I was back here soon after half past four, wasn't I, George?"

Her husband said: "You might have been, dear. And then again you might not. I was asleep."

Ten minutes later Rickards and Oliphant left.

George and Doris watched the police car until it turned the corner of the road and went out of sight.

Doris said: "I can't say I took to that sergeant."

"I can't say I took to either of them."

"You don't think I was wrong, George, telling them about the quarrel?"

"Had no option, did you? This is murder, Doris, and you were one of the last people to see her alive. Anyway, they'll probably get it, or some of it, from Neil Pascoe. No point in keeping back what the police will find out in the end. And you only spoke the truth."

"I wouldn't say that, George, not the whole truth. I may have toned it down a bit. But I didn't tell them any lies."

For a moment they contemplated this nice distinction in silence. Then Doris said: "That mud which Timmy smeared on Miss Robarts's trousers, it came from the patch under the outside tap. Been like that for weeks. Be funny, wouldn't it, if Hilary Robarts was murdered because Neil Pascoe couldn't fix a new washer?"

George said: "Not funny, Doris. I wouldn't exactly say that it was funny."

8

⊠

Jonathan Reeves's parents had moved from their small terraced house in South London to a flat in a modern block overlooking the sea just outside Cromer. His appointment at the power station had coincided with his father's retirement, and the idea had been that they would return to a place that they had known and liked on past holidays and, as his mother had said, "provide a home for you until the right girl comes along." His father had worked for fifty years in the carpet department of a large store in Clapham, starting at fifteen, straight from school, and rising eventually to be head of the department. The firm let him have carpets at less than cost price; the off-cuts, sometimes large enough for a small room, he got for nothing, so that from childhood Jonathan had never known a room at home which wasn't carpeted from wall to wall.

Sometimes it seemed that their thick-pile wool and nylon had absorbed and deadened not only their footsteps. His mother's calm response to any event was either "Very nice," equally appropriate to an enjoyable dinner, a royal engagement or birth or a spectacular sunrise, or "Terrible, terrible, isn't it? You wonder sometimes what the world's coming to," which covered events as diverse as Kennedy's assassination, a particularly gruesome murder, children abused or violated or an IRA bomb. But she didn't wonder what the world was coming to. Wonder was an emotion long since stifled by Axminster, mohair, underfelt. It seemed to him that they lived together in amity because their emotions, debilitated by underuse or undernourishment, couldn't cope with anything as robust as a row. At the first sign of it his mother would say, "Don't raise your voice, dear, I don't like rows." Disagreement, never intense, was expressed in peevish resentment which died through lack of energy to keep it going.

He got on well enough with his sister, Jennifer, eight years his senior but now married to a local authority officer in Ipswich. Once, watching her bending over the ironing board, her features set in their familiar mask of slightly resentful concentration, he had been tempted to say, "Speak to me. Tell me what you think, about death, about evil, about what we're doing here." But her reply would have been predictable. "I know what I'm doing here. Ironing Dad's shirts."

To her acquaintances and to those she might have called friends, his mother would always speak of her husband as Mr. Reeves. "Mr. Reeves is very highly thought of by Mr. Wainwright." "Of course you could say that Mr. Reeves *is* the carpet department of Hobbs and Wainwright." The store represented those aspirations, traditions and orthodoxies that others found in their profession, in their school, regiment or religion. Mr. Wainwright senior was headmaster, colonel, their high priest; their occasional Sunday attendances at the local United Reform Chapel merely a gesture to a lesser God. And they were never regular worshippers. Jonathan suspected that this was deliberate. People might want to get to know them, involve them in mothers' meetings, whist-drives, Sunday-school outings, might even want to visit. On the Friday of his first week at secondary school the form bully had said, "Reeves's dad is shopwalker at Hobbs and Wainwright. He sold my mum a rug last week," and had minced across the room, hands obsequiously clasped. "I know madam will find that mixture extremely hard-wearing. It's a very popular line." The laughter had been sycophantic but uneasy, and the teasing, for lack of popular support, had quickly died. Most of their fathers had even less prestigious jobs.

Sometimes he thought: We can't be as ordinary, as dull as we seem, and wondered if it were some defect in himself which diminished them all so that he invested them with his own inadequacy, his own pessimism. Sometimes, too, he would take from the bureau drawer the family photograph album, which seemed to document their ordinariness: his parents stiffly posed against the rail of Cromer Promenade and at Whipsnade Zoo, himself ridiculous in cap and gown at his degree ceremony. Only one held any real interest for him, the sepia studio photograph of his great-grandfather in the First World War, perched sideways on an artificial wall with, beside him, a huge aspidistra in a Benares jar. He would gaze intensely across seventy-four years at that gentle-faced, vulnerable boy who looked, in the ill-fitting, high-buttoned serge and the grotesquely overlarge cap, more like an orphaned poor-law child than a soldier. He must have been under twenty when it was taken. And he had survived Passchendaele, the Ypres Salient, and had been discharged wounded and gassed early in 1918 with strength enough at least to father a son, but for little else. That life, he told himself, could not have been ordinary. His great-grandfather had survived four years of horror with courage, endurance and a stoical acceptance of what his God or luck had dealt him. But if not ordinary, the life seemed now of absolutely no importance to anyone. It had preserved a family, that was all. And how much did that matter? But now it struck him that his father's life had held a not-dissimilar stoicism. You couldn't, perhaps, equate fifty years with Hobbs and Wainwright with four years in France, but both had required that same dignified and stoical acceptance. He wished that he could talk to his father about his great-grandfather, about his father's early life. But it never seemed possible, and he knew that what held him back was less an inhibiting shyness than the fear that, even if he broke through this strange barrier of reticence and inarticulateness, there would be nothing there. And yet it surely hadn't always been like that. He remembered the Christmas of 1968, when his father had bought him his first science book, *The Wonder Book of Science for Children*. On Christmas morning they had sat for hours together, slowly turning the pages while his father first read and then explained. He still had the book. He still occasionally looked at the diagrams. "How television works," "What happens when we are X-rayed," "Newton and the apple," "The marvel of modern ships." And his father had said, "I would have liked to have been a scientist if things had been different." It was the only time in his life that his father had given any indication that there could have been for him, for them, a fuller, a different life. But things had not been different, and now he knew that they never would be. He thought, "We need, all of us, to be in control of our lives, and we shrink them until they're small and mean enough so that we can feel in control."

Only once had the routine of their predictable days been interrupted by an event which was unexpected, dramatic. Shortly after his sixteenth birthday his father had taken the family Morris and had disappeared. Three days later he was found, sitting in the car on the top of Beachy Head, looking out to sea. It had been called a nervous breakdown due to overwork, and Mr. Wainwright had given him two weeks' holiday. His father had never explained what had happened, colluding in the official view that it had been a temporary amnesia. Neither of his parents had ever referred to it again.

Their flat was on the fourth and top floor of a rectangular modern block. The sitting room at the front had a glass door giving onto a narrow balcony sufficient to hold two chairs. The kitchen was small but had a flap which could be lifted to provide a table just large enough for the three of them to eat at it. There were only two bedrooms, his parents' at the front and his own, much smaller, giving a view of the car-park, the row of breeze-block garages and the town. The sitting room had a wall-mounted gas fire to augment the background central heating and, after they had moved in, his parents had surrounded this with a false mantelshelf on which his mother could display the small treasures brought from the Clapham home. He remembered the morning when they had viewed the flat, his mother stepping out onto the balcony and saying, "Look, Father, it's just like being on the deck of a liner," and turning almost with animation, as if remembering that store of old movie magazines she kept, the pictures of befurred film stars on the gangplanks, the ship festooned with streamers and flags, hearing in imagination the hoots of the pilot boat, the band playing on the quay. And indeed his parents had, from the start, seen the flat as a glamorous change from their small, terraced house. In summer they would move the two easy chairs so that they faced the window and the sea. In winter they reversed them and huddled round the gas fire. But neither the winter gales, nor the uncomfortable heat when summer beat on the glass, ever drew from either of them a word of regret for the old life.

They had sold their car when his father retired, and the single-car garage was used to house Jonathan's second-hand Ford Fiesta. He garaged it and swung back the door. Locking it, he thought how very private the flats were. Nearly all of them were occupied by retired couples whose routine seemed to be to walk during the morning, meet their friends for afternoon tea and be home before 7.00. By the time he returned from work, the block was quiet and the rear curtains drawn. He wondered if Caroline had guessed or had known just how private his comings and goings could be. Outside the flat he hesitated for a moment, key in hand, wishing he could postpone the moment of meeting. But any longer wait would seem unnatural: they must have been listening for the lift.

His mother almost ran towards him.

"It's terrible, isn't it. That poor girl. Dad and I heard it on the local radio. But at least they found the Whistler. That's one worry over. He'll not go on killing again after her."

He said: "They think that he died before Miss Robarts did, so that it may not have been the Whistler."

"But of course it was the Whistler. She died in the same way, didn't she? Who else would it be?"

"That's what the police are trying to find out. They've been at the station all morning. They didn't get round to seeing me until nearly twelve."

"What did they want to see you for? They can't think you had anything to do with it?"

"Of course not, Mother. They're interviewing everyone, everyone who knew her, that is. Anyway, I have an alibi."

"An alibi? What alibi? Why would you want an alibi?"

"I don't want one, but as it happens I have one. I went to supper last night with a girl from the station."

Immediately her face brightened, pleasure at the news momentarily eclipsing the horror of the murder. She said: "Who invited you, then, Jonathan?"

"A girl at the station. I told you."

"Well, I know it's a girl. What kind of girl? Why don't you bring her home? You know that this is your home just as much as it is Dad's and mine. You can always bring your friends here. Why not ask her to tea next Saturday or Sunday? I'd have everything very nice, your granny's best tea-service, I wouldn't let you down."

Torn with a dreadful pity, he said: "Perhaps I will one day, Mum. It's a bit early yet."

"I don't see how it can be too early to meet your friends. It's as well you were with her if they're looking for alibis. What time did you get home, then?"

"About quarter to eleven."

"Well, that's not so very late. You look tired. It must have been a shock for everyone at Larksoken, a girl you knew, Administrative Officer, too, so it said on the radio."

Jonathan said: "Yes, it has been a shock. I suppose that's why I don't feel very hungry. I'd like to wait a little bit before supper."

"It's all ready, Jonathan. Lamb chops. They're half-cooked already. I've only got to slip them under the grill. And the vegetables are cooked. It's only going to spoil."

"All right, I won't be more than five minutes."

He hung his jacket in the hall, then went into his own room and lay on the bed, staring at the ceiling. The thought of food nauseated him, but he had said five minutes and if he lay there much longer she would be knocking at the door. She always knocked, but very gently, two distinct, discreet taps, like an assignation. What, he wondered, did she fear she might find him doing if she came in unannounced? He made himself sit up and swung his legs over the side of the bed but was immediately seized by nausea and weakness, which made him fear for a moment that he was actually going to faint. But he recognized it for what it was: a mixture of tiredness, fear and sheer misery.

And yet so far it hadn't been too bad. There had been three of them, Chief Inspector Rickards; a thickset, serious-faced young man who had been introduced as Detective Sergeant Oliphant and a younger man in the corner apparently taking notes whom no one had bothered to introduce. The small interviewing room attached to the Medical Physics Department had been set aside for them, and they had been sitting side-by-side at a small table, both in plain clothes. The room, as always, smelt faintly of disinfectant. He had never understood why, since no clinical procedures were carried out there. Two white coats still hung behind the door, and someone had left a tray of test tubes on top of the filing cabinet, adding to the air of inadvertence and amateurism. It had all been very low-key, very matter-of-fact. He felt that he was being processed, one of the dozens who had known her or claimed to have known her and who had passed through this or a similar door to answer the same questions. Almost he expected them to ask him to roll up his sleeve and to feel the prick of a needle. He knew that the probing, if there was to be probing, would come later. But he had been surprised at his own initial lack of fear. He had somehow assumed that the police were endowed with an almost supernatural power to sniff out lying, that he would walk into that room bearing an all-too-visible load of guilt, prevarication and conspiracy to defeat the ends of justice.

At their request, he gave his name and address. The sergeant wrote it down. Then he said almost wearily: "If you could tell us, please, where you were yesterday between six and ten-thirty."

He remembered thinking, "Why six and ten-thirty?" She had been found on the beach. She liked to swim most nights just after the nine o'clock news; everyone knew that—at least, everyone who knew her. And the news on Sunday was at 9.10. And then he remembered that they would know exactly when she had been found. There wouldn't have been time yet for the autopsy report. Perhaps they were still uncertain about the time of death, or were playing it safe. Six to 10.30. But 9.00 or shortly after was surely the relevant time. He was surprised that he could work it out so clearly.

He said: "I was at home with my parents until after dinner—after the one o'clock meal, I mean. Then I drove over to spend the evening with my girlfriend, Miss Caroline Amphlett. I was with her until just after ten-thirty. She lives in a bungalow outside Holt. She's PA to the Director, Dr. Mair."

"We know where she lives, sir. And we know who she is. Did anyone see you arrive or leave?"

"I don't think so. The bungalow is very isolated, and there weren't many cars on the road. I think someone in the flats may have seen me leave."

"And you spent the evening doing what?"

The officer in the corner wasn't writing now, only looking, but he didn't seem curious, not even interested, just slightly bored.

"Caroline cooked supper and I helped. She had some home-made soup already made and heated that. We had mushroom omelettes, fruit, cheese, wine. After dinner we chatted. Then we went to bed and made love."

"I don't think we need go into the more intimate parts of the evening, sir. How long have you and Miss Amphlett been friends?"

"About three months."

"And when was this evening together planned?"

"A few days before. I can't remember exactly when."

"And when did you get home, sir?"

"Just after ten-forty-five." He added, "I've no witnesses to that, I'm afraid. My parents were away for the night, visiting my married sister at Ipswich."

"Did you know they would be away when you and Miss Amphlett planned your evening together?"

"Yes. They always visit my sister on the last Sunday of the month. But it wouldn't have made any difference. I mean, I'm twenty-eight. I live with them but I don't have to give them an account of my movements."

The sergeant looked at him and said: "Free, white and twenty-eight," as if he were noting it down. Jonathan had blushed and thought, "That was a mistake. Don't try to be clever, don't explain, just answer their questions."

The Chief Inspector said: "Thank you, sir, that will be all for now."

As he reached the door he heard Rickards's voice.

"She wasn't very nice to you, was she, Miss Robarts, about that local radio programme you took part in, *My Religion and My Job*? Did you hear it, Sergeant?"

The sergeant said stolidly: "No, sir, I didn't hear it. Can't think how I came to miss it. Very fascinating, I'm sure."

He turned and faced them. He said: "She wasn't very kind about it. I'm a Christian. You don't expect it always to be easy."

Rickards said: " 'Blessed are ye when men revile and persecute you for the gospel's sake.' A bit of persecution, was there? Oh well, things could be worse. At least you don't get thrown to the lions any more."

The sergeant seemed to think that it was very funny.

He wondered, for the first time, how they could have known about Hilary's mild persecution of him over the programme. For some reason his brief, rather pathetic notoriety, his affirmation of faith had outraged her. Someone at the station must have mentioned it to the police. After all, they had interviewed plenty of people before they got round to him.

But surely it was over now. He had given the police his alibi, his and hers, and there was no reason why they should be questioned

again. He must put the whole thing out of his mind. But he knew
that this wouldn't be possible. And now, remembering Caroline's
story, he was struck with its inconsistencies. Why had she chosen to
park the car on an isolated part of the road, down a cart-track under
the trees? Why had she chosen to drive with Remus to the headland
when there were plenty of walks nearer home? He could have understood it if she had wanted to let the dog run on the beach and splash
into the sea, but according to her they hadn't gone down to the beach.
And what proof was there that she hadn't reached the cliffs until ten
o'clock, half an hour after Hilary Robarts was thought to have died?

Then there was that story about her mother. He found that he
just didn't believe it, hadn't believed it when she had first told him,
and he believed it even less now. But that, surely, was something he
might be able to check. There were private detectives, firms in London
who could carry out this kind of enquiry. The thought both appalled
and excited him. The idea that he might actually get in touch with
those kind of people, might pay them money to spy on her, astounded
him by its audacity. It wasn't something she would expect him to do,
that anyone would expect him to do; but why shouldn't he? He had
enough money to pay. There was nothing shameful in the enquiry.
But first he must find out her date of birth. That shouldn't be difficult.
He knew Shirley Coles, the junior clerk in the Establishment Division.
Sometimes he even thought that she liked him. She wouldn't let him
see Caroline's personal file, but she might be willing to look up a
harmless piece of information. He could say that he wanted to give
Caroline a birthday present and had a feeling that the date was getting
close. Then, with her name and date of birth, surely her parents could
be traced. It should be possible to know whether her mother was alive,
where she was living, her financial circumstances. There would be a
copy of the London Yellow Pages in the library where private-detective
firms would be listed. He didn't want to do it by letter, but he could
telephone with a preliminary enquiry. If necessary he could take a
day's leave and go up to London. He thought: I've got to know. If this
is a lie, then everything is a lie: the walk on the cliffs, everything she
said to me, even her love.

He heard the two knocks on the door. To his horror he found
that he was crying, not noisily but with a silent welling-forth of tears
which no effort could control. He called out, "I'm coming. I'm coming."

Then he went over to the washbasin and began bathing his face. Looking up, he saw himself in the mirror. It seemed to him that fear and tiredness and a sickness of spirit which lay too deep for healing had stripped away all his pathetic pretences, that the face which had at least been ordinary, familiar, had become as disgusting to him as it must be to her. He stared at his image and saw it through her eyes: the dull brown hair with the clinging specks of scurf which daily shampooing seemed only to exacerbate; the eyes red-rimmed, a little too close together; the damp, pale forehead on which the acne pustules stood out like the stigmata of sexual shame. He thought: She doesn't love me and she never has loved me. She chose me for two reasons: because she knew I loved her and because she thought I was too stupid to discover the truth. But I'm not stupid and I shall discover it. And he would begin with the smallest lie, the one about her mother. And what of his own lies, the lie to his parents, the false alibi to the police? And that greatest lie of all. "I'm a Christian. You don't expect it always to be easy." He wasn't a Christian any more and perhaps he never had been. His conversion had been no more than the need to be accepted, taken seriously, befriended by that little coterie of earnest proselytizers who had at least valued him for himself. But it wasn't true. None of it was true. In one day he had learned that the two most important things in his life, his religion and his love, were delusions.

The two knocks on the door were more insistent this time. His mother called: "Jonathan, are you all right? The chops are getting overcooked."

"It's all right, Mother. I'm coming."

But it took another minute of vigorous splashing before his face looked normal and it was safe to open the door and join them for supper.

'BOOK FIVE

Tuesday 27 September
to
Thursday 29 September

1
⊠

Jonathan Reeves waited until he saw Mrs. Simpson leave her office for coffee before going into the establishment office, where the personnel files were kept. All the personnel records had, he knew, been computerized, but the original files were still in existence, guarded by Mrs. Simpson as if they were repositories of dangerous and actionable information. She was nearing the end of her service and had never come to terms with computer records. For her the only reality was set down in black and white between the manila folders of an official file. Her assistant, Shirley Coles, was a newly appointed junior, a pretty eighteen-year-old who lived in the village. She had early been instructed in the importance of the Director and the heads of departments but hadn't yet assimilated the more subtle law which permeates any organization and which defines those whose wishes are to be taken seriously whatever their grade and those who can be safely ignored. She was a pleasant child, anxious to please and responsive to friendliness.

Jonathan said: "I'm almost sure that her birthday is early next month. I know that the personnel records are confidential, but it's only her date of birth. If you could have a look and let me know."

He knew that he sounded gauche and nervous but that helped: she knew what it was to feel gauche and nervous. He added: "Only the date of birth. Honestly. And I won't tell anyone how I found out. She did tell me, but I've forgotten."

"I'm not supposed to, Mr. Reeves."

"I know, but there isn't any other way that I can find out. She doesn't live at home, so I can't ask her mother. I really would hate her to think I'd forgotten."

"Couldn't you come back when Mrs. Simpson is here? I expect she'd tell you. I'm not supposed to open files when she's away."

"I could ask her, I know, but I'd rather not. You know how she is. I'm afraid she'd laugh at me. About Caroline. I thought you'd understand. Where is she, Mrs. Simpson?"

"Having her coffee break. She always takes twenty minutes."

But he stood instead at the side of the cabinet and watched while she went over to the security cupboard with its combination lock and began twirling the dial. He said: "Can the police see these personnel records if they ask?"

"Oh no, Mr. Reeves, that wouldn't be right. No one sees them except Dr. Mair and Mrs. Simpson. They're confidential. The police did see Miss Robarts's file, though. Dr. Mair asked for it first thing on Monday morning, even before the police arrived. It was the first thing he rang for as soon as he got into his office. Mrs. Simpson took it in to him personally. But that's different. She's dead. There isn't anything private when you're dead."

"No," he said. "Nothing is private once you're dead." And he had a sudden picture of himself in that small rented house in Romford, helping his mother clear out his grandfather's things after the old man's heart attack: the greasy clothes, the smell, the larder with its store of baked beans on which he chiefly lived, the uncovered saucers of stale and mouldy food, those shameful magazines which he had discovered at the bottom of a drawer and which, scarlet-faced, his mother had snatched from him. No, there wasn't anything left private once you were dead.

She said, her back to him, "Awful, isn't it, the murder? You can't sort of realize it. Not someone you actually knew. It's made a lot of extra work for us in Estabs. The police wanted a list of all the staff with their addresses. And everyone's had a form asking where they were on Sunday evening and who they were with. Well, you know. You've had one. We all have."

The combination lock needed precision. Her first effort had been unsuccessful and now she was carefully turning the dial again. Oh

God, he thought, why can't she get on with it? But now, at last, the door swung open. He could glimpse the edge of a small metal box. She took from it a bunch of keys and, returning to the filing cabinet, quickly selected one and inserted it in the lock. The tray slid out at a touch of her fingers. Now she seemed infected with his anxiety. She gave one anxious look at the door and quickly rifled through the suspended files.

"Here it is."

He had to stop himself from snatching it. She opened it and he saw the familiar buff-coloured form which he had himself completed when he first came to the station, her application for her present job. What he wanted was laid out before him in her careful capitals. Caroline Sophia St. John Amphlett, date of birth 14 October 1957, place Aldershot, England, nationality British.

Shirley closed the file and quickly replaced it and slid back the drawer. As she locked it she said: "There you are, then. Fourteenth October. Quite soon really. It's a good thing you checked. What will you do to celebrate? If the weather stays good you could have a picnic on the boat."

He said, puzzled: "What boat? We don't have a boat."

"Caroline does. She bought Mr. Hoskins's old cabin cruiser berthed at Wells-next-the-Sea. I know because he put a card in Mrs. Bryson's window at Lydsett and my Uncle Ted thought he might have a look at it as it was going cheap. But when he rang, Mr. Hoskins told him it had been sold to Miss Amphlett from Larksoken."

"When was that?"

"Three weeks ago. Didn't she tell you?"

He thought: One more secret, innocent perhaps, but still strange. She had never shown the slightest interest in boats or the sea. An old cabin cruiser, going cheap. And it was autumn, hardly the best time to buy a boat.

He heard Shirley's voice: "Sophia's rather a pretty name. Old-fashioned, but I like it. She doesn't look like a Sophia, though, does she?"

But Jonathan had seen more than her full name and the date of birth. Underneath were the names of her parents. Father, Charles Roderick St. John Amphlett, deceased, army officer. Mother, Patricia Caroline Amphlett. He had brought with him a sheet of paper torn from a notebook and quickly wrote down both the dates and the names. They were a bonus. He had forgotten that the application form was so detailed. Surely, with this information, a detective agency would be able to trace her mother without too great difficulty.

It was only when the keys had been replaced in the security cupboard that he could breathe freely. Now that he had gained what he wanted it seemed ungracious to hurry away. It was important to be gone before Mrs. Simpson returned and Shirley was left to face the inevitable question about what he was doing there and might be forced into a lie. But he lingered a moment while she settled herself at her desk. She began threading paper clips together to make a chain.

She said: "I feel really awful about this murder. I really do. Do you know, I was actually there, on Sunday afternoon. I mean the actual place where she died. We went for a picnic so that Christopher could play on the beach. I mean Mum, Dad, Christopher and me. He's my baby brother, he's only four. We parked the car on the headland only about fifty yards from Miss Robarts's cottage, but of course we didn't see her. We didn't see anybody the whole afternoon, except Mrs. Jago in the distance, on her bicycle, delivering the church magazines."

Jonathan said: "Have you told this to the police? I suppose they might be interested. I mean, they'd be interested in hearing that you hadn't actually seen anyone near her cottage."

"Oh yes, I told them. And they were very interested. Do you know, they asked me whether Christopher had spilled any sand on the path. And he had. Wasn't that funny? I mean, it was funny they should think of it."

Jonathan said: "When were you there, then?"

"They asked me that as well. Not very long. Only from about half past one to about half past three. We actually ate our picnic in the car. Mum said it wasn't the time of year to sit around on the beach getting cold. Then we went down the path to that little cove and Christopher made a sand castle near to the sea. He was happy enough, but it wasn't warm enough for the rest of us to sit about. Mum more or less had to drag him away yelling. Dad went on to the car, and we were lagging a bit behind. Mum said: 'I'm not having you carrying that sand into the car, Christopher. You know your dad won't like it.' So she made him tip it out. More yells from Christopher, of course.

Honestly, that kid can be diabolical sometimes. Funny, isn't it? I mean, us being there on that very same afternoon."

Jonathan said: "Why do you think they were so interested in the sand?"

"That's what Dad wanted to know. That detective, the one who was here and interviewed me, said that they might find a footprint and want to eliminate it if it belonged to one of us. Dad reckons they must have found a footprint. A couple of young detectives, very nice they were, came to see Dad and Mum yesterday evening. They asked Dad and Mum what shoes they had been wearing, and they actually asked if they could take them away. Well, they wouldn't do that, would they, if they hadn't found something?"

Jonathan said: "It must have been a terrible worry to your dad and mum."

"Oh no, it didn't bother them. After all, we weren't there when she died, were we? After we left the headland we drove to have tea with Gran at Hunstanton. We didn't leave until half past nine. Far too late for Christopher, Mum said. He slept in the car all the way home, mind you. But it was funny, though, wasn't it? Being there on the very day. If she'd been killed a few hours earlier, we'd actually have seen the body. I don't think we'll go back to that part of the beach again. I wouldn't go there after dark for a thousand pounds. I'd be frightened I might see her ghost. Funny about the sand, though, isn't it? I mean, if they do find a footprint and it helps them to catch the murderer, it will all be because of Christopher wanting to play on the beach and Mum making him spill out the sand. I mean, it was such a little thing. Mum said it reminded her of Vicar's sermon last Sunday when he preached about how even our smallest actions can have immense consequences. I didn't remember it. I mean, I like singing in the choir, but Mr. Smollett's sermons are dead boring."

So small a thing, a footprint in soft sand. And if that footprint was made in the sand spilled by Christopher from his bucket, then it was made by someone who had used that path after 3.30 on Sunday afternoon.

He said: "How many people here know about this? Have you told anyone except the police?"

"No one but you. They said that we weren't to talk and I haven't, not until now. I know Mrs. Simpson was curious why I asked to see

Chief Inspector Rickards. She kept saying that she couldn't see what I could tell them and that I wasn't to waste police time trying to make myself important. I suppose she was worried, thinking I'd tell them about the row she and Miss Robarts had when Dr. Gledhill's personal file was missing and Dr. Mair had it all the time. But you won't tell, will you? Not even Miss Amphlett?"

"No," he promised. "I won't tell. Not even her."

2

⊠

There was a surprising number of detective agencies in the Yellow Pages and apparently very little to choose between them. He chose one of the largest and wrote down the London telephone number. It wouldn't do to telephone from the power station, and he didn't want to wait until he got home, where there would be even less privacy. He was anxious, too, to ring as soon as possible. His plan was to lunch at a local pub and find a public call box.

The morning seemed interminable, but at twelve o'clock he said that he was taking an early lunch hour and left, checking first that he had sufficient small coins. The nearest kiosk was, he knew, in the village, close to the general store. It was a public position, but he told himself that there was no need for particular secrecy.

His call was quickly answered by a woman. He had prepared what he would say, and she seemed to find nothing strange in the request. But it became apparent that it wouldn't be as easy as he had hoped. Yes, she said, the agency could certainly hope to trace an individual from the information provided, but there was no fixed charge. Everything depended on the difficulty and how long it took. Until his request had been formally received, it was impossible even to give an estimate. The cost might be as little as two hundred pounds or as much as four hundred. She suggested that he should write in immediately, setting out all the information in his possession and stating clearly what he required. The letter should be accompanied by a down payment of one hundred pounds. They would certainly deal with it as a matter of urgency, but until the request was received they could give no assurance of how long it would take. He thanked her, said that he would write, and put down the receiver, glad that he hadn't given her his name. Somehow he had imagined that they would take the information down over the telephone, tell him what the cost would be, promise him a quick result. It was all too formal, too expensive, too slow. He wondered whether to try another agency, then told himself that in this highly competitive field they were unlikely to give him any more encouraging news.

By the time he had got back to the power station and parked his car, he had almost persuaded himself not to proceed. And then it occurred to him that he might make his own enquiries. The name was unusual enough; there might be an Amphlett in the London telephone directory, and if not in London it might be worth trying some of the larger cities. And her father had been a soldier. Perhaps there was an army directory—wasn't it called the Army List?—which he could consult. It would be worth doing a little research before committing himself to expenditure he might not be able to meet, and the thought of writing to a detective agency, of actually putting his request down on paper, discouraged him. He began to feel like a conspirator, an unfamiliar role which both excited him and ministered to some part of his nature which he hadn't previously known existed. He would work alone, and if he was unsuccessful it would be time to think again.

And the first step was remarkably straightforward, so simple that he blushed at his folly at not having thought of it earlier. Back in the library he consulted the London telephone directory. There was a P. C. Amphlett with an address in Pont Street, SW1. He stared at it for a moment then, with trembling fingers, took out his notebook and jotted down the telephone number. The initials were those of Caroline's mother, but the entry bore no prefix. The subscriber could easily be a man. It could be a coincidence. And the name Pont Street meant nothing to him, although he didn't think that SW1 could be a poor area of London. But would she have told him a lie which could be detected merely by consulting the telephone directory? Only if she was so confident of her dominance, of his enslavement to her, so certain of his inadequacy and stupidity, that she hadn't needed to care. She had wanted that alibi and he had given it. And if this was a lie, if he visited Pont Street and discovered that her mother wasn't living in poverty, what else that she had told him had been true? When exactly had she been on the headland and for what purpose? But these were suspicions which he knew he could not seriously entertain. The idea that Caroline had killed Hilary Robarts was ridiculous. But why hadn't she been willing to tell the police the truth?

But he knew now what his next move would be. On the way home he would telephone the Pont Street number and ask for Caroline. That at least should prove whether or not it was her mother's address. And if it was, then he would take a day's leave or wait until Saturday, make an excuse to have a day in London and check for himself.

The afternoon dragged endlessly and it was difficult to keep his mind on his work. He was worried too in case Caroline should appear, should suggest that he go home with her. But she seemed to be avoiding him, and he was grateful. He left ten minutes early, making the excuse of a headache, and within twenty minutes was back at the telephone kiosk in Lydsett. The number rang for almost half a minute, and he had nearly given up hope when it was answered. A woman's voice slowly and distinctly spoke the number. He had decided to assume a Scottish accent. He knew himself to be quite a good mimic, and his maternal grandmother had been a Scot. There would be no difficulty in making it convincing. He said: "Is Miss Caroline Amphlett at home, please?"

There was a long silence; then the woman said repressively: "Who is that speaking?"

"My name is John McLean. We're old friends."

"Indeed, Mr. McLean. Then how strange that I don't know you and that you, apparently, don't know that Miss Amphlett no longer lives here."

"Then could you give me her address, please?"

Again there was a silence. Then the voice said: "I hardly think I would care to do that, Mr. McLean. But if you wish to leave a message I will see that it reaches her."

He asked: "Is that her mother speaking?"

The voice laughed. It was not an agreeable laugh. Then she said: "No, I'm not her mother. This is Miss Beasley, the housekeeper, speaking. But did you really need to ask?"

And then it occurred to him that there could be two Caroline

Amphletts, two mothers with the same initials. The chance was surely remote, but it would be as well to make sure. He said: "Does Caroline still work at Larksoken Power Station?"

And this time there could be no mistake. Her voice was harsh with dislike as she answered. "If you know that, Mr. McLean, why bother to ring me."

And the telephone receiver was firmly replaced.

3

It was after 10.30 on the Tuesday night when Rickards came for the second time to Larksoken Mill. He had telephoned his intention shortly after six o'clock and had made it clear that the visit, although late, was official; there were facts he wanted to check and a question he needed to ask. Earlier in the day Dalgliesh had called in at the incident room at Hoveton and made a statement describing the finding of the body. Rickards hadn't been there, but Oliphant, obviously on his way out, had stayed to receive him and had briefly filled him in on the state of the investigation, not unwillingly but with a certain formality which suggested that he was under instructions. And Rickards himself, as he dragged off his jacket and seated himself in the same high-backed chair to the right of the fire, seemed a little chastened. He was wearing a dark pin-striped suit which, for all its over-careful tailoring, had the slightly seedy and rejected air of a suit relegated to second-best. It looked odd and inappropriately citified on his gangling limbs, particularly here on the headland, giving him the citified air of a man dressed for an informal wedding or a job interview from which he had little hope of success. The thinly veiled antagonism, the bitterness of failure after the death of the Whistler and even the restless energy of Sunday night had left him. Dalgliesh wondered whether he had spoken to the Chief Constable and received advice. If so, he could guess what it had been. It was much the same as he himself would have given.

"It's irritating that he's on your patch, but he's one of the Met's senior detectives, the Commissioner's blue-eyed boy. And he knows these people. He was at the Mair dinner party. He found the body. He's got useful information. All right, he's a professional, he's not going to withhold it, but you'll get it more easily and make life more agreeable for both of you if you stop treating him like a rival or, worse, a suspect."

Handing Rickards his whisky, Dalgliesh enquired after his wife.

"She's fine, fine." But there was something forced in his tone.

Dalgliesh said: "I suppose, now the Whistler's dead, she'll be coming home."

"You'd think so, wouldn't you? I'd like it, she'd like it, but there's the little problem of Sue's ma. She doesn't want her ewe-lamb mixed up with any unpleasantness, particularly murder, and particularly just now."

Dalgliesh said: "It's difficult to isolate yourself from unpleasantness, even murder, if you marry a police officer."

"She never intended Sue to marry a police officer."

Dalgliesh was surprised at the bitterness in his voice. Again, he was uncomfortably aware that he was being asked for some kind of assurance which he, of all men, was least competent to give. While he was searching for the anodyne phrase he glanced again at Rickards's face, at the look of weariness, almost of defeat, at the lines which the fitful light of the wood fire made even more cavernous, and took refuge in practicality.

He asked: "Have you eaten?"

"Oh, I'll get myself something from the fridge when I get back."

"There's the remains of a cassoulet, if you'd like it. It won't take a moment to heat up."

"Wouldn't say no, Mr. Dalgliesh."

He ate the cassoulet from a tray on his lap voraciously, as if it were his first meal for days, and afterwards mopped up the sauce with a crust of bread. Only once did he look up from his plate to ask: "Did you cook this, Mr. Dalgliesh?"

"If you live alone you have to learn at least simple cooking if you're not prepared to be always dependent on someone else for one of the essentials of life."

"And that wouldn't suit you, would it? Dependent on someone else for an essential of life?"

But he spoke without bitterness and carried the tray and the empty plate back into the kitchen with a smile. A second later Dalgliesh heard the splash of running water. Rickards was washing up his plate.

He must have been hungrier than he had realized. Dalgliesh knew how mistakenly easy it was, when working a sixteen-hour day, to suppose that one could function effectively on a diet of coffee and snatched sandwiches. Returning from the kitchen, Rickards leaned back in his chair with a small grunt of contentment. The colour had returned to his face, and when he spoke his voice was strong again.

"Her dad was Peter Robarts. Remember him?"

"No, should I?"

"No reason. Nor did I, but I've had time to look him up. He made a packet after the war, in which, incidentally, he served with some distinction. One of those chaps with an eye for the main chance, which in his case was plastics. It must have been quite a time for the wide boys, the 1950s and '6os. She was his only child. He made his fortune quickly and he lost it as fast. The usual reasons: extravagance, ostentatious generosity, women, throwing his money around as if he were printing it, thinking his luck would hold, whatever the odds. He was lucky not to end up inside. The fraud squad had put together a nice little case against him and were within days of making an arrest when he had his coronary. Slumped forward into his lunch plate at Simpson's as dead as the duck he was eating. It must have been difficult for her, daddy's little girl one day, nothing too good, and then near-disgrace, death, poverty."

Dalgliesh said: "Relative poverty, but that, of course, is what poverty is. You've been busy."

"Some but not much we got from Mair, some we had to grub around for. The City of London police have been helpful. I've been speaking to Wood Street. I used to tell myself that nothing about the victim was irrelevant, but I'm beginning to wonder if much of this grubbing about isn't a waste of time."

Dalgliesh said: "It's the only safe way to work. The victim dies because she is uniquely herself."

" 'And once you comprehend the life, you comprehend the death.' Old Blanco White—remember him?—used to drum that into us when I was a young DC. And what do you get in the end? A jumble of facts like an upturned waste-paper basket. They don't really add up to a person. And with this victim the pickings are small. She travelled light. There was little worth finding in that cottage, no diary, no letters except one to her solicitor making an appointment for next weekend and telling him she expected to be married. We've seen him, of course. He doesn't know the name of the man, nor, apparently, does anyone else, including Mair. We found no other papers of importance except a copy of her will. And there's nothing exciting about that. She left everything she had to Alex Mair in two lines of bald lawyer's prose. But I can't see Mair killing her for twelve thousand pounds on NatWest's special reserve account and a practically derelict cottage with a sitting tenant. Apart from the will and that one letter, only the usual bank statements, receipted bills, the place obsessively tidy. You could imagine she knew she was going to die and had tidied away her life. No sign of a recent search, incidentally. If there was something in the cottage the murderer wanted, and he smashed that window to get it, he covered his tracks pretty effectively."

Dalgliesh said: "If he did have to smash the window to get in, then he probably wasn't Dr. Mair. Mair knew that the key was in the locket. He could have taken it, used it and put it back. There would be an additional risk of leaving evidence at the scene, and some murderers dislike returning to the body. Others, of course, feel a compulsion to do so. But if Mair did take the key, he'd have had to put it back, whatever the risk. An empty locket would have pointed directly to him."

Rickards said: "Cyril Alexander Mair, but he's dropped the 'Cyril.' Probably thinks 'Sir Alexander Mair' will sound better than 'Sir Cyril.' What's wrong with 'Cyril'? My grandfather was called Cyril. I've got a prejudice against people who don't use their proper names. She was his mistress, incidentally."

"Did he tell you?"

"More or less had to, didn't he? They were very discreet, but one or two of the senior staff at the station must have known, known or suspected it, anyway. He's too intelligent to keep back information he knows we're bound to discover sooner or later. His story is that the affair was over, a natural end by common consent. He expects to move to London; she wanted to stay here. Well, she more or less had to, unless she gave up her job, and she was a career woman, the job was important. His story is that what they felt for each other wasn't robust enough to be sustained by occasional weekend meetings—his words, not mine. You'd think that the whole affair was a matter of convenience. While he was here he needed a woman, she needed a man. The goods have to be handy. No point if you're a hundred miles apart. Rather like buying meat. He's moving to London, she decided to stay. Find another butcher."

Dalgliesh remembered that Rickards had always been slightly censorious about sex. He could hardly have been a detective for twenty years without encountering adultery and fornication in their various guises, apart from the more bizarre and horrifying manifestations of human sexuality beside which adultery and fornication were comfortingly normal. But this didn't mean that he liked them. He had taken his oath as a police constable and kept it. He had made his marriage vows in church and no doubt intended to keep them. And in a job where irregular hours, drink, macho camaraderie and the propinquity of women police officers made marriages vulnerable, his was known to be solid. He was too experienced and basically too fair to allow himself to be prejudiced, but in one respect at least Mair was unlucky in the detective assigned to the case.

Rickards said: "Her secretary, Katie Flack, has just given notice. Found her too demanding, apparently. There was a recent row over the girl's taking more than her allotted lunch hour. And one of her staff, Brian Taylor, admits that he found her impossible to work for and had asked for a transfer. Admirably frank about it all. He can afford to be. He was at a friend's stag party at the Maid's Head in Norwich with at least ten witnesses from eight o'clock onwards. And the girl hasn't anything to worry about either. She spent the evening watching TV with her family."

Dalgliesh asked: "Just the family?"

"No. Luckily for her the neighbours called in just before nine to discuss the dresses for their daughter's wedding. She's to be a bridesmaid. Lemon dresses with bouquets of small white and yellow chrysanthemums. Very tasteful. We got a full description. I suppose she thought it added to the verisimilitude of the alibi. Anyway, they were neither of them serious suspects. These days if you don't like your boss you pack in the job. Both of them were shocked, of course, and slightly defensive. They probably felt she'd got herself killed on purpose to put them in the wrong. Neither of them pretended that they had liked her. But there was something stronger than dislike about this killing. And this may surprise you, Mr. Dalgliesh. Robarts wasn't particularly unpopular with the senior staff. They respect efficiency and she was efficient. Besides, her responsibilities didn't directly impinge on theirs. It was her job to see that the station was efficiently administered so that the scientific and technical staff could do their job most effectively. Apparently that's what she did. They answered my questions without fuss, but they weren't particularly forthcoming. There's a kind of camaraderie about the place. I suppose if you feel yourself constantly under criticism or attack it makes for a certain wariness in dealing with outsiders. Only one of them said he actually disliked her, Miles Lessingham. But he has produced an alibi of a kind. He claims to have been on his boat at the time of death. And he made no secret of his feelings. He didn't want to eat with her or drink with her or spend his spare time with her or go to bed with her. But, as he pointed out, he feels that about a number of people and hasn't found any impulse to murder them." He paused for a moment, then said, "Dr. Mair showed you round the power station on Friday morning, didn't he?"

Dalgliesh asked: "Did he tell you that?"

"Dr. Mair didn't tell me anything he didn't actually have to tell me. No, it came out when we were talking to one of the junior staff, a local girl who works in the Establishment Division. Chatty little thing. I got a lot of useful stuff out of her, one way or another. I was wondering if anything happened on your visit which could be relevant."

Dalgliesh resisted the temptation to reply that if there had been he would have said so before now. He replied: "It was an interesting visit and the place rather impressive. Dr. Mair attempted to explain to me the difference between the thermal reactor and the new pressurized water reactor. Most of the talk was technical, except when he spoke briefly about poetry. Miles Lessingham showed me the high fuelling machine from which Toby Gledhill plunged to his death. It did strike me that Gledhill's suicide could be relevant, but I don't see how. It was obviously distressing to Lessingham, and not only because he witnessed it. There was a rather cryptic exchange at the Mairs' dinner party between him and Hilary Robarts."

Rickards crouched forward, his huge hand cradling the whisky glass. Without looking up, he said: "The Mair dinner party. I reckon that cosy little gathering—if it was cosy—is at the nub of this case. And there's something I wanted to ask you. That's really why I'm here. That child Theresa Blaney, exactly how much of the conversation about the latest Whistler victim did she overhear?"

It was the question Dalgliesh had been expecting. What surprised him was how long it had taken Rickards to ask it.

He said carefully: "Some of it, undoubtedly. You know that, I've told you already. I couldn't say how long she'd been standing behind the dining-room door before I noticed her, or how much of the conversation she actually heard."

"Can you remember what stage in his account Lessingham had reached at the time you saw Theresa?"

"I can't be certain. I think he was describing the body, exactly what he saw when he returned with his torch."

"So she could have heard about the cut on the forehead and the pubic hair."

"But would she have told her father about the hair? She had a devoutly religious mother, an RC. I don't really know the child, but I imagine that she's unusually modest. Would a gently nurtured, modest girl tell that to any man, even to her father?"

"Gently nurtured? Modest? You're sixty years out of date. Spend half an hour in any secondary-school playground and you'll hear things that'll curl your hair. Today's kids will say anything to anyone."

"Not that child."

"All right, but she could have told her dad about the *L*-shaped cut, and he could have guessed about the hair. Damn it, everyone knew that the Whistler's murders must have had a sexual connotation. He didn't rape them, but that wasn't how he got his kicks. You don't need to be Krafft—what's his name?"

"Krafft-Ebing."

"Sounds like a cheese. You don't need to be Krafft-Ebing, you don't even need to be sexually sophisticated, to guess what kind of hair the Whistler helped himself to."

Dalgliesh said: "But this is important, isn't it, if you're casting Blaney as chief suspect? Would he, or anyone else, kill that way if he wasn't certain about the Whistler's method? He could only hope to pin it on the Whistler by getting all the details right. If you can't prove that Theresa told her father both about the hair and the L-shaped cut, your case is considerably weakened. I would doubt whether you had one. Besides, I thought that Oliphant said that Blaney had an alibi both from Miss Mair, who said he was drunk and at home by nine-forty-five, and from his daughter. Wasn't her story that she went to bed at eight-fifteen and came down just before nine to get herself a drink of water?"

"That's what she said, Mr. Dalgliesh. But I'll tell you this: that child would confirm any story that her dad chose to tell. And the timing is suspiciously accurate. Robarts dies at nine-twenty or as near as damn it. Theresa Blaney goes to bed at eight-fifteen and conveniently needs a drink of water forty-five minutes later. I wish you could have seen her, and seen that cottage. But of course you have. Two WPCs from the juvenile bureau were with me, and they treated her as tenderly as a babe-in-arms. Not that she needed it. We all sat round the fire in a cosy little circle and she held the kid in her lap. Ever tried questioning a child to discover if her dad's a murderer while she's sitting there gazing at you with those huge reproachful eyes and nursing a baby? I suggested that she hand the kid over to one of the WPCs, but as soon as she tried to take him he immediately started up a howling. Wouldn't let his dad take him either. You'd think that Theresa and he had arranged it between them. And Ryan Blaney was there too, of course, throughout the interview. You can't question a child without the parent being present if the parent wants to be. My God, when I arrest someone for this murder—and I shall, Mr. Dalgliesh, this time I shall—I hope it doesn't have to be Ryan Blaney. Those kids have lost enough already. But he's got the strongest motive of all, and he hated Robarts. I don't think he could conceal that hatred if he tried, and he didn't even attempt to try. And it's not only that she was trying to force him out of Scudder's Cottage. It goes deeper than that. I don't know what's at the root of it. Something to do with his wife, maybe. But I'll find out. He left the kids in the cottage and walked out with us to the cars. The last thing he said was: 'She was an evil bitch and I'm glad she's dead. But I didn't kill her, and you can't prove I did.'

"And I know the objections. Jago says he telephoned at about seven-thirty to let him know the Whistler was dead. He spoke to Theresa and the kid says she told her dad. No reason why she shouldn't tell him. I think we take it that she did. He wouldn't have left the kids alone in that cottage with the Whistler alive and on the prowl. No responsible father would, and it's generally admitted he's a responsible father. We've got the local authority's word for that, by the way. A fortnight ago they sent a social worker just to check that everything was all right. And I'll tell you who instigated that, Mr. Dalgliesh. Now, this is interesting. It was Robarts."

"Did she make any specific allegations?"

"None. Her story was that she had to visit from time to time to discuss repairs and so on, and that she was concerned at the weight of responsibility he was carrying and thought he could do with some help. Talked about seeing Theresa lugging heavy shopping home with the twins tagging along, sometimes when Theresa should have been at school. Phoned the local authority to send a social worker along. The social worker satisfied herself, apparently, that things were going as well as could be expected. The twins are already attending a play-group, and she offered additional services including a home help, but she didn't find Blaney either welcoming or co-operative. Don't know that I blame him. I wouldn't want the Welfare on my back."

"Does Blaney know that Hilary Robarts instigated the visit?"

"The local authority didn't tell him; it isn't their policy. And I don't see how he could have found out. But if he did find out, it considerably strengthens his motive, doesn't it? That visit could have been the last straw."

Dalgliesh said: "But would he have killed in that way? Logically, the knowledge that the Whistler was dead negatives the method."

"Not necessarily, Mr. Dalgliesh. Suppose it's a double-bluff. Suppose he's saying in effect, 'Look, I can prove I knew the Whistler was dead. Whoever killed Hilary Robarts didn't know. So why aren't you looking for someone who hadn't been told that the Whistler's body had been found?' And, by God, Mr. Dalgliesh, there's another possibility. Suppose he knew that the Whistler was dead but thought that it was very recent. I asked Theresa precisely what George Jago had said to her. She remembered accurately; anyway, Jago confirmed it. Apparently he said: 'Tell your dad the Whistler is dead. Killed himself. Just now, over at Easthaven.' But no mention of the hotel, or of when the Whistler booked in. Jago didn't know any of that. The message he'd got from his mate at the Crown and Anchor was pretty garbled.

So Blaney could have assumed that the body was found in open country just five miles down the coast. He can kill with impunity. Everyone, including the police, will assume that the Whistler has claimed his last victim, then done away with himself. My God, Mr. Dalgliesh, that's neat."

Dalgliesh privately thought that it was more neat than convincing. He said: "So you're assuming that the smashed portrait isn't directly connected with the murder. I can't see Blaney destroying his own work."

"Why not? From what I saw of it, it wasn't anything special."

"I think it was to him."

"The portrait is a puzzle, I'll grant you that. And that's not the only difficulty. Someone had a drink with Robarts before she took that last swim, someone she let into the cottage, someone she knew. There were those two glasses on the draining board and, in my book, that means two people were drinking. She wouldn't have invited Blaney to Thyme Cottage, and if he turned up I doubt if she would have let him in, drunk or sober."

Dalgliesh said: "But if you believe Miss Mair, your case against Blaney collapses anyway. She claims to have seen him at Scudder's Cottage at nine-forty-five, or shortly afterwards, and he was then half-drunk. All right, he could have feigned his drunkenness; that wouldn't present much difficulty. What he couldn't do was to kill Hilary Robarts at about nine-twenty and get home by nine-forty-five, not without the use of a car or van, which he didn't have."

Rickards said: "Or a bicycle."

"It would need fast pedalling. We know that she died after her swim, not before. Her hair was still damp at the roots when I found her. So you're probably safe enough in putting the time of death at between nine-fifteen and nine-thirty. And he couldn't have taken the bicycle with him and ridden back along the shore. The tide was high; he'd have been riding over the shingle, which would be more difficult than the road. There's only one part of the shore where you get a stretch of sand at high tide, and that's the small cove where Hilary Robarts swam. And if he had been on the road, Miss Mair must have seen him. She's given him an alibi which I don't think you'll be able to break."

Rickards said: "But he hasn't given her one, has he? Her story is that she was alone in Martyr's Cottage until she left just after nine-thirty to collect the portrait. She and that housekeeper at the Old Rectory, Mrs. Dennison, are the only ones who were at the Mairs' dinner party who made no attempt to produce an alibi. And she has a motive. Hilary Robarts was her brother's mistress. I know he tells us it was over, but we've only his word for that. Suppose they'd planned to marry when he goes to London. She's devoted her life to her brother. Unmarried. No other outlet for her emotions. Why give way to another woman just when Mair is about to achieve his ambition?"

Dalgliesh thought that this was an altogether too facile explanation of a relationship which, even on his brief acquaintance, had seemed more complicated. He said: "She's a successful professional writer. I imagine that success provides its own form of emotional fulfilment, assuming she needs it. She seemed to me very much her own woman."

"I thought she wrote cookery books. Is that what you call being a successful professional writer?"

"Alice Mair's books are highly regarded and extremely lucrative. We share the same publisher. If he had to make a choice between us, he'd probably prefer to lose me."

"So you think the marriage might almost be a relief, release her from responsibilities? Let another woman cook and care for him for a change?"

"Why should he need any woman to care for him? It's dangerous to theorize about people and their emotions, but I doubt whether she feels that kind of domestic, quasi-maternal responsibility or whether he either needs or wants it."

"How do you see it, then, the relationship? They live together, after all, most of the time anyway. She's fond of him, that seems to be generally accepted."

"They'd hardly live together if they weren't, if you can call it living together. She's away a great deal, I understand, researching her books, and he has a London flat. How can someone who's only met them together across the table at a dinner party get to the heart of their relationship? I should have thought that there was loyalty, trust, mutual respect. Ask them."

"But not jealousy, of him or his mistress?"

"If there is, she's clever at concealing it."

"All right, Mr. Dalgliesh, take another scenario. Suppose he was tired of Robarts, suppose she's pressing him to marry her, wants to quit the job, move to London with him. Suppose she's making herself a nuisance. Wouldn't Alice Mair feel like doing something about that?"

"Like devising and carrying out a singularly ingenious murder to relieve her brother of a temporary embarrassment? Isn't that carrying sisterly devotion to unreasonable lengths?"

"Ah, but they aren't temporary embarrassments, are they, these determined women? Think. How many men do you know who've been forced into marriage they didn't really want because the woman's will was stronger than theirs? Or because they couldn't stand all the fuss, the tears, recriminations, the emotional blackmail?"

Dalgliesh said: "She could hardly blackmail him with the relationship itself. Neither was married; they weren't deceiving anyone; they weren't causing public scandal. And I can't see anyone, man or woman, coercing Alex Mair into something he didn't want to do. I know it's dangerous to make facile judgements, although that's what we've been doing for the last five minutes, but he seems to me a man who lives his life on his own terms and probably always has."

"Which might make him vicious if someone tried to stop him."

"So now you're casting him as murderer?"

"I'm casting him as a strong suspect."

Dalgliesh asked: "What about that couple at the caravan? Is there any evidence that they knew about the Whistler's methods?"

"None that we could discover, but how certain can you be? The man, Neil Pascoe, gets about in that van of his, drinks in local pubs. He could have heard some talk. Not every policeman on the case has necessarily been discreet. We've kept the details out of the papers, but that doesn't mean that there hasn't been talk. He's got an alibi of sorts. He took the van just south of Norwich to talk to a chap there who'd written to him expressing interest in PANUP, that anti-nuclear organization of his. Had some hopes, apparently, of getting a group started there. I sent a couple of DCs to see the chap. He says they were together until just after eight-twenty, when Pascoe started for home—said he was starting for home, anyway. The girl he lives with, Amy Camm, says he got back to the caravan by nine o'clock and that they were together for the rest of the evening. My guess is that he got back a bit later. In that van he must have been pushing it a bit to get from beyond Norwich to Larksoken in forty minutes. And he's got a motive, one of the strongest. If Hilary Robarts had gone ahead with her libel action, it could have ruined him. And it's in Camm's interest to support his alibi. She's got herself very cosily fixed up with the kid in that caravan. I'll tell you something else, Mr. Dalgliesh: they had a dog once. The lead is still hanging inside the caravan."

"But if one or both of them used it to strangle Robarts, would it be?"

"People might have seen it. They might have thought it would have been more suspicious to destroy or hide it than to leave it there. We took it away, of course, but it was little more than a formality. Robarts's skin was unbroken. There'll be no physical traces. And if we do manage to get prints, they'll be hers and his. We shall go on checking the alibis, obviously. Every blasted employee at that station, and there are over five hundred of them. You'd never believe that, would you? You go in the place and hardly set sight on a soul. They seem to move through the countryside as invisibly as the energy they're generating. Most of them live at Cromer or Norwich. They want to be near schools and shops, presumably. Only a handful choose to live near the station. Most of the Sunday day shift were home well before ten and virtuously watching the telly or out with their friends. We shall check on them, whether or not they had anything to do with Robarts at work. But it's only a formality. I know where to look for my suspects, the guests at that dinner party. Due to Lessingham's inability to keep his mouth shut, they were told two crucial facts: that the hair stuffed into her mouth was pubic hair, and the mark on the forehead was an *L*. So that narrows the field very conveniently. Alex Mair, Alice Mair, Margaret Dennison, Lessingham himself and, assuming that Theresa Blaney reported the conversation to her father, you can add Blaney. All right, I may not be able to break his alibi, his or Mair's, but I shall have a damn good try."

Ten minutes later Rickards got to his feet and said it was time to get home. Dalgliesh walked with him to his car. The cloud level was low, the earth and sky subsumed in the same obliterating darkness in which the cold glitter of the power station seemed to have moved closer, and there lay over the sea a pale-blue luminosity, like the faint semblance of a newly discovered Milky Way. Even to feel the ground strike hard beneath their feet was disorienting in this blackness, and for a few seconds both men hesitated, as if the ten yards to the car, gleaming like some floating spacecraft in the light spilling from the open door, was an odyssey over dangerous and in-substantial ground. Above them the sails of the mill gleamed white and silent, potent with latent power. For a moment Dalgliesh had the illusion that they were about to begin slowly turning.

Rickards said: "Everything on this headland is contrast. After I left Pascoe's caravan this morning I stood on those low sandy cliffs and looked south. There was nothing but an old fishing smack, a coiled rope, an upturned box, that awful sea. It must have looked like that for near on a thousand years. And then I faced north and saw that bloody great power station. There it is, glittering away. And I'm seeing it under the shadow of the mill. Does it work, by the way? The mill, I mean."

Dalgliesh said: "I'm told so. The sails turn but it doesn't grind. The original millstones are in the lower chamber. Occasionally I have a wish to see the sails slowly turning, but I resist. I'm not sure, once started, whether I could stop them. It would be irritating to hear them creaking away all night."

They had reached the car, but Rickards, pausing with his hand on the door, seemed reluctant to get in. He said: "We've moved a long way, haven't we, between this mill and the power station? What is it? Four miles of headland and three hundred years of progress. And then I think of those two bodies in the morgue and wonder if we've progressed at all. Dad would have talked about original sin. He was a lay preacher, was Dad. He had it all worked out."

So had mine, come to that, thought Dalgliesh. He said: "Lucky Dad." There was a moment's silence, broken by the sound of the telephone, its insistent peal clearly heard through the open door. Dalgliesh said: "You'd better wait a moment. It could be for you."

It was. Oliphant's voice asked if Chief Inspector Rickards was there. He wasn't at his home and Dalgliesh's number was one of those which he'd left.

The call was brief. Less than a minute later Rickards joined him at the open door. The slight melancholy of the last few minutes had fallen away and his step was buoyant.

"It could have waited until tomorrow, but Oliphant wanted me to know. This could be the breakthrough we've needed. There's been a call from the lab. They must have been working on it nonstop. Oliphant told you, I imagine, that we found a footprint."

"He did mention it. On the right-hand side of the path, in soft sand. He didn't give any details."

And Dalgliesh, punctilious in not discussing a case with a junior officer in the absence of Rickards, hadn't asked.

"We've just got confirmation. It's the sole of a Bumble trainer, the right foot. Size ten. The pattern on the sole is unique, apparently, and they have a yellow bee on each heel. You must have seen them." Then, when Dalgliesh didn't reply, he said: "For God's sake, Mr. Dalgliesh, don't tell me that you own a pair. That's a complication I can do without."

"No, I don't own them. Bumbles are too fashionable for me. But I've seen a pair recently, and here on the headland."

"On whose feet?"

"They weren't on any feet." He thought for a moment, then said: "I remember now. Last Wednesday morning, the day after I arrived, I took some of my aunt's clothes, including two pairs of her shoes, to the Old Rectory for the church jumble. They keep a couple of tea chests in an old scullery there where people can leave things they don't want. The back door was open, as it usually is in daylight, so I didn't bother to knock. There was a pair of Bumbles among the other shoes. Or, more accurately, I saw the heel of one shoe. I imagine the other was there, but I didn't see it."

"On top of the chest?"

"No, about a third down. I think they were in a transparent plastic bag. As I say, I didn't see the whole pair, but I did glimpse one heel with the unmistakable yellow bee. It's possible that they were Toby Gledhill's. Lessingham mentioned that he was wearing Bumbles when he killed himself."

"And you left the trainers there. You see the importance of what you're saying, Mr. Dalgliesh?"

"Yes, I see the importance of what I'm saying, and yes, I left the shoe there. I was donating jumble, not stealing it."

Rickards said: "If there was a pair, and common sense suggests that there was, anyone could have taken them. And if they're no longer in the chest, it looks as though somebody did." He glanced at the luminous dial of his watch and said: "Eleven-forty-five. What time do you suppose Mrs. Dennison goes to bed?"

Dalgliesh said firmly: "Earlier than this, I imagine. And she'd hardly go to bed without bolting the back door. So if someone did take them and they're still missing, they can't be returned tonight."

They had reached the car. Rickards, with his hand on the door, didn't reply but gazed out over the headland as if in thought. His excitement, carefully controlled and unspoken, was as palpable as if he had banged his fists against the car bonnet. Then he unlocked the door and slipped inside. The headlights cut into the darkness like searchlights.

As he wound down the window to say a final good night, Dalgliesh said: "There's something I ought perhaps to mention about Meg Dennison. I don't know whether you remember, but she was the teacher at the centre of that race-row in inner London. I imagine that she's had about as much interrogation as she can take. That means the interview might not be easy for you."

He had thought carefully before he spoke, knowing that it might be a mistake. It was a mistake. The question, however carefully phrased, had sparked off that latent antagonism of which he was uneasily aware in all his dealings with Rickards.

Rickards said: "What you mean, Mr. Dalgliesh, is that it might not be easy for her. I've already spoken to the lady and I know something about her past. It took a lot of courage to stand up for her principles as she did. Some might say a lot of obstinacy. A woman who is capable of that has guts enough for anything, wouldn't you say?"

4

⊠

Dalgliesh watched the car lights until Rickards reached the coastal road and turned right, then locked the door and began a desultory tidying-up before bed. Looking back over the evening, he recognized that he had been reluctant to talk to Rickards at length about his Friday-morning visit to Larksoken Power Station and less than open about his reactions, perhaps because they had been more complex and the place itself more impressive than he had expected. He had been asked to arrive by 8.45, since Mair wanted to escort him personally and had to leave for a luncheon appointment in London. At the beginning of the visit Mair had asked: "How much do you know about nuclear power?"

"Very little. Perhaps it might be wiser to assume that I know nothing."

"In that case we'd better begin with the usual preamble about sources of radiation, and what is meant by nuclear power, nuclear energy and atomic energy, before we begin our tour of the plant. I've asked Miles Lessingham as Operations Superintendent to join us."

It was the beginning of an extraordinary two hours. Dalgliesh, escorted by his two mentors, was garbed in protective clothing, divested of it, checked for radioactivity, subjected to an almost constant stream of facts and figures. He was aware, even coming as an outsider, that the station was run with exceptional efficiency, that a quietly competent and respected authority was in control. Alex Mair, ostensibly there to escort a man afforded the status of a distinguished visitor, was never uninvolved, always quietly watchful, obviously in charge. And the staff Dalgliesh met impressed him with their dedication as they patiently explained their jobs in terms which an intelligent layman could understand. He sensed beneath their professionalism a commitment to nuclear power amounting in some cases to a controlled enthusiasm combined with a defensiveness which was probably natural given the public's ambivalence about nuclear energy. When one of the engineers said: "It's a dangerous technology but we need it and we can manage it," he heard, not the arrogance of scientific certainty, but a reverence for the element which they controlled, almost the love-hate relationship of a sailor for the sea, which was both a respected enemy and his natural habitat. If the tour had been designed to reassure, then it had to some extent succeeded. If nuclear power was safe in any hands, then it would be safe in these. But how safe, and for how long?

He had stood in the great turbine hall, ears pulsating, while Mair produced his facts and figures about pressures, voltages and breaking capacity; had stood, garbed in protective clothing, and looked down where the spent elements lay like sinister fishes underwater in the fuel-cooling pond for a hundred days before being despatched to Sellafield for reprocessing; had walked to the edge of the sea to look at the cooling-water plant and condensers. But the most interesting part of the visit had been in the reactor house. Mair, summoned by a bleep from his intercom, had temporarily left them, and Dalgliesh was alone with Lessingham. They had stood on a high walkway looking down at the black charge floors of the two reactors. To one side of the reactor was one of the two immense fuelling machines. Remembering Toby Gledhill, Dalgliesh glanced at his companion. Lessingham's face was taut and so white that Dalgliesh feared that he was about to faint. Then he spoke almost like an automaton, reciting a lesson learned by rote.

"There are twenty-six thousand, four hundred and eighty-eight fuel elements in each reactor, and they're charged by the fuelling machinery over a period of five to ten years. Each of the fuelling machines is approximately twenty-three feet high and weighs a hundred and fifteen tons. It can hold fourteen fuel elements, as well as the other components which are necessary for the refuelling cycle. The pressure vessel is heavily shielded, with cast iron and densified wood. What you see mounted on top of the machine is the hoist unit for lifting the fuel elements. There is also a connecting unit which couples the machine to the reactor, and a television camera which allows viewing of the operations above the magazine."

He broke off and, looking at him, Dalgliesh saw that the hands gripping the rail in front of him were shaking. Neither spoke. The spasm lasted less than ten seconds. Then Lessingham said: "Shock is an odd phenomenon. I dreamed of watching Toby fall for weeks afterwards. Then the dream suddenly stopped. I thought I'd be able to look down at the reactor charge floor and put the image out of my mind. Most of the time I can. After all, I work here, this is my place. But the dream still recurs and sometimes, like now, I can see him lying there so clearly that it could be a hallucination."

Dalgliesh felt that nothing he could say would be other than banal. Lessingham went on: "I got to him first. He was lying prone but I couldn't turn him over. I couldn't make myself touch him. But I didn't need to. I knew that he was dead. He looked very small, disjointed, a rag doll. All I was aware of were those ridiculous symbols of a yellow bee on the heels of his trainers. Christ, was I glad to get rid of those bloody shoes."

So Gledhill hadn't been wearing protective clothing. The impulse to suicide hadn't been completely spontaneous.

Dalgliesh said: "He must have been a good climber."

"Oh yes, Toby could climb. That was the least of his talents."

And then, without a perceptible change in his voice, he had continued with the description of the reactor and the procedure for loading new fuel into the reactor core. Five minutes later Mair rejoined them. On their way back to his office at the end of the tour he had suddenly asked: "Have you heard of Richard Feynman?"

"The American physicist? I saw a television programme about him a few months ago; otherwise the name wouldn't have meant anything to me."

"Feynman said: 'Far more marvellous is the truth than any artist of the past imagined. Why do poets of the present not speak of it?' You're a poet, but this place, the power it generates, the beauty of the engineering, the sheer magnificence of it, it doesn't particularly interest you, does it? You or any other poet?"

"It interests me. That doesn't mean that I can make poetry out of it."

"No, your subjects are more predictable, aren't they? How does it go? Twenty percent to God and to His saints, / Twenty percent to nature and her proxies, / And all the rest devoted to the plaints / Of guys pursued by or pursuing doxies."

Dalgliesh said: "The percentage for God and His saints is down, but I'd agree that the doxies are more than holding their own."

"And that poor devil out there, the Norfolk Whistler, he's not poetic either, presumably."

"He's human. That makes him a fit subject for poetry."

"But not one you'd choose?"

Dalgliesh could have replied that a poet doesn't choose his subject, it chooses him. But one reason for escaping to Norfolk had been to avoid discussions about poetry, and even if he had enjoyed talking about his writing, it wouldn't have been with Alex Mair. But he had been surprised how little he had resented the questions. It was difficult to like the man, impossible not to respect him. And if he had murdered Hilary Robarts, then Rickards was faced with a formidable opponent.

As he raked out the last ashes of the fire, he remembered with extraordinary clarity that moment when he had stood with Lessingham and looked down at the dark charge floor of the reactor, beneath which that potent and mysterious power was silently working away. He wondered how long it would be before Rickards asked himself why precisely the murderer had chosen that particular pair of shoes.

5
⊠

Rickards knew that Dalgliesh was right: it would have been an un-
warranted intrusion to call on Mrs. Dennison so late at night. But he
couldn't drive past the Old Rectory without slowing down and glancing to see if there was any sign of life. There was none; the house
stood dark and silent behind the wind-torn bushes. Entering his own
darkened house, he felt a sudden overwhelming tiredness. But there
was paperwork to be got through before he could go to bed, including
his final report on the Whistler enquiry; awkward questions to be
answered, a defence to be argued which would stand a chance of
rebutting the charges, private and public, of police incompetence,
poor supervision, too much reliance on technology and not enough
good old-fashioned detection. And that was before he could begin
scrutinizing the latest reports on the Robarts murder.

It was nearly four o'clock before he tore off his clothes and
slumped face-downwards onto the bed. Sometime during the night
he must have been aware that he was cold, for he awoke to find
himself under the bedclothes and, stretching out his hand to the
bedside lamp, saw with dismay that he had slept through the alarm
and that it was almost eight o'clock. Instantly awake, he threw back
the bedclothes and stumbled over to peer at himself in the glass of
his wife's dressing table. The dressing table, kidney-shaped, was
trimmed with pink-and-white flowered voile, the pretty matching set
of ring-stand and tray still neatly in place, a stuffed doll which Susie

had won at a fair as a child hanging from the side of the glass. Only her jars of make-up were missing, and their absence suddenly struck him as poignantly as if she were dead and they had been disposed of with the unimportant detritus of a life. What, he wondered, bending low to look more closely into the glass, had anything in this pink-and-white, utterly feminine bedroom to do with that gaunt face, that rough, masculine torso? He experienced again what he had felt initially when they first moved in a month after the honeymoon, that nothing in the house was truly his. When he was a young DC he would have been amazed had anyone told him that he would achieve such a house, a gravel sweep of drive, its own half-acre of garden, a drawing room and separate dining room, each with its carefully chosen suite of furniture which still smelt pristine new, reminding him, every time he entered, of the Oxford Street department store in which it had been chosen. But with Susie away he was again as ill at ease in it as if he were a barely tolerated and despised guest.

Dragging on his dressing gown, he opened the door of the small room at the south of the house which was to be the nursery. The cot was in pale lemon and white, matching the curtains. The changing table, with its lower shelf for baby paraphernalia, its hanging bag for clean nappies, stood against the wall. The wallpaper was a riot of rabbits and leaping lambs. It was impossible to believe that any child of his would one day be sleeping here.

And it wasn't only the house which rejected him. With Susie absent it was sometimes difficult even to believe in the reality of his marriage. He had met her on a cultural cruise to Greece on which he had booked as an alternative to the usual solitary walking holiday. She had been one of the few younger women on the ship, travelling with her mother, the widow of a dentist. He realized now that it was Susie who had made the running, who had determined on the marriage, who had chosen him long before he had thought of choosing her. But the realization when it came was flattering rather than disturbing and, after all, he hadn't been unwilling. He had reached that time of life when he would occasionally indulge in an idealized picture of a wife waiting at home, domestic comfort, someone to return to at the end of the day, a child who would be his stake in the future, someone to work for.

And she had married him despite the opposition from her mother,

who at first had seemed to collude in the enterprise, perhaps reminding herself that Susie was twenty-eight and time not on her side,
but who, once the engagement had been secured, had made it plain
that her only child could have done better, and had embarked on a
policy of ostentatiously making the best of it while undertaking a
vigorous campaign of his social re-education. But even she hadn't
been able to find fault with the house. It had cost him all his savings,
and the mortgage was the largest his income could support, but it
stood as a solid symbol of the two things that mattered most to him,
his marriage and his job.

Susie had been trained as a secretary but had seemed glad to
give it up. If she had wanted to carry on working, he would have
supported her, as he would in any interest she cared to take up. But
he preferred her to be happily satisfied with the house and the garden,
to find her waiting for him when he returned at the end of the day.
It was not the kind of marriage that was currently fashionable, nor
the kind that most couples could afford; but it was his kind of marriage
and he was grateful that it was hers.

He hadn't been in love with her at the time of the marriage, he
knew that now. He would, indeed, have said that he hardly knew the
meaning of the word, since it had certainly nothing to do with the
half-shameful affairs, the humiliations of his earlier experiences with
women. And yet not only poets and writers, the whole world used the
word, seeming to know by instinct if not by direct experience exactly
what it meant. Sometimes he felt uniquely disadvantaged, excluded
from a universal birthright, as a man might be who had been born
without a sense of taste or smell. And when, three months after the
honeymoon, he had fallen in love with Susie, it had seemed like the
revelation of something known but never experienced, as blinded eyes
might suddenly open to the reality of light and colour and form. It
was one night when, for the first time, she had found joy in his
lovemaking and, half-crying, half-laughing, had clung to him, whis-
pering incoherent endearments. Tightening his arms about her, he
had known in what seemed a moment of amazed recognition that this
was love. That moment of affirmation had been both a fulfilment and
a promise, not the end of searching but the beginning of discovery.
It left no room for doubts; his love, once acknowledged, seemed to
him indestructible. Their marriage might have its moments of shared

unhappiness and anxiety, but it could never be less than it was at this moment. Was it really possible, he thought now, that it could be seriously threatened if not destroyed by its first serious test, her decision to give in to her mother's calculated mixture of bullying and entreaty and leave him when their first child was about to be born? When the baby was first placed in her arms he wanted to be there. Now he might not even be told when she went into labour. The picture which persistently haunted his imagination before he fell asleep and at waking, of his mother-in-law standing triumphantly in the labour ward with his child in her arms, deepened his dislike of her almost to paranoia.

To the right of the dressing table was one of their wedding photographs in a silver-plated frame, taken after a marriage ceremony which could have been specifically designed to emphasize the social differences between the two families. Susie was leaning a little towards him, her peaked, vulnerable face looking younger than her twenty-eight years, the fair head with its chaplet of flowers barely reaching his shoulder. The flowers had been artificial, rosebuds and lilies of the valley, but in memory, as on the day, there rose from them a transitory sweetness. Her face, gravely smiling, revealed nothing, not even what the whole white mystique surely symbolized: This is what I worked for, what I want, what I've achieved. He was looking straight at the camera, stolidly enduring what had after all been the last of the seemingly endless photographs taken outside the church. The family group had at last been released. Here were Susie and himself, legally yoked, an accepted pair. The photographic session had, it seemed in retrospect, been the most important part of the ceremony, the service merely a preliminary to this complicated arranging and rearranging of incongruously garbed strangers according to some hierarchy not wholly understood by him but of which the hectoring photographer was obviously master. He heard again his mother-in-law's voice: "Yes, a bit of a rough diamond, I'm afraid, but he's really very able. Chief Constable material, I'm told."

Well, he wasn't Chief Constable material and she had known it, but at least she hadn't been able to criticize the house which he had provided for her only child.

It was an early hour to telephone, and he knew that his mother-in-law, who was a late riser, would make the most of the first grievance of the day. But if he didn't speak to Susie now, it might well be late at night before he had another opportunity. For a moment he stood looking down at the bedside telephone, unwilling to stretch out his hand. If things had been different, if it hadn't been for this new murder, he could have got in the Rover, driven north to York and brought her home. Face-to-face with him, she might have found the strength to resist her mother. Now she would have to travel alone, or with Mrs. Cartwright if her mother insisted on accompanying her. Well, he would put up with her if she insisted on coming, and it might be better for Susie than facing the long train journey alone. But he wanted her home; he wanted her here in this house.

The ringing tone seemed to last for an inordinate time and it was his mother-in-law who answered, enunciating the number with weary resignation, as if this had been the twentieth call of the morning.

He said: "This is Terry, Mrs. Cartwright. Is Susie awake?"

He had never called her Mother. That was a nonsense which he had never been able to get his tongue round and, to do her justice, she had never suggested it.

"Well, she will be now, won't she? Not very considerate, Terry, to ring before nine. Susie isn't sleeping very well just now, and she needs her lie-in. And she was trying to get you all last evening. Hold on."

And then, at least a minute later, came the small, tentative: "Terry?"

"Are you all right, darling?"

"Yes, everything's fine. Mummy took me to Dr. Maine yesterday. He used to look after me when I was a child. He's keeping an eye on me, and he says that everything's going on very well. He's booked me a bed in the local hospital just in case."

So she's even got that fixed up, he thought bitterly, and for a moment the treacherous thought lodged in his mind that the two of them might have planned it together, that this was what Susie wanted. He said: "I'm sorry I couldn't spend longer on the phone yesterday. Things got pretty hectic. But I wanted you to know that the Whistler was dead."

"It's been in all the papers, Terry. It's wonderful news. Are you all right? Are you feeding yourself properly?"

"Fine. I'm fine. Tired, but I'm OK. Look, darling, this new murder, it's different. We haven't got another serial murderer on the loose. The danger's over now. I'm afraid there's no chance I can get away to fetch you, but I could meet you at Norwich. Do you think you could make it today? There's a fast train at two minutes past three. If your mother would like to come, stay until after the baby is born, well, that's all right, of course."

It wasn't all right, but it was a small price to pay.

"Hold on, Terry. Mummy wants to talk to you."

Then, after another long delay, he heard her mother's voice.

"Susie is staying here, Terry."

"The Whistler is dead, Mrs. Cartwright. The danger's over."

"I know that the Whistler's dead. But you've had another murder down there, haven't you? There's still a killer at large, and you're the man who's hunting him. This baby is due in less than two weeks, and what Susie needs now is to get away from murder and death. Her health has to be my first consideration. What she needs is a little cosseting and kindness."

"She's had that here, Mrs. Cartwright."

"I dare say you did your best, but you're never there, are you? Susie rang you four times last night. She really needed to talk to you, Terry, and you weren't there. It isn't good enough, not now, it isn't. Out half the night catching murderers, or not catching them. I know that's your job, but it's hardly fair on Susie. I want my grandchild born safely. A girl's place is with her mother at a time like this."

"I thought that a wife's place was with her husband."

Oh God, he thought, that I should ever hear myself speaking those words. A wave of utter misery swept over him compounded of self-disgust, anger and despair. He thought, If she doesn't come today she'll never come. The baby will be born in York and her mother will hold him in her arms before I do. She'll get her clutches into both of them, now and forever. He knew how strong was that bond between widow and only child. There wasn't a day when Susie didn't telephone her mother, sometimes more than once. He knew with what difficulty and patience he had begun to wean her away from that obsessive maternal embrace. Now he had given Mrs. Cartwright another weapon. He heard the triumph in her voice.

"Don't you talk about a wife's place to me, please, Terry. You'll be talking about Susie's duty next. And what about your duty to her?

You've told her that you can't get away to fetch her, and I'm certainly not having my grandchild born on a British Rail train. Susie is staying here until this latest murder is solved and you can find time to fetch her."

And then he was cut off. Slowly he replaced the receiver and stood waiting. Perhaps Susie would ring back. He could, of course, ring again, but he knew with a sick hopelessness that there would be no use. She wasn't going to come. And then the telephone rang. He snatched up the receiver and said eagerly: "Hello? Hello?"

But it was only Sergeant Oliphant ringing from the incident room at Hoveton, an early call letting him know that Oliphant either had been up all night or had snatched even less sleep than he. His own four hours now seemed an indulgence.

"The Chief Constable's trying to get you, sir. I told his PA there'd be no point in ringing home. You'd be on your way here by now."

"I shall be on my way in five minutes. Not to Hoveton, but to the Old Rectory at Larksoken. Mr. Dalgliesh has given us a strong lead on the Bumble trainers. Meet me outside the rectory in three-quarters of an hour. And you'd better ring Mrs. Dennison now. Tell her to keep the back door locked and not to admit anyone to the house until we come. Don't alarm her; just say that there are one or two questions we have to put to her and we'd rather she spoke to us this morning before she talked to anyone else."

If Oliphant was excited at the news he managed to conceal it. He said: "You haven't forgotten that PR have fixed a press conference for ten, sir? Bill Starling from the local radio has been on to me, but I told him he'll have to wait until then. And I think the CC wants to know if we're going to release the approximate time of death."

And the Chief Constable wasn't the only one. It had been useful to fudge the approximate time of the murder, to avoid stating categorically that this couldn't have been the work of the Whistler. But sooner or later they would have to come clean, and once the postmortem report was to hand it would be difficult to parry the media's insistent questions. He said: "We shan't release any forensic information until we get the written report of the autopsy."

"We've got that now, sir. Doc Maitland-Brown dropped it in about twenty minutes ago on his way to the hospital. He was sorry he couldn't wait to see you."

I'll bet he was, thought Rickards. Nothing, of course, would have been said; Dr. Maitland-Brown didn't gossip with junior police officers. But there must have been a cosy atmosphere of mutual self-congratulation in the incident room on their joint early start to the day. He said: "There's no reason why he should have waited. All the stuff we need from him will be in the report. Better open it now, give me the gist."

He heard the receiver being placed down on the desk. There was a silence of less than a minute; then Oliphant spoke: "No sign of recent sexual activity. She wasn't raped. Seems she was an exceptionally healthy woman until someone slung a ligature round her neck and strangled her. He can be a bit more precise about the time of death now he's seen the stomach contents, but he hasn't changed his first estimate. Between eight-thirty and nine-forty-five, but if we want to make it nine-twenty he won't object. And she wasn't pregnant, sir."

"All right, Sergeant. I'll be with you outside the Old Rectory in about forty-five minutes."

But he was damned if he was going to face a heavy day without breakfast. Quickly he peeled a couple of rashers from the packet in the refrigerator and placed them under the grill, turning it to full power, then switched on the kettle and reached for a mug. Time for one mug of strong coffee; then he'd put the rashers between two hunks of bread and eat them in the car.

Forty minutes later, driving through Lydsett, he thought about the previous evening. He hadn't suggested to Adam Dalgliesh that he should come with the police to the Old Rectory. It wasn't necessary; his information had been precise and specific, and it hardly needed a Commander of the Metropolitan Police to point out a tea chest of discarded shoes. But there was another reason. He had been happy enough to drink Dalgliesh's whisky, eat his stew, or whatever it was he had called it, to discuss the salient points of the investigation. What else, after all, had they in common except their jobs? But that certainly didn't mean that he wanted Dalgliesh present while he was actually doing it. He had been glad the previous evening to call at the mill, grateful that he hadn't had to return to an empty house, had sat companionably by the wood fire and had felt, by the end of the evening, at least comfortably at ease. But once he was away from Dalgliesh's physical presence, the old uncertainties returned, as they had with such disconcerting force at the deathbed of the Whistler. He knew he would never be totally at one with the man and he knew why. He had only to think of the incident now and the old resentment would come flooding back. And yet it had happened nearly twelve years ago, and he doubted whether Dalgliesh even remembered it. That, of course, was the greater part of the injury, that words which had remained in his memory for years, which at the time had humiliated him and almost destroyed his confidence as a detective, could be so easily spoken and apparently so quickly forgotten.

The place was a small top room in a narrow warren of a house behind the Edgware Road, the victim a fifty-year-old prostitute. She had been dead for over a week when they found her, and the stink in the cluttered, airless hovel had been so disgusting that he had had to press his handkerchief against his mouth to hold back the vomit. One of the DCs had been less successful. He had rushed to throw open the window and might have made it if the pane hadn't been grimed fast. He himself had been unable to swallow, as if his own spittle had become contaminated. The handkerchief held against his mouth was soaked with saliva. She had been lying naked among the bottles, the pills, the half-eaten food, an obscene putrefying lump of flesh only a foot from the brimming chamber-pot which she hadn't in the end been able to reach. But that had been the least of the stench in the room. After the pathologist had left, Rickards had turned to the nearest DC and said: "For God's sake, can't we get this thing out of here?"

And then he had heard Dalgliesh's voice from the doorway like a whiplash.

"Sergeant, the word is 'body.' Or, if you prefer, there's 'cadaver,' 'corpse,' 'victim,' even 'deceased' if you must. What you are looking at was a woman. She was not a thing when she was alive and she is not a thing now."

He could still react physically to the memory of it, feel the tightening of the stomach muscles, the hot surge of anger. He shouldn't have let it pass, of course, not a public rebuke like that, not in front of the DCs. He should have looked the arrogant bastard in the face and spoken the truth, even if it had cost him his stripes.

"But she isn't a woman now, is she, sir? She's not a human being any more, is she? So if she isn't human, what is she?"

It had been the unfairness that had rankled. There were a dozen of his colleagues who would have merited that cold rebuke, but not he. He had never at any time since his promotion to the CID seen the victim as an unimportant lump of flesh, never taken a prurient, half-shameful pleasure in the sight of a naked body, had rarely seen even the most degraded, most disgusting of victims without some pity, and often with pain. His words had been totally out of character, torn from him out of hopelessness, tiredness after a nineteen-hour day, out of uncontrollable physical disgust. It was bad luck that they should have been overheard by Dalgliesh, a DCI whose cold sarcasm could be more devastating than another officer's bawled obscenities. They had continued working together for another six months. Nothing further had been said. Apparently Dalgliesh had found his work satisfactory; at least there hadn't been any further criticism. There hadn't been any praise either. He had been scrupulously correct to his superior officer; Dalgliesh had acted as if the incident had never taken place. If he later regretted his words, he had never said so. Perhaps he would have been amazed to know how bitterly, almost obsessively, they had been resented. But now, for the first time, Rickards wondered whether Dalgliesh too might not have been under strain, driven by his own compulsions, finding relief in the bitterness of words. After all, hadn't he at the time recently lost his wife and newborn child? But what had that to do with a dead prostitute in a London whorehouse? And he should have known better. That was the nub of it. He should have known his man. It seemed to Rickards that to remember the incident for so long and with such anger was almost paranoid. But the thought of Dalgliesh on his patch had brought it all back. Worse things had happened to him, more serious criticisms accepted and forgotten. But this he couldn't forget. Sitting by the wood fire in Larksoken Mill, drinking Dalgliesh's whisky, nearly equal in rank, secure on his own patch, it had seemed to him that the past might be put aside. But he knew now that it couldn't. Without that memory, he and Adam Dalgliesh might have become friends. Now he respected him, admired him, valued his opinion, could even feel at ease with him. But he told himself that he could never like him.

6

Oliphant was waiting outside the Old Rectory, not sitting in the car but lolling cross-legged against the bonnet and reading a tabloid newspaper. The impression given and no doubt intended was that he had been wasting time there for the past ten minutes. As the car approached he straightened up and handed over the paper. He said: "They've gone to town a bit, sir. Only to be expected, I suppose."

The story hadn't made the front page but was spread over the two centre pages with black headlines and a screamer: "Not again!" The byline was that of the paper's crime correspondent. Rickards read: "I have today learned that Neville Potter, the man now identified as the Whistler, who killed himself in the Balmoral Hotel at Easthaven on Sunday, had been interviewed by the police early in their enquiry and eliminated. The question is, why? The police knew the type of man they were looking for. A loner. Probably unmarried or divorced. Unsociable. A man with a car and a job that took him out at night. Neville Potter was just such a man. If he had been caught when he was first interviewed, the lives of four innocent women could have been saved. Have we learned nothing from the Yorkshire Ripper fiasco?"

Rickards said: "The usual predictable nonsense. Female murder victims are either prostitutes, who presumably deserve what they get, or innocent women."

Walking up the drive to the Old Rectory, he quickly scanned the rest of the article. Its argument was that the police relied too much on computers, on mechanical aids, fast cars, technology. It was time to get back to the bobby on the beat. What use was feeding interminable data into a computer when an ordinary DC wasn't competent to spot an obvious suspect? The article was no more acceptable to Rickards because it expressed some of his own views.

He threw it back at Oliphant and said: "What are they suggesting, that we could have trapped the Whistler by stationing a uniformed bobby on the beat at every country-road intersection? You told Mrs. Dennison that we were coming and asked her to keep out visitors?"

"She sounded none too pleased, sir. Said the only visitors who were likely to call were the headlanders, and what reason could she give for turning away her friends. No one has called so far, at least not at the front door."

"And you checked on the back door?"

"You said to wait outside for you, sir. I haven't been round the back."

It was hardly a promising beginning. But if Oliphant, with his usual tactlessness, had managed to antagonize Mrs. Dennison, she showed no sign of displeasure on opening the door but welcomed them in with grave courtesy. Rickards thought again how attractive she was, with a gentle, old-fashioned prettiness which he supposed people used to call the English-rose type when English-rose prettiness was in fashion. Even her clothes had an air of anachronistic gentility, not the ubiquitous trousers but a grey pleated skirt and a matching cardigan over a blue blouse with a single row of pearls. But despite her apparent composure she was very pale, the carefully applied pink lipstick almost garish against the bloodless skin, and he saw that her shoulders were rigid under the thin wool.

She said: "Won't you come into the drawing room, Chief Inspector, and explain what this is all about? And I expect you and your sergeant would like some coffee."

"It's good of you, Mrs. Dennison, but I'm afraid we haven't the time. I hope we won't have to keep you for long. We're looking for a pair of shoes, Bumble trainers, which we have reason to believe may be in your jumble box. Could we see it, please?"

She gave them one quick glance, then, without speaking, led them through a door at the rear of the hall and down a short passage leading to another door, which was bolted. She reached up to the bolt, which slid easily, and they found themselves in a second and shorter passage, stone-flagged, facing a formidably stout back door, which was also bolted at the top and bottom. There was a room on either side. The door on the right stood open.

Mrs. Dennison led them in. She said: "We keep the jumble here. As I told Sergeant Oliphant when he telephoned, the back door was double-locked at five last evening and has remained bolted. During the daytime I usually open it, so that anyone who has jumble can come in and leave it without bothering to knock."

Oliphant said: "Which means they could help themselves to the stuff as well as leave it. Aren't you afraid of theft?"

"This is Larksoken, Sergeant, not London."

The room, stone-floored, brick-walled and with a single high window, must originally have been either a pantry or perhaps a storeroom. Its present use was immediately apparent. Against the wall were two tea chests, the left one about three-quarters full of shoes and the right containing a jumble of belts, bags and men's ties knotted together. Next to the door were two long shelves. On one stood an assortment of bric-à-brac: cups and saucers, fairings, small statuettes, saucers and plates, a portable radio, a bedside lamp with a cracked and grubby shade. The second shelf held a row of old and rather tattered books, most of them paperbacks. A row of hooks had been screwed into the lower shelf, on which hung hangers holding a variety of better-quality clothes: men's suits, jackets, women's dresses and children's clothes, some of them already priced on small scraps of paper pinned to the hem. Oliphant stood for no more than a couple of seconds surveying the room, and then turned his attention to the box of shoes. It took less than a minute of rummaging to confirm that the Bumbles weren't there, but he began a systematic search, watched by Rickards and Mrs. Dennison. Each pair, most tied together by the laces, was taken out and placed on one side until the box was empty and then as methodically replaced. Rickards took a right-foot Bumble trainer from his briefcase and handed it to Mrs. Dennison.

"The shoes we are looking for are like this. Can you remember if a pair were ever in the jumble box and, if so, who brought them in?"

She said at once: "I didn't realize they were called Bumbles but, yes, there was a pair like this in the box. Mr. Miles Lessingham, from the power station, brought them in. He was asked to dispose of the clothes of the young man who killed himself at Larksoken. Two of the suits hanging up here also belonged to Toby Gledhill."

"When did Mr. Lessingham bring in the shoes, Mrs. Dennison?"

"I can't remember exactly. I think it was late afternoon a week or so after Mr. Gledhill died, sometime towards the end of last month. But you'd have to ask him, Chief Inspector. He may remember more precisely."

"And he brought them to the front door?"

"Oh yes. He said he wouldn't stay to tea but he did have a word in the drawing room with Mrs. Copley. Then he brought the suitcase of clothes out here with me and we unpacked them together. I put the shoes in a plastic bag."

"And when did you last see them?"

"I can't possibly remember that, Chief Inspector. I don't come out here very often, except occasionally to price up some of the clothes. And when I do I don't necessarily look in the shoe box."

"Not even to see what's been brought in?"

"Yes, I do that from time to time, but I don't make any kind of regular inspection."

"They're very distinctive shoes, Mrs. Dennison."

"I know that, and if I'd rummaged about in the box recently I must have seen them or even noticed that they were missing. But I didn't. I'm afraid I can't possibly say when they were taken."

"How many people know about the system here?"

"Most of the headlanders know, and any staff at Larksoken Power Station who regularly donate jumble. They usually come by car, of course, on their way home, and sometimes, like Mr. Lessingham, ring at the front door. Occasionally I take the bags from them at the door, or they may say that they'll drop them in at the back. We don't actually hold the jumble sale here; that takes place in the village hall in Lydsett in October. But this is a convenient collecting place for the headland and for the power station, and then Mr. Sparks or Mr. Jago from the Local Hero comes in a van and loads it up a day or two before the sale."

"But I see you price up some of the stuff here."

"Not all of it, Chief Inspector. It's just that occasionally we know of people who might like some of the items and who buy them before the sale."

The admission seemed to embarrass her. Rickards wondered whether the Copleys might not benefit in this way. He knew about jumble sales. His ma had helped with the annual one at the chapel. The helpers expected to get the pick of the goods; that was their perk. And why not? He said: "You mean that anyone local wanting clothes, maybe for his kids, would know that he could buy them here?"

She flushed. He could see that the suggestion and perhaps his choice of pronoun had embarrassed her. She said: "Lydsett people usually wait until the main sale. After all, it wouldn't be worthwhile, people coming in from the village just to see what we're collecting. But sometimes I sell to people on the headland. After all, the jumble is given in aid of the church. There's no reason why it shouldn't be sold in advance if someone local happens to want it. Naturally they pay the proper price."

"And who has from time to time wanted it, Mrs. Dennison?"

"Mr. Blaney has occasionally bought clothes for the children. One of Mr. Gledhill's tweed jackets fitted Mr. Copley, so Mrs. Copley paid for that. And Neil Pascoe called in about a fortnight ago to see if we had anything suitable for Timmy."

Oliphant asked: "Was that before or after Mr. Lessingham brought in the trainers?"

"I can't remember, Sergeant. You'd better ask him. We neither of us looked in the shoe box. Mr. Pascoe was interested in warm jumpers for Timmy. He paid for two. There's a tin with the money on a shelf in the kitchen."

"So people don't just help themselves and leave the cash?"

"Oh no, Chief Inspector. No one would dream of doing that."

"And what about the belts? Would you be able to say whether one of the belts or straps is missing?"

She said with a sudden spurt of impatience: "How could I possibly do that? Look for yourself. This box is literally a jumble: straps, belts, old handbags, scarves. How could I possibly say if anything is missing or when it was taken?"

Oliphant said: "Would it surprise you to be told that we have a witness who saw the trainers in this box last Wednesday morning?"

Oliphant could make the simplest and most innocuous question sound like an accusation. But his crudeness, sometimes bordering on insolence, was usually carefully judged, and Rickards seldom attempted to discipline it, knowing that it had its uses. It had, after all, been Oliphant who had got close to shaking Alex Mair's composure. But now he should perhaps have remembered that he was talking to an ex-schoolmistress. Mrs. Dennison turned on him the mildly reproving look more appropriate to a delinquent child.

"I don't think you can have been listening carefully to what I've been saying, Sergeant. I have no idea when the shoes were taken. That being so, how could it surprise me to learn when they were last seen?" She turned to Rickards: "If we're going to discuss this further, wouldn't it be more comfortable for all of us in the drawing room than standing about here?"

Rickards hoped that it might at least be warmer.

She led them across the hall into a room at the front of the house which faced south, over the lumpy lawn and the tangle of laurels, rhododendrons and wind-stunted bushes, which effectively screened the road. The room was large and barely warmer than the one they had left, as if even the strongest autumn sun had been unable to penetrate the mullioned windows and the heavy drapes of the velvet curtains. And the air was a little stuffy, smelling of polish, pot pourri and faintly of rich food, as if still redolent with long-eaten Victorian afternoon teas. Rickards almost expected to hear the rustle of a crinoline.

Mrs. Dennison didn't switch on the light and Rickards felt that he could hardly ask her. In the gloom he had an impression of solid mahogany furniture, side tables laden with photographs, of comfortably upholstered armchairs in shabby covers and of so many pictures in ornate frames that the room had the air of an oppressive and rarely visited provincial gallery. Mrs. Dennison seemed aware of the cold, if not of the gloom. She stooped to plug in a two-bar electric fire to the right of the huge carved grate, then seated herself with her back towards the window and gestured Rickards and Oliphant to the sofa, on which they sat side-by-side solidly upright on stiff unyielding cushions. She sat quietly waiting, her hands folded in her lap. The room, with its weight of dark mahogany, its air of ponderous respectability, diminished her, and it seemed to Rickards that she gleamed like a pale and unsubstantial wraith dwarfed by the huge arms of the chair. He wondered about her life on the headland and in this remote and surely unmanageable house, wondered what she had been seeking when she fled to this wind-scoured coast and whether she had found it.

He asked: "When was it decided that the Reverend and Mrs. Copley should go to stay with their daughter?"

"Last Friday, after Christine Baldwin was murdered. She'd been very anxious about them for some time and pressing them to leave, but it was the fact that the last murder was so very close that persuaded them. I was to drive them to Norwich to catch the eight-thirty on Sunday evening."

"Was that generally known?"

"It was talked about, I expect. You could say it was generally known in as far as there are people here to know it. Mr. Copley had to make arrangements for the services he normally takes. I told Mrs. Bryson at the stores that I would only be needing half a pint of milk a day instead of the normal two and a half pints. Yes, you could say it was generally known."

"And why didn't you drive them to Norwich as arranged?"

"Because the car broke down while they were finishing the packing. I thought I'd explained that already. At about half past six I went to get it out of the garage and drove it to the front door. It was all right then, but when I finally got them into it at seven-fifteen and we were ready to go it wouldn't start. So I rang Mr. Sparks at Lydsett garage and arranged for him to take them in his taxi."

"Without you?"

Before she could answer, Oliphant got to his feet, walked over to a standard lamp close to his chair and, without a word, switched it on. The strong light flowed down on her. For a moment Rickards thought that she was about to protest. She half-rose from the chair, then sat down again and went on as if nothing had happened.

"I felt bad about that. I would have been much happier to have seen them on the train, but Mr. Sparks could only take the job if he could go straight on to Ipswich, where he had to pick up a fare. But he promised he wouldn't leave them until he'd seen them into the carriage. And, of course, they're not children, they're perfectly capable of getting out at Liverpool Street. It's the terminus, after all; and their daughter was meeting them."

Why, Rickards wondered, was she so defensive? She could hardly suppose herself a serious suspect. And yet, why not? He had known less likely murderers. He could see fear in the dozen small signs which no experienced policeman could miss: the tremble of the hands, which she tried to control when his glance fell on them; the nervous tic at the corner of the eye; the inability to sit still one moment, followed by an unnatural, controlled stillness the next; the note of strain in the voice; the way in which she was resolutely meeting his eyes with a look compounded of defiance and endurance. Taken singly, each was a sign of natural stress; together they added up to something close to terror. He had resented Adam Dalgliesh's warning the previous night. It had been uncomfortably close to teaching him his job. But perhaps he had been right. Perhaps he was facing a woman who had suffered more aggressive interrogations than she could take. But he had his job to do.

He said: "You phoned for the taxi straight away? You didn't try to find out what was wrong with the car?"

"There was no time to fuss about under the bonnet. I'm not a mechanic anyway. I've never been particularly good with a car. It was lucky that I found out in time that it wouldn't go, and even luckier that Mr. Sparks could oblige. He came at once. Mr. and Mrs. Copley were getting very agitated. Their daughter was expecting them; all the arrangements had been made. It was important to catch the train."

"Where was the car normally kept, Mrs. Dennison?"

"I thought I told you that, Chief Inspector. In the garage."

"Locked?"

"There's a padlock. Quite a small one. I don't suppose it's very secure if someone really wanted to break it, but no one has ever tried. It was locked when I went for the car."

"Three-quarters of an hour before you needed to leave."

"Yes. I don't understand what you're getting at. Is that significant?"

"I'm just curious, Mrs. Dennison. Why so much time?"

"Have you ever had to load a car with the luggage required by two elderly people leaving for an indefinite stay? I had been helping Mrs. Copley with the final part of her packing. I wasn't needed for a minute or so, and it seemed a good opportunity to get the car out."

"And while it stood there in front of the house, was it constantly under your eye?"

"Of course not. I was busy checking that the Copleys had every-thing that they needed, going over the things I needed to do while they were away, parish business, a few telephone calls."

"Where was this happening?"

"In Mr. Copley's study. Mrs. Copley was in her bedroom."

"And the car was unattended in the drive?"

"Are you suggesting that someone sabotaged it?"

"Well, that would be a little fanciful, wouldn't it? What gave you that idea?"

"You did, Chief Inspector. It wouldn't otherwise have occurred to me. And I agree, it's fanciful."

"And when, at nine-forty-five, Mr. Jago rang from the Local Hero to tell you that the Whistler's body had been found, what did you do then?"

"There was nothing I could do. There was no way of stopping the Copleys; they were over an hour into their journey. I rang their daughter at her London club and managed to catch her before she set out for Liverpool Street. She said that she'd made all her arrange-ments, so that they might as well stay for a week since they were on their way. Actually, they're coming home tomorrow afternoon. Mrs. Duncan-Smith has been called to help nurse a sick friend."

Rickards said: "One of my officers has seen Mr. Sparks. He was anxious to reassure you that the Copleys were safely on their way. He rang you as soon as convenient for him but could get no reply. That was at about nine-fifteen, about the same time as Mr. Jago first tried to get through to you."

"I must have been in the garden. It was a beautiful moonlit night and I was restless. I needed to get out of the house."

"Even with the Whistler, as you thought, still at large?"

"Strangely enough, Chief Inspector, I've never been very fright-ened of the Whistler. The threat always seemed remote, a little unreal."

"You went no farther than the garden?"

She looked at him straight in the eyes.

"I went no farther than the garden."

"Yet you didn't hear the telephone?"

"It is a large garden."

"But it was a quiet night, Mrs. Dennison."

She didn't reply.

He asked: "And when did you come in from wandering alone in the dark?"

"I wouldn't describe a stroll around the garden as wandering alone after dark. I suppose I was out for about half an hour. I had been back about five minutes when Mr. Jago rang."

"And when did you hear about the Robarts murder, Mrs. Dennison? Obviously it wasn't news to you when we met at Martyr's Cottage."

"I thought you already knew that, Chief Inspector. Miss Mair telephoned me shortly after seven on Monday morning. She herself knew when her brother returned late on Sunday night after seeing the body, but she didn't want to disturb me at midnight, particularly with such distressing news."

Oliphant asked: "And was it distressing news, madam? You hardly knew Miss Robarts. Why should it be so distressing?"

Mrs. Dennison gave him a long look, then turned away. She said: "If you really have to ask that question, Sergeant, are you sure you're in the right job?"

Rickards rose to go. She came with them to the front door. As they were leaving she turned to him and said with sudden urgency: "Chief Inspector, I'm not stupid. All these questions about the shoes. Obviously you've found a print at the scene and you think it could have been made by the murderer. But surely Bumbles aren't uncommon. Anyone could have been wearing them. The fact that Toby Gledhill's pair are missing could be simply coincidence. They weren't necessarily taken with evil purpose. Anyone needing a pair of trainers could have stolen them."

Oliphant looked at her. "Oh, I don't think so, madam, do you? As you said yourself only half an hour ago, this is Larksoken, not London." And he smiled his thick-lipped, self-satisfied smile.

7

Rickards wanted to see Lessingham at once, but the press conference called for 10.00 meant that the interview had to be postponed and, to complicate matters further, a telephone call to Larksoken Power Station revealed that Lessingham had taken a day's leave but had left a message saying he could be reached at his cottage outside Blakeney. Luckily he was at home and, without explanation, Oliphant made an appointment for midday.

They were less than five minutes late, and it was the more frustrating, therefore, to find when they arrived at the low-built wood-and-brick cottage set back on the coastal road a mile to the north of the village that he wasn't at home. A note in pencil was tacked to the front door.

"Anyone wanting me, try the *Heron*, berthed at Blakeney quay. That includes the police."

"Bloody cheek!" complained Oliphant. As if unwilling to believe that any suspect could be as wilfully uncooperative, he tried the door, peered in at the window, then disappeared round the back. Returning, he said: "Ramshackle. Could do with a lick of paint. Funny place to choose to live. These marshes are pretty dreary in winter. You'd think he'd want a bit of life around him."

Rickards privately agreed that it was an odd place for Lessingham to choose. His cottage looked as if it had once been a pair, now converted into a single dwelling and, although agreeably proportioned with a certain melancholy charm, it looked at first sight unoccupied and neglected. Lessingham was a senior engineer after all, or technician, he couldn't for the moment remember which. Anyway, he hardly lived here because he was poor.

Rickards said: "He probably wants to be close to his boat. There's not much choice of harbour on this coast. It was either there or Wells-next-the-Sea."

As they got back into the car, Oliphant gazed back at the cottage resentfully, as if it were concealing behind the peeling paint some secret which a few vigorous kicks on the door might persuade it to divulge. Fastening his seat belt, he grumbled: "And when we get to the quay I suppose there'll be a notice telling us to try the pub."

But Lessingham was where he said he'd be. Ten minutes later they came up to him, sitting on an upturned crate on the deserted quay, an outboard motor in front of him. Berthed beside him was a thirty-foot sailing boat with a central cabin. It was obvious that he hadn't yet started to work. A relatively clean rag drooped from fingers which seemed too listless to hold it, and he was regarding the engine as if it posed an intractable problem. He looked up as they stood over him, and Rickards was shocked at the change in him. In only two days he seemed to have aged ten years. He was barefoot and wore a faded dark-blue guernsey over knee-length denim shorts fashionably tattered at the edges. But this informal garb seemed only to emphasize his urban pallor, the skin taut over the wide cheekbones, the smudges like bruises under the deep-set eyes. He was a part-time sailor after all, thought Rickards. Extraordinary that even this bad summer hadn't produced more than a biscuit-coloured tan.

Lessingham didn't get up, but said without preamble: "You were lucky to catch me when you rang. A day's leave is too good to waste indoors, particularly now. I thought we could talk here as well as anywhere."

Rickards said: "Not altogether. Somewhere more private would be better."

"This is private enough. The locals can recognize the police when they see them. Of course, if you want me to make a formal statement or were thinking of arresting me, I'd prefer the police station. I like to keep my house and my boat uncontaminated." He added: "I mean, uncontaminated by disagreeable sensations."

Oliphant said stolidly: "Why do you suppose we would want to arrest you? Arrest you for what exactly?" He added: "Sir," and made the word sound like a threat.

Rickards felt a spurt of irritation. It was like the man not to miss an easy opening, but this childish preliminary sparring would hardly smooth the interrogation. Lessingham looked at Oliphant, seriously considering whether the question needed a reply.

"God knows. I suppose you could think of something if you put your minds to it." Then, seeming to realize for the first time that they were having to stand, he got up. "All right, better come on board."

Rickards wasn't a sailor, but it seemed to him that the boat, all wood, was old. The cabin, which they had to crouch low to enter, had a narrow mahogany table down the whole length and a bench on either side. Lessingham seated himself opposite them, and they re-garded each other across two feet of polished wood, their faces so close that Rickards felt he could smell his companions, a masculine amalgam of sweat, warm wool, beer and Oliphant's aftershave, as if all three were claustrophobically caged animals. It could hardly have been a more unsuitable place in which to conduct an interview, and he wondered whether Adam Dalgliesh would have engineered things better and despised himself for the thought. He was aware of Oliphant's great bulk beside him, their thighs touching, Oliphant's un-naturally warm, and had to resist an impulse to edge farther away.

He said: "Is this your boat, sir? The one you were sailing last Sunday night?"

"Not sailing, Chief Inspector, for much of the time; there wasn't enough wind. But, yes, this is my boat and this is the one I was on last Sunday."

"You seem to have damaged the hull. There's a long fresh-looking scratch on the starboard side."

"Clever of you to notice. I scraped the water tower offshore from the power station. Careless of me. I've sailed these waters often enough. If you'd come a couple of hours later it would have been repainted."

"And do you still say that you were never at any time within sight of the beach where Miss Robarts took her last swim?"

"You asked me that question when you saw me on Monday. It depends what you mean by 'in sight of.' I could have seen the beach through my binoculars if I'd happened to look, but I can confirm that I never got to within half a mile of it and that I didn't land. Since I could hardly murder her without landing, that seems to me conclusive. But I don't suppose you've come all this way just to hear me repeat my alibi."

Reaching down with difficulty, Oliphant dragged his grip onto the seat beside him, took out a pair of Bumble trainers and placed them on the table neatly, side-by-side. Rickards watched Lessingham's face. He controlled himself immediately but he hadn't been able to disguise the shock of recognition in the eyes, the tensing of the muscles around the mouth. The pair of trainers, pristine, new, grey and white, with the small bumblebee on each heel, seemed to dominate the cabin. Having placed them there, Oliphant ignored them.

He said: "But you were south of the water towers at the power station. The scratch is on the starboard side. You must have been travelling north, sir, when you got that scrape."

"I turned for home when I was about fifty yards beyond the towers. I'd planned to make the power station the limit of the journey."

Rickards said: "These trainers, sir, have you seen a pair like these?"

"Of course. They're Bumbles. Not everyone can afford them, but most people have seen them."

"Have you seen them worn by anyone who worked at Larksoken?"

"Yes, Toby Gledhill had a pair. After he killed himself, his parents asked me if I'd clear out his clothes. There weren't very many. Toby travelled light, but I suppose there were a couple of suits, the usual trousers and jackets and half a dozen pairs of shoes. The trainers were among them. Actually, they were almost new. He bought them about ten days before he died. He only wore them once."

"And what did you do with them, sir?"

"I bundled up all the clothes and took them to the Old Rectory for the next church jumble sale. The Copleys have a small room at the back of the house where people can leave their junk. From time to time Dr. Mair puts a notice on the notice board asking people to donate anything they don't want. It's part of the policy of being part of the community, all one happy family on the headland. We may not always go to church but we show goodwill by bestowing on the righteous our cast-off clothes."

"When did you take Mr. Gledhill's clothes to the Old Rectory?"

"I can't remember exactly, but I think it was a fortnight after he died. Just before the weekend, I think. Probably on Friday, twenty-sixth August. Mrs. Dennison may remember. I doubt whether it's worth asking Mrs. Copley, although I did see her."

"So you handed them over to Mrs. Dennison?"

"That's right. Actually, the back door of the rectory is usually kept open during daylight hours and people can walk in and drop anything they want to leave. But I thought on this occasion that it would be better to hand the things over formally. I wasn't entirely sure they'd be welcome. Some people are superstitious about buying the clothes of the recently dead. And it seemed, well, inappropriate just to drop them."

"What happened at the Old Rectory?"

"Nothing very much. Mrs. Dennison opened the door and showed me into the drawing room. Mrs. Copley was there and I explained why I had called. She produced the usual meaningless platitudes about Toby's death, and Mrs. Dennison asked me if I would like tea. I declined and I followed her through the hall to the room at the back where they store the jumble. There's a large tea chest there which holds the shoes. The pairs are just tied by the laces and thrown in. I had Toby's clothes in a suitcase, and Mrs. Dennison and I unpacked it together. She said that the suits were really too good for the jumble sale and asked if I'd mind if she sold them separately, provided, of course, the money went to church funds. She thought she might get a better price. I had a feeling that she was wondering whether Mr. Copley might not use one of the jackets. I said she could do what she liked with them."

"And what happened to the trainers? Were they put into the tea chest with the rest of the shoes?"

"Yes, but in a plastic bag. Mrs. Dennison said they were in too good a condition to be thrown in with the others and get dirty. She went off and returned with the bag. She seemed to be uncertain what to do with the suits, so I said I'd leave the suitcase. It was Toby's after all. It could be sold at the jumble sale with the rest of the things. Ashes to ashes, dust to dust, jumble to jumble. I was glad to see the end of it."

Rickards said: "I read about Dr. Gledhill's suicide, of course. It must have been particularly distressing for you, who actually saw it happen. He was described as a young man of brilliant promise."

"He was a creative scientist. Mair will confirm that, if you're interested one way or the other. Of course, all good science is creative, whatever the humanities try to tell you, but there are scientists who have this special vision, genius as opposed to talent, inspiration as well as the necessary patient conscientiousness. Someone, I forget who, described it rather well. Most of us edge forward, painfully advancing, yard by yard; they parachute behind enemy lines. He was young, only twenty-four. He could have become anything."

Rickards thought, Anything or nothing, like most of these young geniuses. Early death usually conferred a brief vicarious immortality. He'd never known a young DCI, accidentally killed, who wasn't at once proclaimed a potential Chief Constable. He asked: "What exactly was he doing at the power station, what was his job?"

"Working with Mair on his PWR safety studies. Briefly, it's to do with the behaviour of the core in abnormal conditions. Toby never discussed it with me, probably because he knew I couldn't understand the complicated computer codes. I'm just a poor bloody engineer. Mair is due to publish the study before he leaves for his rumoured new job, no doubt under both their names and with a suitable acknowledgement to his collaborator. All that will last of Toby is his name under Mair's on a scientific paper."

He sounded utterly weary and, looking towards the open door, made a half-movement as if to get up, out of the claustrophobic little cabin and into the air. Then he said, his eyes still on the door: "It's no use trying to explain Toby to you, you wouldn't understand. It would be a waste of your time and mine."

"You seem very sure of that, Mr. Lessingham."

"I am sure, very sure. I can't explain why without being offensive. So why don't we keep it simple, stick to the facts. Look, he was an exceptional person. He was clever, he was kind, he was beautiful. If you find one of these qualities in a human being, you're lucky; if you find all three, then you get someone rather special. I was in love with him. He knew, because I told him. He wasn't in love with me and he wasn't gay. Not that it's any business of yours. I'm telling you because it was a fact and you're supposed to deal in facts, and because if you're determined to be interested in Toby you may as well get him right.

And there's another reason. You're obviously grubbing about for all the dirt you can find. I'd rather you had facts from me than rumours from other people."

Rickards said: "So you didn't have a sexual relationship."

Suddenly the air was rent with a wild screeching and there was a beating of white wings against the porthole. Outside someone must be feeding the seagulls.

Lessingham started up as if the sound were alien to him. Then he collapsed back in his seat and said with more weariness than anger: "What the *hell* has that to do with Hilary Robarts's murder?"

"Possibly nothing at all, in which case the information will be kept private. But at this stage it's for me to decide what may or may not be relevant."

"We spent one night together two weeks before he died. As I said, he was kind. It was the first and the last time."

"Is that generally known?"

"We didn't broadcast it over local radio or write to the local paper or put up a notice in the staff canteen. Of course it wasn't generally known, why the hell should it be?"

"Would it have mattered if it had been? Would either of you have cared?"

"Yes, I would, we both would. I would care in the way you would care if your sex life was sniggered about in public. Of course we would have cared. After he died, it ceased to matter as far as I was concerned. There's this to be said for the death of a friend: it frees you from so much you thought was important."

Frees you for what? thought Rickards. For murder, that iconoclastic act of protest and defiance, that single step across an unmarked, undefended frontier which, once taken, sets a man apart forever from the rest of his kind? But he decided to defer the obvious question.

Instead he asked: "What sort of family had he?" The question sounded innocuous and banal, as if they were casually discussing a common acquaintance.

"He had a father and a mother. That sort of family. What other sort is there?"

But Rickards had resolved on patience. It was not a ploy that came easily to him, but he could recognize pain when its taut and naked sinews were thrust so close to his face. He said mildly: "I mean, what sort of background did he come from? Had he brothers or sisters?"

"His father is a country parson. His mother is a country parson's wife. He was an only child. His death nearly destroyed them. If we could have made it look like an accident, we would have. If lying could have helped, I would have lied. Why the hell didn't he drown himself? That way there would at least have been room for doubt. Is that what you meant by background?"

"It's helping to fill in the picture." He paused and then, almost casually, asked the seminal question. "Did Hilary Robarts know that you and Tobias Gledhill had spent a night together?"

"Whatever possible relevance . . . ? All right, it's your job to do the scavenging. I know the system. You trawl up everything you can get your nets to and then throw away what you don't want. In the process you learn a lot of secrets you've no particular right to know and cause a lot of pain. Do you enjoy that? Is that what gives you your kicks?"

"Just answer the question, sir."

"Yes, Hilary knew. She found out by one of those coincidences which seem a one-in-a-million chance when they happen but which aren't really so remarkable or unusual in real life. She drove past my house when Toby and I were leaving just after seven-thirty in the morning. She had taken a day's leave, apparently, and must have left home early to drive off somewhere. It's no use asking me where, because I don't know. I suppose, like most other people, she has friends she visits from time to time. I mean, someone somewhere must have liked her."

"Did she ever speak about the encounter, to you or to anyone else you know?"

"She didn't make it public property. I think she regarded it as too valuable a piece of information to cast before the swine. She liked power, and this was certainly power of a kind. As she drove past, she slowed down almost to walking pace and stared straight into my eyes. I can remember that look: amusement, changing to contempt, then triumph. We understood each other all right. But she never subsequently spoke a word to me."

"Did she talk about it to Mr. Gledhill?"

"Oh yes, she spoke to Toby all right. That's the reason he killed himself."

"How do you know that she spoke to him? Did he tell you?"

"No."

"You're suggesting that she blackmailed him?"

"I'm suggesting that he was unhappy, muddled, uncertain about every aspect of his life, his research, his future, his sexuality. I know that she attracted him sexually. He wanted her. She was one of those dominant, physically powerful women who do attract sensitive men like Toby. I think she knew that and she used it. I don't know when she got hold of him or what she said to him, but I'm bloody sure that he'd be alive now if it weren't for Hilary Robarts. And if you think that gives me a motive for her murder, you're damned right. But I didn't kill her and, that being so, you won't find any evidence that I did. Part of me, a very small part, is actually sorry that she's dead. I didn't like her and I don't think she was a happy woman, or even a particularly useful one. But she was healthy and intelligent and she was young. Death ought to be for the old, the sick and the tired. What I feel is a touch of *lacrimae rerum.* Even the death of an enemy diminishes us, apparently, or so, in certain moods, it seems. But that doesn't mean I'd want her alive again. But it's possible I'm prejudiced, perhaps even unjust. When Toby was happy, no one was more joyous. When he was miserable, he went down into his private hell. Perhaps she could reach him there, could help him. I know I couldn't. It's difficult to comfort a friend when you suspect that he sees it as a ploy to get him into your bed."

Rickards said: "You've been remarkably frank in suggesting a motive for yourself. But you haven't given us a single piece of concrete evidence to support your allegation that Hilary Robarts was in any way responsible for Toby Gledhill's death."

Lessingham looked straight into his eyes and seemed to be considering; then he said: "I've gone so far, I may as well tell you the rest. He spoke to me when he passed me on his way to death. He said, 'Tell Hilary she doesn't have to worry any more. I've made my choice.' The next time I saw him he was climbing the fuelling machine. He balanced on it for a second, then dived down on top of the reactor. He meant me to see him die, and I saw him die."

Oliphant said: "A symbolic sacrifice."

"To the terrifying god of nuclear fission? I thought one of you might say that, Sergeant. That was the vulgar reaction. It's altogether too crude and histrionic. All he wanted, for God's sake, was the quickest way to break his neck." He paused, seemed to consider, then went on: "Suicide is an extraordinary phenomenon. The result is irrevocable. Extinction. The end of all choice. But the precipitating action often seems so commonplace. A minor setback, momentary depression, the state of the weather, even a poor dinner. Would Toby have died if he'd spent the previous night with me instead of alone? If he was alone."

"Are you saying that he wasn't?"

"There was no evidence either way, and now there will never be. But, then, the inquest was remarkable for the lack of evidence about anything. There were three witnesses, myself and two others, to the way he died. No one was near him, no one could have pushed him, it couldn't have been an accident. There was no evidence from me or anyone else about his state of mind. You could say that it was a scientifically conducted inquest. It stuck to the facts."

Oliphant said quietly: "And where do you think he spent the night before he died?"

"With her."

"On what evidence?"

"None that would stand up in a court. Only that I rang him three times between nine and midnight and he didn't reply."

"And you didn't tell that to the police or the coroner?"

"On the contrary. I was asked when I'd last seen him. That was in the canteen on the day before he died. I mentioned my telephone call, but no one regarded it as important. Why should they? What did it prove? He could have been out walking. He could have decided not to answer the phone. There was no mystery about how he died. And now, if you don't mind, I'd like to get out of here and on with cleaning that bloody engine."

They walked in silence back to the car. Rickards said: "Arrogant bastard, isn't he? He made his view brutally plain. No point in trying to explain anything to the police. He can't say why without being offensive. You bet he can't. We're too thick, ignorant and insensitive to understand that a research scientist isn't necessarily an unimaginative technocrat, that you can be sorry a woman is dead without necessarily wishing her alive again and that a sexually attractive boy might actually be prepared to go to bed with either sex."

Oliphant said: "He could have done it if he used the engine at full power. He'd have had to come ashore north of where she bathed and kept to the tide line, or we'd have seen his footprints. It was a thorough search, sir, at least a mile north and south. We identified Mr. Dalgliesh's prints, but otherwise the upper beach was clean."

"Oh yes, he'd have kept pretty clear of the killing ground. But he could have beached the inflatable dinghy on shingle without much problem. There are stretches which are practically all pebbled, or with narrow strips of sand which he could leap over."

"What about the old beach defences, the hunks of concrete? It would be difficult to come close to shore anywhere north within easy walking distance without risking the boat."

"He has risked the boat recently, hasn't he? There's this scrape along the bow. He can't prove that he made it on the water towers. Cool about it, too, wasn't he? Calmly admitted that if we'd been an hour later he'd have repaired it. Not that repainting would have done him much good; the evidence would still be there. All right, so he manages to manoeuvre the boat as close in shore as he can—say, a hundred yards north of where she was found—makes his way along the shingle and into the trees and waits quietly in their shadow. Or he could have loaded the folding bicycle into the dinghy and landed at a safer distance. He couldn't cycle along the beach at high tide, but he'd have been safe enough on the coast road if he cycled without a light. He gets back to the boat and berths her again at Blakeney, just catching the high tide. No trouble about the knife or the shoes: he drops them overboard. We'll get the boat examined, with his consent, of course, and I want a single-handed chap to make that journey. If we've got an experienced sailor among our chaps, use him. If not, get someone local and accompany him. We've got to time it to the minute. And we'd better make enquiries of the crab fishermen down Cromer way. Someone may have been out that night and seen his boat."

Oliphant said: "Obliging of him, sir, to hand us his motive on a plate."

"So obliging that I can't help wondering whether it isn't a smoke screen for something he didn't tell us."

But as Rickards fastened his seat belt another possibility occurred to him. Lessingham had said nothing about his relationship with Toby Gledhill until he had been questioned about the Bumble trainers. He must know—how could he fail to?—that these linked the murder even more strongly to the headlanders and, in particular, to the Old Rectory. Was his new openness with the police less a compulsion to confide than a deliberate ploy to divert suspicion from another suspect? And if so, which of the suspects, Rickards wondered, was most likely to evoke this eccentric act of chivalry?

8
⊠

On Thursday morning Dalgliesh drove to Lydsett to shop at the village store. His aunt had shopped locally for most of her main provisions and he continued the practice, partly, he knew, to assuage a nagging guilt about having a second home, however temporary. The villagers did not on the whole resent weekenders, despite the fact that their cottages remained empty for most of the year and their contribution to village life was minimal, but preferred them not to arrive with their car boots loaded with provisions from Harrods or Fortnum and Mason.

And patronizing the Brysons in their corner shop entailed no particular sacrifice. It was an unpretentious village store with a clanging bell on the door which, as the sepia photographs of the Victorian village showed, had hardly altered externally in the last 120 years. Inside, however, the last four years had seen more changes than in the whole of its history. Whether because of the growth of holiday homes or the more sophisticated tastes of the villagers, it now offered fresh pasta, a variety of French as well as English cheeses, the more expensive brands of jams, marmalade and mustard and a well-stocked delicatessen, while a notice proclaimed that fresh croissants were delivered daily.

As he drew up in the side street, Dalgliesh had to manoeuvre past an old and heavily built bicycle with a large wicker basket which was propped against the kerb, and as he entered he saw that Ryan Blaney was just completing his purchases. Mrs. Bryson was ringing up and bagging three large brown loaves, packets of sugar, cartons of milk and an assortment of tins. Blaney gave Dalgliesh a glance from his bloodshot eyes, a curt nod, and was gone. He was still without his van, thought Dalgliesh, watching him load his basket with the contents of one carrier and hang the other two on the handlebars. Mrs. Bryson turned on Dalgliesh her welcoming smile but did not comment. She was too prudent a shopkeeper to get a reputation as a gossip or to become too openly involved in local controversies, but it seemed to Dalgliesh that the air was heavy with her unspoken sympathy for Blaney, and, as a policeman, he felt obscurely that she held him partly responsible, although he was unsure precisely why and for what. Rickards or his men must have questioned the villagers about the headlanders, Ryan Blaney in particular. Perhaps they had been less than tactful.

Five minutes later he stopped to open the gate barring entry to the headland. On the other side a tramp was sitting on the bank which separated the narrow road from the reed-enclosed dyke. He was bearded and wearing a checked tweed cap beneath which two neat plaits of strong grey hair bound with a rubber band fell almost to his shoulders. He was eating an apple, slicing it with a short-handled knife and throwing the sections into his mouth. His long legs, clad in thick corduroy trousers, were stretched out widely in front of him, almost as if he were deliberately displaying a pair of black, white and grey trainers, their obvious newness in stark contrast to the rest of his clothes. Dalgliesh closed the gate, then walked over to him and looked down into a pair of bright and intelligent eyes set in a drawn and weatherbeaten face. If this was a tramp, the keenness of that first glance, his air of confident self-sufficiency and the cleanliness of his white rather delicate hands made him an unusual one. But he was surely too encumbered to be a casual hiker. His khaki coat looked like army surplus and was bound with a wide leather belt from which was suspended by string an enamel mug, a small saucepan and a frying pan. A small but tightly packed backpack lay on the verge beside him.

Dalgliesh said: "Good morning. I'm sorry if I seem impertinent, but where did you get those shoes?"

The voice that answered him was educated, a little pedantic, a voice, he thought, that might have once belonged to a schoolmaster.

"You are not, I hope, about to claim ownership. I shall regret it if our acquaintanceship, although no doubt destined to be brief, should begin with a dispute about property."

"No, they're not mine. I was wondering how long they've been yours."

The man finished his apple. He threw the core over his shoulder into the ditch, cleaned the blade of his clasp-knife on the grass and pushed it with care deep into his pocket. He said: "May I ask if this enquiry arrives from—forgive me—an inordinate and reprehensible curiosity, an unnatural suspicion of a fellow mortal or a desire to purchase a similar pair for yourself. If the last, I am afraid I am unable to help you."

"None of these things. But the enquiry is important. I'm not being either presumptuous or suspicious."

"Nor, sir, are you being particularly candid or explicit. My name, incidentally, is Jonah."

"Mine is Adam Dalgliesh."

"Then, Adam Dalgliesh, give me one good reason why I should answer your question and you shall have an answer."

Dalgliesh paused for a moment. There was, he supposed, a theoretical possibility that here before him was the murderer of Hilary Robarts, but he did not for a moment believe it. Rickards had telephoned him the previous evening to inform him that the Bumbles were no longer in the jumble chest, obviously feeling that he owed Dalgliesh this brief report. But that did not mean that the tramp had taken them, nor did it prove that the two pairs were the same. He said: "On Sunday night a girl was strangled here on the beach. If you recently found, or were given, those shoes, or were wearing them on the headland last Sunday, the police will need to know. They have found a distinct footprint. It is important to identify it if only to eliminate the wearer from their enquiries."

"Well, that at least is explicit. You talk like a policeman. I should be sorry to hear that you are one."

"This isn't my case. But I am a policeman, and I know that the local CID are looking for a pair of Bumble trainers."

"And these, I take it, are Bumble trainers. I had thought of them as shoes."

"They don't have a label except under the tongue. That's the firm's sales gimmick. Bumbles are supposed to be recognizable without a blatant display of the name. But if these are Bumbles, there will be a yellow bee on each heel."

Jonah didn't reply, but with a sudden vigorous movement swung both feet into the air, held them for a couple of seconds, then dropped them again.

Neither spoke for a few moments; then Jonah said: "You are telling me that I now have on my feet the shoes of a murderer?"

"Possibly, but only possibly, these are the shoes he was wearing when the girl was killed. You see their importance?"

"I shall no doubt be made to see it, by you or another of your kind."

"Have you heard of the Norfolk Whistler?"

"Is it a bird?"

"A mass murderer."

"And these shoes are his?"

"He's dead. This latest killing was made to look as if he were responsible. Are you telling me you haven't even heard of him?"

"I sometimes see a newspaper when I need paper for other, more earthy purposes. There are plenty to pick up from the waste bins. I seldom read them. They reinforce my conviction that the world is not for me. I seem to have missed your murdering Whistler." He paused, then added: "What now am I expected to do? I take it that I am in your hands."

Dalgliesh said: "As I said, it isn't my case. I'm from the Metropolitan Police. But if you wouldn't mind coming home with me, I could telephone the officer in charge. It isn't far. I live in Larksoken Mill, on the headland. And if you care to exchange these trainers for a pair of my shoes, it seems the least I can offer. We're about the same height. There should be a pair to fit you."

Jonah got to his feet with surprising agility. As they walked to the car Dalgliesh said: "I've really no right to question you, but satisfy my curiosity. How did you come by them?"

"They were bestowed on me—inadvertently, I might say—sometime on Sunday night. I had arrived on the headland after dark and made my way to my usual night shelter in these parts. It's the half-buried concrete bunker near the cliff. A 'pillbox,' I think it's called. I expect you know it."

"I know it. Not a particularly salubrious place to spend the night, I should have thought."

"I have known better, certainly. But it has the advantage of privacy. The headland is off the usual route for fellow wayfarers. I usually visit once a year and stay for a day or two. The pillbox is completely weatherproof, and as the slit window faces the sea I can light a small fire without fear of discovery. I push the rubbish to one side and ignore it. It is a policy I would recommend to you."

"Did you go straight there?"

"No. As is my custom, I called at the Old Rectory. The elderly couple who live there are usually very obliging in allowing me to use their tap. I wanted to fill up my water bottle. As it happens, there was no one at home. There were lights on in the lower windows, but no one responded to the bell."

"What time would this be, do you remember?"

"I have no watch and I take little account of time between sunset and sunrise. But I did notice that St. Andrew's Church clock in the village showed eight-thirty as I passed. I was probably at the Old Rectory by nine-fifteen, or shortly afterwards."

"What did you do then?"

"I knew that there was an outside tap close to the garage. I took the liberty of filling my bottle without permission. They would hardly, I think, begrudge me clean water."

"Did you see a car?"

"There was one standing in the drive. The garage was open but, as I have said, I saw no human beings. I then went straight to the shelter. I was by then exceedingly tired. I drank some of the water, ate a crust of bread and some cheese and fell asleep. The shoes were thrown in through the door of the bunker sometime during the night."

Dalgliesh said: "Thrown in rather than placed?"

"I imagine so. Anyone who actually entered the bunker must have seen me. It is surely more likely that they were thrown in. There is a wayside pulpit at a church in Ipswich. Last week it said: 'God gives every bird his worm, but He does not throw it into the nest.' On this occasion, apparently, He did."

"And they hit you without waking you? They're heavy shoes."

"As I have said, you talk like a policeman. I had walked twenty miles on the Sunday. I have an easy conscience and I sleep sound. If they had fallen on my face, I have no doubt they would have wakened me. As it was, I found them next morning when I woke up."

"Neatly placed?"

"Not at all. What happened was that I woke and turned over from my left side onto my back. I felt something hard beneath me and lit a match. The lump was one of the shoes. The other I found near my foot."

"They weren't tied together?"

"Had they been tied, my dear sir, it would hardly have been possible for me to find one near the small of my back and the other at my feet."

"And you weren't curious? After all, the trainers were practically new, hardly the kind of shoe anyone would chuck away."

"Naturally I was curious. But, unlike members of your profession, I am not obsessed by the need to find explanations. It did not occur to me that I had a responsibility to find the owner or take the shoes into the nearest police station. I doubt whether they would have thanked me for my trouble. I took gratefully what fate or God had provided. My old shoes were nearing the end of their usefulness. You will find them in the pillbox."

"And you put on these."

"Not immediately. They were too damp. I waited until they were dry."

"Damp in parts or all over?"

"Damp all over. Someone had washed them very thoroughly, probably by holding them under a tap."

"Or by walking into the sea."

"I smelt them. It was not sea water."

"Could you tell?"

"My dear sir, I have the use of my senses. My nose is particularly keen. I can tell the difference between sea and tap water. I can tell you what county I'm in by the smell of the earth."

They had turned left at the crossroads, and the soaring white sails of the Mill were in sight. They sat in companionable silence for a few moments.

Then Jonah said: "You have, perhaps, a right to know what manner of man you are inviting under your roof. I am, sir, a modern remittance man. I know that originally my kind were banished to the colonies, but they are a little more discriminating now and, in any case, banishment from the smells and colours of the English countryside would not have suited me. My brother, a model of civil rectitude and a prominent member of his community, transfers a thousand pounds per annum from his bank account into mine, providing I never embarrass him by intruding on his presence. The interdict, I may say, extends to the town of which he is mayor, but since he and his fellow planners have long destroyed whatever character it once possessed, I have deleted it from my itinerary without regret. He is indefatigable in good works, and you could say that I am among the recipients of his charity. He has been honoured by Her Majesty. An OBE merely, but he has, I am sure, hope of higher things."

Dalgliesh said: "Your brother seems to be getting off rather lightly."

"You yourself would willingly pay more to ensure my perpetual absence?"

"Not at all. It's just that I assume that the thousand pounds is to enable you to keep yourself, and I was wondering how you managed to do it. One thousand pounds as an annual bribe could be considered generous; as a living allowance it's surely inadequate."

"To do him justice, my brother would willingly make an annual increase in line with the Retail Price Index. He has an almost obsessive sense of bureaucratic propriety. But I have told him that twenty pounds a week is more than adequate. I have no house, no rent, no rates, no heating, no lighting, no telephone, no car. I pollute neither my own body nor the environment. A man who cannot feed himself on nearly three pounds a day must either be lacking in initiative or be the slave of inordinate desires. An Indian peasant would regard it as luxury."

"An Indian peasant would have less problem in keeping warm. The winters must be trying."

"A hard winter is, indeed, a discipline in endurance. Not that I complain. I am always healthiest in winter. And matches are cheap. I have never learned those Boy Scout tricks with a magnifying glass and rubbed sticks. Happily I know half a dozen farmers who are willing to let me sleep in their barns. They know that I don't smoke, that I am tidy, that I shall be gone by the morning. But one should never trespass on kindness. Human kindness is like a defective tap: the first gush may be impressive, but the stream soon dries up. I have my annual routine and that, too, reassures them. In a farmhouse twenty miles north of here they will be saying soon, 'Isn't this the time of year that Jonah drops in?' They greet me with relief rather than tolerance. If I am still alive, then so are they. And I never beg. An offer to pay is far more efficacious. 'Could you sell me a couple of eggs and half a pint of milk,' spoken at the farm door—provided the cash is proffered—will usually produce six eggs and a full pint. Not necessarily of the freshest, but one must not expect too much of human generosity."

Dalgliesh said: "What about books?"

"Ah, there, sir, you have hit on a difficulty. Classics I can read in public libraries, although it is sometimes a little irritating to have to break off when it is time to move on. Otherwise I depend on second-hand paperbacks from market stalls. One or two stall-holders allow you to exchange the book or get your money back at the second visit. It is a remarkably cheap form of public lending library. As for clothes, there are jumble sales, Oxfam and those useful shops that deal in army surplus. I save from my allowance for a new ex-army winter coat every three years."

Dalgliesh said: "How long have you been living this life?"

"Nearly twenty years now, sir. Most tramps are pitiful, because they are the slaves of their own passions, usually drink. A man who is free of all human desires except to eat, sleep and walk is truly free."

Dalgliesh said: "Not entirely. You have a bank account, apparently, and you rely on that thousand pounds."

"True. You think I would be freer if I didn't take it?"

"More independent, perhaps. You might have to work."

"I cannot work; to beg I am ashamed. Luckily the Lord has tempered the wind to His shorn lamb. I should be sorry to do my brother out of the satisfaction of his benevolence. True, I have a bank account to receive my annual subsidy, and to that extent I conform. But since my income depends on my separation from my brother, it would hardly be possible to receive the money personally, and my cheque book and accompanying plastic card have a most gratifying effect on the police when, as occasionally happens, they take a presumptuous interest in my doings. I had no idea that a plastic card was such a guarantee of respectability."

Dalgliesh asked: "No luxuries? No other needs? Drink? Women?"

"If by women you mean sex, then the answer is no. I am escaping, sir, from drink and sex."

"Then you are on the run from something. I could argue that a man on the run is never entirely free."

"And I could ask you, sir, from what you are escaping on this isolated headland. If from the violence of your job, you have been singularly unlucky."

"And now that same violence has touched your life. I'm sorry."

"You needn't be. A man who lives with nature is used to violence and is companionable with death. There is more violence in an English hedgerow than in the meanest streets of a great city."

When they reached the mill Dalgliesh telephoned Rickards. He wasn't at the incident room, but Oliphant was and said that he would immediately drive over. Then Dalgliesh took Jonah upstairs to look over the half-dozen pairs of shoes he had with him at the mill. There was no problem over fit, but Jonah tried them all on and examined each shoe minutely before making his choice. Dalgliesh was tempted to say that a life of simplicity and self-abnegation hadn't spoilt his guest's eye for good leather. With some regret he saw his favourite and most expensive pair chosen.

Jonah walked up and down the bedroom, looking down at his feet with complacency. He said: "I seem to have the best of the bargain. The Bumbles came at an opportune time but they were hardly suitable for serious walking, and I intended to replace them as opportunity offered. The rules of the road are few and simple, but they are imperative. I commend them to you. Keep your bowels open; bathe once a week; wear wool or cotton next to the skin and leather on the feet."

Fifteen minutes later his guest was ensconced in an armchair, a mug of coffee in hand, still regarding his feet with satisfaction. Oliphant was prompt in arriving. Apart from his driver, he was alone. He came into the sitting room bringing with him an aura of masculine menace and authority. Even before Dalgliesh had made the introduction he said to Jonah: "You must have known you'd no right to those trainers. They're new. Ever heard of stealing by finding?"

Dalgliesh said: "A moment, Sergeant." Drawing Oliphant aside, he said in a low voice: "You'll treat Mr. Jonah with courtesy." And before Oliphant could protest, he added, "All right, I'll save you the trouble of saying it. This isn't my case. But he is a guest in my house. If your men had searched the headland more thoroughly on Monday, all three of us might have been saved some embarrassment."

"He has to be a serious suspect, sir. He's got the shoes."

Dalgliesh said: "He also has a knife, and he admits to having been on the headland on Sunday night. Treat him as a serious suspect, by all means, if you can find a motive or proof that he knew how the Whistler killed or even knew that he existed. But why not listen to his story before you jump to conclusions about his guilt?"

Oliphant said: "Guilty or not, Mr. Dalgliesh, he's an important witness. I don't see how we can allow him to go wandering off."

"And I don't see how, legally, you can prevent him. But that's your problem, Sergeant."

A few minutes later Oliphant was leading Jonah towards the car. Dalgliesh went out to see him off. Before climbing in at the back, Jonah turned to him.

"It was an ill day for me when I met you, Adam Dalgliesh."

"But a good day, perhaps, for justice."

"Oh, justice. Is that the business you're in? I think you may have left it rather late. This planet earth is hurtling now to its destruction. That concrete bastion on the edge of a polluted sea may bring about the final darkness. If not it will be by some other folly of man. There comes a time when every scientist, even God, has to write off an experiment. Ah, I see a certain relief on your face. You are thinking, So he is mad after all, this peculiar tramp. I need no longer take him seriously."

Dalgliesh said: "My mind agrees with you. My genes are more optimistic."

"You know it. We all know it. How else can one explain the modern sickness of man. And when the final darkness falls I shall die as I have lived, in the nearest dry ditch." And then he gave a singularly sweet smile and added: "Wearing your shoes, Adam Dalgliesh."

9

The encounter with Jonah had left Dalgliesh curiously restless. There were plenty of jobs still to be done in the mill, but he felt disinclined to tackle any of them. His instinct was to get into the Jaguar and drive very fast and very far. But he had tried that expedient too often to have any faith in its efficacy. The mill would still be standing when he returned, the problems still unsolved. He had no difficulty in recognizing the basis of his discontent: the frustrating involvement with a case which would never be his yet from which it was impossible to distance himself. He remembered some words of Rickards's spoken before they had finally parted on the night of the murder.

"You may not want to be involved, Mr. Dalgliesh, but you are involved. You may wish that you had never been near the body, but you were there."

He seemed to remember using much the same words to a suspect in one of his own cases. He was beginning to understand why they had been so ill received. On an impulse, he unlocked the mill and climbed up the ladders to the top storey. Here, he suspected, his aunt had found her peace. Perhaps some of that lost contentment might seep into him. But any hope of being left undisturbed was due to be frustrated.

As he looked over the headland from the southern window, a bicycle came into sight. At first it was too distant to see who was riding, but then he recognized Neil Pascoe. They had never spoken but, like all the headlanders, they knew each other by sight. Pascoe seemed to be cycling with a ponderous determination, his head low over the handlebars, his shoulders working. But as he came close to the mill, he suddenly stopped, put both feet on the ground, stared towards the mill as if seeing it for the first time, then dismounted and began wheeling the bicycle over the sandy scrubland.

For one second Dalgliesh was tempted to pretend that he wasn't home. Then he realized that the Jaguar was parked at the side of the mill and that it was possible that Pascoe in that long stare had glimpsed his face at the window. Whatever the purpose of this visit, it looked as if it were one he couldn't avoid. He moved over to the window above the door, opened it and called down: "Are you looking for me?"

The question was rhetorical. Who else would Pascoe expect to find at Larksoken Mill? Looking down at the upturned face, the thin jutting beard, Dalgliesh saw him curiously diminished and foreshortened, a vulnerable, rather pathetic figure clutching his bicycle as if for protection.

Pascoe shouted up against the wind: "Could I talk to you?"

An honest reply would have been "If you must," but it was not one that Dalgliesh felt he could shout down against the noise of the wind without sounding ungracious. He mouthed, "I'll be down."

Pascoe propped the machine against the wall of the mill and followed him into the sitting room.

He said: "We haven't actually met, but I expect you've heard of me. I'm Neil Pascoe, from the caravan. I'm sorry if I'm butting in when you want some peace." He sounded as embarrassed as a door-to-door salesman trying to reassure a prospective customer that he wasn't a con man.

Dalgliesh was tempted to say, "I might want some peace but it doesn't look as if I'm likely to get it." He asked: "Coffee?"

Pascoe gave the predictable reply: "If it isn't too much trouble."

"No trouble. I was thinking of making it."

Pascoe followed him into the kitchen and stood leaning against the doorpost in an unconvincing assumption of ease as Dalgliesh ground the coffee beans and put on the kettle. It struck him that he had spent a considerable time since his arrival at the mill providing food and drink for uninvited visitors. When the grinding had ceased, Pascoe said almost truculently: "I need to talk to you."

"If it's about the murder, then you ought to be speaking to Chief Inspector Rickards, not me. This isn't my case."

"But you found the body."

"That might in certain circumstances make me a suspect. But it doesn't give me the right to interfere professionally in another officer's case outside my own force area. I'm not the investigating officer. But you know that, you're not stupid."

Pascoe kept his eyes on the bubbling liquid. He said: "I didn't expect you to be particularly pleased to see me. I wouldn't have come if there were anyone else I could talk to. There are things I can't discuss with Amy."

"As long as you remember whom you are talking to."

"A policeman. It's like the priesthood, is it? Never off-duty. Once a priest, always a priest."

"It isn't in the least like the priesthood. No guarantee of confidentiality in the confessional and no absolution. That's what I'm trying to tell you."

They said nothing else until the coffee had been poured into the two mugs and carried by Dalgliesh into the sitting room. They sat, one each side of the fireplace. Pascoe took his mug but seemed uncertain what to do with it. He sat twisting it in his hands, looking down at the coffee, making no attempt to drink. After a moment he said: "It's about Toby Gledhill, the boy—well, he was a boy, really— who killed himself at the power station."

Dalgliesh said: "I've heard about Toby Gledhill."

"Then I expect you know how he died. He hurled himself down on top of the reactor and broke his neck. That was on Friday, twelfth August. Two days before, on the Wednesday, he came to see me at about eight o'clock in the evening. I was on my own in the caravan; Amy had taken the van into Norwich to shop and said she wanted to see a film and would be back late. I was looking after Timmy. Then there was this knock and there he stood. I knew him, of course. At least, I knew who he was. I'd seen him on one or two of those open days at the power station. I usually make time to go to those. They can't stop me, and it gives me an opportunity of putting one or two awkward questions, countering their propaganda. And I think he was present at some of the meetings of the new pressurized-water-reactor enquiry. But, of course, I'd never really met him. I couldn't think what he wanted of me, but I invited him in and offered him a beer. I'd lit the stove, because there were a lot of Timmy's clothes which needed drying, so the caravan was very hot and rather damp. When I remember that night I seem to see him through a haze of steam. After the beer he asked if we couldn't go out. He seemed restless, as if he found the caravan claustrophobic, and he asked more than once when Amy was expected back. So I lifted Timmy out of his cot and put him into the backpack and we set off to walk north along the shore. It was when we had got as far as the abbey ruins that he told me what he'd come to say. He came out with it quite baldly, without any preamble. He'd come to the conclusion that nuclear power was too dangerous to use and that, until we've solved the problem of radioactive waste, we ought not to build any more nuclear-power stations. There was one rather odd expression he used. He said: 'It's not only dangerous, it's corrupting.' "

Dalgliesh asked: "Did he say why he'd come to this conclusion?"

"I think it had been building up for quite a few months, and Chernobyl had probably brought it to a head. He said that something else had recently happened that had helped to make up his mind. He didn't say what, but he promised he would tell me when he'd had more time to think. I asked him if he was merely going to give up his job and opt out or whether he was prepared to help us. He said he thought that he had to help. It wouldn't be enough just to resign his job. It was difficult for him, and I could see just how difficult. He admired and liked his colleagues. He said they were dedicated scientists and very intelligent men who believed in what they were doing. It was just that he couldn't believe any more. He hadn't thought about the way ahead, not very clearly anyway. He was like I am now: he just needed to talk it through. I suppose I seemed to be the natural person. He knew about PANUP, of course." He looked up at Dalgliesh and said rather naïvely: "That stands for 'People Against Nuclear Power.' When the proposal was put forward for the new reactor here, I formed a little local group to oppose it. I mean a group of ordinary concerned local residents, not the more powerful national protest bodies. It hasn't been easy. Most people try to pretend that the power station isn't really there. And of course quite a number welcome it because it does bring in some employment, new customers for the shops and pubs. Most of the opposition to the new reactor wasn't local, anyway; it was people from CND, Friends of the Earth and Green-peace. Of course we welcomed them. They're the ones with the heavy guns. But I thought it important to get something going locally, and I suppose I'm not really a joiner. I like to do my own thing."

Dalgliesh said: "And Gledhill would have been quite a catch for you." The words were almost brutal in their implication.

Pascoe flushed, then looked him in the eyes. "There was that too. I suppose I realized it at the time. I wasn't entirely disinterested. I mean, I did know how important it would be if he came over. But I was, well, flattered, I suppose, that he'd come first to me. PANUP hasn't made much impact, really. Even the initials were a mistake. I wanted something that people would easily remember, but PANUP— a bit of a laugh. I can guess what you're thinking, that I might have done more good for the cause by joining an existing pressure group instead of ministering to my own ego. You'd be right."

Dalgliesh asked: "Did Gledhill say whether he'd spoken to anyone at the station?"

"He said that he hadn't, not yet. I think that was what he most dreaded. He particularly hated the thought of telling Miles Les-singham. While we walked along the beach, with Timmy half-asleep bumping on my back, he felt free to talk, and I think he found it a release. He told me that Lessingham was in love with him. He wasn't gay himself but he was ambivalent. But he did tremendously admire Lessingham and felt that in some way he was letting him down. He gave the impression that everything was a muddle, his feelings about atomic power, his personal life, his career, everything."

Suddenly Pascoe seemed to realize that he was holding his coffee mug and, lowering his head, began to drink from it with great slurps, like a man desperate with thirst. When the cup was drained, he put it down on the floor and wiped his mouth with his hand.

He said: "It was a warm night after a rainy day, the night of the new moon. Funny how I remember that. We were walking just above the tide mark on the shingle. And then, suddenly, there she was, Hilary Robarts, splashing out of the foam. She was only wearing the bottom half of her bikini, and she stood there for a moment, with the water running off her hair, glistening in that eerie light which seems to come off the sea on a starry night. Then she came slowly up the beach towards us. I suppose we stood there almost as if mesmerized.

She had lit a small fire of brushwood on the shingle, and the three of us moved towards it. She picked up her towel but didn't wrap it round her. She looked—well, she looked marvellous, the drops of water glistening on her skin, and that locket thing she wears resting between her breasts. I know it sounds ridiculous and, well, corny, but she looked like some goddess risen from the sea. She took absolutely no notice of me, but she looked at Toby. She said: 'Nice to see you, Toby. Why not come down to the cottage for a drink and a meal?' Such ordinary words. Harmless-sounding words. But they weren't.

"I don't think he could resist her. I don't suppose I would have been able to either. Not at that moment. And I knew exactly what she was doing, and so did she. She was asking him to make a choice. On my side nothing but trouble, a lost job, personal anguish, possibly even disgrace. And on hers security, professional success, the respect of peers, colleagues. And love. I think she was offering him love. I knew what would happen in the cottage if he went with her, and he knew too. But he went. He didn't even say good night to me. She slung her towel over her shoulder and turned her back on us as if absolutely confident that he would follow her. And he did follow her. And two days later, on Friday twelfth August, he killed himself. I don't know what she said to him. No one will know now. But after that meeting I think he just couldn't take any more. It was not what she threatened him with, or even if she threatened him at all. But if it hadn't been for that meeting on the beach I think he'd be alive now. She killed him."

Dalgliesh said: "None of this came out at the inquest?"

"No, none. There was no reason why it should. I wasn't called as a witness. It was all handled very discreetly. Alex Mair was anxious that there shouldn't be any publicity. As you've probably noticed, there hardly ever is when something goes wrong at an atomic-power station. They all become experts at the cover-up."

"And why are you telling me this?"

"I want to be sure that this is something Rickards needs to be told. But I suppose I'm really telling you because I need to share it with someone. I'm not sure why I picked on you. Sorry."

A true, if hardly kind, reply would have been: "You picked on me in the hope that I'd undertake to pass it on to Rickards and save you the responsibility." Instead Dalgliesh said: "You realize, of course, that this is information Chief Inspector Rickards should have."

"But is it? That's what I want to be sure of. I suppose it's the usual fear when dealing with the police. What use are they going to make of it? Are they going to get the wrong idea? Could it point to someone who could be innocent? I suppose you have to have confidence in the integrity of the police, you wouldn't go on being a detective if you hadn't. But the rest of us know that things can go wrong, that the innocent can be harried, the guilty get off, that the police aren't always as scrupulous as they pretend to be. I'm not asking you to tell him for me, I'm not that childish. But I don't really see how it's relevant. Both of them are dead. I can't see how telling Rickards about that meeting can help to catch Miss Robarts's killer. And it can't bring either of them back to life."

Dalgliesh refilled Pascoe's mug. Then he said: "Of course it's relevant. You're suggesting that Hilary Robarts might have blackmailed Gledhill into staying in his job. If she could do it to one person, she could do it to another. Anything about Miss Robarts could be relevant to her death. And don't worry too much about innocent suspects. I'm not going to pretend that the innocent don't suffer in a murder investigation. Of course they do. No one even remotely touched by murder goes unscathed. But Chief Inspector Rickards isn't a fool and he's an honest man. He's only going to use what is relevant to his enquiry, and it's for him to decide what is relevant and what isn't."

"I suppose that's the reassurance I wanted to hear. All right, I'll tell him."

He finished his coffee very quickly, as if anxious to be gone, and, with only a final word of goodbye, mounted his bicycle and pedalled furiously down the path, bending himself against the wind. Dalgliesh took the two mugs back into the kitchen thoughtfully. That verbal picture of Hilary Robarts rising like a glistening goddess from the waves had been remarkably vivid. But one detail had been wrong. Pascoe had spoken of the key locket resting between her breasts. He remembered Mair's words as he stood looking down at the body. "That locket round her neck, I gave it to her on twenty-ninth August for her birthday." On Wednesday 10 August Hilary Robarts couldn't have been wearing it. Pascoe had undoubtedly seen Hilary Robarts walking out of the sea with the locket resting between her naked breasts; but it couldn't have been on 10 August.

BOOK SIX

Saturday 1 October
to
Thursday 6 October

1
⊠

Jonathan had decided to wait until Saturday to visit London and continue his enquiries. His mother was less likely to question him about a trip on Saturday to visit the Science Museum, whereas taking a day's leave always provoked enquiries about where he was going and why. But he thought it prudent to spend half an hour in the museum before setting off to Pont Street, and it was after three o'clock before he was outside the block of flats. One fact was immediately apparent: no one who lived in this building and employed a housekeeper could possibly be poor. The house was part of an imposing Victorian terrace, half-stone, half-brick, with pillars each side of the gleaming black door and ornate glass, like green bottle tops, in the two ground-floor windows. The door was open and he could see a square hall tiled with black-and-white marble, the lower balustrade of an ornate wrought-iron staircase and the door of a golden cage lift. To the right was a porter's desk with a uniformed man on duty. Anxious not to be seen loitering, he walked quickly on, considering his next move.

In one sense none was necessary except to find his way to the nearest tube station, return to Liverpool Street and take the first train to Norwich. He had done what he had set out to do: he knew now that Caroline had lied to him. He told himself that he should be feeling shocked and distressed, both at her lie and at his own duplicity in discovering it. He had thought himself in love with her. He was in love with her. For the past year there had been hardly an hour in which she had been absent from his thoughts. That blond, remote, self-contained beauty had obsessed him. Like a schoolboy, he had waited at the corners of corridors where she might pass, had welcomed his bed because he could lie undisturbed and indulge his secret erotic fantasies, would wake wondering where and how they might next meet. Surely neither the physical act of possession nor the discovery of deceit could destroy love. So why was this confirmation of her deception almost agreeable, even pleasant? He should be devastated; instead he was filled with a satisfaction close to triumph. She had lied, almost carelessly, confident that he was too much in love, too enthralled, too stupid even to question her story. But now, with the discovery of the truth, the balance of power in their relationship had subtly shifted. He wasn't sure yet what use he would make of the information. He had found the energy and courage to act, but whether he would have the courage to confront her with his knowledge was another matter.

He walked quickly to the end of Pont Street, his eyes on the paving stones, then turned and retraced his steps, trying to make sense of his turbulent emotions, so tangled that they seemed to jostle each other for dominance: relief, regret, disgust, triumph. And it had been so easy. Every dreaded obstacle, from contacting the detective agency to finding an excuse for this day in London, had been surmounted with greater ease than he could believe possible. So why not chance one further step? Why not make absolutely sure? He knew the name of the housekeeper, Miss Beasley. He could ask to see her, say that he had met Caroline a year or two ago, in Paris perhaps, had lost her address, wanted to get in touch. If he kept his story simple, resisted the temptation to embroider, there was no possible danger. He knew that Caroline had taken her summer holiday in France in 1986, the year he too had been there. It was one of the facts that had come up in conversation on their early dates together, innocuous chats about travel and paintings, the attempt to find some common ground, a shared interest. Well, at least he had been in Paris. He had seen the Louvre. He could say that that was where they had met.

He would need a false name, of course. His father's Christian name would do. Percival. Charles Percival. It was better to choose something slightly unusual; a too-common name would sound obviously false. He would say that he lived in Nottingham. He had been at the university there and knew the town. Somehow being able to picture those familiar streets made the fantasy believable. He needed to root his lies in a semblance of truth. He could say that he worked at the hospital there, a laboratory technician. If there were any other questions he could parry them. But why should there be any other questions?

He made himself walk with confidence into the hall. Only a day ago he would have found difficulty in meeting the porter's eyes. Now, filled with the self-assurance of success, he said: "I want to visit Miss Beasley in Flat Three. Would you say that I'm a friend of Miss Caroline Amphlett."

The porter left the reception desk and went into his office to telephone. Jonathan thought, What's to prevent me just going up the stairs and knocking at the door? Then he realized that the porter would immediately telephone Miss Beasley and warn her not to let him in. There was security of a kind, but it wasn't particularly tight.

Within half a minute the man was back. He said: "That's all right, sir. You can go up. It's on the first floor."

He didn't bother to take the lift. The double mahogany door with its numeral of polished brass, its two security locks and central spy hole was at the front of the house. He smoothed back his hair, then rang the bell and made himself stare at the peephole with an assumption of ease. He could hear nothing from inside the flat and the heavy door seemed as he waited to grow into an intimidating barricade which only a presumptuous fool would attempt to breach. For a second, picturing that single eyeball scrutinizing him through the peephole, he had to fight an impulse to flee. But then there was the faint clink of a chain, the sound of a lock turning, and the door was opened.

Since his decision to call at the flat he had been too preoccupied with fabricating his story to give much conscious thought to Miss Beasley. The word "housekeeper" had conjured up a soberly dressed middle-aged woman, at worst a little condescending and intimidating, at best deferential, chatty, eager to help. The reality was so bizarre that he gave a perceptible start of surprise, then blushed at his own betrayal. She was short and very thin with straight red-gold hair, white at the roots and obviously dyed, falling in a gleaming helmet to her shoulders. Her pale-green eyes were immense and shallowly set, the lower lids inverted and bloodshot so that the eyeballs seemed to be swimming in an open wound. Her skin was very white and crêped with innumerable small lines, except over the jutting cheekbones, where it was stretched as fine as paper. In contrast to the skin's unpainted fragility, her mouth was a thin gash of garish crimson. She was wearing high-heeled slippers and a kimono and was carrying a small, almost hairless dog with bulging eyes, its thin neck encircled with a jewelled collar. For a few seconds she stood silently regarding him, the dog pressed against her cheek.

Jonathan, his carefully husbanded confidence rapidly draining, said: "I'm sorry to trouble you. It's just that I'm a friend of Miss Caroline Amphlett and I'm trying to trace her."

"Well, you won't find her here." The voice, which he recognized, was unexpected from so frail a woman, deep and husky, and not unattractive.

He said, "I'm sorry if I've got the wrong Amphlett. You see, Caroline did give me her address two years ago, but I've lost it, so I tried the telephone directory."

"I didn't say that you'd got the wrong Amphlett, only that you won't find her here. But, as you look harmless enough and are obviously unarmed, you had better come in. One cannot be too careful in these violent times, but Baggott is very reliable. Very few imposters get past Baggott. Are you an imposter, Mr. . . . ?"

"Percival. Charles Percival."

"You must excuse my *déshabillé*, Mr. Percival, but I do not normally expect afternoon visitors."

He followed her across a square hall and through double doors into what was obviously the drawing room. She pointed imperiously to a sofa set in front of the fireplace. It was uncomfortably low and as soft-cushioned as a bed, each drop-end festooned with thick tasselled cords. Moving slowly, as if deliberately taking her time, she placed herself opposite to him in an elegant high winged chair, settled the dog on her lap and gazed down on him with the fixed unsmiling intensity of an inquisitor. He knew that he must look as gauche and ungainly as he felt, his thighs enclosed in the softness of the cushion, his sharp knees almost touching his chin. The dog, as naked as if it had been skinned and shivering perpetually like a creature demented with cold, turned first on him and then up at her its pleading exophthalmic eyes. The leather collar, with its great dollops of red and blue stones, lay heavily on the animal's frail neck.

Jonathan resisted the temptation to look round at the room, but it seemed that every feature had entered his consciousness: the marble fireplace with above it a full-length oil painting of a Victorian army officer, a pale, arrogant face with one lock of blond hair falling almost to the cheek, which bore an uncanny resemblance to Caroline; the four carved chairs with embroidered seats set against the wall; the pale, polished floor with its wrinkled carpets; the drum-shaped table in the centre of the room and the side tables with their photographs in silver frames. There was a strong smell of paint and turpentine. Somewhere in the flat a room was being decorated. After a moment's silent scrutiny, the woman spoke.

"So you're a friend of Caroline's. You surprise me, Mr. . . . Mr. . . . I'm afraid I have already forgotten your name."

He said firmly: "Percival. Charles Percival."

"Mine is Miss Oriole Beasley. I am the housekeeper here. As I said, you surprise me, Mr. Percival. But if you say you are Caroline's friend, naturally I accept your word."

"Perhaps I shouldn't say friend. I only met her once, in Paris in 1986. We went round the Louvre together. But I would like to see her again. She did give me her address, but I lost it."

"How careless. So you waited two years and then decided to trace her. Why now, Mr. Percival? You have managed, apparently, to control your impatience for two years."

He knew how he must look and sound to her: unconfident, shy, ill at ease. But that, surely, was what she would expect from a man gauche enough to believe that he could revive a dead and fleeting passion. He said: "It's just that I'm in London for a few days. I work in Nottingham. I'm a technician at the hospital there. I don't often get the chance to come south. It was an impulse really, trying to trace Caroline."

"As you see, she's not here. She has not, in fact, lived in this house since she was seventeen, and as I am only the housekeeper it is hardly my place to hand out information about the family's whereabouts to casual enquirers. Would you describe yourself as a casual enquirer, Mr. Percival?"

Jonathan said: "Perhaps it seems like that. It's just that I found the name in the telephone directory and thought it was worth a try. Of course she might not want to see me again."

"I should imagine that is more than likely. And, of course, you have some identification, something to confirm that you are Mr. Charles Percival of Nottingham."

Jonathan said: "Not really, I'm afraid. I didn't think . . ."

"Not even a credit card or a driving license? You seem to have come singularly unprepared, Mr. Percival."

Something in the deep, arrogantly upper-class voice, the mixture of insolence and contempt, stung him into defiance. He said: "I'm not from the Gas Board. I don't see why I need to identify myself. It was just a simple enquiry. I was hoping to see her, or perhaps Mrs. Amphlett. I'm sorry if I've offended you."

"You haven't offended me. If I were easily offended I wouldn't work for Mrs. Amphlett. But I'm afraid you can't see her. Mrs. Amphlett goes to Italy in late September and then flies to Spain for the winter. I'm surprised Caroline didn't tell you. In her absence I look after the flat. Mrs. Amphlett dislikes the melancholy of autumn and the cold of winter. A wealthy woman need suffer neither. I'm sure you are perfectly well aware of that, Mr. Percival."

And here, at last, was the opening he needed. He made himself look into those terrible bleeding eyes and said: "I thought Caroline told me that her mother was poor, that she'd lost all her money investing in Peter Robarts's plastics company."

The effect of his words was extraordinary. She flushed scarlet, the mottled stain travelling like a rash from her neck to her forehead. It seemed a long time before she could bring herself to speak, but when she did her voice was perfectly under control.

"Either you wilfully misunderstood, Mr. Percival, or your memory is as unreliable for financial facts as it is for addresses. Caroline could have told you nothing of the sort. Her mother inherited a fortune from her grandfather when she was twenty-one and has never lost a penny of it. It was my small capital—ten thousand pounds, in case you are interested—which was unwisely invested in the schemes of that plausible rogue. But Caroline would hardly confide that small personal tragedy to a stranger."

He could think of nothing to say, could find no credible explanation, no excuse. He had the proof he wanted: Caroline had lied. He should have been filled with triumph that his suspicions had been justified, his small enterprise crowned with success. Instead, he was swept with a momentary but overwhelming depression and a conviction which seemed to him as frightening as it was irrational, that the proof of Caroline's perfidy had been bought at a terrible price.

There was a silence in which she continued to regard him but did not speak. Then she suddenly asked: "What did you think of Caroline? Obviously she made an impression on you or you wouldn't be wishing to renew the acquaintance. And no doubt she has been in your mind during the last two years."

"I think—I thought she was very lovely."

"Yes, isn't she? I'm glad you feel that. I was her nurse—her nanny, if one must use that ridiculous expression. You could say that I brought her up. Does that surprise you? I'm hardly the popular idea of a nanny. Warm lap, aproned bosom, *Winnie-the-Pooh, The Wind in the Willows*, prayers at bedtime, eat up your crusts or your hair won't curl. But I had my methods. Mrs. Amphlett accompanied the Brigadier on his overseas postings and we stayed here together, just the two of us. Mrs. Amphlett believed that a child should have stability provided she was not required to provide it. Of course, if Caroline had been a son it would have been different. The Amphletts have never valued daughters. Caroline did have a brother, but he was killed in a friend's car when he was fifteen. Caroline was with them but survived almost without a scratch. I don't think her parents ever forgave her. They could never look at her without making it plain that the wrong child had been killed."

Jonathan thought: I don't want to hear this, I don't want to listen. He said: "She never told me that she had a brother. But she did mention you."

"Did she indeed? She talked about me to you. Now you do surprise me, Mr. Percival. Forgive me, but you are the last person I should have expected her to talk to about me."

He thought: She knows; not the truth, but she knows that I'm not Charles Percival from Nottingham. And it seemed to him, meeting those extraordinary eyes in which the mixture of suspicion and contempt was unmistakable, that she was allied to Caroline in a female conspiracy in which he had from the first been the hapless and despised victim. The knowledge fuelled his anger and gave him strength. But he said nothing.

After a moment she went on: "Mrs. Amphlett kept me on after

Caroline left home, even after the Brigadier passed on. But 'passed on' is hardly an appropriate euphemism for a soldier. Perhaps I should say 'was called to higher service,' 'recalled to the Colours,' 'promoted to glory.' Or is that the Salvation Army? I have a feeling that it's only the Salvation Army who get promoted to glory."

He said: "Caroline did tell me that her father was a professional soldier."

"She has never been a very confiding girl, but you seem to have gained her confidence, Mr. Percival. So now I call myself a house-keeper rather than a nanny. My employer finds plenty to keep me occupied even when she isn't here. It would never do for Maxie and me to live here on board wages and enjoy ourselves in London, would it, Maxie? No indeed. A little skilled sewing. Private letters to be posted on. Bills to be paid. Her jewels to be taken to be cleaned. The flat to be redecorated. Mrs. Amphlett particularly dislikes the smell of paint. And, of course, Maxie has to be exercised daily. He never thrives in kennels, do you, my treasure? I wonder what will happen to me when Maxie is promoted to glory?"

There was nothing he could say to that, nor, apparently, did she expect him to. After a moment's silence, during which she lifted the dog's paw and rubbed it gently against her face, she said: "Caroline's old friends seem very anxious to get in touch with her all of a sudden. Someone telephoned to ask for her only on Tuesday. Or was it Wednesday? But perhaps that was you, Mr. Percival?"

"No," he said, and was amazed at the ease with which he could lie. "No, I didn't telephone. I thought it better just to take my chance and call."

"But you knew who to ask for. You knew my name. You gave it to Baggott."

But she wasn't going to catch him like that. He said: "I remem-bered it. As I said, Caroline did talk about you."

"It might have been sensible to telephone first. I could have explained that she wasn't here, saved you time. How odd that it didn't occur to you. But that other friend didn't sound like you. Quite a different voice. Scottish, I think. If you will excuse my saying so, Mr. Percival, your voice is without either character or distinction."

Jonathan said: "If you don't feel you can give me Caroline's ad-dress, perhaps I'd better go. I'm sorry if I came at an inconvenient time."

"Why not write a letter to her, Mr. Percival? I can let you have the writing paper. I don't think it would be right to give you her address, but you can be confident that I will post on any communication that you care to trust to me."

"She isn't in London, then?"

"No, she hasn't lived in London for over three years, and she hasn't lived here since she was seventeen. But I do know where she is. We keep in touch. Your letter will be safe with me."

He thought: This is an obvious trap. But she can't make me write. There must be nothing in my handwriting. Caroline would recognize it even if I tried to disguise it. He said: "I think I'd rather write later, when I've more time to think what to say. If I post it to this address, then you can send it on."

"I will do that with pleasure, Mr. Percival. And now, I expect, you will want to be on your way. Your visit may have been less productive than you hoped, but I expect you have learned what you came to learn."

But she didn't move, and for a moment he felt himself trapped, immobilized, as if the disagreeably soft and yielding cushions held him in a vise. He half-expected her to leap up and bar his way to the door, to denounce him as an imposter, to keep him locked in the flat while she telephoned the police or the porter. What then would he do: attempt to seize the keys by force and make his escape, wait for the police and try to bluff his way to freedom? But the momentary panic subsided. She got to her feet and led the way to the door and, without speaking, held it open. She did not close it and he was aware that she was standing there, the dog shivering in her arms, both of them watching him leave. At the head of the stairs he turned to smile a final goodbye. What he then saw made him stand for a second immobile before he almost ran down the stairs and through the hall to the open door. He had never in all his life seen such concentrated hatred on a human face.

2

⊠

The whole enterprise had been more of a strain than Jonathan could have believed possible, and by the time he reached Liverpool Street he was very tired. The station was in the process of being rebuilt—"improved," as the large displays designed to reassure and encourage proclaimed—and had become a clanging and confusing maze of temporary walkways and direction signs in which it was difficult to actually find the trains. Taking a false turn, he found himself in a glossily floored piazza and felt momentarily as disorientated as if he were in a foreign capital. His arrival that morning had been less confusing, but now even the station reinforced his sense of having ventured both physically and emotionally onto alien ground.

Once the journey had started he leaned back, his eyes closed, and tried to make sense of the day and of his conflicting emotions. But instead, and almost immediately, he fell asleep, and didn't stir into consciousness until the train was drawing into Norwich station. But the sleep had done him good. He strode towards the castle car-park filled with renewed energy and optimism. He knew what he would do: drive at once to the bungalow, and confront Caroline with the evidence and ask her why she had lied. He couldn't go on seeing her and pretend not to know. They were lovers; they should be able to trust each other. If she was worried or frightened he was there to reassure and comfort her. He knew that she couldn't have murdered Hilary. The very thought was profanation. But she wouldn't have lied unless she was frightened. Something was dreadfully wrong. He would persuade her to go to the police, explain why she had lied and persuaded him to lie. They would go together, confess together. He didn't ask himself whether she would want to see him or even whether, late on a Saturday, she would be at home. All he knew was that the matter between them had to be settled now. There was a rightness and an inevitability about his decision and he felt, too, a small surge of power. She had thought him a gullible and ineffectual fool. Well, he would show her that she was wrong. From now on there would be a subtle change in their relationship; she would have a more confident, less malleable lover.

Forty minutes later he was driving through the darkness across flat, undistinguished country towards the bungalow. Slowing down as it came into sight on his left, he was struck afresh by how remote and unattractive it was and wondered again why, with so many villages closer to Larksoken, with the attractions of Norwich and the coast, she should have rented this forbidding, almost sinister little box of crude red brick. And the very word "bungalow" seemed to him ridiculous, evoking a picture of suburban ribbon development, of cosy respectability, of old people who could no longer manage stairs. Caroline should live in a tower with a wide view of the sea.

And then he saw her. The silver Golf came out from the drive very fast and accelerated eastwards. She was wearing what looked like a woollen cap pulled down over her yellow hair, but he knew her immediately. He didn't know whether she had recognized him or the Fiesta, but instinctively he braked and let her get almost out of sight before he followed. And, waiting in the quietness of that flat landscape, he could hear Remus barking hysterically.

He was surprised how easy it was to keep her in sight. Sometimes another car passing him would obscure his view of the silver Golf, and occasionally, when she slowed for traffic lights or because they had reached a village, he had quickly to reduce speed in case she realized that he was on her tail. They passed through Lydsett Village and she took the right turn across the headland. By now he feared that she must have recognized him, must know that she was being followed, but she went on, apparently uncaring. When she had negotiated the gate, he waited until she was out of sight over the ridge before following, then stopped, put out the car lights and went a little way on foot. He saw that she was picking someone up; a slim girl with spiked yellow hair, orange at the tips, was briefly illuminated in the headlights. The car turned north along the coast road, inland at the power station, then north again. Forty minutes later their destination was known, the quay at Wells-next-the-Sea.

He parked the Fiesta beside the Golf and followed them, keeping Caroline's blue-and-white cap in sight. They walked quickly, unspeaking, and neither of them looked back. At the quay he momentarily lost them, and then he saw that they were getting on a boat. And now was his chance; he had to speak to Caroline. He almost ran towards them. They were already on board. It was a small craft, no more than fifteen feet long, with a low central cabin and an outboard motor. Both girls were standing in the cockpit. As he came up Caroline turned to him.

"What the hell do you think you're doing?"

"I want to talk to you. I've been following you since you left the bungalow."

"I know that, you fool. You've been in my mirror practically the whole way. If I'd wanted to throw you off it wouldn't have been difficult. You should give up this cloak-and-dagger business. It doesn't suit you and you're no good at it."

But there was no anger in her voice, only a kind of irritated weariness. He said: "Caroline, I have to talk to you."

"Then wait until tomorrow. Or stay where you are if you must. We'll be back in an hour."

"But where are you going? What are you doing?"

"For Christ's sake, what do you think I'm doing? This is a boat, my boat. Out there is the sea. Amy and I are planning a short trip."

Amy, he thought. Amy who? But Caroline didn't introduce her. He said weakly: "But it's so late. It's dark and it's getting misty."

"So it's dark and misty. This is October. Look, Jonathan, why don't you mind your own business and get off home to Mother."

She was busying herself in the cockpit. He leaned over and clutched the side of the boat, feeling the gentle rock of the tide. He said: "Caroline, please talk to me! Don't go. I love you."

"I doubt it."

Both of them seemed to have forgotten Amy. He said desperately: "I know that you lied about your mother being ruined by Hilary's father. That wasn't true, any of it. Look, if you're in trouble I want to help. We've got to talk. I can't go on like this."

"I'm not in trouble, and if I were you'd be the last person I'd turn to. And take your hands off my boat."

He said, as if it were the most important thing between them: "Your boat? You never told me you had a boat."

"There are a great many things that I didn't tell you."

And then, suddenly, he knew. There was no longer room for doubt. "So it wasn't real, was it, any of it? You don't love me, you never did love me."

"Love, love, love. Stop bleating that word, Jonathan. Look, go home. Stand in front of your glass and take a good long look at yourself. How could you ever have supposed that it was real? This is real, Amy and me. She is why I stay at Larksoken and I am why she stays. Now you know."

"You used me."

He knew that he sounded like a querulous child.

"Yes, I used you. We used each other. When we went to bed, I was using you and you were using me. That's what sex is. And, if you want to know, it was bloody hard work and it made me sick."

Even in the throes of his misery and humiliation he could sense an urgency in her that had nothing to do with him. The cruelty was deliberate but it had no passion in it. It would have been more bearable if it had. His presence was merely an irritating but minor intrusion into more important preoccupations. Now the end of the rope had whipped clear of the bollard. She had started the engine, and the boat was edging away from the quay. And for the first time he really noticed the other girl. She hadn't spoken since he arrived. She stood silently beside Caroline in the cockpit, unsmiling, shivering slightly, and somehow vulnerable, and he thought he saw on her childish face a look of puzzled compassion before his tears began to sting and the boat and its occupants became an amorphous blur. He waited until they were almost out of sight moving on the dark water, and then he made another decision. He would find a pub, have a beer and some food and be there when they returned. They couldn't be away long or they would miss the tide. And he had to know the truth. He couldn't spend another night in this uncertainty. He stood on the quay staring out to sea as if the little boat with its two occupants were still in sight, then turned away and dragged his feet towards the nearest pub.

3

The throb of the engine, unnaturally loud, shook the quiet air. Amy half-expected doors to open, people to come running down to the quay, to hear protesting voices calling after them. Caroline made a movement, and the noise died in a gentle murmur. The boat gently moved away from the quay. Amy said angrily: "Who is he? Who is that creep?"

"Just a man from Larksoken. His name's Jonathan Reeves. He's unimportant."

"Why did you tell him lies? Why did you tell him lies about us? We're not lovers."

"Because it was necessary. What does it matter anyway? It isn't important."

"It's important to me. Look at me, Caroline. I'm talking to you."

But still Caroline didn't meet her eyes. She said calmly: "Wait until we get clear of the harbour. There's something I have to tell you, but I want to get into deep water and I need to concentrate. Get up to the prow and keep a lookout."

Amy stood for a moment irresolute, and then she obeyed, working her way carefully along the narrow deck, clutching the rim of the low cabin roof. She wasn't sure she liked the hold that Caroline apparently had over her. It was nothing to do with the money, which was paid irregularly and anonymously into her post-office account or left hidden in the abbey ruins. It wasn't even the excitement and the secret sense of power which she gained from being part of a conspiracy. Perhaps after that first meeting in the pub at Islington, which had led to her recruitment to Operation Birdcall, she had subconsciously made a decision to give her loyalty and obedience, and now that the test had come she was unable to shake off that unspoken allegiance.

Looking back, she could see that the lights in the harbour were growing fainter, the windows becoming little squares of light and then pinpricks. The engine stuttered into greater life and, standing on the prow, she could feel the great power of the North Sea beneath her, the hiss of the parting water, see the unbroken waves smooth and black oil emerging out of the mist, could feel the boat lifting, shuddering and then settling. After ten minutes of watching, she left her post and made her way back to the cockpit. She said: "Look, we're well away from land now. What's going on? Did you have to tell him that? I know I'm supposed to keep away from people at Larksoken, but I'll find him, and I'll tell him the truth."

Caroline was still standing motionless at the tiller, looking straight ahead. In her left hand she held a compass. She said: "We won't be going back. That's what I have to tell you."

Before Amy could even open her mouth she said: "Look, don't start getting hysterical and don't argue. You're entitled to an explanation, and if you keep quiet you'll get it. I've no option now; you have to know the truth, or some of the truth."

"What truth? What are you talking about? And why aren't we going back? You said we'd only be gone about an hour. You said we were going out to meet some comrades offshore and get some new instructions. I left a note for Neil saying I wouldn't be long. I've got to get back to Timmy."

But still Caroline didn't look at her. She said: "We're not going back because we can't. When I recruited you from that London squat I didn't tell you the truth. It wasn't in your interest and I didn't know how far I could trust you. And I didn't know the whole truth myself, only as much as I needed to know. That's the way the operation works. Operation Birdcall is nothing to do with taking over Larksoken in the cause of animal rights. It's nothing to do with animals. It's nothing to do with threatened whales and sick seals and tormented laboratory animals and abandoned dogs and all the other spurious miseries you agonize about. It's to do with something far more important. It's to do with human beings and their future. It's to do with the way we organize our world."

She was speaking very low and with an extraordinary intensity.

Amy said above the noise of the engine: "I can't hear you! I can't hear you properly. Turn off that engine!"

"Not yet. We've still a long way to go. We're meeting them at a precise spot. We have to sail straight southeast, then take a bearing on the power-station offshore structures and the Happisburgh Light. I hope this mist doesn't thicken."

"Who? Who are we meeting?"

"I don't know their names and I don't know their place in the organization. As I said, we are all of us told only as much as we actually need to know. My instructions were that if Operation Birdcall was blown I was to ring a number and activate the emergency procedure for getting me out. That's why I bought this boat and made sure it was always ready. I was told precisely where they'll pick us up. Then they'll get us into Germany, provide false papers, a new identity, incorporate us into the organization, find us a job."

"Not for me they bloody well won't!" Amy looked at Caroline with horror. "They're terrorists, aren't they? And you're one too. You're a bloody terrorist!"

Caroline said calmly: "And what else are the agents of capitalism? What are the armies, the police, the courts? What are the industrialists, the multinational corporations who hold down three-quarters of the world's population and keep them poor and hungry? Don't use words you don't understand."

"I understand that word. And don't you patronize me. You crazy or something? What were you planning, for Christ's sakes, to sabotage the reactor, release all that radioactivity, worse than Chernobyl, kill everyone on the headland, Timmy and Neil, Smudge and Whisky?"

"We wouldn't need to sabotage the reactors or release any radioactivity. The threat would be sufficient once we'd taken over the power stations."

"The stations? How many? Where?"

"One here, one in France, one in Germany. The action would be co-ordinated and it would be sufficient. It's not what we could do when we had taken them over, it's what people would think we could do. War is out of date and unnecessary. We don't need armies. All we need are a few trained, intelligent and dedicated comrades with the necessary skills. What you call terrorism can change the world, and it's more cost-effective in human life than the militaristic industry of death which my father made his career. They've only one thing in common. A soldier, in the end, has to be prepared to die for his cause. Well, so are we."

Amy cried: "It can't happen! Governments won't let it happen!"

"It is happening and they can't stop it. They aren't united enough and they haven't the will. This is just the beginning."

Amy looked at her. She said: "Stop this boat. I'm getting off."

"And swim ashore? You'd either drown or freeze to death. And in this mist."

Amy hadn't noticed the thickening mist. One moment it seemed to her that she could see the distant lights of the shore, like stars, almost she could see the blackness of the slopping waves, could peer ahead. But now, slowly and inexorably, there was a clammy wetness. She cried: "Oh God, take me back. You've got to get me off. Get me off. I want Timmy. I want Neil."

"I can't do that, Amy. Look, if you don't want to be part of all this, just say so when the boat arrives. They'll put you ashore somewhere. It won't be on this coast necessarily, but somewhere. We don't want reluctant recruits. There would be enough trouble as it is, fitting you up with a new identity. But if you didn't want to be part of it, didn't want to be committed, why did you kill Hilary Robarts? D'you think we wanted a murder investigation centred on Larksoken, police attention, Rickards actually on the site, every suspect's past scrutinized, nothing left private? And if Rickards had arrested you, how sure could I be that you wouldn't crack, tell him about Operation Birdcall, turn Queen's evidence?"

Amy cried: "Are you crazy? I'm on this boat with a bloody crazy woman. I didn't kill her."

"Then who did? Pascoe? That's almost as dangerous."

"How could he? He was on his way back from Norwich. We lied to Rickards about the time but he was back at the caravan by nine-fifteen, and we were there together all the evening with Timmy. And all that business about the Whistler cutting her forehead, the hair, we never knew any of that. I thought you killed her."

"Why should I?"

"Because she discovered Operation Birdcall. Isn't that why you're running, because you've got no option?"

"You're right that I've got no option. But it's not because of Robarts. She didn't find out. How could she? But someone did. It isn't only the Hilary Robarts murder. They've started checking up on me, the security services. Somehow they've got a lead, probably from one of the German cells or from a mole in the IRA."

"How do you know? You could be running away for nothing."

"There are too many coincidences. That last postcard you hid in the abbey ruins. I told you it was put back the wrong way. Someone had read it."

"Anyone could have found it. And the message wouldn't have meant anything. It never meant anything to me."

"Found it in late September, when the picnic season's well over? Found it and carefully put it back? And that wasn't all. They've checked on my mother's flat. She has a housekeeper who used to be my nanny. She rang to let me know earlier today. I didn't wait after that. I sent the signal to say I was getting out."

On their starboard side the occasional lights of the shore were blurred by the mist but still visible. And the throb of the engine sounded less intrusive now, almost a gentle, companionable hum. Or perhaps, thought Amy, she had got used to it. But it seemed extraordinary to be moving so quietly and steadily through the darkness, hearing Caroline's voice saying unbelievable things, talking about terrorism and flight and betrayal as calmly as if she were discussing the details of a picnic. And Amy needed to hear, needed to know. She found herself saying: "Where did you meet them, these people you're working for?"

"In Germany when I was seventeen. My nanny was ill and I had to spend the summer holiday with my parents. My father was stationed there. He didn't take much notice of me, but someone else did."

"But that was years ago."

"They know how to wait, and so do I."

"And this nanny housekeeper, is she a member of Birdcall too?"

"She knows nothing, absolutely nothing. She's the last person I'd choose. She's a silly old fool who's hardly worth her bed and board, but my mother finds a use for her, and so do I. She hates my mother, and I've told her that Mummy is checking on my life and to let me know at once if there are any telephone calls for me or any visitors. It helps make her life with Mummy tolerable. It makes her feel important, helps her to believe that I care about her, that I love her."

"Do you? Do you love her?"

"I did once. A child has to love someone. I grew out of it and I grew out of her. Well, there was a call and there was a visitor. On Tuesday a Scot, or someone pretending to be a Scot, rang. And today a visitor came."

"What sort of visitor?"

"A young man who said he'd met me in France. It was a lie. He was an imposter. He was from MI5. Who else could have sent him?"

"But you can't be sure. Not sure enough to send that signal, leave everything, put yourself in their mercy."

"I can. Look, who else could it have been? There were three separate incidents, the postcard, the telephone call, the visitor. What else should I wait for? The security services kicking down my door?"

"What was he like, this man?"

"Young. Nervous. Not very attractive. Not particularly convincing either. Even Nanny didn't believe him."

"Funny kind of MI5 officer. Couldn't they do better than that?"

"He was supposed to be someone I'd met in France who fancied me and wanted to see me again and had steeled himself actually to call at the flat. Of course he appeared young and nervous. That's the kind of man they'd send. They'd hardly choose a seasoned forty-year-old veteran from Curzon Street. They know how to select the right man for the job. That's their business. He was the right man, all right. Perhaps he wasn't even meant to be convincing. Perhaps they were trying to scare me, get me to react, flush me out."

"Well, you have reacted, haven't you? But if you're wrong, wrong about it all, what will they do, the people you work for? You've blown Operation Birdcall by running away."

"This operation has been aborted, but the future won't be jeopardized. My instructions were to telephone if there was firm evidence that we'd been discovered. And there was. And that's not all. My telephone is being bugged."

"You can't possibly tell that."

"I can't tell it for certain, but I know."

Suddenly Amy cried: "What did you do about Remus? Did you feed him, leave him water?"

"Of course not. This has to look like an accident. They've got to believe that we're lesbian lovers who went for an evening boat trip and were drowned. They've got to believe that we only intended to be away for a couple of hours. He gets fed at seven. They've got to find him hungry and thirsty."

"But they might not start looking for you until Monday! He'll be frantic, barking and whining. There's no one close to hear. You bloody bitch!"

Suddenly she flew at Caroline, screaming obscenities, clawing at her face. But the girl was too strong for her. Hands gripped her wrists like steel bands, and she found herself hurled back against the boards. Through the tears of rage and self-pity she whispered: "But why? Why?"

"For a cause worth dying for. There aren't many of those."

"Nothing's worth dying for, except maybe another person, someone you love. I'd die for Timmy."

"That's not a cause, that's sentimentality."

"And if I want to die for a cause I'll bloody well choose it myself. And it won't be for terrorism. It won't be for bastards who put bombs in pubs and blow up my friends and don't give a damn about ordinary people because we're not important, are we?"

Caroline said: "You must have suspected something. You're not educated but you're not stupid either. I wouldn't have chosen you if I couldn't be sure of that. You never questioned me and you wouldn't have got an answer if you had, but you couldn't have thought that we were going to all that trouble for frightened kittens or butchered seal pups."

Had she thought that? Amy wondered. Perhaps the truth was that she had believed in the intention but never that it would actually be carried out. She hadn't doubted their will, only their ability. And in the meantime it had been fun to be part of the conspiracy. She had enjoyed the excitement, the knowledge that she had a secret from Neil, the half-simulated *frisson* of fear as she left the caravan after dark to plant the postcards in the ruins of the abbey. She had hidden behind a broken breakwater almost laughing aloud that night when she had nearly been caught by Mrs. Dennison and Mr. Dalgliesh. And the money had been useful, too—generous payment for so small a task. And there had been the dream, the picture of a flag whose design was as yet unknown, but which they would raise over the power station and which would command respect, obedience, instant response. They would be saying to the whole world, "Stop it. Stop it now." They would be speaking for the captive zoo animals, the threatened whales, the polluted, sick seals, the tormented laboratory animals, the terrified beasts driven into the abattoirs to the smell of blood and their own death, the hens crowded together, unable even to peck, for the whole of the abused and exploited animal world. But it had been only a dream. This was reality: the unsubstantial boards under her feet, the dark, suffocating mist, the oily waves slapping against their frail craft. The reality was death; there was no other. Everything in her life, from the moment she had met Caroline in that Islington pub and they had walked back to the squat together, had led to this moment of truth, this terror.

She moaned: "I want Timmy. What about my baby? I want my baby."

"You won't have to leave him, not permanently. They'll find a way of reuniting you."

"Don't be daft. What sort of life would he have with a terrorist gang? They'll write him off like they write off everyone else."

Caroline said: "What about your parents? Won't they take him? Can't they look after him?"

"Are you crazy? I ran away from home because my stepfather knocked Ma about. When he started on me I walked out. Do you think I'd let him have Timmy, him or her?"

Her mother had seemed to like the violence, or at least had liked what came after it. Those two years before she ran away had taught Amy one lesson: have sex only with men who want you more than you want them.

Caroline asked: "What about Pascoe? Are you sure he knows nothing?"

"Of course he doesn't. We weren't even lovers. He didn't want me and I didn't want him."

But there was someone she had wanted, and she had a sudden vivid memory of lying with Alex in the dunes, the smell of sea and sand and sweat, his grave, ironic face. Well, she wasn't going to tell Caroline about Alex. She had one secret of her own. She would keep it.

She thought of the curious paths by which she had come to this moment in time, to this place. Perhaps if she drowned her whole life would flash before her, as it was said to do, everything experienced, understood, made sense of in that final annihilating moment. But now she saw the past as a series of coloured slides, clicking in quick succession, an image briefly received, an emotion barely experienced before it disappeared. Suddenly she was shivering violently. She said: "I'm cold."

"I said to come with warm clothes and nothing else. That jumper isn't enough."

"These are the only warm clothes I've got."

"On the headland? What do you wear in winter?"

"Sometimes Neil lends me his greatcoat. We share. Whichever one of us goes out gets the coat. We were thinking we might get one for me from the Old Rectory jumble."

Caroline took off her jacket. She said: "Here, put this round you."

"No, that's yours. I don't want it."

"Put it on."

"I said I don't want it."

But, like a child, she let Caroline push her arms into the sleeves, stood obediently while the jacket was fastened. Then she crouched down, almost wedging herself under the narrow seat which ran round the boat, shutting out the horror of those silently advancing waves. It seemed to Amy that she felt for the first time and with every nerve the inexorable power of the sea. She saw in imagination her pale and lifeless body plummeting through the miles of wet darkness to the seabed, to the skeletons of long-drowned sailors, where the uncaring creatures swam between the ribs of ancient ships. And the mist, less thick now but mysteriously more frightening, had become a living thing, gently swirling and soundlessly breathing, stealing her own breath, so that she found herself panting, insinuating its damp horror into every pore. It seemed impossible to believe that somewhere there was land, lighted windows behind the drawn curtains, light spilling from the doors of pubs, laughing voices, people sitting in warmth and safety. She saw the caravan as she had seen it so often, returning from Norwich after dark, a sturdy rectangle of wood which seemed rooted to the headland, defying the gales and the sea, the warm glow from its windows, the twist of smoke rising from the stack. She thought of Timmy and Neil. How long would Neil wait until he called the police? He wasn't one to act in a hurry. After all, she wasn't a child, she had a right to leave. He might do nothing until morning, and perhaps even then he would wait. But it wouldn't matter. There was nothing the police could do. No one except that desolate figure on the quay knew where they were, and if he raised the alarm it would be too late. It was useless to believe even in the reality of the terrorists. They were marooned here in black dampness. They would circle and circle until the fuel ran out and then drift out to sea until a coaster ran them down.

She no longer had any sense of passing time. The rhythmic throbbing of the engine had lulled her not into peace, but into a dulled acquiescence in which she was aware only of the wood hard against her back, of Caroline standing intent and motionless in the cockpit. And then the engine died.

For a few seconds the silence was absolute. Then, as the boat gently lurched, Amy heard the creak of wood, the slap of water. She breathed a suffocating wetness, felt its cold seeping through the jacket, into her bones. It seemed impossible that anyone could find them in this bleak expanse of water and emptiness, and she had ceased to care whether they did.

Caroline said: "This is the place. This is where they're going to meet us. We'll just have to wait here until they come."

Amy heard the engine again, but this time it was an almost imperceptible throb. And suddenly she knew. There was no conscious process of reasoning, only a blinding and terrifying certainty that burst upon her with the clarity of a vision. There was a second in which her heart froze, then leapt, and its strong drumming powered her body into life. She almost sprang to her feet. "They're not going to put me ashore, are they? They're going to kill me. You know it. You've known it all along. You've brought me here to be killed."

Caroline's eyes were fixed on the two lights, the intermittent flash from the lighthouse, the glitter from the offshore structures. She said coldly: "Don't be hysterical."

"They can't risk letting me go, I know too much. And you said yourself that I wouldn't be much use to them. Look, you've got to help me. Tell them how useful I was, make believe I'm worth keeping. If I can only get ashore, somehow I'll make a break for it. But I have to have a chance. Caroline. You've got me into this. You must help me. I have to get ashore. Listen to me! Listen to me, Caroline! We've got to talk."

"You are talking. And what you're saying is ludicrous."

"Is it? Is it, Caroline?"

She knew now that she mustn't plead. She wanted to throw herself at Caroline's feet and scream: "Look at me. I'm human. I'm a woman. I want to live. My child needs me. I'm not much of a mother, but I'm the only one he has. Help me." But she knew with an instinctive wisdom born of desperation that abject pleading, clutching hands, sobs, whining entreaties would only repel. She was speaking for her life. She had to stay calm, to rely on reason. She had somehow to find the right words. She said: "It isn't only me, it's you too. This could be a choice of life or death for both of us. They won't want you either. You were only useful to them while you worked at Larksoken, while you could pass on to them details of how the place was run, who was on duty and when. Now you're a liability, the same as me. There's no difference. What kind of work can you do for them that will make it worthwhile supporting you, setting you up with a new identity? They can't find you a job in another power station. And if MI5 are really on to you they'll still be looking. They might not believe so easily in the accident, not if our bodies aren't washed up. And our bodies won't be washed up, will they? Not unless they kill us, and that's what they're planning to do. What are two more bodies to them? Why meet us here? Why so far? They could have picked us up much closer to land. They could have got us out by air if they'd really needed us. Caroline, go back. It isn't too late. You could tell the people you work for that it wasn't safe to come, the mist was too thick. They'll find another way to get you out if you want to go. I won't talk, I wouldn't dare. I promise you with my life. We can go back now, and it will just have been two friends who took a boat trip and came back safely. It's my life, Caroline, and it could be yours. You gave me your jacket. I'm asking for my life."

She didn't touch Caroline. She knew that the wrong gesture, perhaps any gesture, could be fatal. But she knew, too, that the silent figure staring rigidly ahead was at the moment of decision. And, gazing at that carved intent face, Amy realized for the first time in her life that she was utterly alone. Even her lovers, seen now as a passing procession of strained, beseeching faces and grasping, exploring hands, had been only casual strangers giving her the fleeting illusion that a life could be shared. And she had never known Caroline, could never know her, never begin to understand what in her past, perhaps in her childhood, had led to this dangerous conspiracy, this moment of decision. They were physically so close that each could hear, could almost smell, the other's breath. But each was alone, as much alone as if this wide sea held no other craft, no other living soul. They might be fated to die together, but each could suffer only her own death, as each had lived only her own life. And there was nothing left to say. She had pleaded her cause and the words were all spent. Now she waited in the darkness and the silence to know whether she would live or die.

It seemed to her that even time had stopped. Caroline put out her hand and switched off the engine. In the eerie silence Amy could hear, like a low insistent pounding, the beating of her heart. And then Caroline spoke. Her voice was calm, reflective, as if Amy had posed her a difficult problem which needed thought to solve.

"We have to get away from the meeting place. We haven't enough power to outrun them if they find us and give chase. Our hope is to put out all the lights, get away from this place and lie silent, hoping they won't find us in the mist."

"Can't we get back to the harbour?"

"There isn't time. It's over ten miles, and they'll have a powerful engine. If they find us they'll be on to us in seconds. The mist is our only chance."

And then they heard, blunted by the fog but clearly, the sound of an approaching boat. Instinctively they moved closer together in the cockpit and waited, not daring even to whisper. Each knew that their only chance now lay in silence, the mist, the hope that their small craft would be undetected. But the engine noise increased and became a regular, directionless, vibrating throb. And then, when they had thought that the boat would loom out of the darkness and be on them, the noise grew no louder and Amy guessed that they were being slowly circled. Then suddenly she screamed. The searchlight cut through the mist and shone full on their faces. The light dazzled so that she could see nothing but its own giant cone, in which the particles of mist swam like motes of silver light. A rough foreign voice called: "Is that the *Lark* out of Wells harbour?"

There was a moment's silence and then Amy heard Caroline's voice. It was clear and loud but to Amy's ears it signalled a high note of fear. "No. We're a party of four friends from Yarmouth, but we'll probably put in at Wells. We're all right. No help needed, thank you."

But the searchlight didn't move. The boat was held as if suspended between sea and sky in a blaze of light. The seconds passed. Nothing more was said. Then the light was switched off and they heard again the sound of the engines, this time retreating. For a minute, still waiting, still frightened to speak, they shared a common desperate hope that the ruse had worked. And then they knew. The light held them again. And now the engines were roaring and the boat came straight at them out of the mist, with only time for Caroline to place an icy cheek against Amy's. She said: "I'm sorry. I'm sorry."

And then the great hull towered above them. Amy heard the crack as the wood splintered and the boat leapt out of the water. She felt herself hurled through an eternity of wet darkness and then falling, endlessly falling, spread-eagled in time and space. And then there was the smack of the sea and a coldness so icy that for a few seconds she felt nothing. She came back to consciousness as she surfaced, gasping and fighting for breath, no more aware of the cold, feeling only the agony of a metal band crushing her chest, terror and the desperate fight to keep her head above water, to survive. Something hard scraped against her face, then floated free. She thrashed out with flailing arms and fastened on a plank of wood from the boat. It offered at least a chance. She rested her arms on it and felt the blessed release of strain. And now she was capable of rational thought. The plank might support her until morning light and the fog lifted. But she would be dead of cold and exhaustion long before then. Somehow to swim ashore was her only hope, but which way lay the shore? If the mist lifted she would be able to see the lights, perhaps even the light of the caravan. Neil would be there waving to her. But that was silly. The caravan was miles away. Neil would be desperately worried by now. And she had never finished those envelopes. Timmy might be crying for her. She had to get back to Timmy.

But in the end the sea was merciful. The cold that numbed her arms so that she could no longer hold on to the plank numbed also her mind. She was slipping into unconsciousness when the search-light again found her. She was beyond thought, beyond fear when the boat turned and came driving at full power into her body. And then there was silence and darkness and a single plank of wood gently bobbing where the sea was stained red.

4

⊠

It was after 8.00 before Rickards got home on Saturday night, but
this was still earlier than usual and, for the first time in weeks, he
was able to feel that an evening stretched ahead with its choices: a
leisurely meal, television, radio, a gentle, undemanding catching-up
with household chores, telephoning Susie, an early bed. But he was
restless. Faced with a few hours of leisure, he was uncertain what to
do with them. For a moment he wondered whether to go out for a
solitary restaurant meal, but the effort of choosing, the expense, even
the bother of booking seemed disproportionate to any possible pleasure. He showered and changed as if the steaming water were a ritual
cleansing-away of his job, of murder and failure, which might give
the evening before him some meaning, some pleasure. Then he
opened a tin of baked beans, grilled four sausages and a couple of
tomatoes and carried his tray into the sitting room to eat while watching the television.

At 9.20 he switched off the set and, for a few minutes, sat immobile with the tray still on his lap. He thought that he must look
like one of those modern paintings, *Man with a Tray*, a stiff figure
immobilized in an ordinary setting made unordary, even sinister.
As he sat, trying to summon the energy even to wash up, the familiar
depression settled on him, the sense that he was a stranger in his
own house. He had felt more at home in that fire-lit, stone-walled

room at Larksoken Mill, drinking Dalgliesh's whisky, than he did here in his own sitting room, in his familiar, tightly upholstered chair, eating his own food. And it wasn't only the absence of Susie, the heavily pregnant ghost in the opposite chair. He found himself comparing the two rooms, seeking in his different responses a clue to the deepening depression of which the sitting room seemed partly a symbol, partly a cause. It wasn't only that the mill had a real wood fire, hissing and spitting real sparks and smelling of autumn, while his was synthetic, or that Dalgliesh's furniture was old, polished by centuries of use, arranged purely for convenience, not for show, not even that the paintings were real oils, genuine water-colours, or that the whole room had been put together with no apparent sense that anything in it was particularly highly regarded for its own sake. Above all, he decided, the difference surely lay in the books, the two walls covered with shelves holding books of every age and description, books for use, for pleasure in the reading and the handling. His own small collection, and Susie's, was in the bedroom. Susie had decreed that the books were too diverse, too tattered to be worthy of a place in what she called the "lounge," and there weren't many of them. In recent years he had had so little time for reading: a collection of modern adventure novels in paperback, four volumes from a book club to which, for a couple of years, he had belonged, a few hardback travel books, police manuals, Susie's school prizes for neatness and needlework. But a child should be brought up with books. He had read somewhere that it was the best possible beginning to life, to be surrounded with books, to have parents who encouraged reading. Perhaps they could fit shelves each side of the fireplace and make a start. Dickens: he had enjoyed Dickens at school; Shakespeare, of course, and the major English poets. His daughter—neither he nor Susie doubted that the baby would be a girl—would learn to love poetry.

But all that would have to wait. He could at least make a start with the housework. The room's air of dull pretentiousness was partly due, he realized, to dirt. It looked like an uncleaned hotel room in which no one took pride because no guest was expected and those few who came wouldn't care. He realized now that he should have kept on Mrs. Adcock, who came in to clean for three hours every Wednesday. But she had only worked for them in the last two months of Susie's pregnancy. He had hardly met her, and he disliked the thought of handing over house keys to a comparative stranger, more from his love of privacy than from any lack of trust. So, despite Susie's misgivings, he had paid Mrs. Adcock a retainer and had said that he could cope. Now he added his supper things to a load of crockery in the dishwasher and took a duster from those neatly folded in the drawer. Dust lay heavy on every surface. In the sitting room he drew the duster along the windowsill and saw with wonder the black line of grimed dirt.

He moved next to the hall. The cyclamen on the table beside the telephone had unaccountably wilted, despite his hurried daily watering, perhaps because of it. He was standing, duster in hand, wondering whether to throw it out or whether rescue was possible, when his ears caught the crunch of wheels on the gravel. He opened the door, then flung it wide with such force that it swung back and the latch clicked. Then he was at the taxi door, gently receiving the swollen figure into his arms.

"My darling, oh, my darling, why didn't you ring?"

She leaned against him. He saw with compassion the white, transparent skin, the smudges under her eyes. He seemed to feel even beneath the thick tweed of her coat the stirring of his child.

"I didn't wait. Mummy had only gone up the road to see Mrs. Blenkinsop. I just had time to ring for a taxi and leave her a note. I had to come. You're not cross?"

"Oh, my love, my darling. Are you all right?"

"Only tired." She laughed. "Darling, you've let the door close. You'll have to use my key."

He took her handbag from her, rummaged for the key and her purse, paid the driver, who had placed her one case by the door. His hands were shaking so that he could hardly fit the key in the lock. He half-lifted her over the threshold and lowered her onto the hall chair.

"Sit there a moment, darling, while I see to the case."

"Terry, the cyclamen is dead. You've overwatered it."

"No, I haven't. It died missing you."

She laughed. The sound was strong, a happy, contented peal. He wanted to lift her up into his arms and shout aloud. Suddenly serious, she said: "Has Mummy phoned?"

"Not yet, but she will."

And then, as if on cue, the telephone rang. He snatched it up. This time, awaiting the sound of his mother-in-law's voice, he was totally without fear, without anxiety. By that one magnificent affirming action Susie had placed them both for ever beyond her mother's destructive reach. He felt that he had been lifted out of misery as if by a huge wave and set for ever with his feet firmly on a rock. There was a second in which he saw Susie's look of anxiety, so acute that it was a spasm of pain, and then she got clumsily to her feet and leaned against him, slipping her hand into his. But the caller wasn't Mrs. Cartwright.

Oliphant said: "Jonathan Reeves has rung headquarters, sir, and they've put him on to me. He says that Caroline Amphlett and Amy Camm have gone boating together. They've been gone three hours now, and the mist is getting thicker."

"Then why did he ring the police? He should have got on to the Coast Guard."

"I've already done that, sir. That wasn't really why he phoned. He and Amphlett didn't spend last Sunday evening together. She was on the headland. He wanted to tell us that Amphlett lied. So did he."

"I don't suppose they're the only ones. We'll pull them in first thing tomorrow morning and hear their explanations. I've no doubt she'll come up with one."

Oliphant said stolidly: "But why should she lie if she's got nothing to hide? And it isn't just the false alibi. Reeves says that their love affair was only pretence, that she only pretended to care for him to cover up her lesbian affair with Camm. I reckon the two women were in it together, sir. Amphlett must have known that Robarts swam at night. All the staff at Larksoken knew that. And she worked closely with Mair, none closer. She's his PA. He could have told her all the details of that dinner party, how the Whistler operated. There'd be no problem in getting hold of the Bumbles. Camm knew about the jumble box even if Amphlett didn't. Her kid had clothes from it."

Rickards said: "There'd be no trouble in getting hold of the shoes. There might be trouble in wearing them. Neither woman is tall."

Oliphant dismissed what he probably felt was a puerile objection. He said: "But they would have had no time to try them on. Better to grab a pair too large than too small, a soft shoe rather than unyielding leather. And Camm's got a motive, sir. A double motive. She threatened Robarts after her kid was pushed over. We've got Mrs. Jago's evidence of their quarrel. And if Camm wanted to stay on in the caravan, close to her lover, it was important to put a stop to Robarts's libel action against Pascoe. And Camm almost certainly knew exactly where Robarts took her nightly swim. If Amphlett didn't tell her, Pascoe probably did. He admitted to us that he used to sneak out occasionally to spy on her. Dirty-minded little devil. And there's another thing. Camm has a dog lead, remember. So has Amphlett, come to that. Reeves said that she was exercising her dog on the headland Sunday night."

"There were no paw marks at the scene, Sergeant. Don't let's get too excited. She might have been at the scene, but the dog wasn't."

"Kept in the car, sir. Maybe she didn't have him with her, but I reckon she used the lead. There's another thing. Those two wine-glasses in Thyme Cottage. I reckon Caroline Amphlett was with Robarts before she went for that last swim. She's Mair's PA. Robarts would have let her in without question. It all adds up, sir. It's a water-tight case, sir."

Rickards thought that it was as water-tight as a sieve. But Oliphant was right. There was a case, even if there wasn't as yet a scintilla of proof. He mustn't let his feelings about the man cloud his judgement. And one fact was depressingly obvious. If he arrested another suspect, this theory, for all the lack of firm evidence, would be a gift to any defence counsel.

He said: "Ingenious, but it's totally circumstantial. Anyway, it can wait until tomorrow. There's nothing we can do tonight."

"We ought to see Reeves, sir. He may change his story before morning."

"You see him. And let me know when Camm and Amphlett get back. I'll see you at Hoveton at eight. We'll pull them in then. And I don't want them questioned, either of them, until I see them tomorrow. Is that understood?"

"Yes sir. Good night, sir."

When he had replaced the receiver, Susie said: "If you think you ought to go, darling, don't worry about me. I'll be all right now I'm home."

"It's not urgent. Oliphant can cope. He likes being in charge. Let's make him a happy Jumbo."

"But I don't want to be a trouble to you, darling. Mummy thought that life would be better for you with me away."

He turned and took her in his arms. He felt his own tears warm on her face. He said: "Life is never better for me when you're away."

5
⊠

The bodies were washed up two days later, two miles south of Hunstanton, or enough of them to make identification certain. On the Monday morning a retired tax officer, exercising his dalmatian dog on the beach, saw the animal sniffing round what looked like a white slab of lard entwined with seaweed, rolling and gliding at the edge of the tide. As he drew close the object was sucked back by the receding wave, then taken up by the next surge and flung at his feet, and he found himself gazing in incredulous horror at the torso of a woman neatly severed at the waist. For a second he stood petrified, staring down as the tide boiled in the empty socket of the left eye and swayed the flattened breasts. Then he turned away and was violently sick before shambling like a drunkard up the shingle of the beach, dragging the dog by its collar.

The body of Caroline Amphlett, unmutilated, was washed up on the same tide together with planks from the boat and part of the roof of the cabin. They were found by Daft Billy, a harmless and amiable beachcomber, on one of his regular sorties. It was the wood which first caught his eye, and he dragged the planks ashore with squeals of glee. Then, his prize secure, he turned his puzzled attention to the drowned girl. It was not the first body he had found in forty years of beachcombing and he knew what he must do, whom he must tell. First he placed his hands under the arms and pulled the body out of the reach of the tide. Then, moaning softly, as if mourning his clumsiness, her lack of response, he knelt beside her and, pulling off his jacket, spread it over the torn rags of her shirt and slacks.

"Comfy?" he asked. "Comfy?"

Then, putting out his hand, he carefully moved the strands of hair out of her eyes and, rocking himself gently, began crooning to her as he might to a child.

6
⊠

Dalgliesh made three visits on foot to the caravan after lunch on Thursday, but on no occasion was Neil Pascoe at home. He was unwilling to telephone to check whether the man had returned. He could think of no valid excuse for wanting to see him, and it seemed best to make the visit part of a walk, as if the decision to call at the caravan were merely an impulse. In one sense he supposed it could be a visit of condolence, but he had only known Amy Camm by sight and that excuse seemed to him dishonest as well as unconvincing. Shortly after five o'clock, when the light was beginning to fade, he tried again. This time the door of the caravan was wide open, but there was no sign of Pascoe. While he stood hesitating, a billow of smoke rose from above the edge of the cliff, followed by a brief flash of flame, and the air was suddenly filled with the acrid smell of bonfire.

From the edge of the cliff he looked down on an extraordinary scene. Pascoe had built a fireplace of large stones and chunks of concrete and had lit a fire of brushwood, onto which he was emptying papers, box files, cartons, bottles and what looked like an assortment of clothes. The pile awaiting burning was caged down against the strengthening wind by the bars of Timmy's cot; that too, no doubt, destined for the flames. A soiled mattress lay curled to one side like a makeshift and ineffectual windbreak. Pascoe, wearing only a pair of grubby shorts, was working like a demented demon, his eyes white saucers in his blackened face, his arms and naked chest glistening with sweat. As Dalgliesh slithered down the sandy slope of the cliff and moved up to the fire, he nodded a brief acknowledgement of his presence, then began dragging a small, scuffed suitcase from under the cot bars with desperate haste. Then he sprang up and balanced himself on the wide rim of the fireplace, his legs wide apart. In the ruddy glow of the flames his whole body gleamed, seeming for a moment transparent, as if it were lit from within, and the great dollops of sweat ran from his shoulders like blood. With a shout he swung the case high over the fire and wrenched it open. The baby clothes fell in a brightly coloured shower, and the flames leapt like living tongues to snatch at the woollen garments in mid-air, spinning them into briefly burning torches before they fell blackened into the heart of the fire. Pascoe stood for a moment breathing heavily, then sprang down with a cry half-exultant, half-despairing. Dalgliesh could understand and partly shared his exultation in this tumultuous juxtaposition of wind, fire and water. With each gust the tongues of flame roared and hissed so that he saw through a shimmering haze of heat the veins of the tumbling waves stained as if with blood. As Pascoe emptied into the fire yet another box file of papers, the charred fragments rose and danced like frantic birds, blew gently against Dalgliesh's face and settled over the dry stones of the upper shingle like a black contagion. He could feel his eyes prickling with the smoke.

He called out: "Aren't you polluting the beach?"

Pascoe turned to him and spoke for the first time, shouting above the roar of the fire.

"What does it matter? We're polluting the whole bloody planet."

Dalgliesh shouted back: "Shove some shingle on it and leave it until tomorrow. It's too windy for a bonfire this evening."

He had expected Pascoe to ignore him, but to his surprise the words seemed to recall his companion to reality. The exultation and vigour seemed to drain out of him. He looked at the fire and said dully: "I suppose you're right."

There were a spade and a rusty shovel thrown down by the pile of rubbish. Together the two men scooped up a mixture of shingle and sand and flung it onto the flames. When the last red tongue had died with an angry hiss, Pascoe turned and began scrunching his way up the beach towards the cliff. Dalgliesh followed. The question he had half-feared—"Are you here on purpose? Why do you want to see me?"—was unspoken and apparently unthought.

In the caravan Pascoe kicked the door shut and slumped down

at the table. He said: "Want a beer? Or there's tea. I'm out of coffee."

"Nothing, thanks."

Dalgliesh sat and watched as Pascoe groped his way over to the refrigerator. Returning to the table, he wrenched open the seal, threw back his head and poured the beer down his throat in an almost continuous stream. Then he slumped forward, silent, still clutching the tin. Neither spoke and it seemed to Dalgliesh that his companion hardly knew that he was still there. It was dark in the caravan, and Pascoe's face across the two feet of wood was an indistinguishable oval in which the whites of the eyes gleamed unnaturally bright. Then he stumbled to his feet murmuring something about matches, and a few seconds later there was a scrape and hiss and his hands stretched towards the oil lamp on the table. In its strengthening glow his face, beneath the dirt and smudges of smoke, looked drained and haggard, the eyes dulled with pain. The wind was shaking the caravan, not roughly but with a regular gentle sway, as if it were being rocked by an unseen hand. The sliding door of the end compartment was open and Dalgliesh could see, on the narrow bed, a pile of female clothes topped with a jumble of tubes, jars and bottles. Apart from this, the caravan looked tidy but denuded, less a home than a temporary, ill-equipped refuge but holding still the unmistakable milky and faecal smell of a child. The absence of Timmy and his dead mother filled the caravan as it did both their minds.

After minutes of silence, Pascoe looked up at him. "I was burning all my PANUP records out there with the rest of the rubbish. You probably guessed. It was never any use. I was only using PANUP to pander to my own need to feel important. You more or less said so that time I called at the mill."

"Did I? I hadn't any right to. What will you do now?"

"Go to London and look for a job. The university won't extend my grant for a further year. I don't blame them. I'd prefer to go back to the north-east, but I suppose London offers me more hope."

"What sort of job?"

"Any job. I don't give a damn what I do as long as it makes money for me and is no possible use to anyone else."

Dalgliesh asked: "What happened to Timmy?"

"The local authority took him. They got a Place of Safety Order or something of the sort. A couple of social workers came for him yesterday. Decent enough women, but he didn't want to go with them. They had to tear him screaming from my arms. What sort of a society does that to its children?"

Dalgliesh said: "I don't suppose they had any choice. They have to make long-term plans for his future. After all, he couldn't have stayed here indefinitely with you."

"Why not? I cared for him for over a year. And at least I would have had something out of all this mess."

Dalgliesh asked: "Have they traced Amy's family?"

"They haven't had much time, have they? And when they do I don't expect they'll tell me. Timmy lived here for over a year, but I'm of less account than the grandparents he never saw and who probably don't give a damn about him."

He was still holding the empty beer can. Twisting it slowly in his hands, he said: "What really gets to me is the deception. I thought she cared. Oh, not about me, but about what I was trying to do. It was all pretence. She was using me, using this place to be near Caroline."

Dalgliesh said: "But they can't have seen very much of each other."

"How do I know? When I wasn't here she probably sneaked out to meet her lover. Timmy must have spent hours alone. She didn't even care for him. The cats were more important than Timmy. Mrs. Jago has taken them now. They'll be all right. Sometimes on Sunday afternoons she used to go out, blatantly telling me that she was off to meet her lover in the sand dunes. I thought it was a joke, I needed to believe that. And all the time she and Caroline were out there together making love, laughing at me."

Dalgliesh said: "You've only got Reeves's evidence to suggest they were lovers. Caroline could have been lying to him."

"No. No, she wasn't lying. I know that. They used us both, Reeves and me. Amy wasn't—well, she wasn't undersexed. We lived here together for over a year. On the second night she—well, she did offer to come to my bed. But it was just her way of paying for board and lodging. It wouldn't have been right then for either of us. But after a time I suppose I began to hope. I mean, living here together, I suppose I grew fond of her. But she never really wanted me to be near her. And when she came in from those Sunday walks I knew. I pretended to myself that I didn't, but I knew. She looked exultant. She was shining with happiness."

Dalgliesh said: "Look, is it really so important to you, the affair with Caroline, even if it is true? What you had here together, the affection, friendship, comradeship, caring for Timmy, does all that go for nothing because she found her sexual life outside the walls of this caravan?"

Pascoe said bitterly: "Forget and forgive? You make it sound so easy."

"I don't suppose you can forget, or perhaps even want to. But I can't see why you have to use the word 'forgive.' She never promised more than she gave."

"You despise me, don't you?"

Dalgliesh thought how unattractive it was, the self-absorption of the deeply unhappy. But there were questions he still had to ask. He said: "And she left nothing, no papers, no records, no diary, nothing to say what she was doing on the headland?"

"Nothing. And I know what she was doing here, why she came. She came to be near Caroline."

"Did she have any money? Even if you fed her, she must have had something of her own."

"She always had some cash, but I don't know how she got it. She never said and I didn't like to ask. I know she didn't draw any Welfare payments. She said she didn't want the DHSS snooping round here to check whether we were sleeping together. I didn't blame her. Nor did I."

"And she got no post."

"She got postcards from time to time. Pretty regularly, really. So she must have had friends in London. I don't know what she did with them. Threw them away, I suppose. There's nothing in the caravan but her clothes and make-up, and I'm going to burn those next. After that there'll be nothing left to show that she was ever here."

Dalgliesh asked: "And the murder. Do you think that Caroline Amphlett killed Robarts?"

"Perhaps. I don't care. It doesn't matter any more. If she didn't, Rickards will make her a scapegoat, her and Amy together."

"But you can't really believe that Amy committed a murder?"

Pascoe looked at Dalgliesh with the frustration and anger of an uncomprehending child. "I don't know! Look, I really never knew her. That's what I'm telling you. I don't know! And now that Timmy's gone, I don't really care. And I'm in such a muddle, anger at what she did to me, at what she was, and grief that she's dead. I didn't think you could be angry and grieving at the same time. I ought to be mourning her, but all I can feel is this terrible anger."

"Oh yes," said Dalgliesh. "You can feel anger and grief together. That's the commonest reaction to bereavement."

Suddenly Pascoe began crying. The empty beer can rattled against the table, and he bent his head low over it, his shoulders shaking. Women, thought Dalgliesh, are better at coping with grief than we are. He had seen them so many times, the women police officers moving unconsciously to take the grieving mother, the lost child in their arms. Some men were good at it too, of course. Rickards had been in the old days. He himself was good with the words, but, then, words were his trade. What he found difficult was what came so spontaneously to the truly generous at heart, the willingness to touch and be touched. He thought: I'm here on false pretences. If I were not, perhaps I too could feel adequate.

He said: "I think the wind is less strong than it was. Why don't we finish the burning and clear up that mess on the beach?"

It was over an hour later before Dalgliesh was ready to set off for the mill. As he said goodbye to Pascoe at the door of the caravan, a blue Fiesta with a young man at its wheel came bumping over the grass.

Pascoe said: "Jonathan Reeves. He was engaged to Caroline Am-phlett, or thought he was. She fooled him like Amy fooled me. He's been round once or twice to chat. We thought we might walk to the Local Hero for a game of bar billiards."

It was not, thought Dalgliesh, an agreeable picture, the two men, bound by a common grievance, consoling each other for the perfidy of their women with beer and bar billiards. But Pascoe seemed to want to introduce him to Reeves, and he found himself grasping a sur-prisingly firm hand and making his formal condolences.

Jonathan Reeves said: "I still can't believe it, but I suppose people always say that after a sudden death. And I can't help feeling that it was my fault. I should have stopped them."

Dalgliesh said: "They were adult women. Presumably they knew what they were doing. Short of physically dragging them off the boat, which would hardly have been practicable, I don't see how you could have stopped them."

Reeves reiterated obstinately: "I should have stopped them." Then he added: "I keep having this dream, well, nightmare really. She's standing at the side of my bed with the child in her arms and saying to me, 'It's all your fault. All your fault.' "

Pascoe said: "Caroline comes with Timmy?"

Reeves looked at him as if surprised that he could be so obtuse. He said: "Not Caroline. It's Amy who comes. Amy, whom I never met, standing there with water streaming from her hair, holding the child in her arms and telling me that it's all my fault."

7

⊠

Just over an hour later Dalgliesh had left the headland and was driving
west along the A1151. After twenty minutes he turned south along a
narrow country road. Darkness had fallen and the low, scudding
clouds, torn by wind, moved like a tattered blanket over the moon and
the high stars. He drove fast and unhesitatingly, hardly aware of the
tug and howl of the wind. He had taken this route only once before,
early that same morning, but he had no need to consult the map; he
knew where he was going. On either side of the low hedges stretched
the black, unbroken fields. The lights of the car silvered an occasional
distorted tree flailing in the wind, briefly illuminated as if with a
searchlight the blank face of an isolated farm cottage, picked out the
pin-bright eyes of a night animal before it scuttled to safety. The drive
was not long, less than fifty minutes, but, staring straight ahead and
shifting the gear lever as if he were an automaton, he felt for a moment
disorientated as if he had driven through the bleak darkness of this
flat, secretive landscape for interminable hours.

The brick-built, early-Victorian villa stood on the outskirts of a
village. The gate to the gravel drive lay open, and he drove slowly
between the tossing laurels and the high, creaking boughs of the
beech trees and manoeuvred the Jaguar between the three cars already discreetly parked at the side of the house. The two rows of
windows in the front were dark, and the single bulb which illuminated
the fanlight seemed to Dalgliesh less a welcoming sign of occupation

than a private signal, a sinister indication of secretive life. He did not need to ring. Ears had been alert for the approaching car, and the door was opened just as he reached it by the same stocky, cheerful-faced janitor who had greeted him on his first summons, earlier that morning. Now, as then, he was wearing blue overalls so sprucely well cut that they looked like a uniform. Dalgliesh wondered what was his precise role: driver, guard, general factotum? Or had he, perhaps, a more specialized and sinister function?

He said: "They're in the library, sir. I'll bring in the coffee. Will you be wanting sandwiches, sir? There's some beef left, or I could put up a bit of cheese."

Dalgliesh said: "Just the coffee, thank you."

They were waiting for him in the same small room at the back of the house. The walls were panelled in pale wood and there was only one window, a square bay heavily curtained with faded blue velvet. Despite its name, the function of the room was unclear. Admittedly the wall opposite the window was lined with bookshelves, but they held only half a dozen leather-bound volumes and piles of old periodicals which looked as if they were Sunday colour supplements. The room had an oddly disturbing air of being makeshift yet not devoid of comfort, a staging post in which the temporary occupants were attempting to make themselves at home. Ranged round the ornate marble fireplace were six assorted armchairs, most of them leather and each with a small wine table. The opposite end of the room was occupied by a modern dining table in plain wood with six chairs. This morning it had held the remains of breakfast and the air had been oppressively heavy with the smell of bacon and eggs. But the debris had been cleared and replaced by a tray of bottles and glasses. Looking at the variety provided, Dalgliesh thought that they had been doing themselves rather well. The loaded tray gave the place the air of a temporary hospitality room in which little else was hospitable. The air struck him as rather chill. In the grate an ornamental fan of paper rustled with each moan of the wind in the chimney, and the two-bar electric fire which stood in the fender was barely adequate even for so meanly proportioned and cluttered a room.

Three pairs of eyes turned on him as he entered. Clifford Sowerby was standing against the fireplace in exactly the same pose as when Dalgliesh had last seen him. He looked, in his formal suit and immaculate linen, as fresh as he had at nine o'clock that morning. Now, as then, he dominated the room. He was a solid-fleshed, conventionally handsome man with the assurance and controlled benevolence of a headmaster or a successful banker. No customer need fear to enter his office, provided his account was well in credit. Meeting him for only the second time, Dalgliesh felt again an instinctive and seemingly irrational unease. The man was both ruthless and dangerous, and yet, in their hours apart, he had been unable accurately to recall either his face or his voice.

The same could not be said of Bill Harding. He stood over six feet tall and, with his pale freckled face and thatch of red hair, had obviously decided that anonymity was impossible and that he might as well opt for eccentricity. He was wearing a checked suit in heavy tweed with a spotted tie. Raising himself with some difficulty out of the low chair, he ambled over to the drinks and, when Dalgliesh said he'd wait for coffee, stood holding the whisky bottle as if unsure what to do with it. But there was one addition since the morning. Alex Mair, whisky glass in hand, stood against the bookcase, as if interested in the assortment of leather-bound volumes and piled periodicals. He turned as Dalgliesh entered and gave him a long, considering look, then nodded briefly. He was easily the most personable and the most intelligent of the three waiting men, but something, confidence or energy, seemed to have drained out of him, and he had the diminished, precariously contained look of a man in physical pain.

Sowerby said, his heavily lidded eyes amused: "You've singed your hair, Adam. You smell as if you've been raking a bonfire."

"I have."

Mair didn't move, but Sowerby and Harding seated themselves each side of the fire. Dalgliesh took a chair between them. They waited until coffee had arrived and he had a cup in hand. Sowerby was leaning back in his chair and looking up at the ceiling and seemed to be prepared to wait all night.

It was Bill Harding who said: "Well, Adam?"

Putting down his cup, Dalgliesh described what exactly had happened since his arrival at the caravan. He had total verbal recall. He had made no notes, nor was it necessary. At the end of his account he said: "So you can relax. Pascoe believes what will, I imagine, become the official line, that the two girls were lovers, went for an unwise boat trip together and were accidentally run down in the fog. I don't think he'll make any trouble for you or for anyone else. His capacity for troublemaking seems to be over."

Sowerby said: "And Camm left nothing incriminating in the caravan?"

"I doubt very much whether there was anything to leave. Pascoe said that he read one or two of the postcards when they arrived, but they were mostly the usual meaningless phrases, tourist's chat. Camm apparently destroyed them. And he, with my help, has destroyed the detritus of her life on the headland. I helped him carry the last of her clothes and make-up down to the fire. While he was busy burning it, I had a chance to return and make a fairly thorough search. There was nothing there."

Sowerby said formally: "It was good of you to do this for us, Adam. Obviously, as Rickards isn't in the picture as far as our interest is concerned, we could hardly rely on him. And you, of course, had an advantage he lacked. Pascoe would see you more as a friend than a policeman. That's obvious from his previous visit to Larksoken Mill. For some reason he trusts you."

Dalgliesh said: "You explained all that this morning. The request you made then seemed to me to be reasonable in the circumstances. I'm neither naïve nor ambivalent about terrorism. You asked me to do something and I've done it. I still think you should put Rickards in the picture, but that's your business. And you've got your answer. If Camm was involved in Amphlett's conspiracy, she didn't confide in Pascoe and he has no suspicions of either woman. He believes that Camm only stayed with him to be near her lover. Pascoe, for all his liberal ideas, is as ready as the next man to believe that a woman who persists in not wanting to go to bed with him must be either frigid or a lesbian."

Sowerby permitted himself a wry smile. He said: "While you were playing Ariel to his Prospero on the beach, I suppose he didn't confess to killing Robarts. It's of small importance, but one has a natural curiosity."

"My brief was to talk to him about Amy Camm, but he did mention the murder. I don't think he really believes that Amy helped to kill Robarts, but he doesn't really care whether the two girls did or did not. Are you satisfied yourselves that they did?"

Sowerby said: "We don't have to be. It's Rickards who has to be satisfied, and I imagine that he is. Incidentally, have you seen or spoken to him today?"

"He telephoned briefly about midday, principally, I think, to tell me that his wife has come home. For some reason, he thought I'd be interested. As far as the murder is concerned, he seems to be coming round to the view that Camm and Amphlett were in it together."

Harding said: "And he's probably right."

Dalgliesh asked: "On what evidence? And since he's not allowed to know that one of them at least is a suspected terrorist, where's the motive?"

Harding said impatiently: "Come off it, Adam, what real evidence does he expect to get? And since when was motive the first consideration? Anyway, they had a motive, at least Camm did. She hated Robarts. There's one witness at least to a physical fight between them on the Sunday afternoon of the murder. And Camm was fiercely protective of Pascoe and connected to that pressure group he started. That libel action would have ruined him and put PANUP out of business for ever. It's precarious enough as it is. Camm wanted Robarts dead, and Amphlett killed her. That will be the general belief locally, and Rickards will go along with it. To do him justice, he probably believes it."

Dalgliesh said: "Camm fiercely protective of Pascoe? Who says so? That's supposition, not evidence."

"But he's got some evidence, hasn't he? Circumstantial evidence, admittedly, but that's all he's likely to get now. Amphlett knew that Robarts went swimming at night; practically everyone at the power station knew that. She concocted a false alibi. Camm had access like anyone else to the jumble room at the Old Rectory. And Pascoe now admits that it could have been nine-fifteen when he got back from Norwich. All right, the timing is tight, but it's not impossible if Robarts swam earlier than usual. It adds up to a reasonable case. Not one which would have justified arresting them if they were still living, but enough to make it difficult to get a conviction against anyone else."

Dalgliesh said: "Would Amy Camm have left the child?"

"Why not? He was probably asleep, and if he wasn't and started yelling, who would hear? You're not suggesting, Adam, that she was a good mother, for God's sake? She left him at the end, didn't she? Permanently, as it happens, although that may not have been intentional. If you ask me, that kid had a pretty low priority with his mother."

Dalgliesh said: "So you're postulating a mother who is so outraged by a minor assault on her child that she avenges it with murder, and that same mother leaves him alone in a caravan while she goes sailing with her girlfriend. Wouldn't Rickards find that difficult to reconcile?"

Sowerby said, with a touch of impatience: "God knows how Rickards reconciles anything. Luckily we're not required to ask him. Anyway, Adam, we know of a positive motive. Robarts could have suspected Amphlett. After all, she was Acting Administrative Officer. She was intelligent, conscientious—overconscientious, didn't you say, Mair?"

They all looked towards the silent figure standing against the bookcase. Mair turned to face them. He said quietly: "Yes, she was conscientious. But I doubt whether she was conscientious enough to detect a conspiracy which had eluded me." He turned back to his contemplation of the books.

There was a moment's embarrassed silence which was broken by Bill Harding. He said briskly, as if Mair hadn't spoken: "So who was better placed to smell out a spot of treason? Rickards may have no firm evidence and an inadequate motive, but essentially he'll probably get it right."

Dalgliesh got to his feet and walked over to the table. He said: "It would suit you to get the case closed, I see that. But if I were the investigating officer, the file would stay open."

Sowerby said wryly: "Obviously. Then let us be grateful that you aren't. But you'll keep your doubts to yourself, Adam? That doesn't need saying."

"Then why say it?"

He placed his coffee cup back on the table. He was aware of Sowerby and Harding watching his every move as if he were a suspect who might suddenly make a break for it. Returning to his chair, he said: "And how will Rickards or anyone else explain the boat trip?"

It was still Harding who answered: "He doesn't have to. They were lovers, for God's sake. They fancied a sea trip. It was Amphlett's boat after all. She left her car on the quay perfectly openly. She took nothing with her and neither did Amy. She left a note to Pascoe saying she'd be back in a couple of hours. In Rickards's eyes and everyone else's, that adds up to an unfortunate accident. And who is to say that it wasn't? We were nowhere near close enough to have scared Amphlett into making a run for it; not yet."

"And your people have found nothing at the house?"

Harding looked at Sowerby. It was a question they preferred not to answer, and one which should not have been asked. After a pause, Sowerby answered: "Clean. No radio, no documents, no evidence of trade craft. If Amphlett did intend to do a bunk, she cleaned up efficiently before she left."

Bill Harding said: "OK, if she did panic and was getting out, the only mystery is, why so precipitous? If she killed Robarts and thought that the police were getting close, that might have tipped the balance. But they weren't getting close. It could, of course, have been a genuine boat trip, and a genuine accident. Or their own side could have killed them both. Once the Larksoken plan was obsolete, they were expendable. What were the comrades going to do with them, for God's sake? Fit them out with new personalities, new papers, infiltrate them into a power station in Germany? They were hardly worth the trouble, I should have thought."

Dalgliesh said: "Is there any evidence that it was an accident? Has any ship reported bow damage in the fog, a possible collision?"

Sowerby said: "None so far. I doubt whether there will be. But if Amphlett really was part of the organization we suspect recruited her, they'd have no compunction in providing a couple of involuntary martyrs for the cause. What sort of people did she think she was dealing with? The fog would have helped them, but they could have run down that boat without the fog. Or, for that matter, taken them off and killed them elsewhere. But to fake an accident was the sensible course, particularly given the bonus of the fog. I'd have done it that way myself." And he would, thought Dalgliesh. He would have done it without compunction.

Harding turned to Mair. He said: "You never had the least suspicion of her?"

"You asked me that before. None. I was surprised—a little irritated even—that she preferred not to stay as my PA when I got the new job, and even more surprised at the reason. Jonathan Reeves was hardly the man I thought she'd have chosen."

Sowerby said: "But it was clever. An ineffectual man, one she could dominate. Not too intelligent. Already in love with her. She could have chucked him whenever she chose, and he wouldn't have the wit to know why. And why should you suspect? Sexual attraction is irrational anyway."

There was a pause, then he added: "Did you ever see her, the other girl, Amy? I'm told that she did visit the power station on one of those open days, but I don't suppose you'd remember her."

Mair's face was like a white mask. He said: "I did see her once, I think. Blond dyed hair, a chubby, rather pretty face. She was carrying the child. What will happen to him, incidentally? Or is it a she?"

Sowerby said: "Taken into care, I suppose, unless they can trace the father or the grandparents. He'll probably end up fostered or adopted. I wonder what the hell his mother thought she was doing."

Harding spoke with sudden vehemence: "Do they think? Ever? No faith, no stability, no family affection, no loyalty. They're blown like paper with every wind. Then, when they do find something to believe in, something to give them the illusion that they're important, what do they choose? Violence, anarchy, hatred, murder."

Sowerby looked at him, surprised and a little amused. Then he said: "Ideas some of them think worth dying for. In that, of course, lies the problem."

"Only because they want to die. If you can't cope with living, look for an excuse, a cause you can kid yourself is worth dying for, and indulge your death-wish. With luck you can take a dozen or so poor sods with you, people who can cope with living, who don't want to die. And there's always the ultimate self-deception, the final arrogance. Martyrdom. Lonely and inadequate fools all over the world will clench their fists and shout your name and carry placards with your picture and start looking round themselves for someone to bomb and shoot and maim. And that girl, Amphlett. She hadn't even the excuse of poverty. Dad a senior army officer, security, a good education, privilege, money. She'd had it all."

It was Sowerby who replied. He said: "We know what she had. What we can't know is what she didn't have."

Harding ignored him. "And what did they expect to do with Larksoken if they did take it over? They wouldn't have lasted for more than half an hour. They'd have needed experts, programmers."

Mair said: "I think you can take it they knew what and who they'd need and had planned how they could get them."

"Into the country? How?"

"By boat, perhaps."

Sowerby looked at him and then said a little impatiently: "They didn't do it. They couldn't have done it. And it's our job to see that they never can do it."

There was a moment's silence; then Mair said: "I suppose Amphlett was the dominant partner. I wonder what arguments or what inducements she used. The girl—Amy—struck me as an instinctive creature, not likely to die for a political theory. But that is obviously a superficial judgement. I only saw her once."

Sowerby said: "Without knowing them, we can't be sure who was the dominant partner. But I'd say it was almost certainly Amphlett. Nothing is known or suspected about Camm. She was probably recruited as a runner. Amphlett must have had a contact in the organization, must have met him occasionally, if only to receive instructions. But they'd be careful never to get in touch directly. Camm probably received the coded messages setting out time and place for the next meeting and passed them on. As for her reasons, she found life unsatisfactory, no doubt."

Bill Harding lunged over to the table and poured himself a large whisky. His voice was thick, as if he were drunk. "Life has always been unsatisfactory for most people for most of the time. The world isn't designed for our satisfaction. That's no reason for trying to pull it down about our ears."

Sowerby smiled his sly, superior smile. He said easily: "Perhaps they thought that's what we're doing."

Fifteen minutes later Dalgliesh left with Mair. As they stood unlocking their cars, he looked back and saw that the janitor was still waiting at the open door. Mair said: "Making sure that we actually leave the premises. What extraordinary people they are! I wonder how they got on to Caroline. There seemed no point in asking, as they made it obvious that they had no intention of saying."

"No, they wouldn't say. Almost certainly they got a tip-off from the security services in Germany."

"And this house. How on earth do they find these places? D'you suppose that they own it, borrow it, rent it or just break into it?"

Dalgliesh said: "It probably belongs to one of their own officers—retired, I imagine. He, or she, lets them have a spare key for such an occasional use."

"And now they'll be packing up, I suppose. Dusting down the furniture, checking for fingerprints, finishing up the food, turning off the power. And in an hour no one will know that they were ever there. The perfect temporary tenants. They've got one thing wrong, though. There wasn't a physical relationship between Amy and Caroline. That's nonsense."

He spoke with such extraordinary strength and conviction, almost with outrage, that Dalgliesh wondered for a moment whether Caroline Amphlett had been more than his PA. Mair must surely have sensed what his companion was thinking, but he neither explained nor denied. Dalgliesh said: "I haven't congratulated you yet on your new job."

Mair had slipped into his seat and turned on the engine. But the car door was still open, and the silent warder at the door still waited patiently.

He said: "Thank you. These tragedies at Larksoken have taken away some of the immediate satisfaction, but it's still the most important job I'm ever likely to hold."

Then, as Dalgliesh turned away, he said: "So you think we still have a killer alive on the headland."

"Don't you?"

But Mair didn't reply. Instead he asked: "If you were Rickards, what would you do now?"

"I'd concentrate on trying to find out whether Blaney or Theresa left Scudder's Cottage that Sunday night. If either of them did, then I think my case would be complete. It isn't one that I'd be able to prove, but it would stand up in logic and I think that it would be the truth."

8

Dalgliesh drove first out of the drive but Mair, accelerating sharply, overtook him on the first stretch of straight road and remained ahead. The thought of following the Jaguar all the way back to Larksoken was, for some reason, intolerable. But there was no danger of it: Dalgliesh even drove like a policeman, inside, if only just inside, the speed limit. And by the time they reached the main road, Mair could no longer see the lights of the Jaguar in his mirror. He drove almost automatically, eyes fixed ahead, hardly aware of the black shapes of the tossing trees as they rushed past like an accelerated film, of the cat's eyes unfolding in an unbroken stream of light. He was expecting a clear road on the headland and, cresting a low ridge, saw almost too late the lights of an ambulance. Violently twisting the wheel, he bumped off the road and braked on the grass verge, then sat there listening to the silence. It seemed to him that emotions which for the last three hours he had rigorously suppressed were buffeting him as the wind buffeted the car. He had to discipline his thoughts, to arrange and make sense of these astonishing feelings which horrified him by their violence and irrationality. Was it possible that he could feel relief at her death, at a danger averted, a possible embarrassment prevented, and yet at the same time be torn as if his sinews were being wrenched apart by a pain and regret so overwhelming that it could only be grief? He had to control himself from beating his head against the wheel of the car. She had been so uninhibited, so gallant, so entertaining. And she had kept faith with him. He hadn't been in touch with her since their last meeting on the Sunday afternoon of the murder, and she had made no attempt to contact him by letter or telephone. They had agreed that the affair must end and that each would keep silent. She had kept her part of the bargain, as he had known she would. And now she was dead. He spoke her name aloud, Amy, Amy, Amy. Suddenly he gave a gasp which tore at the muscles of his chest as if he were in the first throes of a heart attack and felt the blessed releasing tears flow down his face. He hadn't cried since he was a boy and even now, as the tears ran like rain and he tasted their surprising saltiness on his lips, he told himself that these minutes of emotion were good and therapeutic. He owed them to her and, once they were over, the tribute of grief paid, he would be able to put her out of his mind as he had planned to put her out of his heart. It was only thirty minutes later, when switching on the engine, that he gave thought to the ambulance and wondered which of the few inhabitants of the headland was being rushed to hospital.

9

As the two ambulance men wheeled the stretcher down the garden path, the wind tore at the corner of the red blanket and billowed it into an arc. The straps held it down, but Blaney almost flung himself across Theresa's body, as if desperately shielding her from something more threatening than the wind. He shuffled crab-like down the path beside her, half-bent, his hand holding hers under the blanket. It felt hot and moist and very small, and it seemed to him that he was aware of every delicate bone. He wanted to whisper reassurance but terror had dried his throat and when he tried to speak his jaw jabbered as if palsied. And he had no comfort to give. There was a too-recent memory of another ambulance, another stretcher, another journey. He hardly dared look at Theresa in case he saw on her face what he had seen on her mother's: that look of pale, remote acceptance which meant that she was already moving away from him, from all the mundane affairs of life, even from his love, into a shadow land where he could neither follow nor was welcome. He tried to find reassurance in the memory of Dr. Entwhistle's robust voice.

"She'll be all right. It's appendicitis. We'll get her to hospital straight away. They'll operate tonight and with luck she'll be back with you in a few days. Not to do the housework, mind; we'll discuss all that later. Now, let's get to the telephone. And stop panicking, man. People don't die of appendicitis."

But they did die. They died under the anaesthetic, they died because peritonitis intervened, they died because the surgeon made a mistake. He had read of these cases. He was without hope.

As the stretcher was gently lifted and slid with easy expertise into the ambulance, he turned and looked back at Scudder's Cottage. He hated it now, hated what it had done to him, what it had made him do. Like him, it was accursed. Mrs. Jago was standing at the door holding Anthony in her unpractised arms with a twin standing silently on each side. He had telephoned the Local Hero for help, and George Jago had driven her over immediately to stay with the children until he returned. There had been no one else to ask. He had telephoned Alice Mair at Martyr's Cottage, but all he had got was the answerphone. Mrs. Jago lifted Anthony's hand and waved it in a gesture of goodbye, then bent to speak to the twins. Obediently they too waved. He climbed into the ambulance and the doors were firmly shut.

The ambulance bumped and gently swayed up the lane, then accelerated as it reached the narrow headland road to Lydsett. Suddenly it swerved and he was almost thrown from his seat. The paramedic sitting opposite him cursed.

"Some bloody fool going too fast."

But he didn't reply. He sat very close to Theresa, his hand still in hers, and found himself praying as if he could batten on the ears of the God he hadn't believed in since he was seventeen. "Don't let her die. Don't punish her because of me. I'll believe. I'll do anything. I can change, be different. Punish me but not her. Oh God, let her live."

And suddenly he was standing again in that dreadful little churchyard hearing the drone of Father McKee's voice with Theresa at his side, her hand still cold in his. The earth was covered with synthetic grass but there was one mound left bare and he saw again the newly sliced gold of the soil. He hadn't known that Norfolk earth could be so rich a colour. A white flower had fallen from one of the wreaths, a small, tortured, unrecognized bud with a pin through the wrapped stalk, and he was seized with an almost uncontrollable compulsion to pick it up before it was shovelled with the earth into the grave, to take it home, put it in water and let it die in peace. He had to hold himself tautly upright to prevent himself bending to retrieve it. But he hadn't dared, and it had been left there to be smothered and obliterated under the first clods.

He heard Theresa whisper and bent so low to listen that he could smell her breath.

"Daddy, am I going to die?"

"No. No."

He almost shouted the word, a howled defiance of death, and was aware of the paramedic half-rising to his feet. He said quietly: "You heard what Dr. Entwhistle said. It's just appendicitis."

"I want to see Father McKee."

"Tomorrow. After the operation. I'll tell him. He'll visit you. I won't forget. I promise. Now lie still."

"Daddy, I want him now, before the operation. There's something I have to tell him."

"Tell him tomorrow."

"Can I tell you? I have to tell someone now."

He said almost fiercely: "Tomorrow, Theresa. Leave it till tomorrow." And then, appalled by his selfishness, he whispered: "Tell me, darling, if you must," and closed his eyes so that she should not see the horror, the hopelessness.

She whispered: "That night Miss Robarts died. I crept out to the abbey ruins. I saw her running into the sea. Daddy, I was there."

He said hoarsely: "It doesn't matter. You don't have to tell me any more."

"But I want to tell. I ought to have told you before. Please, Daddy."

He put his other hand over hers. He said: "Tell me."

"There was someone else there, too. I saw her walking over the headland towards the sea. It was Mrs. Dennison."

Relief flowed through him, wave after wave, like a warm, cleansing summer sea. After a moment's silence he heard her voice again: "Daddy, are you going to tell anyone, the police?"

"No," he said. "I'm glad you've told me, but it isn't important. It doesn't mean anything. She was just taking a walk in the moonlight. I'm not going to tell."

"Not even about me being on the headland that night?"

"No," he said firmly, "not even that. Not yet, anyway. But we'll talk about it, what we ought to do, after the operation."

And for the first time he could believe that there would be a time for them after the operation.

10

⊠

Mr. Copley's study was at the back of the Old Rectory, looking out over the unkempt lawn and the three rows of wind-crippled bushes which the Copleys called the "shrubbery." It was the only room in the rectory which Meg would not dream of entering without first knocking, and it was accepted as his private place as if he were still in charge of a parish and needing a quiet sanctum to prepare his weekly sermon or counsel those parishioners who sought his advice. It was here that each day he read Morning Prayer and Evensong, his only congregation his wife and Meg, whose low feminine voices would make the responses and read alternate verses of the psalms. On her first day with them he had said gently but without embarrassment: "I say the two main offices every day in my study, but please don't feel that you need to attend unless you wish to."

She had chosen to attend, at first from politeness but later because this daily ritual, the beautiful, half-forgotten cadences, seducing her into belief, gave a welcome shape to the day. And the study itself, of all the rooms in the solidly ugly but comfortable house, seemed to represent an inviolable security, a great rock in a weary land, against which all the rancorous, intrusive memories of school, the petty ir-ritations of daily living, even the horror of the Whistler and the menace of the power station beat in vain. She doubted whether it had greatly changed since the first Victorian rector had taken possession. One wall was lined with books, a theological library which she thought

Mr. Copley now rarely consulted. The old mahogany desk was usually bare, and Meg suspected that he spent most of his time in the easy chair which looked out over the garden. Three walls were covered with pictures: the rowing eight of his university days with ridiculously small caps above the grave moustached young faces; the ordinands of his theological college; insipid water-colours in golden mounts, the record by some Victorian ancestor of his grand tour; etchings of Norwich Cathedral, the nave at Winchester, the great octagon of Ely. To one side of the ornate Victorian fireplace was a single crucifix. It seemed to Meg to be very old and probably valuable, but she had never liked to ask. The body of Christ was a young man's body, stretched taut in its last agony, the open mouth seeming to shout in triumph or defiance at the God who had deserted Him. Nothing else in the study was powerful or disturbing; furniture, objects, pictures all spoke of order, of certainty, of hope. Now, as she knocked and listened for Mr. Copley's gentle "Come in," it occurred to her that she was seeking comfort as much from the room itself as from its occupant.

He was sitting in the armchair, a book in his lap, and made to get up with awkward stiffness as she entered. She said: "Please don't get up. I wonder if I could talk to you privately for a few minutes."

She saw at once the flare of anxiety in the faded blue eyes and thought, He's afraid I'm going to give notice. She added quickly but with gentle firmness: "As a priest. I wish to consult you as a priest."

He lay down his book. She saw that it was one he and his wife had chosen the previous Friday from the travelling library, the newest H.R.F. Keating. Both he and Dorothy Copley enjoyed detective stories, and Meg was always slightly irritated that husband and wife took it for granted that he should always have first read. This inopportune reminder of his mild domestic selfishness assumed for a moment a disproportionate importance, and she wondered why she had ever thought he could be of help. Yet was it right to criticize him for the marital priorities which Dorothy Copley had herself laid down and gently enforced over fifty-three years? She told herself, I am consulting the priest, not the man. I wouldn't ask a plumber how he treated his wife and children before letting him loose on the leaking tank.

He gestured towards a second easy chair and she drew it up opposite him. He marked his page with his leather bookmark with

careful deliberation and laid down the novel as reverently as if it were
a book of devotions, folding both hands over it. It seemed to her that
he had drawn himself together and was leaning slightly forward, head
to one side, as if he were in the confessional. She had nothing to
confess to him, only a question which in its stark simplicity seemed
to her to go to the very heart of her orthodox, self-affirming but not
unquestioning Christian faith. She said: "If we are faced with a decision, a dilemma, how do we know what is right?"

She thought she detected in his gentle face an easing of tension,
as if grateful that the question was less onerous than he had feared.
But he took his time before he replied.

"Our conscience will tell us if we will listen."

"The still, small voice, like the voice of God?"

"Not *like*, Meg. Conscience *is* the voice of God, of the indwelling
Holy Spirit. In the Collect for Whit Sunday we do indeed pray that
we may have a right judgement in all things."

She said with gentle persistence: "But how can we be sure that
what we're hearing isn't our own voice, our own subconscious desires?
The message we listen for so carefully must be mediated through our
own experience, our personality, our heredity, our inner needs. Can
we ever break free of the devices and desires of our own hearts? Might
not our conscience be telling us what we most want to hear?"

"I haven't found it so. Conscience has usually directed me against
my own desires."

"Or what at the time you thought were your own desires."

But this was pressing him too hard. He sat quietly, blinking rapidly, as if seeking inspiration in old sermons, old homilies, familiar
texts. There was a moment's pause and then he said: "I have found
it helpful to think of conscience as an instrument, a stringed instrument perhaps. The message is in the music, but if we don't keep it
in repair and use it constantly in regular and disciplined practice we
get only an imperfect response."

She remembered that he had been an amateur violinist. His hands
were too rheumatic now to hold the instrument, but it still lay in its
case on top of the bureau in the corner. The metaphor might mean
something to him, but for her it was meaningless.

She said: "But even if my conscience tells me what is right—I
mean, right according to the moral law or even the law of the country

—that doesn't necessarily mean the end of responsibility. Suppose if I obey it, do what conscience tells me, I cause harm, even danger to someone else."

"We must do what we know is right and leave the consequences to God."

"But any human decision has to take account of the probable consequences; that is surely what decision means. How can we separate cause from effect?"

He said: "Would it be helpful if you told me what is troubling you—that is, if you feel you can?"

"It isn't my secret to tell, but I can give an example. Suppose I know that someone is regularly stealing from his employer. If I expose him he'll be sacked, his marriage will be at risk, his wife and children injured. I might feel that the shop or firm could afford to lose a few pounds each week rather than cause all that hurt to innocent people."

He was silent for a moment, then said: "Conscience might tell you to speak to the thief rather than to his employer. Explain that you know, persuade him to stop. Of course the money would have to be returned. I can see that that might present a practical difficulty."

She watched as he wrestled with the difficulty for a moment, brow creased, conjuring up the mythical thieving husband and father, clothing the moral problem in living flesh. She said: "But what if he won't or can't stop his stealing?"

"Can't? If stealing is an irresistible compulsion, then, of course, he needs medical help. Yes, certainly, that would have to be tried, although I'm never very sanguine about the success of psychotherapy."

"Won't, then, or promises to stop and then goes on stealing."

"You must still do what your conscience tells you is right. We cannot always judge the consequences. In the case you have postulated, to let the stealing go on unchecked is to connive at dishonesty. Once you have discovered what is happening, you can't pretend not to know, you can't abdicate responsibility. Knowledge always brings responsibility; that is as true for Alex Mair at Larksoken Power Station as it is in this study. You said that the children would be injured if you told; they are being injured already by their father's dishonesty, and so is the wife who benefits from it. Then there are the other staff to consider: perhaps they might be wrongly suspected. The dishonesty, if undetected, could well get worse, so that at the end the wife and children would be in deeper trouble than if it were stopped now. That is why it is safer if we concentrate on doing what is right and leave the consequences to God."

She wanted to say, "Even if we're not sure any longer if He exists? Even if that seems only another way of evading the personal responsibility which you have just told me we can't and shouldn't evade?" But she saw with compunction that he was suddenly looking tired, and she didn't miss the quick glance down at his book.

He wanted to get back to Inspector Ghote, Keating's gentle Indian detective, who, despite his uncertainties, would get there in the end, because this was fiction: problems could be solved, evil overcome, justice vindicated and death itself only a mystery which would be solved in the final chapter. He was a very old man. It was unfair to bother him. She wanted to put her hand on his sleeve and tell him that it was all right, he mustn't worry. Instead she got up and, using for the first time the name that came naturally to her, spoke the comforting lie.

"Thank you, Father, you have been very helpful. It's plainer to me now. I shall know what to do."

11
⊠

Every turn and hazard of the overgrown garden path leading to the gate which gave access to the headland was so familiar to Meg that she hardly needed to follow the jerking moon of her torch's beam, and the wind, always capricious at Larksoken, seemed to have abated the worst of its fury. But when she reached a slight ridge, and the light at the door of Martyr's Cottage came in sight, it renewed its strength and came swooping down on her as if it would pluck her from the earth and send her whirling back to the shelter and peace of the rectory. She didn't give battle but leaned against it, her head bent, her shoulder-bag bumping at her side, clutching her scarf to her head with both hands until the fury passed and she could again stand upright. The sky too was turbulent, the stars bright but very high, the moon reeling frantically between the shredded clouds like a blown lantern of frail paper. Fighting her way towards Martyr's Cottage, Meg felt as if the whole headland were whirling in chaos about her so that she could no longer tell whether the roaring in her ears was the wind, her blood or the crashing sea. When at last, breathless, she reached the oak door, she thought for the first time about Alex Mair and wondered what she would do if he were at home. It struck her as strange that the possibility hadn't previously occurred to her. And she knew that she couldn't face him, not now, not yet. But it was Alice who answered her ring. Meg asked: "Are you alone?"

"Yes, I'm alone. Alex is at Larksoken. Come in, Meg."

Meg took off and hung up her coat and headscarf in the hall and followed Alice to the kitchen. She had obviously been occupied in correcting her proofs. Now she reseated herself at her desk, swivelled round and looked gravely at Meg as she took her usual fireside chair. For a few moments neither spoke. Alice was wearing a long brown skirt of fine wool with a blouse high-buttoned to the chin and over it a sleeveless, pleated shift in narrow stripes of brown and fawn which reached almost to the floor. It gave her a hieratic dignity, an almost sacerdotal look of composed authority which was yet one of total comfort and ease. A small fire of logs was burning in the hearth, filling the room with a pungent autumnal smell, and the wind, muted by thick seventeenth-century walls, sighed and moaned companionably in the chimney. From time to time it gushed down and the logs flared into hissing life. The clothes, the firelight, the smell of burning wood overlaying the subtler smell of herbs and warm bread were familiar to Meg from their many quiet evenings together, and they were dear to her. But tonight was dreadfully different. After tonight the kitchen might never be home to her again.

She asked: "Am I interrupting?"

"Obviously, but that doesn't mean that I don't welcome interruption."

Meg bent to extract a large brown envelope from her shoulderbag.

"I've brought back the first fifty pages of proofs. I've done what you asked, read the text and checked for printing errors only."

Alice took the envelope and, without glancing at it, placed it on the desk. She said: "That's what I wanted. I'm so obsessed with the accuracy of the recipes that errors in the text sometimes slip through. I hope it wasn't too much of a chore."

"No, I enjoyed it, Alice. It reminded me of Elizabeth David."

"Not too much, I hope. She's so marvellous that I'm always afraid of being overinfluenced by her."

There was a silence. Meg thought: "We're talking as if the dialogue has been scripted for us, not as strangers exactly, but as people who are careful of their words because the space between them is loaded with dangerous thoughts. How well do I really know her? What has she ever told me about herself? Just a few details of her life with her father, snatches of information, a few phrases dropped into our conversations like a falling match, briefly illuminating the contours of a vast unexplored terrain. I've confided almost everything about myself, my childhood, the racial trouble at the school, Martin's death. But has it ever been an equal friendship? She knows more about me than any other living creature does. All I really know about Alice is that she's a good cook."

She was aware of her friend's steady, almost quizzical look. Alice said: "But you didn't fight your way in this wind just to bring back fifty pages of proofs."

"I have to talk to you."

"You are talking to me."

Meg held Alice's own unflinching gaze. She said: "Those two girls, Caroline and Amy, people are saying that they killed Hilary Robarts. Is that what you believe?"

"No. Why do you ask?"

"Nor do I believe it. Do you suppose the police will try to pin it on them?"

Alice's voice was cool. "I shouldn't think so. Isn't that rather a dramatic idea? And why should they? Chief Inspector Rickards strikes me as an honest and conscientious officer, if not particularly intelligent."

"Well, it's convenient for them, isn't it? Two suspects dead. The case closed. No more deaths."

"Were they suspects? You seem to be more in Rickards's confidence than I am."

"They didn't have alibis. The man at Larksoken Caroline was supposed to be engaged to—Jonathan Reeves, isn't it?—apparently he's confessed that they weren't together that night. Caroline forced him to lie. Most of the staff at Larksoken know that now. And it's all over the village, of course. George Jago rang to tell me."

"So they didn't have alibis. Nor did other people—you, for example. Not having an alibi isn't proof of guilt. Nor did I, incidentally. I was at home all that evening, but I doubt whether I could prove it."

And this at last was the moment which had filled Meg's thoughts since the murder, the moment of truth which she had dreaded. She said through dry unyielding lips: "But you weren't at home, were you? You told Chief Inspector Rickards that you were when I was here sitting in this kitchen on the Monday morning, but it wasn't true."

There was a moment's silence. Then Alice said calmly: "Is that what you've come to say?"

"I know that it can be explained. It's ridiculous even to ask. It's just that I've had it on my mind for so long. And you are my friend. A friend should be able to ask. There should be honesty, confidence, trust."

"Ask what? Do you have to talk like a marriage guidance counsellor?"

"Ask why you told the police you were here at nine o'clock. You weren't. I was. After the Copleys left, I had a sudden need to see you. I tried to telephone but got only the answerphone. I didn't leave a message; there was no point. I walked down. The cottage was empty. The light was on in the sitting room and the kitchen, and the door was locked. I called out for you. The record player was on, very loud. The cottage was filled with triumphant music. But there was no one here."

Alice sat in silence for a moment. Then she said calmly: "I went for a walk to enjoy the moonlight. I didn't expect a casual caller. There are never casual callers except you, and I thought that you were in Norwich. But I took the obvious precaution against an intruder, I locked the door. How did you get in?"

"With your key. You can't have forgotten, Alice. You gave me a key a year ago. I've had it ever since."

Alice looked at her, and Meg saw in her face the dawning of memory, chagrin, even, before she turned briefly away, the beginning of a rueful smile. She said: "But I had forgotten; completely. How extraordinary! It might not have worried me, even if I had remembered. After all, I thought you were in Norwich. But I didn't remember. We've got so many keys to the cottage, some here, some in London. But you never reminded me that you had one."

"I did once, early on, and you told me to keep it. Like a fool I thought that the key meant something: trust, friendship, a sign that Martyr's Cottage was always open to me. You told me that I might one day need to use it."

And now Alice did laugh aloud. She said: "And you did need to use it. How ironic. But it isn't like you to come in uninvited, not while I wasn't here. You never have before."

"But I didn't know you weren't here. The lights were on and I rang and I could hear the music. When I rang the third time and you still didn't come, I was afraid that you might be ill, unable to summon help. So I unlocked the door. I walked into a surge of wonderful sound. I recognized it, Mozart's Symphony in G minor. It was Martin's favourite. What an extraordinary tape to choose."

"I didn't choose it. I just turned on the player. What do you think I should have chosen? A requiem mass to mark the passing of a soul I don't believe in?"

Meg went on as if she hadn't heard: "I walked through to the kitchen. The light was on here too. It was the first time I'd been in this room on my own. And suddenly I felt like a stranger. I felt that nothing in it had anything to do with me. I felt that I had no right here. That's why I went away without leaving you any message."

Alice said sadly: "You were quite right. You had no right here. And you needed to see me so badly that you walked alone over the headland before you knew that the Whistler was dead?"

"I didn't walk in fear. The headland is so deserted. There's nowhere anyone can lurk, and I knew when I reached Martyr's Cottage I'd be with you."

"No, you're not easily frightened, are you? Are you frightened now?"

"Not of you but of myself. I'm frightened of what I'm thinking."

"So the cottage was empty. What else is there? Obviously there is something else."

Meg said: "That message on your answerphone—if you'd really received it at ten past eight, you would have telephoned Norwich station and left a message for me to ring back. You knew how much the Copleys disliked the thought of going to their daughter. No one else on the headland knew that. The Copleys never spoke of it, nor did I, not to anyone except you. You would have rung, Alice. There could have been an announcement over the station loudspeaker and I could have driven them home. You would have thought of that."

Alice said: "One lie to Rickards, which could have been a matter of convenience, a wish to avoid trouble, and one instance of insensitive neglect. Is that all?"

"The knife. The middle knife in your block. It wasn't here. It meant nothing at the time, of course, but the block looked odd. I was so used to seeing the five carefully graded knives, each in its sheath.

It's back now. It was back when I called in on the Monday after the murder. But it wasn't here on the Sunday night."

She wanted to cry out: "You can't be going to use it! Alice, don't use it!" Instead she made herself go on, trying to keep her voice calm, trying not to plead for reassurance, understanding.

"And next morning, when you telephoned to say that Hilary was dead, I didn't say anything about my visit. I didn't know what to believe. It wasn't that I suspected you; that would have been impossible for me, it still is. But I needed time to think. It was late morning before I could bring myself to come to you."

"And then you found me here with Chief Inspector Rickards and heard me lying. And you saw that the knife was back in the block. But you didn't speak then and you haven't spoken since, not even, I presume, to Adam Dalgliesh."

It was a shrewd thrust. Meg said: "I've told no one. How could I? Not until we'd spoken. I knew that you must have had what seemed to you a good reason for lying."

"And then, I suppose, slowly, perhaps unwillingly, you began to realize what that reason might be?"

"I didn't think you'd murdered Hilary. It sounds fantastic, ludicrous even to speak those words, to think of suspecting you. But the knife was missing and you weren't here. You did lie and I couldn't understand why. I still can't. I wonder who it is you're shielding. And sometimes—forgive me, Alice—sometimes I wonder whether you were there when he killed her, kept guard, stood there watching, might even have helped him by cutting off her hair."

Alice sat so still that the long-fingered hands resting in her lap, the folds of her shift, might have been carved in stone. She said: "I didn't help anyone—and no one helped me. There were only two people on that beach, Hilary Robarts and I. I planned it alone and I did it alone."

For a moment they sat in silence. Meg felt a great coldness. She heard the words and she knew that they were true. Had she, perhaps, always known? She thought: "I shall never be with her in this kitchen again, never again find the peace and security which I found in this room." And there fell into her mind an incongruous memory: herself sitting quietly in the same chair and watching while Alice made short pastry, sieving the flour onto a marble slab, adding the squares of soft butter, breaking in the egg, her long fingers delicately dabbling the mixture, drawing in the flour, lightly forming the glistening ball of dough. Meg said: "They were your hands. Your hands tightening the belt round her throat, your hands cutting off her hair, your hands slicing that *L* into her forehead. You planned it alone and you did it alone."

Alice said: "It took courage, but perhaps less than you would imagine. And she died very quickly, very easily. We shall be lucky to go with so little pain. She hadn't even time to feel terror. She had an easier death than most of us can look forward to. And as for what followed, that didn't matter. Not to her. Not even much to me. She was dead. It's what you do to the living that takes the strong emotions, courage, hatred and love."

She was silent for a moment; then she said: "In your eagerness to prove me a murderess, don't confuse suspicion with proof. You can't prove any of this. All right, you say the knife was missing, but that's only your word against mine. And if it was missing, I could say that I went for a short walk on the headland and the murderer saw his chance."

"And put it back afterwards? He wouldn't even know that it was there."

"Of course he would. Everyone knows that I'm a cook, and a cook has sharp knives. And why shouldn't he put it back?"

"But how would he get in? The door was locked."

"There's only your word for that. I shall say that I left it open. People on the headland usually do."

Meg wanted to cry out: "Don't, Alice. Don't begin planning more lies. Let there at least be truth between us." She said: "And the portrait, the smashed window, was that you too?"

"Of course."

"But why? Why all that complication?"

"Because it was necessary. While I was waiting for Hilary to come out of the sea, I glimpsed Theresa Blaney. She suddenly appeared on the very edge of the cliff, by the abbey ruins. She was only there for a moment, and then she disappeared. But I saw her. She was unmistakable in the moonlight."

"But if she didn't see you, if she wasn't there when you . . . when Hilary died . . ."

"Don't you see? It meant that her father wouldn't have an alibi. She has always struck me as a truthful child, and she has had a strict religious upbringing. Once she told the police that she was out on the headland that night, Ryan would be in terrible danger. And even if she had sense enough to lie, for how long could she keep it up? The police would be gentle questioning her. Rickards isn't a brute. But a truthful child would find it difficult to lie convincingly. When I got back here after the murder I played back the message on the answerphone. It occurred to me that Alex might change his plans and telephone. And it was then, too late, that I got George Jago's message. I knew that the murder could no longer be pinned on the Whistler. I had to give Ryan Blaney an alibi. So I tried to ring him to say that I'd collect the picture. When I couldn't get through I knew I had to call at Scudder's Cottage, and as quickly as possible."

"You could just have collected the portrait, knocked at the door to say what you'd done, seen him then. That would be proof enough that he was at home."

"But it would have looked too deliberate, too contrived. Ryan had made it plain that he didn't want to be disturbed, that I was merely to collect the portrait. He made that very clear. And Adam Dalgliesh was with me when he said it. Not any casual caller, but Scotland Yard's most intelligent detective. No, I had to have a valid excuse to knock and speak to Ryan."

"So you put the portrait in the boot of your car and told him that it wasn't in the shed?" It seemed to Meg extraordinary that horror could briefly be subsumed by curiosity, by the need to know. They might have been discussing complicated arrangements for a picnic.

Alice said: "Exactly. He was hardly likely to think that it was I who had taken it only a minute earlier. It was convenient, of course, that he was half-drunk. Not as drunk as I described to Rickards, but obviously incapable of killing Robarts and getting back to Scudder's Cottage by a quarter to ten."

"Not even in the van or on his bicycle?"

"The van was out of commission, and he couldn't have stayed on the bicycle. Besides, I would have passed him cycling home. My evidence meant that Ryan would be safe even if Theresa confessed that she'd left the cottage. After I left him, I drove back over a deserted headland. I stopped briefly below the pillbox and threw the shoes inside. I had no way of burning them except on an open fire where I had burned the paper and string from the wrapped portrait, but I had an idea that burning rubber could leave some trace and a persistent smell. I didn't expect the police to search for them, because I didn't believe they would find a print. But even if they did, there would be nothing to link those particular shoes with the murder. I washed them thoroughly under the outside tap before I disposed of them. Ideally, I could have returned them to the jumble box, but I daren't wait, and that night I knew that, with you gone to Norwich, the back door would be locked."

"And then you threw the picture through Hilary's window?"

"I had to get rid of it somehow. That way it looked like a deliberate act of vandalism and hatred, and there were plenty of possible suspects for that, not all of them on the headland. It complicated matters even further, and it was one more piece of evidence to help Ryan. No one would believe that he would deliberately destroy his own work. But it had a double purpose: I wanted to get into Thyme Cottage. I smashed enough of the window to get through."

"But that was terribly dangerous. You might have cut yourself, got a sliver of glass on your shoes. And they were your own shoes then; you had disposed of the Bumbles."

"I examined the soles very thoroughly. And I was particularly careful where I trod. She had left the downstairs lights on, so I didn't have to use my torch."

"But why? What were you looking for? What did you hope to find?"

"Nothing. I wanted to get rid of the belt. I curled it very carefully and put it in the drawer in her bedroom among her belts, stockings, handkerchiefs, socks."

"But if the police examined it, it wouldn't have her prints on it."

"Nor would it have mine. I was still wearing my gloves. And why should they examine it? One would assume that the murderer had used his own belt and had taken it away again. The least likely hiding place for the killer to choose would be the victim's own cottage. That's why I chose it. And even if they did decide to examine every belt and dog lead on the headland, I doubt whether they'd get any useful prints from half an inch of leather which dozens of hands must have touched."

Meg said bitterly: "You took a lot of trouble to give Ryan an alibi. What about the other innocent suspects? They were all at risk; they still are. Didn't you think of them?"

"I only cared about one other, Alex, and he had the best alibi of all. He would go through security to get into the station, and again when he left."

Meg said: "I was thinking of Neil Pascoe, Amy, Miles Lessingham, even myself."

"None of you is a parent responsible for four motherless children. I thought it very unlikely that Lessingham wouldn't be able to provide an alibi, and if he couldn't there was no real evidence against him. How could there be? He didn't do it. But I have a feeling that he guesses who did. Lessingham isn't a fool. But even if he knows, he'll never tell. Neil Pascoe and Amy could give each other an alibi, and you, my dear Meg, do you really see yourself as a serious suspect?"

"I felt like one. When Rickards was questioning me it was like being back in that staff room at school, facing those cold, accusing faces, knowing I'd already been judged and found guilty, wondering if perhaps I wasn't guilty."

"The possible distress of innocent suspects, even you, was very low on my list of priorities."

"And now you'll let them blame the murder on Caroline and Amy, both dead and both innocent?"

"Innocent? Of that, of course. Perhaps you're right and the police will find it convenient to assume they did it, one of them or together in collusion. From Rickards's point of view it's better to have two dead suspects than no arrest. And it can't hurt them now. The dead are beyond harm, the harm they do and the harm that is done to them."

"But it's wrong and it's unjust."

"Meg, they are dead. Dead. It can't matter. 'Injustice' is a word, and they have passed beyond the power of words. They don't exist. And life is unjust. If you feel called upon to do something about injustice, concentrate on injustice to the living. Alex had a right to that job."

"And Hilary Robarts, hadn't she a right to life? I know that she wasn't likable, or even very happy. There's no immediate family to mourn, apparently. She doesn't leave young children. But you've taken from her what no one can ever give back. She didn't deserve to die.

Perhaps none of us do, not like that. We don't even hang the Whistler now. We've learnt something since Tyburn, since Agnes Poley's burning. Nothing Hilary Robarts did deserved death."

"I'm not arguing that she deserved to die. It doesn't matter whether she was happy, or childless, or even much use to anyone but herself. What I'm saying is that I wanted her dead."

"That seems to me so evil that it's beyond my understanding. Alice, what you did was a dreadful sin."

Alice laughed. The sound was so full-throated, almost happy, as if the amusement were genuine. "Meg, you continue to astonish me. You use words which are no longer in the general vocabulary—not even in the Church's, so I'm told. The implications of that simple little word are outside my comprehension. But if you want to see this in theological terms, then think of Dietrich Bonhoeffer. He wrote: 'We have at times to be willing to be guilty.' Well, I'm willing to be guilty."

"To be guilty, yes. But not to feel guilt. That must make it easier."

"Oh, but I do feel it. I've been made to feel guilty from childhood. And if at the heart of your being you feel that you've no right even to exist, then one more cause of guilt hardly matters."

Meg thought, I shall never be able to unlearn, never forget what's happening here this evening. But I have to know the whole of it. Even the most painful knowledge is better than half-knowledge. She said: "That afternoon I came here to tell you the Copleys were going to their daughter . . ."

Alice said: "On the Friday after the dinner party. Thirteen days ago."

"Is that all? It seems in a different dimension of time. You asked me to come and have supper with you when I got back from Norwich. Was that planned as part of your alibi? Did you use even me?"

Alice looked at her. She said: "Yes. I'm sorry. You would have been here about half past nine, just time for me to get back and be ready with a hot meal in the oven."

"Which you would have cooked earlier in the evening. Safe enough with Alex at the power station, out of the way."

"That's what I planned. When you declined I didn't press it. That would have looked suspicious later, too like trying to establish an alibi. Besides, you wouldn't have been persuaded to change your mind, would you? You never do. But the very fact of the invitation would have helped. A woman wouldn't normally invite a friend even to an informal supper party if she were simultaneously planning a murder."

"And if I had accepted, if I had turned up here at half past nine, that would have been awkward, wouldn't it, given your later change of plan? You wouldn't have been able to drive over to Scudder's Cottage to give Ryan Blaney his alibi. And you would have been left in possession of the shoes and the belt."

"The shoes would have been the greatest problem. I didn't think they'd ever be connected with the crime, but I needed to get rid of them before next morning. I couldn't possibly explain my possession of them. I would probably have washed them and hidden them away, hoping for a chance to get them back to the jumble box the next day. Though I would have to have found a way of giving Ryan his alibi. Probably I would have told you that I couldn't get through by telephone and that we ought to drive over at once to tell him that the Whistler was dead. But it's all academic. I didn't worry. You said you wouldn't come and I knew you wouldn't."

"But I did. Not to supper. But I came."

"Yes. Why did you, Meg?"

"A feeling of depression after a heavy day, hating seeing the Copleys go, the need to see you. I wasn't looking for a meal. I had an early supper and then walked over the headland."

But there was something else she needed to ask. She said: "You knew that Hilary swam after watching the beginning of the main news. I suppose most people knew that who knew that she liked swimming at night. And you were taking trouble to see that Ryan had his alibi for nine-twenty or shortly after. But suppose the body hadn't been discovered until the next day? Surely she wouldn't normally be missed until she didn't turn up at the power station on Monday morning, and then they would telephone to see if she were ill. It might even have been Monday evening before anybody made any enquiries. She could have swum in the morning and not at night."

"The pathologist can usually estimate the time of death with reasonable accuracy. And I knew she'd be found that night. I knew that Alex had promised to visit her when he got back from the power station. He was on his way to the cottage when he met Adam Dalgliesh. And now, I think, you know it all except for the Bumble trainers. I came through the back garden at the Old Rectory late on Sunday afternoon. I knew that the back door would be open, and it was the time when you would be having high tea. I had a bag with me with a few items of jumble in case I was seen. But I wasn't seen. I took soft shoes, easy to wear, a pair that looked roughly my size. And I took one of the belts."

But there was one more question to ask, the most important of all. Meg said: "But why? Alice, I have to know. Why?"

"That's a dangerous question, Meg. Are you sure you really want the answer?"

"I need the answer, need to try to understand."

"Isn't it enough that she was determined to marry Alex and I was determined that she shouldn't?"

"That isn't why you killed her. It can't be. There was something more than that, there had to be."

"Yes, there was. I suppose you have a right to know. She was blackmailing Alex. She could have stopped him getting that job, or, if he had got it, could have made it impossible for him to function successfully. She had the power to destroy his whole career. Toby Gledhill had told her that Alex had deliberately held up publishing the result of their research because it might have prejudiced the success of the enquiry into Larksoken's second reactor. They discovered that some of the assumptions made in generating the mathematical models were more critical than had been thought. People opposing the building of the new PWR at Larksoken could have exploited it to cause delay, whip up fresh hysteria."

"You mean that he deliberately falsified the results?"

"That's something he's incapable of doing. All he did was to delay publishing the experiment. He'll publish it within the next month or two. But that's the kind of information which, once it got into the press, would have done irreparable harm. Toby was almost prepared to hand it over to Neil Pascoe, but Hilary dissuaded him. It was far too valuable for that. She meant to use it to persuade Alex to marry her. She faced him with the knowledge when he walked home with her after the dinner party, and late that night he told me. I knew then what I had to do. The only way he might have been able to buy her off was by promoting her from Acting Administrator to Administrative Officer of Larksoken, and that was almost as impossible for him as deliberately falsifying a scientific result."

"You mean he might actually have married her?"

"He might have been forced to. But how safe would he have been even then? She could have held that knowledge over his head until the end of his life. And what would that life have been, tied to a woman who had blackmailed him into marriage, a woman he didn't want, whom he could neither respect nor love?"

And then she said, in a voice so low that Meg only just heard it: "I owed Alex a death."

Meg said: "But how could you be sure, sure enough to kill her? Couldn't you have talked to her, persuaded her, reasoned with her?"

"I did talk to her. I went to see her on that Sunday afternoon. It was I who was with her when Mrs. Jago arrived with the church magazine. You could say that I went to give her a chance of life. I couldn't murder her without making sure that it was necessary. That meant doing what I'd never done before, talking to her about Alex, trying to persuade her that the marriage wouldn't be in either of their interests, to let him go. I could have saved myself the humiliation. There was no argument, she was beyond that. She was no longer even rational. Part of the time she railed at me like a woman possessed."

Meg said: "And your brother, did he know about the visit?"

"He knows nothing. I didn't tell him at the time, and I haven't told him since. But he told me what he planned: to promise her marriage and then, when the job was secure, to renege. It would have been disastrous. He never understood the woman he was dealing with, the passion, the desperation. She was a rich man's only child, alternately overindulged and neglected, trying all her life to compete with her father, taught that what you want is yours by right if you've only got the courage to fight for it and take it. And she had courage. She was obsessed by him, by her need for him, above all by her need for a child. She said that he owed her a child. Did he think she was like one of his reactors, tamable, that he could let down into that turbulence the equivalent of his rods of boron steel and control the force which he'd let loose? When I left her that afternoon I knew I had no choice. Sunday was the deadline. He had arranged to call at Thyme Cottage on his way home from the power station. It was fortunate for him that I got to her first.

"Perhaps the worst part of all was waiting for him to come home that night. I daren't ring the power station. I couldn't be sure that he would be alone in his office or in the computer room, and I had never before telephoned him to ask when he would be home. I sat there and waited for nearly three hours. I expected that it would be Alex who would find the body. When he discovered that she wasn't in the cottage, the natural move would be to check at the beach. He would find the body, telephone the police from the car and ring home to tell me. When he didn't I began to fantasize that she wasn't really dead, that somehow I'd bungled it. I pictured him desperately working on her, giving her the kiss of life, saw her eyes slowly open. I turned off the lights and moved to the sitting room to watch the road. But it wasn't an ambulance that arrived, it was the police cars, the paraphernalia of murder. And still Alex didn't come."

Meg asked: "And when he did?"

"We hardly spoke. I'd gone to bed; I knew I must do what I would normally have done, not wait up for him. He came to my room to tell me that Hilary was dead and how she had died. I asked, 'The Whistler?' and he answered, 'The police think not. The Whistler was dead before she was killed.' Then he left me. I don't think either of us could have borne to be together, the air heavy with our unspoken thoughts. But I did what I had to do, and it was worth it. The job is his. And they won't take it away from him, not after it's been confirmed. They can't sack him because his sister is a murderess."

"But if they found out why you did it?"

"They won't. Only two people know that, and I wouldn't have told you if I couldn't trust you. On a less elevated level, I doubt if they'd believe you in the absence of confirmation from another witness; and Toby Gledhill and Hilary Robarts, the only two who could give it, are dead."

After a minute's silence she said: "You would have done the same for Martin."

"Oh no, no."

"Not as I did. I can't see you managing to use physical force. But when he drowned, if you could have stood on that riverbank and had the power to choose which one should die and which live, would you have hesitated?"

"No, of course not. But that would have been different. I wouldn't have planned a drowning, wouldn't have wanted it."

"Or if you were told that millions of people would live more safely if Alex got a job which he is uniquely capable of filling but at the cost of one woman's life, would you hesitate then? That was the choice which faced me. Don't evade it, Meg. I didn't."

"But murder, how could it solve anything? It never has."

Alice said with sudden passion: "Oh, but it can, and it does. You read history, don't you? Surely you know that."

Meg felt exhausted with weariness and pain. She wanted the talking to stop. But it couldn't. There was still too much to be said. She asked: "What are you going to do?"

"That depends on you."

But out of horror and disbelief Meg had found courage. And she had found more than courage: authority. She said: "Oh no it doesn't. This isn't a responsibility I asked for and I don't want it."

"But you can't evade it. You know what you know. Call Chief Inspector Rickards now. You can use this telephone." When Meg made no move to use it she said: "Surely you aren't going to do an E. M. Forster on me. 'If I had a choice between betraying my country and my friend, I hope I would have the guts to betray my country.' "

Meg said: "That is one of those clever remarks that, when you analyse them, either mean nothing or mean something rather silly."

Alice said: "Remember, whatever you choose to do, you can't bring her back. You've got a number of options, but that isn't one. It's very satisfying to the human ego to discover the truth; ask Adam Dalgliesh. It's even more satisfying to human vanity to imagine you can avenge the innocent, restore the past, vindicate the right. But you can't. The dead stay dead. All you can do is to hurt the living in the name of justice or retribution or revenge. If that gives you any pleasure, then do it, but don't imagine that there's virtue in it. Whatever you decide, I know that you won't go back on it. I can believe you and I can trust you."

Looking at Alice's face, Meg saw that the look bent on her was serious, ironic, challenging; but it was not pleading. Alice said: "Do you want some time to consider?"

"No. There's no point in having time. I know now what I have to do. I have to tell. But I'd rather you did."

"Then give me until tomorrow. Once I've spoken, there'll be no more privacy. There are things I need to do here. The proofs, affairs to arrange. And I should like twelve hours of freedom. If you can give me that, I'll be grateful. I haven't the right to ask for more, but I am asking for that."

Meg said: "But when you confess, you'll have to give them a motive, a reason, something they can believe in."

"Oh, they'll believe it all right. Jealousy, hatred, the resentment of an aging virgin for a woman who looked as she did, lived as she did. I'll say that she wanted to marry him, take him from me after all I've done for him. They'll see me as a neurotic, menopausal woman gone temporarily off her head. Unnatural affection. Suppressed sexuality. That's how men talk about women like me. That's the kind of motive that makes sense to a man like Rickards. I'll give it to him."

"Even if it means you end up in Broadmoor? Alice, could you bear it?"

"Well, that's a possibility, isn't it? It's either that or prison. This was a carefully planned murder. Even the cleverest counsel won't be able to make it look like a sudden, unpremeditated act. And I doubt whether there's much to choose between Broadmoor and prison when it comes to the food."

It seemed to Meg that nothing ever again would be certain. Not only had her inner world been shattered but the familiar objects of the external world no longer had reality. Alice's roll-top desk, the kitchen table, the high-backed cane chairs, the rows of gleaming pans, the stoves all seemed insubstantial, as if they would disappear at her touch. She was aware that the kitchen round which her eyes ranged was now empty. Alice had left. She leaned back, faint, and closed her eyes, and then, opening them, she was aware of Alice's face bending low over hers, immense, almost moon-like. She was handing Meg a tumbler. She said: "It's whisky. Drink this, you need it."

"No, Alice, I can't. I can't really. You know I hate whisky, it makes me sick."

"This won't make you sick. There are times when whisky is the only possible remedy. This is one of them. Drink it, Meg."

She felt her knees tremble, and simultaneously the tears started like burning spurts of pain and began flowing unchecked, a salt stream over her cheeks, her mouth. She thought, This can't be happening. This can't be true. But that was how she had felt when Miss Mortimer, calling her from her class, had gently seated her in the chair opposite to her in the Head's private sitting room and had broken the news of Martin's death. The unthinkable had to be thought, the unbelievable believed. Words still meant what they had always meant: "murder," "death," "grief," "pain." She could see Miss Mortimer's mouth moving, the odd, disconnected phrases floating out, like balloons in a cartoon, noticing again how she must have wiped off her lipstick before the interview. Perhaps she had thought that only naked lips could give such appalling news. She saw again those restless blobs of flesh, noticed again that the top button on Miss Mortimer's cardigan was hanging loose on a single thread and heard herself say, actually say, "Miss Mortimer, you're going to lose a button."

She clasped her fingers round the glass. It seemed to her to have grown immensely large and heavy as a rock and the smell of the whisky almost turned her stomach. But she had no power to resist. She lifted it slowly to her mouth. She was aware of Alice's face still very close, of Alice's eyes watching her. She took the first small sip and was about to throw back her head and gulp it down when, firmly but gently, the glass was taken out of her hands, and she heard Alice's voice: "You're quite right, Meg, it was never your drink. I'll make coffee for both of us, then walk with you back to the Old Rectory."

Fifteen minutes later Meg helped wash up the coffee cups as if this were the end of an ordinary evening. Then they set out together to walk over the headland. The wind was at their back, and it seemed to Meg that they almost flew through the air, their feet hardly touching the turf, as if they were witches. At the door of the rectory Alice asked: "What will you do tonight, Meg, pray for me?"

"I shall pray for both of us."

"As long as you don't expect me to repent. I'm not religious, as you know, and I don't understand that word unless, as I suppose, it means regret that something we've done has turned out less well for us than we hoped. On that definition I have little to repent of except ill luck that you, my dear Meg, are an incompetent car mechanic."

And then, as if on impulse, she grasped Meg's arms. The grip was so fierce that it hurt. Meg thought for a moment that Alice was going to kiss her, but her hold loosened and her hands fell. She said a curt goodbye and turned away.

Putting her key in the lock and pushing the door open, Meg looked back, but Alice had disappeared into the darkness, and the wild sobbing, which for an incredible moment she thought was a woman weeping, was only the wind.

12

⊠

Dalgliesh had just finished sorting the last of his aunt's papers when the telephone rang. It was Rickards. His voice, strong, high with euphoria, came over the line as clearly as if his presence filled the room. His wife had given birth to a daughter an hour earlier. He was ringing from the hospital. His wife was fine. The baby was wonderful. He only had a few minutes. They were carrying out some nursing procedure or other, and then he'd be able to get back to Susie.

"She's got home just in time, Mr. Dalgliesh. Lucky, wasn't it? And the midwife says she's hardly known such a quick labour for a first pregnancy. Only six hours. Seven and a half pounds, just a nice weight. And we wanted a girl. We're calling her Stella Louise. Louise is after Susie's mother. We may as well make the old trout happy."

Replacing the receiver after warm congratulations which he suspected Rickards felt were hardly adequate, Dalgliesh wondered why he had been honoured with such early news and concluded that Rickards, possessed by joy, was ringing everyone who might have an interest, filling in the minutes before he was allowed back to his wife's bedside. His last words were: "I can't tell you what it feels like, Mr. Dalgliesh."

But Dalgliesh could remember what it had felt like. He paused for a moment, the receiver still warm under his hand, and faced reactions which seemed to him overcomplicated for such ordinary and expected news, recognizing with distaste that part of what he was feeling was envy. Was it, he wondered, his coming to the headland, the sense there of man's transitory but continuing life, the everlasting cycle of birth and death, or was it the death of Jane Dalgliesh, his last living relative, that made him for a moment wish so keenly that he too had a living child?

Neither he nor Rickards had spoken about the murder. Rickards would no doubt have felt it an almost indecent intrusion into his private, almost sacrosanct, rapture. And there was, after all, little more to be said. Rickards had made it plain that he considered the case closed. Amy Camm and her lover were both dead, and it was unlikely now that their guilt would ever be proved. And the case against them was admittedly imperfect. Rickards still had no evidence that either woman had known details of the Whistler killings. But that, apparently, now assumed less importance in the police mind. Someone could have talked. Scraps of information picked up by Camm in the Local Hero could have been pieced together. Robarts herself could have told Amphlett, and what they hadn't learned they could have guessed. The case might officially be classified as unsolved, but Rickards had now persuaded himself that Amphlett, helped by her lover, Camm, had killed Hilary Robarts. Dalgliesh, when they had briefly met on the previous evening, had felt it right to put another view and had argued it calmly and logically, and Rickards had turned his own arguments against him.

"She's her own woman. You said so yourself. She's got her own life, a profession. Why the hell should she care who he marries? She didn't try to stop him when he married before. And it's not as if he needs protection. Can you imagine Alex Mair doing anything he doesn't want to do? He's the sort of man who'll die at his own convenience, not God's."

Dalgliesh had said: "The absence of motive is the weakest part of the case. And I admit there isn't a single piece of forensic or other physical evidence. But Alice Mair fulfils all the criteria. She knew how the Whistler killed; she knew where Robarts would be shortly after nine o'clock; she has no alibi; she knew where she could find those trainers and she is tall enough to wear them; she had an opportunity of throwing them into the bunker on her way back from Scudder's Cottage. But there's something else, isn't there? I think this crime was committed by someone who didn't know that the Whistler was dead when she did the murder and did know shortly afterwards."

"It's ingenious, Mr. Dalgliesh."

Dalgliesh was tempted to say that it wasn't ingenious, merely logical. Rickards would feel obliged to question Alice Mair again, but he would get nowhere. And it wasn't his case. Within two days he would be back in London. Any more dirty work which MI5 wanted done they would have to do themselves. He had already interfered more than was strictly justified and certainly more than he had found agreeable. He told himself that it would be dishonest to blame either Rickards or the murderer for the fact that most of the decisions he had come to the headland to make were still undecided.

That unexpected spurt of envy had induced a mild self-disgust which wasn't helped by the discovery that he had left the book he was currently reading, A. N. Wilson's biography of Tolstoy, in the room at the top of the tower. It was providing satisfaction and consolation of which at the present he felt particularly in need. Shutting the front door of the mill firmly against the wind, he fought his way round the curve of the tower, switched on the lights and climbed up to the top storey. Outside, the wind whooped and screamed like a pack of demented demons, but here, in this small domed cell, it was extraordinarily quiet. The tower had stood for over 150 years. It had resisted far worse gales. On an impulse he opened the eastward window and let the wind rush in like a wild cleansing force. It was then that he saw, over the flint wall which bounded the patio at Martyr's Cottage, a light in the kitchen window. It was no ordinary light. As he watched, it flickered, then died, flickered again and then strengthened into a ruddy glow. He had seen that kind of light before and knew what it meant. Martyr's Cottage was on fire.

He almost slid down the two ladders linking the mill floors and, dashing into the sitting room, paused only to telephone for the fire brigade and ambulance, grateful that he hadn't yet garaged the car. Seconds later he was hurtling at top speed across the rough grass of the headland. The Jaguar rocked to a stop and he rushed to the front door. It was locked. For a second he considered battering it open with the Jaguar. But the frame was solid sixteenth-century oak, and valuable seconds could be lost in futile manoeuvring and accelerating. Racing to the side, he sprang at the wall, grasped the top, swung his body over and dropped onto the rear patio. It took only a second to check that the back door, too, was bolted top and bottom. He had no doubt who was inside; he would have to get her out through the window. He tore off his jacket and wrapped it round his right arm while, at the same time, turning on full the outside tap and drenching his head and upper body. The icy water dripped from him as he flexed his elbow and crashed it against the glass. But the pane was thick, designed to keep out the winter gales. He had to stand on the sill, supporting himself by the window frame, and kick violently and repeatedly before the glass crashed inwards and the flames leapt at him.

Inside the window was a double sink. He rolled over it and, gasping in the smoke, dropped to his knees and began to crawl towards her. She was lying between the stove and the table, the long body rigid as an effigy. Her hair and clothes were alight and she lay there staring upwards, bathed in tongues of fire. But her face was as yet untouched, and the open eyes seemed to gaze at him with such an intensity of half-crazed endurance that there flashed into his mind unbidden the image of Agnes Poley, so that the blazing tables and chairs were the crackling fagots of her excruciating martyrdom, and he smelled above the acrid smoke the dreadful stink of burning flesh.

He tugged at Alice Mair's body, but it was awkwardly wedged and the edge of the burning table had fallen across her legs. Somehow he had to buy a few seconds of time. He staggered, coughing through the smoke, to the sink, turned both taps full on and, seizing a pan, filled it and threw water over the flames again and again. A small area of fire hissed and began to die. Kicking away the burning debris, he managed to lift her over his shoulder, then stumbled to the window. But the bolts, almost too hot to touch, were jammed fast. He would have to get her out through the broken window. Gasping with the effort, he pushed the dead weight forward over the sink. But the rigid body caught on the taps, and it took an eternity of agonizing time before he was able to free her, shove her forward to the window and at last see her tip forward out of sight. He gasped in the fresh air and, grasping the edge of the sink, tried to raise himself. But suddenly his legs had no strength. He felt them buckle and had to rest his arms on the sink edge to prevent himself from falling back into the strengthening fire. Until this minute he had been unaware of pain, but now it clawed and bit at his legs and back as if he were being savaged by a pack of dogs. He couldn't stretch his head to reach the running taps, but he cupped his hands and threw the water against his face, as if this cool benison could assuage the agony in his legs. And suddenly he was visited with an almost overwhelming temptation to let go, to fall back into the fire rather than make the impossible effort to escape. It was only a second's folly, but it spurred him to a last, desperate attempt. He seized the taps, one with each hand, and slowly and painfully lifted himself across the sink. And now his knees had a purchase on the hard edge and he could thrust himself forward to the windows. Smoke billowed around him, and the great tongues of flame roared at his back. His ears hurt with the roaring. It filled the headland, and he no longer knew whether he was hearing fire, wind or the sea. Then he made the last effort and felt himself falling onto the softness of her body. He rolled away from her. She was no longer burning. Her clothes had been burnt away and now clung like blackened rags to what was left of the flesh. He managed to get to his feet and half-crawled, half-stumbled towards the outside tap. He reached it just before he lost consciousness, and the last thing he heard was the hiss as the stream of water quenched his burning clothes.

A minute later he opened his eyes. The stones were hard against his burnt back, and when he tried to move the spasm of agony made him cry aloud. He had never known such pain. But a face, pale as the moon, was bending over him, and he recognized Meg Dennison. He thought of that blackened thing by the window and managed to say: "Don't look. Don't look."

But she answered gently: "She's dead. And it's all right, I had to look."

And then he ceased to know her. His mind, disorientated, was in another place, another time. And suddenly, among the crowd of gaping spectators, the soldiers with their pikes guarding the scaffold, there was Rickards saying: "But she isn't a thing, Mr. Dalgliesh. She's a woman." He closed his eyes. Meg's arms enclosed him. He turned his face and pressed it into her jacket, biting the wool so that he would not disgrace himself by groaning aloud. And then he felt her cool hands on his face.

She said: "The ambulance is coming. I can hear it. Lie still, my dear. It's going to be all right."

The last sound he heard was the clanging of the fire engine's bell as he let himself slide again into unconsciousness.

EPILOGUE
Wednesday 18 January

⊠

It was mid-January before Adam Dalgliesh came again to Larksoken Mill, a sunny day of such warmth that the headland lay bathed in the bright translucence of a premature spring. Meg had arranged to meet him at the mill in the afternoon to say goodbye and, passing through the rear garden gate to walk across the headland, she saw that the first snowdrops were already in bloom and squatted to gaze with pure pleasure at their delicate green-and-white heads trembling in the breeze. The turf of the headland was springy to her feet and, in the far distance, a flock of seagulls wheeled and swooped like a shower of white petals.

The Jaguar stood outside the mill, and through the open door a swathe of sunlight lay over the denuded room. Dalgliesh was on his knees, packing the last of his aunt's books into tea chests. The pictures, already wrapped, were propped against the wall. Meg knelt beside him and began to help by passing him the corded volumes. She said: "How are your legs and back?"

"A little stiff, and the scars still itch occasionally. But they seem fine."

"No more pain?"

"No more pain."

They worked for a few minutes in companionable silence. Then Meg said: "I know you don't want to be told this, but we're all grateful for what you are doing for the Blaneys. The rent you're charging for the mill is derisory, and Ryan knows it."

Dalgliesh said: "I'm doing him no favours. I wanted a local family to live here, and he was the obvious choice. It isn't everyone's house, after all. If he's worried about the size of the rent, he can regard himself as a caretaker. You could argue that I should be paying him."

"Not many men looking for a caretaker would choose an eccentric artist with four children. But this place will be just right for them: two bathrooms, a proper kitchen and the tower for Ryan to paint in. Theresa is transformed. She's been so much stronger since her operation, and now she looks radiant with happiness. She called in at the Old Rectory yesterday to tell us all about it and how she's been measuring up the rooms and planning where they'll put the furniture. It's much more suitable for them than Scudder's Cottage, even if Alex hadn't wanted to sell and get rid of it for good. I can't blame him. Did you know that he's selling Martyr's Cottage, too? Now that he's so busy with the new job, I think he wants to cut himself off from the headland and its memories. I suppose that's natural. And I don't think you know about Jonathan Reeves. He's engaged to a young girl from the power station, Shirley Coles. And Mrs. Jago has had a letter from Neil Pascoe. After a couple of false starts, he's got a temporary job as a social worker in Camden. She says he seems happy enough. And there's good news about Timmy, at least I suppose it's good news. The police have traced Amy's mother. She and her common-law husband don't want Timmy, so he's being placed for adoption. He'll go to a couple who'll give him love and security."

And then she stopped, afraid that she was prattling on, that he might not be interested in all this local gossip. But there was one question that had been in her mind for the last three months which she needed to ask, and which only he could answer. She watched for a moment in silence as the long sensitive hands fitted the corded books expertly into the case, then said: "Does Alex accept that his sister killed Hilary? I've never liked to ask Inspector Rickards, and he wouldn't tell me if I did. And I can't possibly ask Alex. We've never discussed Alice or the murder since her death. At the funeral we hardly spoke."

But she knew that Rickards would have confided in Adam Dalgliesh. He said: "I don't think Alex Mair is a man to deceive himself about uncomfortable facts. He must know the truth. But that doesn't mean that he'll admit it to the police. Officially he accepts their view that the murderess is dead but that it's now impossible to prove whether that murderess was Amy Camm, Caroline Amphlett or Alice Mair. The difficulty is that there still isn't a single piece of concrete evidence to connect Miss Mair with Hilary Robarts's death, and certainly not enough circumstantial evidence posthumously to brand her as the killer. If she had lived and withdrawn her confession to you, I doubt whether Rickards would have been justified even in making an arrest. The open verdict at the inquest means that even the suicide theory is unproved. The fire investigator's report confirms that the fire was caused by the overturn of a pan of boiling fat, probably while she was cooking, perhaps trying out a new recipe."

Meg said bitterly: "And it all rests on my story, doesn't it? The not-very-likely tale told by a woman who has made trouble before and who has a history of mental breakdown. That came out clearly when I was being questioned. Inspector Rickards seemed obsessed with the relationship, whether I had a grudge against Alice, whether we had quarrelled. By the time he had finished, I didn't know whether he saw me as a malicious liar or her accomplice."

Even three and a half months after the death it was difficult to think of those long interrogations without the familiar destructive mixture of pain, fear and anger. She had been made to tell her story over and over again under those sharp and sceptical eyes. And she could understand why he had been so reluctant to believe her. She had never found it easy to lie convincingly, and he had known that she was lying. But why? he had asked. What reason did Alice Mair give for the murder? What was her motive? Her brother couldn't be forced to marry Hilary Robarts. And it's not as if he hadn't been married before. His ex-wife is alive and well, so what made this marriage so impossible for her? And she hadn't told him, except to reiterate obstinately that Alice had wanted to prevent it. She had promised not to tell, and she never would, not even to Adam Dalgliesh, who was the only man who might possibly have been able to make her. She guessed that he knew that too, but that he would never ask. Once when she was visiting him in hospital she had suddenly said: "You know, don't you?"

And he had replied: "No, I don't know, but I can guess. Blackmail isn't an uncommon motive for murder."

But he had asked no questions, and for that she was grateful.

She knew now that Alice had told her the truth only because she had planned that Meg wouldn't be alive the next day to reveal it. She had meant them to die together. But in the end she had drawn back. The whisky, almost certainly drugged with her sleeping tablets, had been gently but firmly taken from her hand. In the end Alice had kept faith with their friendship, and she would keep faith with her friend. Alice had said that she owed her brother a death. Meg had pondered on those words but could still find no real meaning in them. But if Alice had owed Alex a death, she, for her part, owed Alice her loyalty and her silence. She said: "I'm hoping to buy Martyr's Cottage when the repairs are finished. I have some capital from the sale of the London house and the promise of a small mortgage, which is all I'll need. I thought I could let it in summer to help with the expenses. And then, when the Copleys no longer need me, I could move in and live there. I'd like the thought that it would be waiting for me."

If he was surprised that she should want to return to a place with such traumatic memories, he didn't say so. As if she had a need to explain, Meg went on: "Terrible things have happened in the past to people living on this headland, not only to Agnes Poley, to Hilary, to Alice, to Amy and Caroline. But I still feel at home here. I still feel that this is my place. I still feel that I want to be part of it. And if there are ghosts at Martyr's Cottage, they will be friendly spirits."

He said: "It's a stony soil in which to put down roots."

"Perhaps that's the kind of soil my roots need."

An hour later she had said her last goodbye. The truth lay between them, unspoken, and now he was leaving and she might never see him again. She realized with a smile of happy surprise that she was a little in love with him. But it didn't matter. It was as devoid of pain as it was of hope. When she reached a low ridge on the headland, she turned and looked north at the power station, the generator and symbol of the potent and mysterious power which she could never separate from the image of that curiously beautiful mushroom cloud, symbol too of the intellectual and spiritual arrogance which had led Alice to murder, and it seemed to her for a second that she heard the echo of the last warning siren screaming its terrible message over the headland. And evil didn't end with the death of one evil-doer. Somewhere at this moment a new Whistler could be planning his dreadful revenge against a world in which he had never been at home. But that was in the unforeseeable future, and the fear had no reality. Reality was here, in a single moment of sunlit time, in the shivering grasses of the headland, the sparkling sea layered in blue and purple to the horizon and winged with a single sail, the broken arches of the abbey, in which the flints struck gold from the mellowing sun, the great sails of the mill, motionless and silent, the taste of the sea-salted air. Here the past and the present fused, and her own life, with its trivial devices and desires, seemed only an insignificant moment in the long history of the headland. And then she smiled at these portentous imaginings and, turning to wave a final goodbye to the tall figure still standing at the mill door, she strode out resolutely for home. The Copleys would be waiting for their afternoon tea.

A Note About the Author

P. D. James spent thirty years in various branches of the British Civil Service, retiring in 1979 to devote herself full-time to writing. She is the author of eleven novels and one work of non-fiction, many of which have been filmed and broadcast on television, and the recipient of numerous honors, including the Order of the British Empire. She lives in London, where she has served as a magistrate and is a governor of the BBC.

A NOTE ON THE TYPE

This book was set in a digitized version of a face called
Primer, designed by Rudolph Ruzicka (1883–1978). Mr.
Ruzicka was also responsible for the design of Fairfield and
Fairfield Medium, Linotype faces whose virtues have for
some time been accorded wide recognition.

The complete range of sizes of Primer was first made
available in 1954, although the pilot size of 12-point was
ready as early as 1951. The design of the face makes general
reference to Linotype Century—long a serviceable type, totally lacking in manner or frills of any kind—but brilliantly
corrects its characterless quality.

Composed by
PennSet, Inc.
Bloomsburg, Pennsylvania

Printed and bound by
The Haddon Craftsmen, Inc.
Scranton, Pennsylvania